Praise for T. I. Lowe

T. I. Lowe is a master of Southern storytelling, and *South of Somewhere* is her best book yet. Captivating, atmospheric, and filled with complex family dynamics, a vibrant community, romance, and healing, this is a beautiful story about how to step away from the person you have always been to become the person you were meant to be.

JOY CALLAWAY, international bestselling author of *Sing Me Home to Carolina*

South of Somewhere is an earnest, thought-provoking story that should be lauded not only for its relevance but for its powerful message of resilience and hope. Written with humor, empathy, and a generous dose of Southern charm, Lowe's latest quickly immerses the reader in the story world and further proves she's a writer who excels at her craft.

DONNA EVERHART, *USA TODAY* bestselling author of *When the Jessamine Grows*

T. I. Lowe delivers a soul-stirring, unforgettable romance, pairing a couple's redemption story with the restoration of a deserted town.

***BOOKPAGE*,** starred review on *Lowcountry Lost*

[A] heartfelt tale of loss, healing, and second chances . . . this story will also attract the HGTV crowd, particularly fans of shows like *Fixer Upper* and *Home Town*.

BOOKLIST on *Lowcountry Lost*

T. I. Lowe has created an impeccably researched, emotionally compelling new novel. You will root for Avalee as you immerse yourself in the restoration of not just a forgotten town, but of a heart that could never be forgotten.

MARYBETH MAYHEW WHALEN, author of *Every Moment Since* and cofounder of The Book Tide, on *Lowcountry Lost*

Immersive, transportive, and divinely transformational, *Lowcountry Lost* lays the blueprint for hope after loss. An up-close-and-personal renovation of the heart, with a generous smattering of Lowe's signature Southern charm and cheeky wit. Please don't miss this one.

NICOLE DEESE, Christy Award–winning author

T. I. Lowe mixes serious issues with her own unique sense of humor and style, and her Sonny Bates is a force to reckon with. . . . A terrific read!

FRANCINE RIVERS, *New York Times* bestselling author of *Redeeming Love* and *The Lady's Mine*, on *Indigo Isle*

With beautiful themes and strong writing, Lowe delivers a romance that lifts up women and men and shows how love can overcome the walls built around secrets.

LIBRARY JOURNAL on *Indigo Isle*

A powerful coming-of-age story set on a Magnolia, SC, tobacco farm in the 1980s. . . . Lowe's fans will be thrilled.

PUBLISHERS WEEKLY on *Under the Magnolias*

SOUTH OF SOMEWHERE

Tyndale House Publishers
Carol Stream, Illinois

SOUTH OF SOMEWHERE

T. I. LOWE

Visit Tyndale online at tyndale.com.

Visit T. I. Lowe's website at tilowe.com.

South of Somewhere

Cover design by Faceout Studio, Tim Green

Interior design by Brandi Davis

Edited by Kathryn S. Olson

Published in association with the literary agency of Browne & Miller Literary Associates, LLC, 52 Village Place, Hinsdale, IL 60521

For information about special discounts for bulk purchases, please contact Tyndale House Publishers at csresponse@tyndale.com, or call 1-855-277-9400.

Library of Congress Cataloging-in-Publication Data

A catalog record for this book is available from the Library of Congress.

ISBN 979-8-4005-0780-9 (HC)
ISBN 979-8-4005-0781-6 (SC)

Printed in the United States of America

32 31 30 29 28 27 26
7 6 5 4 3 2 1

In memory of my sister, Shanna. I love you. I miss you.

I was given a thorn in my flesh, a messenger from Satan to torment me and keep me from becoming proud.

2 CORINTHIANS 12:7

1

I died once, and I didn't find it all that unpleasant. Coming back, though . . . well, that's an entirely different story. Facing the aftermath of it seemed so much worse than death itself. Today, years in the making, I would have to start facing more of the aftermath head-on. No more hiding behind locked doors and security. I just had to get around this skunk first.

Not a real one, but her hair reminded me of a skunk. Two inches of white tracks zipping right down the middle on either side of her parted brassy-red hair. *I'm going natural,* the lead addiction counselor had said last week when she attended my exit plan meeting. It didn't look all that natural and, really, why did natural actually matter? Boring, if you asked me, but no one asked for my opinion.

"Just sign here, hon." Gail offered a pen, but the offer meant so much more than that. The offer also included my freedom. A freedom I wrestled with being ready for.

Don't screw this up, I thought, signing *Juniper Wilder* on the line at the bottom of the page that stated I was ready to reenter the real world and act like I had some sense this time around. Heaven help me, I sure hoped I wasn't signing a lie.

"Your brother dropped off your car." Gail handed me the key chain with the mini picture frame still holding on for dear life.

I accepted the key chain and stared at the small photo. A set of green eyes, identical to mine, stared back. The picture of pure sweet innocence and a reminder of the worst mistake of my life. Blinking back tears, I mumbled, "Thanks."

"Oh, and here's the paperwork for your new license. Good job on finishing the course and getting it reinstated." Gail smiled encouragingly, as if I'd completed a college course and not an alcoholism and drug safety action program. "Be sure to go by the DMV as soon as possible."

"I will. Thanks again." I turned to leave.

"Junie," Gail called out, putting my escape on pause. "You're going to be okay."

I met her light-brown eyes that were *naturally* warm with compassion I didn't deserve. I only nodded before walking toward a life of unknowns. Did I believe her simple declaration, that I would be okay? Absolutely not.

My silver car sat in a spot in the visitors' section right out front. I pushed the button on the key fob and the trunk opened smoothly, but there wasn't any room for my luggage. Boxes of my belongings filled most of the space, telling me all I needed to know. *Stay away. Move on. Don't come back.* Next to the boxes, a case of sparkling waters was frosty with condensation, indicating it hadn't been there long, which also meant my brother could have waited for me. Did I blame my brother? Not at all. Did it hurt anyway? Much more than I cared to admit.

"Thanks, jerk." I stabbed the plastic wrapping with a house key that no longer welcomed me and pried an ice-cold can from the case. Chilling the waters had been considerate, I gave him that much.

I'd just cracked open the can and taken a deep drink from it when a shadow crept over me. Bracing myself, I lowered the can and met a set of heavy-lidded, bloodshot eyes.

"You breaking out today, Sassy?" Deaton licked his lips and moved closer.

I put my luggage between us. "Yep."

"Sweet." Deaton tucked his long blond hair behind his ear, the shade dark and dull. If I squinted my eyes, I could almost imagine him pre-drugs. He reminded me of Arlo, both handsome in a worn way and charismatic with a heavy dose of crazy. I considered myself crazy as well after making that terrible mistake the night we were both admitted. A mistake he hadn't once let me forget in the past six months. A mistake that haunted me as much as Arlo did.

I barely remembered the night I arrived here, but the next day remained crystal clear in my memory. I had to take my first of many drug tests. I straight-up admitted I wouldn't pass it—who knew how easily accessible drugs were in prison—but the woman administering the test laughed it off. *No one passes the first, but you better pass all the rest.* Despite Deaton's constant access to contraband which he constantly offered to me, I managed to stay clean.

"Whelp. I gotta go, so . . ." I maneuvered around Deaton and slung my suitcase and duffel bag in the backseat.

"Where are you off to? Sullivan's Island, right?"

I opened the car door, but he blocked me from getting in. "Yep." *Why on earth did I tell him about that?* I blamed it on being stuck in this facility, day in and day out. I had to admit Deaton helped me pass time with hours of card games and dumb jokes. Once he finally understood nothing more could happen between us, he settled for surface-level friendship. Sort of. Every now and then he'd try coming on to me, but I kept on shutting that down.

"Take me with you." His breath smelled of stale cigarettes and coffee, two things I couldn't stand. I told him time and time again he should quit smoking, but, as with all things, no one told Deaton James what to do. We'd both made it through the program, but it was time for me to move on.

I huffed a laugh. "You get to go jet-setting or laze on a yacht somewhere, while I'm strapped with a year's worth of probation, AA meetings, and random drug tests." I thumped his shoulder, hoping the light banter helped get me out of this. "Trust me. You don't want to go with me."

"Deaton! We have paperwork to do before you can leave!" Standing at the entrance, Gail waved for him to get back inside.

He turned and I took the opportunity to slide inside the car. Before I could get the door shut, he grabbed it. "You got a number?"

"I don't own a phone anymore, remember?" He'd somehow snuck a phone in, like other things we weren't allowed to have, but I stuck to the rules. Prison and rehab will do that to a girl. Scared me straight into obeying everything, that's for dang sure.

"Well, when you get one, add my number first." Deaton placed a torn piece of paper in my hand. "Don't forget me, Sassy." He winked and then walked away.

Once Deaton disappeared inside, I tossed the paper on the ground and shut my door. I know some people formed lasting friendships in rehab, but I couldn't afford to do that with him. He hadn't learned a darn thing while we were stuck here, but I had. Mainly, I'd learned the life I'd been living wasn't living at all, but today I wanted a real shot at it.

My steady—something new to me—index finger pressed the start button, and the sedan came to life. Strapped for cash, I'd have to look into selling it, but I was too weary to even consider that daunting task at the moment. Driving away from this place of reckoning and toward more consequences took all the strength I had.

I put the car in reverse and looked into the rearview mirror. Flinching, I kept my foot on the brake and relived the last time I had looked into that mirror. The scene had been much different than an unassuming parking lot. No, last time the view had been lit with flashing blue lights as my life imploded.

2

Between my rusty driving skills and worrying about being pulled over, the trip to Sullivan's Island turned out to be a slow one. While on the interstate, I wondered about the traffic going the opposite direction. Were they on the way out of our little state, going on vacation, a new adventure? My probation prohibited me from leaving South Carolina. Funny how I'd never left this state before but really wanted to now that I'd been told I couldn't. *Just like a young'un,* I heard my grandmother say in my thoughts. *Always wanting what you can't have.*

As soon as I spotted the Ben Sawyer swing bridge, thoughts of going elsewhere faded. I rolled the window down and breathed in the savory humid air, so thick the flavor settled on the back of my tongue. It tasted like home. I'd spent more time here with Olla than with my own parents in all the places they'd lived over the years. My parents could be best described as nomads. Although their passion in life dealt with maintaining healthy root systems in the world of botany, they had no desire to lay down roots of their own anywhere in particular.

I took a right at the stop sign and slowly passed the short stretch of quaint shops and restaurants in the heart of the island's business district. On the right, one of the most popular places to eat, Poe's Tavern, already had a line out the door. I continued down Middle Street, edging slowly in the heavy traffic, until reaching Grandma's house. Even though she'd been gone for close to three years now, it would always be Olla's place. Not mine. Not my brother's.

Parking in the driveway, I began smoothing my thumb along each fingernail while taking a moment to just look at the three-story home on stilts named Lady Indigo. Most every home had a unique name showcased on a plaque, either on the porch rail or by the front door. Oleander Cottage, Crossed Fish, Willie's Whistle Stop, and Brady's Bungalow were a few I could recall right off the top of my head. Grandma told me once that in the early days of Sullivan's Island, mail was typically addressed by the name of the house instead of the address. I'd always found that tidbit quite charming.

The shaker siding had a fresh coat of navy-blue paint with a gray tin roof. Two shaggy palmetto trees bookended either side of the house in the front yard, swaying to the rhythm of the ocean breeze.

I exited the car and the coast embraced me like an old friend. I closed my eyes and tilted my head, letting the sun kiss my face and the breeze wash over me until the sound of movement next door interrupted. Glancing to the right at the large white house, I noticed a man sitting hunched in the shade of its deep porch. He wore a ball cap shrouding most of his face, which was buried in a book. Thank goodness he didn't seem the social type, not even raising his head when I shut the car door. We were close enough that I heard him cough, so he had to have heard me also.

I moved to the trunk of my car to start unloading it just as a shiny black Corvette pulled in behind me. A white-headed man, more fit than most men half his age, exited the low-slung car with very little effort.

I shook my head. "You know you look ridiculous in that thing."

"Do I look like I care?" Gilbert pulled off his aviators and huffed. "And you're a fine one to talk, Miss Mercedes."

Touché.

"I'm not ready to deal with you. I haven't even gone inside yet." I gestured toward the house, widening my eyes. "And I have to pee."

"Sounds like perfect timing to me." Gilbert leaned into the car and came back with a brown paper bag. "Let's get you tested." He held the bag out but I crossed my arms.

"I took one before I left the"—remembering the neighbor, I lowered my voice—"facility."

"That was hours ago. Plenty of time to get high or down a bottle of booze." Gilbert shoved the drug test into my grasp and waved a hand. "Lead the way."

I snuck another peek next door, disappointed to find the guy still there on his porch. He didn't look my way, but I was pretty sure he'd heard every word just now. Humiliated, I stomped up the stairs and punched in the code for the door. I rushed to get inside and plowed into the faint scent of patchouli, an essential oil my grandmother swore by, saying it had calm-inducing properties. Needing as much of that as possible, I took a deep inhale and made my way to the guest bathroom to handle this first order of business. I wondered how disappointed Olla would be in me over the awful mess I'd made of my life. What would she say if she could see me unscrewing a plastic cup with barcodes on the side? Face heated and tears threatening, I turned to the toilet and went on autopilot.

Finishing up, I washed my hands and opened the door. Gilbert stood there waiting. "Have at it, sir." I stepped aside and left him to do the testing.

I'm not sure how I ended up with this seventy-three-year-old man as my probation officer and sponsor. He retired a while back, but he claimed his friend and judge asked him to come out of retirement to help me stay on the straight and narrow. And darned if the man hadn't made that his mission. He'd visited me once, sometimes twice, a week since I met him eight months ago. We had a love/hate relationship and had made a game out of razzing each other.

"You passed!" Gilbert declared, striding into the living room while stripping off a pair of latex gloves.

"What a wonderful surprise! I didn't even study!" I did a silly little clap.

Gilbert rolled his eyes. "Don't be a smart aleck."

"I'm afraid I know no other way to be." I flipped the overhead light on even though enough sunshine poured through the giant windows without it. "Now that the fun is over, you can head on out, sir. I need to unpack and—"

"You have plenty of time for that." Gilbert returned to the bathroom and I listened to the sink turn on as he called out, "I heard that Mexican place down the street is popular."

"I'm sure you'll like it." I moved to the front door, ready to send him on his merry way.

Gilbert came out of the bathroom. "You're going too."

I crossed my arms and took in the large yet quaint living room, dressed in vibrant teal, coral, and dark navy tones. I got my love of color from my grandmother, for sure. "Thanks, but I'm good."

"I didn't ask. I'm telling." He swept a hand in an ushering motion.

"Look, I haven't been out in public in like forever. I'm not sure I'm ready for that."

"No time like the present to get it over with and I'll be with you, so that's a bonus." Gilbert frowned. "If it's too much, just say so, and we'll leave."

"Fine." I stomped past him. "But you're paying."

*

We ended up at a table smack-dab in the middle of the busy cantina. After being locked away for the better part of the last year, this place was sensory overload with its colorful décor, lots of people talking and laughing, and lively music playing over the speakers. I felt itchy inside and out, but I tried not to show it.

A young guy sidled up to the table with an offering of chips and salsa. "I'm Derrick. Can I start you off with something to drink?"

"Can I have a frozen strawberry margarita?"

Gilbert choked on his chip.

The waiter said, "Sure," like it was no big deal. In the normal world with normal folks, I guess that should have been the truth but not with me.

"A nonalcoholic one," I clarified, ignoring the huffing sounds coming from Gilbert. "We're both alcoholics, so please make sure it's a mocktail."

Derrick managed to hide his reaction rather well, even though his cheeks reddened. "Sure thing. And you, sir?"

"Just water." Tapping a finger on the table, Gilbert waited until the guy moved away. "You don't just go around blurtin' that mess out to just anybody."

"Why not? I bet he'll make sure to get my drink order correct."

Gilbert grumbled incoherently, apparently out of patience with me. Good. Hopefully, he'd dump me out in my driveway after lunch.

"Lighten up, Gilly." I searched the basket for a folded chip, my favorite, and dunked it in the salsa.

"You make me sound like a dang fish. *Gilly.*" He made a face.

I angled my head and studied him. "You kinda look like a catfish, now that you've mentioned it."

Gilbert didn't dignify my lie with a response. Truthfully, he was a good-looking man and a sharp dresser. Today, he wore a navy sports coat with a crisp white button-down and dark-wash jeans. If Grandma Olla was still alive, I'd encourage her to flirt with him.

"Here ya go." Derrick placed the hot-pink beverage in front of me.

I gave it a sniff, not detecting any booze, just strawberries. "You sure this is a mocktail, right?" My joke now had me a little nervous.

He nodded. "Yes."

I took a cautious sip of the super-sweet slushie and wrinkled my nose. "Something's . . . something's not right with this . . ." I tested it again, almost giving myself a brain freeze.

Derrick's eyes widened. "What's wrong?"

"It's missing the tequila."

"Good grief." Gilbert kicked me under the table.

The waiter's brow furrowed. "But I thought you said . . ."

I held a palm up. "I'm just joking. It's fine. I'd like the carnitas, please. With a side of guacamole." An overly sweet smile stretched my face to full capacity, almost painfully so, reminding me I'd not used that expression in quite a long time.

"Oh. Okay." Derrick took our orders and wasted no time getting away from our table.

Gilbert swiped another chip and aggressively dunked it in the salsa. It's a wonder the poor chip didn't break. "Your joke sucked."

"Gotta keep ya on your toes, ole Gilly." I winked just to annoy him, even though my heart wasn't really into it.

He wiped his mouth with a napkin and gave me a pointed glare. "Young lady, you need to take your sobriety seriously and stop actin' like a ninny."

"I don't believe I'm acting."

"You are and it's not funny."

I stared at the frosty margarita glass. "But if I don't figure out a way to laugh through this, I'll be crying." My vision blurred as my composure began to slip underneath the deluge of guilt and shame.

Gilbert placed his hand on top of mine. "Breathe, Junie." He waited until I complied. "It's okay to laugh. More than okay. We just need to get you signed up for some comedy lessons. I'm sure your joke telling can improve with the right help." He patted my hand before letting go.

"You're not funny either," I muttered, grabbing an extra napkin to dry my eyes. "Gosh, I'm such a stupid, terrible person."

"No, you're not. You're just a typical human, who made a stupid, terrible mistake."

"Gee, thanks."

"Just truth-speaking." He pointed a finger at me. "When God created you, he factored in that stupidity. Even though you made all those bad decisions, he still claims you and cares deeply for you. If he can, then I think it's high time you start caring for yourself too." Gilbert looked like he wanted to say more, but our food arrived, shutting us both up while we ate in amicable silence. I had a feeling the reprieve would be short-lived.

Once the plates were clear, Gilbert handed over a paper. "This is the address to the AA meeting I found for us to attend. They meet Fridays at six. There's a few locations that hold NA meetings if you'd like to check those out too."

"One's just as good as the other." My main vice was alcohol with a small side of narcotics, so AA seemed the better fit for me. I folded the paper without looking at it and shoved it into my back pocket. It was one of those things I knew I had to face, like all the rest of the consequences that came from my bad choices, but chose to do so later. Maybe tomorrow . . .

"You know you have to go to them."

"Yes, sir." I sighed, slumping heavily in my chair. "I know."

Gilbert gave me a concerned look, bordering on pity. "It'll get easier, Junie. Just stick this out, okay?"

I shrugged. "What other choice do I have?"

We settled the bill—Gilbert paid, thank goodness—then he offered another gift by dropping me off in the driveway instead of barging his way back in the house.

I'd gotten no further than closing the door good when someone knocked.

Groaning, I turned around and yanked the door open. "Go away, Gil—! Oh!" Static raised the fine hairs on my neck as I gazed at a man who was definitely not my probation officer. I lifted a shoulder and used my chin to brush the tingle away. "Sorry. I thought you were my . . . uh . . . personal trainer. He just left." Shifting in my Birkenstocks, I willed him not to notice my white peasant blouse and bell-bottom jeans with decorative patches I'd hand-sewn on them myself—far from workout gear. "May I help you?"

He straightened his glasses but the frames went right back to where they were, sitting somewhat askew. "Oh, I just wanted to introduce myself. I'm Henry." He had a deep velvety voice, the kind that reaches even when spoken quietly. He pointed a long index finger to his right while holding my gaze. "I live next door. I'm your neighbor."

"Nice to meet you. I'm Juniper but everyone calls me Junie."

"This is a nice place you have." Henry nodded. He reminded me of a scruffy version of Clark Kent, who looked a day or two late on shaving. He was no longer wearing the hat from earlier, so now a shock of dark-chocolate curls spilled around his ears and onto his forehead.

"It was my grandmother's house. My brother and I inherited it from her." Grandma Olla left the house to us equally with a stipulation that we couldn't sell it. She knew Cy and I were no longer close, so I've often thought she probably did this to ensure we maintained some sort of relationship long after she was gone. Sadly, a house with strong studs secured in a firm foundation isn't a guarantee to keep a family together.

Henry cleared his throat, glancing past me, then returning his bright-blue eyes to mine. "I'm sorry for your loss."

"Thanks." Chitchatting wasn't my forte, especially when meeting someone new. I racked my brain until settling on, "Your place is nice too." *Brilliant.* "How long have you lived here?"

"About two years. I like it out here. It's quiet. Well, this end of the island is anyway."

"Yep." I could have told him how it hadn't always been so touristy, that back in my younger years the entire island held this peaceful quiet, but then that might encourage more conversation and I'd already reached my daily limit.

We stared at each other until it grew awkward. I needed to take a weeklong nap, not socialize with strangers. Looking for an out, I yawned deliberately.

Henry's eyebrows rose above the black frame of his glasses, picking up on my cue, mercifully. He took a few steps back. "I won't keep you. I just wanted to say hey and let you know if you ever need anything, like sugar, I probably won't have it."

His handsome face remained completely serious as his broad shoulders lifted apologetically. I wished Gilbert could have seen it. I would have pointed out, *Now that's how to cut a joke.*

"Good to know." I began closing the door. "Same goes here too. Bye now." I caught sight of a slight smile and his hand lifting to wave before the door shut with a firm click. Locking it, I shook off the weird encounter and wandered to the kitchen. I stood at the long island and let the silence of the house and the earthy scent of patchouli soothe me.

It had been eight months since I'd had a moment of privacy. Now I suddenly had all the privacy one could wish for. No check-ins, no cellmates, no roommates, no intercom announcements, no surprise room inspections. Just total solitude.

Such a gift and I feared ruining it.

3

Standing at only five feet tall with an aged white exterior, this monumental part of Lady Indigo appeared dead. At one time, she had the sole duty of being the heartbeat of this home. As long as she ticked, life continued. Laying my hands on either side, I felt the cold realization that life had not continued. Seemed with her passing, a lot had died right along with her.

I wiped a palm over the face of the antique grandmother clock, removing the layer of dust, and read the time. Two thirty-two. Had it been morning or afternoon when the clock drew her last breath, I didn't know. Arlo's time of death happened midday. Olla passed away early evening, so the house's time of death didn't correlate with either of theirs.

I couldn't bring either of them back, as much as I longed to, but I had the ability to resurrect this clock. Cy used to be the clock keeper until I turned eight and all but demanded he pass his duties down to me. My brother was a meticulous person, and he took teaching me the intricacies of maintaining the clock seriously. He drew diagrams in a small notebook he labeled *Grandmother Clock Responsibilities* and he would stand by me to supervise, critiquing as I went along. He could have played his I'm-older trump card, but he seemed to enjoy teaching me something. I wished he would pop in now and stand over my shoulder with instructions while I wound the clock, but nowadays the only instruction he'd given me was to stay away.

Brushing my hands together, I made my way to the laundry room and retrieved a dust rag. Returning to the clock in the back hallway, I began wiping away the last two years' worth of neglect. I took my time, cleaning the clock until the glass panels were sparkly clear. I tucked the rag into my back pocket, opened the bottom case, and pulled the first chain until the weight reached the top. The zipping sound interrupted the quiet of the house in a familiar way. So familiar and nostalgic, my chest and throat tightened with a fresh hit of grief. Sniffing, I pulled the other two chains, repeating the process to wind the clock. A gentle shove set the pendulum into motion and the tick-tock began, bringing the heartbeat of the house back to existence. I closed the bottom and opened the clockface to set the time to fifteen after four.

With the clock restored to order, I took a step back and watched the pendulum sway while listening to the rhythmic *tick-tock, tick-tock*.

"Sure wish it was that easy to restore my life . . ." I mumbled under my breath.

Eventually, I gave up staring at the clock and moved on to nothing much of anything. I found myself in the kitchen staring out the window, then sitting on one of the bottom steps of the staircase. For the first time in forever, I didn't have a schedule to adhere to nor did I have to do anything in particular. For some reason, that made me anxious. The idea of all this freedom should have given me a celebratory vibe, not this deep-seated dread.

You could sneak a drink and no one would know.

I bolted off the step. "No, no, no . . ."

Meditation and yoga were two tools I learned in rehab to reduce stress and to divert my attention to something besides my anxieties and cravings. Feeling the tides of restlessness rise, I made quick work of opening up the windows facing the Atlantic. Dropping onto the area rug, I crossed my legs into a half chair pose and centered my thoughts on the crashing waves just outside. With measured breaths, in and out, I pictured myself sitting on the deck of a boat, my body swaying from the sea's current and not my panicking nerves.

A sudden noise jolted me out of the boat. I rose to my feet and followed the sound to the kitchen. An iPhone on the counter by the fridge with a note beside it was lighting up with an incoming call. I'd totally missed seeing both the note and the phone earlier. Tentatively, I picked up the phone, read Cy's name on the screen, then slid my finger across the green button. "Hello?"

"Good. You found the phone I bought you." No greetings, straight to the point. Typical Cypress Wilder.

"Uh . . . yeah." I looked around to see if I'd missed anything else, like maybe a family member who wanted to help me celebrate my freedom, but found nothing. "You didn't have to do that."

"Of course I did. You didn't have one." The sharpness in his tone sent an instant wave of humiliation over me.

"I really appreciate it. Thank you."

"The six-month termite inspection and treatment was done two weeks ago . . ." Cy plowed forward with the facts. The math professor couldn't help himself, I supposed.

I scanned the note as my brother continued going over other things I already knew, like where the key to the lawn mower was, and how to put gas in it.

Lana stocked the fridge and pantry but from here on out, that's your responsibility. Olla's Caddy is in the garage. Taxes and insurance are up-to-date. Take it out for a drive at least once a week. The number to your new phone is below. FYI, the tracking is on. Don't turn it off.

Cy

I opened the fridge, revealing completely stocked shelves of everything I would need, undeservedly. A variety of condiments, fresh fruits and veggies in the crisper, a half gallon of two-percent milk, deli meats and cheeses. "Thank you for the phone and groceries." I shut the fridge and leaned against the stainless steel door. "Let me know how much I owe you."

"Don't worry about it." His sigh had a weight to it, the cumbersome sound speaking of how much of a burden I was on him. "Did you get settled in?"

"Pretty much." All of my belongings still sat untouched in the car, but I would get to that later. I'd also be adding the phone and groceries to the amount I already owed him. Just paying off my debt wouldn't make things right with him, but I had to start somewhere. "I miss y'all. Why don't you come down for the weekend? The weather is supposed to be nice."

"I'm stuck teaching a Maymester last minute. It starts on Monday, so I have to prepare—"

"I could go to y'all." Sullivan's Island was just far enough away from my family in Columbia to keep me at arm's length. Out of sight, out of mind. Exactly how Cy said he wanted it. But it's not what I wanted at all. I wanted my family. Needed them, more precisely.

Cy didn't respond right away, so I already knew the answer before he said, "Now isn't a good time."

Swallowing the lump in my throat, I nodded to the empty room. "No worries. Another time then." I waited a few beats to see if he would add a little bit of kindness to soften his rejection, but he remained quiet so I asked, "How's Lana and the kids?"

"They're fine."

I rolled my stinging eyes. Apparently, my brother had no plans on cutting me any slack. Not that I deserved any, but darned if it wouldn't have been nice all the same. "Will you let Fernie know I sent her a letter out yesterday? She should get it tomorrow, I think." It was a drawing she could color in, something I'd been doing every other week since going to rehab.

"Sure. By the way, Fern doesn't want to be called Fernie anymore. She just goes by Fern now."

I laughed, barely bringing any actual humor to the sound. "She's not even three, Cy. I doubt she's old enough to be deciding such."

Cy didn't laugh at all.

"I'd really like to see her."

He let out another long-suffering sigh. "We both know that's not a good idea."

"Why is that?"

"Seriously, Junie? What did I promise you after your arrest?"

I squeezed my eyes shut and rubbed my forehead. "To protect Fern. To always put her first in decisions about me."

"This is me putting her first. Let me keep that promise without you holding it against me. For your daughter's sake, I will not agree to you being around her until I know she'll be safe with you. Take this summer to prove yourself, that you can stay clean and out of trouble."

I sniffed, using the sleeve of my blouse to wipe my nose. Cy was right, but danged if it didn't hurt.

"Listen. I need to go. But be sure and call Mom and Dad and let them know you've been released."

Let them know you've been released. I filed that away under things I never wanted to hear again, along with *you are under arrest.*

"Okay." I shifted my weight from one foot to the other, growing agitated. "Thanks again for everything. Call me soon and maybe I could speak to Fern next—" He ended the call before I finished, dismissive as always. A bubble of indignation hiccupped out of me. Sniffing, I pulled up the contacts in the phone and saw that the good son had already added my parents' numbers. I looked at the clock on the stove and did the math. They were five hours ahead of us, past their bedtime, so I settled on a text in a group chat.

I'm a free bird!

At the moment, my arborist father and botanist mother were in England aiding in the world's largest seed conservationist project at Wakehurst. I really didn't know much about Rupert and Rose Wilder beyond that, so it always felt like communicating with distant relatives.

I stared at the unanswered message until my eyes blurred, growing more upset over something else I had no control over. My parents were who they were, brilliant yet neglectful, successful contributors to society yet forgetful parents. As I set the phone down, another piece of paper underneath Cy's note caught my eye. I slid it out and what I saw sent a sharp pang through my chest.

Local Woman Arrested

Twenty-five-year-old Juniper Wilder was arrested Thursday morning, charged with DUI and Child Endangerment DUI. Wilder's young daughter was taken in by protective services but has now been placed in emergency custody of family.

At the top of the printout Cy had written: *Let this be a reminder.*

A flash of shame heated my face. I didn't need a physical reminder. One lived rent-free in my head daily. I balled the paper up and tossed it.

Thinking better of it, I fished the paper from the trash can and smoothed it out. Maybe this needed to be a part of my punishment, to see my mistake in black and white. I grabbed a roll of tape and went upstairs, skipping the fourth step to avoid the perpetual creak. Crossing my room, I stopped in front of the dresser and taped the piece of paper to the bottom right corner of the mirror.

I read it once again as an anxious energy coursed through me. I needed to work it out of my system. Lugging in boxes and suitcases would have to do, considering most of the day had disappeared into long shadows.

Grandma's house stood a good bit taller than the one next door, which always made it easy to spy on the neighbors. A middle-aged couple used to own the house, the Palmers, who hosted a radio show that gave relationship advice. Olla used to get up early to listen, just to be supportive, even though she expressed to me more than once that their advice should be taken with a grain of salt. They'd been married three times and divorced twice from *each other*, so that made them an authority on the topic, in my opinion. I wondered if my calling might be to give advice on how not to completely ruin your life.

Leaving the disgraceful reminder on the mirror, I moved over to the window and took a peek. With a good view of Henry's house, I found the front porch clear. I entered my connecting bathroom and pulled the curtain to the side, checking his back pool patio and upper deck. Both clear as well, so I went outside to get on with it.

It only took three trips to complete the task. I should have been grateful for the little amount of work it took, but a sadness pressed over me instead as I surveyed the paltry collection of things piled in the living room. Two cardboard boxes, a duffel bag, a white garbage bag, and two suitcases represented my life. *Paltry indeed.*

I tore open one of the boxes and found exactly what I needed sitting right on top. I picked up the lavender scrapbook with delicate fern fronds painted on the front. The only piece of Fern I freely owned at the moment.

Leaving everything else for another day, I went upstairs to my room and plopped on the edge of the bed and opened the book. The first page was the ultrasound image of my little peanut, then a picture of Olla sitting beside me at my baby shower. I studied the image of Olla in the picture, trying to find a clue as to what was soon to shatter our entire family, but Olla looked perfectly healthy, grinning ear to ear as she held up a pink baby gown. No sign of the deadly beast lying in wait inside her. I moved my focus to me in the picture, wearing a floral dress, clutching my round belly. I wasn't hiding my despair all that well. Sure, I looked healthy too, but there were dark circles under my swollen eyes and the smile on my lips appeared a bit forced. It had been such a conundrum to be mourning my husband while celebrating the upcoming birth of our daughter at the same time. I never could reconcile the two emotions.

Turning the page, I blinked back tears and looked at the hospital photo of my newborn baby. She was blotchy and tiny, so different from what she looked like by the time we went home. No one took any of those traditional pictures of me holding my baby in the hospital bed, but I wouldn't have wanted that anyway. It was also the day of Olla's funeral, so once again I had been plunged into the wildly uncomfortable state of mourning and celebrating at the same time. Losing Arlo had been devastating, but I sensed I could survive it with Olla as my lifeline. Then my lifeline was snatched away before I resurfaced.

Using the collar of my shirt to dry my face, I turned the page and studied the picture of me and Fern snuggled together asleep in my bed. I didn't even know Lana had taken it until the next day when she gave me the print. Fern had slept tucked under my chin every night since coming home from the hospital, as if she were my doll baby. I wondered how she slept without me now. Had she adjusted easily to my absence? I hoped so, for her sake. I sure hadn't adjusted well to sleeping without her.

My daughter and I had been robbed in so many ways. And then, two years after her birth, I went and robbed her of her mother too. My eyes darted up to the dresser mirror, to that piece of paper, then I flipped several pages to the last photo I had of Fern. Sitting under an umbrella on the very beach just outside, with a red shovel in her chubby fist, and grinning at the camera.

I removed the photo from the little corner brackets and moved to the dresser. It needed to join the article about my arrest. I taped it to the center of the mirror, so every day I could see both my best achievement in life, and my worst.

4

Growing up, my brother took it upon himself to be my keeper from the get-go, and I did everything to prove he wasn't. Cy took it upon himself to assign me chores and I took it upon myself to hide from him and his orders. My favorite hiding spot was either the open-air crow's nest on top of Grandma Olla's house or underneath my bed. I would hunker down and pretend nothing existed beyond my hiding place until my big brother showed up and demanded I get to whatever task I had been avoiding.

After carrying in my belongings the other night, I debated making a bed in the crow's nest but it started raining, of course. And scooting underneath a bed wasn't nearly as appealing as back in my childhood, so I chose to cling to the lavender scrapbook and hide away underneath the blankets instead.

There I remained while hours turned into days, sleeping then flipping through the memories of Fern. I kept promising myself I'd get up out of this bed and get on with it as soon as Cy called or showed up to make me. How foolish that ended up being. And, yeah, I knew being an adult meant making myself do the adulting things, but sometimes it would've been nice to have someone around to nudge me in that direction with some encouragement. Some support.

I rolled over and adjusted the pillow under my head, wrinkling my nose as a waft of unwashed hair and stale breath hit me. Not caring enough to do anything about it, I shut my eyes and let my thoughts drift until the doorbell rang.

After getting my bearings, I shuffled to the bathroom and turned on the sink faucet. Ignoring the doorbell and whoever it was knocking incessantly, I slurped several gulps of water, then splashed my face a few times to wash away the fatigue. A shower would do a better job, but I decided to go downstairs and figure out who the heck was trying to break down the front door.

I yanked it open and glared at my unwanted guest. Just beyond him, dark clouds hung heavily in the sky, fittingly so. "I should have known it was you." No one else bothered to visit me.

Gilbert gave me an assessing once-over and made a sound much like a rumble of thunder. "You didn't, Junie. *Please* say you didn't."

I crossed my arms and leaned on the doorjamb, hoping he'd pick up on the fact that he wasn't welcome inside. "What are you talking about?"

He gave a resigned shake of his head and walked to his car.

I closed the door and started to the kitchen. Some tea would be good, but before I could start the kettle, I heard the front door open and shut with a little force, then a brown bag landed on the counter beside me.

"It's not what you think." I snatched up the bag and marched to the bathroom and yelled, "I can't wait to prove you wrong!"

"Me too!"

Ten minutes and another clean test later, I tried to direct Gilbert to the door, but he made it no farther than a barstool at the kitchen island and refused to budge.

"Have a seat and let's you and me have a talk." He motioned to the stool beside him.

Defiant and also aware of needing a shower, I moved to the other side of the island and remained standing. "Just say what you need to say."

Gilbert swiveled on the stool and craned his neck, surveying the living room and all my stuff still stacked up and waiting to be put away. "What have you been doing since I saw you last week?"

"Catching up on my rest."

"That's it?"

I shrugged. "Between prison and rehab, I had a lot to catch up on."

Gilbert scrubbed a hand down his face. "There's more to it than just needing rest. What's this hibernating really about?"

I stared past him, watching the ocean waves crash onto the shore. *My family acts like I don't exist and . . . I'm wondering if that would be for the best.* I chose not to say this out loud for fear he'd haul me back to rehab or some other facility, and I'd had my fill of such.

"Junie?"

I shrugged. "As my Grandma Olla used to say, this is just my winter, ya know."

"No. It's May in the South. Ain't no winter in sight."

"You know very well that's an expression, old man." I combed my hair over my shoulder and began plaiting it in a loose braid. "I'm staying clean and that's all you need to concern yourself with."

Gilbert leaned his elbows on the counter and frowned. "I've come out of retirement for the sole purpose of concerning myself with all things Juniper Wilder. So, let's be clear here, *young* lady, you are my main priority. If you stumble, just keep in mind I'm a seventy-three-year-old geezer. I'm liable to break a hip when I go down with you."

I suppressed a snort. As much as I hated to admit it, I liked Gilbert and found him quite endearing. He'd shared a little bit about himself in our initial meeting. Served in the military, did two tours in

Vietnam, lost a lot of his friends in an air strike, came home, and fell into a bottle. It took a childhood friend named Valerie to get him to sober up. After marrying her, Gilbert made a career in law enforcement. He'd worked enough, if you asked me, and shouldn't have to be dealing with a recovering alcoholic at this stage of life. Yet here we were.

Gilbert glanced over his shoulder and around the room as if searching for something. "What's that creaking sound?"

I tipped my head to the side and listened for a moment, hearing the faint groaning from a strong gust coming off the ocean. "Just the house complaining like any coastal home. It's never liked windy days. And it really has a sore spot for hurricanes. You live on Isle of Palms, you should know this."

"I live in a condo. It doesn't creak." Gilbert tapped his knuckles against the gray and white marble. "Anyway, we need to hit the road soon, so go get yourself cleaned up."

Instantly on guard, I narrowed my eyes at him. "Where are we going?"

"To go make some new friends."

Looking heavenward, I whined. "I'm not feeling social."

"Too bad. We have an AA meeting to get to." He wore that stubborn look on his face. The one that didn't allow any lip, so I stomped upstairs like a pouty child to shower.

*

Filled with dread, I descended the back stairs of a community center near Mount Pleasant. I had done group therapy in rehab. I wasn't much of a fan of it then and had no desire to do it now. I never considered the whole opening-up-to-strangers thing as a fun pastime.

"Stop dragging your feet and wipe that grimace off your face." Gilbert held the door and beckoned me to hurry up, nodding his head and waving his hand, which had me slowing down to a snail's pace. "Today, Junie, *today*."

I skulked past him and as soon as I crossed the threshold into the dimly lit room, the grimace returned to my face as the smell of burned coffee and mildew hit me. I opened my mouth to complain to Gilbert, but raised voices by the refreshment table distracted me.

"I said take it back!" A wiry guy with dark circles under his puffy eyes jabbed a finger into a much bigger guy's chest. The scrawny man seemed too frail to be yelling and jabbing someone.

"You don't tell me what to do!" burly guy shouted back.

Gilbert held out his arm, directing me to stay behind him. Unsure of what to do, we remained rooted in place. The arguing escalated and a few others ended up being pulled into it when their efforts to intervene backfired.

"Stay put," Gilbert ordered, then moved in the direction of the conflict, yelling at the crowd to knock it off.

Of course no one listened. Seemed this whole crowd had a chip on their shoulder. A few shoves in, chairs started toppling over and a box of donuts shot through the air in an explosion of pink frosting and sprinkles. Wiry guy launched himself at burly guy, only to bounce off the big guy's barrel chest, sending him on a crash course toward me. It all happened so fast. One moment it was raining donuts, the next I was flat on my back, seeing stars.

5

Apparently, an elbow made for a pretty serious weapon. My mouth stood no chance. Pain shot from my face all the way down to my toes.

"Junie!" Gilbert stood over me, offering a hand.

Ears ringing, it took a moment to get my bearings. Finally, I accepted his hand and he slowly helped me to my feet.

"I'm so sorry, miss!" The scrawny man's entire body shook. From withdrawals or the fight, I'm not sure.

Disoriented, I dabbed my wet lip, wincing from the sting. I pulled my hand back and found my fingertips painted red. Without acknowledging the now-sobbing assailant and the uproar of the room, I turned on my heels and beat a path out of there.

Gilbert caught up with me and shoved a handful of paper towels into my hand. "Here, let me see." He tilted my chin and inspected my mouth. "It's split pretty good, but I think you'll live."

"Gee, that's wonderful," I said with a slight lisp. Pressing the towels to my lip, I got into the car and waited until Gilbert settled in the driver's seat to launch my complaint. "If this is what AA meetings entail, it's gonna drive me back to drinking."

"That wasn't normal for a meeting. Sure, talks can get heated, but I've never seen it escalate to that point." Gilbert put the car into gear and left the awful place behind. Several minutes down Highway 17, he turned on his blinker and veered into the Sonic parking lot. "Let's get you a slushie. My treat."

I huffed a laugh, being mindful to not stretch my lips. "Like a child being rewarded after a doctor's visit?"

He pulled up to one of the menu boards and put the car in park. "More like it'll help numb your lip."

"Oh." I leaned forward and read over the endless options, but nothing sounded like it would pair too well with a mouth full of blood. "Just a cup of ice."

Gilbert frowned. "That's it? Last time I offered to buy, you ordered one of everything on the menu."

"Because I hadn't had Taco Bell in like four months when you offered. *Duh.*" I shrugged. It made perfect sense to me.

Gilbert kept frowning, his thumb tapping the top of the steering wheel. "Have you eaten anything today?"

I moved the paper towels away and pointed at my mangled mouth. "I don't have much of an appetite."

"That didn't answer my question." His expectant gaze waited for my reply that I stubbornly held back. Sighing, he shook his head. "You have blood all over your chin. Use one of those napkins to clean up some so you don't scare the server." He reached over and pushed the button, ordering the cup of ice I requested along with an iced coffee for himself.

"Iced coffee? I figured you for hot black coffee."

Gilbert scoffed. "Just because iced coffee is on *trend* doesn't mean it's a new invention. I've been making iced coffees since way back to my military days. My cup would get cold before I could drink it most of the time, so I started putting ice in it and found it was more refreshing that way."

"Good for you," I muttered.

The server showed up with our two cups, barely glancing my way, thank goodness.

On the drive home, I kept adding nuggets of ice behind my bottom lip, like the coldest tobacco dip ever, while Gilbert rambled on and on about other so-called trends and how they had also been around since the dinosaurs.

"Those high-water pants were a sign of poverty back in my day. It showed folks you couldn't afford new pants when you got to growin'. But you people wear them now to show off that you got more money than sense."

I leaned my head against the window and let him rant, not pointing out the fact that I preferred flared jeans that dragged the ground or flowy maxi skirts.

"And why is it these new generations act like big ole headphones are something new? They were invented before even I was born."

My eyes slid shut and an image of a blond-haired, brown-eyed teenage boy wearing a pair of red headphones materialized. Arlo always preferred them instead of earbuds. The first time I saw him, he was sitting in art class my sophomore year wearing that red pair while working on a charcoal drawing. As silly as it sounded, it was love at first sight. Our infatuation with each other caught like a firecracker and followed the path of one as well—bright and all-consuming before burning out.

"You asleep over there?"

Opening my eyes, I lifted my head and realized we'd arrived home. I reached for the door handle but hesitated when I noticed the neighbor checking his mail.

Gilbert leaned forward and peered around me. "Who's that?"

"My neighbor."

"Hmm . . . The meeting didn't work out, but you still need to make some friends."

"Don't even think about it," I hissed.

Still staring, Gilbert mumbled, "How do you know what I'm thinking about?"

"I see it in your beady eyes."

Gilbert narrowed said beady eyes, still focused on the guy. "Here's your homework assignment, invite your neighbor over for coffee."

I scoffed. "You can't make me do that."

Gilbert opened his door. "I just did."

We exited the car and I made sure to keep my face turned away from Henry.

"That's so not fair!" My fists balled, wanting nothing more than to punch this crazy man.

"Remember, sweetheart, we are in good ole boy country. I shouldn't even be your probation officer yet here I am. So, don't make me put in my report that you're being uncooperative."

"You can't be serious, Gill. I have other relationships to fix before I even think about a relationship with a *man*. I'm not sure I'll ever want something like that again." I discreetly motioned toward Henry. "Plus he looks a good bit older than me."

"I'm talking friendship, not proposing marriage." Gilbert crossed my yard and into the neighbor's. "Excuse me, young man, do you mind telling me how old you are?"

I all but ran inside the house. "This cannot be my life!" I dumped the cup of melted ice into the kitchen sink and went into the guest bathroom to check my face. "Ugh!" Leaning closer to the mirror, I angled my face one way and then the other, the overhead light catching on the nasty split at the corner of my bottom lip. A bruise darkened my swollen chin, but at least the bleeding had finally stopped. I grabbed a washcloth from under the sink and cleaned it up as best as I could.

"He's only thirty-four!" Gilbert hollered, slamming the front door. "Not old at all."

"Not old? That's close to a decade older than me." I shared an eye roll with my disfigured reflection.

"Doesn't matter with friendship. I'm near 'bout a century older than you and we're friends."

I left the bathroom and met Gilbert in the living room. "Are we, though?"

"Of course." Gilbert declaring that so easily and without pause made my chest tighten. This old man was my only friend.

He snapped his fingers. "Oh, and his name is Henry Morrison. That's a good name!"

"Much better than Gilbert, for sure." I decided not to tell Mr. Busy Britches I already knew Henry's name.

Ignoring my sass, Gilbert continued, "Henry is a fan of coffee. He likes flavored creamers. Caramel is his favorite." He nodded encouragingly, seeming so proud of himself.

"Well, good for him, but I don't drink coffee, remember?" I took a seat across from Gilbert as he sat on the coral chenille sofa.

"Henry likes it, so make it for him. It's called being considerate of others." He zeroed in on my lip. "How ya feelin'?"

"Like someone tried to remove my bottom lip with his elbow." I licked across the wound and cringed. "Elbows should be outlawed."

"You got some Tylenol or ibuprofen?"

"Yeah, but a Percocet or three sure would hit the spot right about now."

Gilbert grunted. "Get some better jokes, kid." He scanned the room, his gaze landing on my boxes and bags scattered about. "You need to unpack and then work on a game plan."

"A game plan for what?"

He waved a hand, gesturing at nothing in particular. "To get your life back in order."

Feeling the threat of tears, I closed my eyes and rubbed my forehead.

"Look, I know you're in a bad place, losing your husband, then your grandmother . . ." Each word he spoke ripped into me more severely than my split lip. "And then losing custody of Fernie—"

"Just stop!" Hand held up, I took a painful breath. My pulse pounded through my head and against my swollen lip. "I'd rather not talk about that." I rose to my feet and headed to the kitchen. I rummaged in the pantry, finding a plastic bag and filling it with ice cubes from the freezer.

Gilbert joined me in the kitchen with a huff and a puff, as if he was the disgruntled one. Maybe he was, considering the poor guy had to put up with the likes of me. "Fine, then let's talk about your plans for income."

I pressed the ice pack to my mouth, the cold sting soon eased into numbness. A numbness I sure wished would envelop my entire body.

"Junie, you need to work."

Glaring, I lowered the ice pack. "I know this, Gilly."

"Okay, so do you have anything in mind?"

"Yeah. I want to start an online boutique, customizing hats."

His brow furrowed. "Customizing hats?"

"Mostly cowboy hats. I'll use all sorts of material to customize them, like ribbon, lace, feathers. Maybe paint or stain them. The creative possibilities are endless. It's really on *trend* right now." I loved to draw and do watercolors but knew, realistically, I didn't have much of a chance making a living with canvas art. At least the hats would keep me in the creative world.

Gilbert propped his elbows on the counter. "How do you get that up and going?"

I returned the ice pack to my lips and gave it some thought before lowering it again. "I'll need money for supplies, so I'm gonna sell my car. It's fairly new and should be worth a good bit." I owed Cy a pretty penny, so paying him back would be my first priority. Hopefully, there would be enough left for the hats.

"If you sell your car, how do you plan on getting around to sell these custom hats of yours?"

"I still have my grandmother's vehicle. It's in the garage."

"Okay. Add getting a phone to your list. I need to be able to reach you."

"My brother got me one already." I plucked Cy's note off the counter and handed it to Gilbert. "Here's the number."

Gilbert took a moment to program my contact info into his phone. "I guess that's a good start. You work on the hat business and I'll work on finding another meeting." He hitched a thumb toward the living room. "You need help moving your stuff?"

"No thanks. I got it."

Gilbert left soon after without me having to shove him out the door. Grateful for that, I decided to listen to him for a change and put away my meager belongings.

Belongings that didn't really belong anywhere . . . Or maybe that was just me who didn't belong.

I moved everything upstairs into my room and started sorting through the box I'd opened the other night. The contents were mostly art and stationary supplies. I found the pack of paint pens and plucked the white one out. Shaking it, I crossed to the dresser and studied Fern's sweet face and then the article about my arrest while working the cap off. It was time to work on that game plan. One I could see every day.

Above Fern's picture, I wrote: *Operation Get Fern Back!* Below the picture, I began writing the plan of action.

1. Sell car
2. Get a job
3. Work on hat and jewelry business
4. Prepare house for Fern
5. Set up Fern's room
6. Make amends with Cy

I capped the pen and reread the list several times. It was only six items, didn't seem all that complicated, but isn't that how things go? The whole looks-can-be-deceiving thing?

6

How could something smell so good yet taste so disgusting? As I scooped another spoonful of coffee and dumped it into the filter, I inhaled deeply. I liked just about anything but coffee. That and celery, which used to be my go-to food for crunch until burning myself out on it. When stressed out, I had the bad habit of clenching and grinding my teeth. Used to be, a stiff cocktail or a Xanax kept my anxiety at bay but always brought along other problems. Like blackouts, hangovers, and burned bridges. Since sobering up, I had to find crunchy food to relieve the ache in my jaw.

"Shut up!" I growled at the room. The thing about being sober was that I felt everything, painfully so. My skin crawled with it.

I pushed the brew button on the coffeepot and took a moment to wipe down the marble countertops. The faint gray veining reminded me of bare tree branches in winter. The design sparked a sudden need to draw, but I'd have to wait to do that until after Gilbert's coffee assignment. Speaking of, I headed next door to get it over with.

Henry was on his front porch again, a book in one hand while shoveling a spoonful of cereal into his mouth with the other.

"Uh, hi." I waved at him like a doofus as he looked up at me with a perplexed expression. "I'm Junie, your neighbor. Remember?"

He nodded his head while chewing away. "Of course I remember."

I peeked inside his bowl. "Is that Frosted Flakes?"

"They're great." Henry saluted me with his spoon. The phrase and spoon salute were straight from a familiar commercial but he delivered it in such a matter-of-fact tone instead of mimicking Tony the Tiger, making it even more funny.

I huffed a faint laugh. "So I've heard."

Henry closed the book and placed it on the table, giving me his full attention. "What happened to your lip?"

"A boxing lesson gone awry." I waved it off and glanced at the book beside his bowl. "I just read that one not too long ago." I tipped my head toward the bestselling suspense novel. I'd devoured H. M. Rossi's entire backlist while in rehab after Lana sent me his first two.

Henry tilted his head to the side. "What'd you think?"

"Rossi's other books were much better. This one was a little slow for my liking and the romance was all but missing. Not his best." I lifted my gaze and was surprised by the frown on his face. "Oops. Did I spoil it for you? The pacing picks up eventually. Just stick with it."

"No. I've already finished it." He sat back in his chair and rubbed his scruffy jaw. "But I agree with your critique."

It sure doesn't sound like it.

Clearing my throat, I motioned toward my house. "I just made a pot of coffee and was wondering if you'd like a cup or . . . two?"

From his expression, I fully expected Henry to decline my offer, but he rose to his feet and said, "I'd love a cup . . . or two."

"Oh, okay then." Begrudgingly, I turned around and led the way. Neither of us said a word until we reached the kitchen. I pointed to a stool. "Have a seat."

I expected him to begin a conversation or perhaps he expected me to since I was the hostess, but that had never been my strong suit. I gathered a carton of milk and a small bag of sugar and set it in front of him. I opened the cabinet and my eyes landed briefly on the hand-painted cup covered in purple and fuchsia hydrangeas. Grandma Olla's cup. Skipping hers, I selected a plain blue one, filled it with steaming coffee, placed it on the counter, and stood across from Henry while he doctored it.

"What do you do for a living?" I asked, attempting the small talk against my better judgment.

Henry stirred a good amount of sugar into his coffee. "I'm a math professor at the College of Charleston."

"No way."

"Yep." He said, making the *p* pop.

"My brother is a math professor at the University of South Carolina."

"Go Gamecocks!" He faux toasted me with his cup. With the coffee raised to his lips, Henry gave me a confused look. "You're not having any?"

I shook my head. "Nah. I hate coffee."

Without tasting it, he set the cup down and adjusted his glasses. "Then why make it?"

"My—" I caught the words *probation officer* just before they spilled from my busted lips. "Uh, life coach challenged me to invite you over for coffee."

Henry fixed his glasses once again, making me wonder if it was a tic instead of necessity, because the frames seemed to have a favorite angle to sit and reverted back to it as soon as he stopped fiddling with them. "Are you talking about Gilbert?"

"Uh . . . yes." I fidgeted with the stack of bracelets on my wrist.

Henry's eyes narrowed. "I thought he was your personal trainer."

"Well, he sucked at that, so we've given him a new job."

Lips twitching, Henry finally picked up the cup and took a sip. "And why exactly did he present you with this coffee challenge?"

I settled my fingertips on one of the bracelets and began tracing the tiny seed beads. "Because I don't have any friends."

Head nodding, as if that was a completely acceptable answer, Henry brought the cup to his lips for another sip. I liked that he didn't slurp it like my brother always did. Seemed this guy did everything in a quiet, mild-mannered fashion. "And what is it you do for a living?"

"I umm . . ." I looked around the kitchen and decided to go with honesty. "I'm still trying to figure that out, but I want to work toward opening a custom hat and accessory boutique."

"That sounds interesting."

I hummed and lifted a shoulder.

Small talk complete, we grew quiet again.

While Henry worked his way through the cup of coffee, I stole a glance at the microwave clock. How long did this coffee thing need to last, anyway? As soon as the cup was empty, I quickly refilled it like a good hostess. To make the two-cup maximum clear, I dumped the rest of the pot down the sink.

With my back to Henry, I said, "I'm not looking for friends, so don't think you're obligated to offer your friendship. Just like you said when you introduced yourself about probably not having sugar or such, I'm like that with friendship. I just want my pro—*life coach* to see that I'm making an effort."

Henry didn't respond, just kept drinking his coffee as if I hadn't babbled a bunch of bull.

I pulled my phone out of my pocket. "Speaking of my life coach. You mind me taking a picture to prove you were here?"

Henry studied me. He owned a set of eyes that saw more than what was before them. It made me nervous. "I guess."

"Great." I held the phone up and centered him on the screen. "Say cheese."

His expression remained neutral as he muttered, "Cheese."

I assessed the photo, figuring he didn't look too miserable, and sent it to Gilbert while Henry went back to drinking his coffee. The man was basically guzzling it like it was his life's mission to reach the bottom of that mug.

Henry kept staring at my lip. "What really happened to your face?"

I pulled my bottom lip into my mouth and tested the scab with the tip of my tongue. It didn't hurt so bad anymore. "I got into a brawl at an AA meeting."

Henry blinked slowly, his brows puckering. "Come again?"

"Just kidding." I coughed a laugh and tucked my hair behind my ears. "About the brawl, not the meeting. I'm in recovery. And well, there *was* an argument between these two guys at the meeting. I was minding my own business but my face got in the way of an elbow." I shrugged as if saying, *It happens. What can ya do?*

Once the cup was empty, Henry slid it toward me. "May I leave now?"

"Absolutely." Straightening, I grabbed the cup and washed it out, wishing I could wash down the drain and escape my own weirdness.

By the time I turned from the sink Henry was gone. Poor guy. That had to have been the oddest coffee date he'd ever had.

Staring at his empty stool, I shook my head and sighed. "No wonder I have no friends."

More pressing issues needed my attention than me dwelling on the fact that I was an embarrassment to myself, so I climbed the stairs up to the third-floor attic. As soon as I opened the door, a strong whiff of drywall dust and patchouli hit me, followed by a memory of Olla standing in the middle of the room with her arms out wide while she explained her vision for the space.

This can be your creative space, Junie Bug. You can set up your paints and canvases over by the space in front of the dormer windows. It has good light.

This came after a season of tumultuous mistakes at the ripe old age of nineteen. I'd left Arlo and was staying with Grandma Olla, one of many on-again-off-again moments in our short marriage. Wanting to blow off some steam and just forget for a little while, I went to a beach party. My friend Lizzy offered me what she called a chill pill. Yeah, it chilled me out alright. So much so I went into cardiac arrest. I all but threw my life away for a high. After the paramedics brought me back to life, I went to rehab. And when I was released, Olla was there, offering me this space and another chance.

I walked farther into the room, shutting the door on those awful memories. We'd only gotten as far as drywalling the room and priming the walls before I made the asinine decision to go back to Arlo. I couldn't help but wonder if I'd stayed and accepted this gift she tried giving me, how different things could have been. But then there'd be no Fern and I just couldn't fathom a world without her.

A blank canvas, a fresh start. That's what Grandma called this room. Too bad she wouldn't be here to finally see me accept her gift.

Various cans of paint and supplies lined the wall to the right. I wasn't all that sure how long paint kept. "Only one way to find out."

As the white primed walls began transforming, I imagined each stroke of the paintbrush covering the humiliating parts of my past and creating a new future I could be proud of.

If only it were that easy.

7

There were times when I used to drink myself into such a stupor I would misplace days, having no idea where they went. The only time I've ever experienced anything close to this while sober was when I held a paintbrush in my hand, creating.

I stood back from the wall, stretching my neck and back while surveying the botanical garden I'd planted and landscaped with a great deal of paint and a brush. This wall had a selection of ferns. Horsetails, eagle ferns, the Java fern, and leatherleaf. Colorful perennials in rich purples, deep oranges, pinks, and yellows bloomed amongst the green plants.

I was toying with the idea of planting a garden of poisonous plants on a small area of wall by the bookcases, a nod to the toxic parts of my life story. Most people wouldn't even know what it meant. My parents would, but it was unlikely they would ever lay eyes on this room.

College sweethearts, Rupert and Rose put the cart before the horse when my mother got pregnant with Cy her junior year. They married the following year after graduation and focused the next ten years of their lives on raising Cy and advancing their careers. They had worked at the top botanical gardens in the US: Dallas Arboretum and Botanical Garden, New York Botanical Garden, Brookgreen Gardens. They spent a few years near their hometown of Columbia, doing consulting work for the Riverbanks Zoo, after Mom gave birth to me. Even though they had been absent a good chunk of my life, focusing on work above everything, their children included, I was darn proud of my parents. I just wish they could have figured out how to let us be a part of their world instead of spectators.

I barely heard the doorbell from way up here, but it was enough of a disruption to snap me out of my creative zone. Dropping the paintbrush in the pail of water, I wiped a smear of green off my finger and onto my ruined jeans and went down to open the door.

Gilbert lowered his sunglasses and gave me a once-over. "What did you do, fall into a bucket of paint?" He pointed toward my head. "You even got it in your hair."

Having paint on myself didn't bother me, so I chose not to address his snark. "May I help you, sir?"

Gilbert eased around me, being careful to not come into contact with any of the paint. "You need to get cleaned up." He checked his shiny gold watch. "We have a meeting to get to."

Grumbling under my breath, I moved to the kitchen and started scrubbing the paint from my hands. "Feels like we just went to one."

"It's been four days since that last meeting."

I glanced over my shoulder, continuing to scrub. "You sure?"

Gilbert inclined his head toward the stairs. "We need to leave in twenty minutes."

"But my face is still busted and bruised."

"It ain't that bad. Just put some face goop over it."

"You mean foundation, concealer?"

"Sure."

"Sure," I mimicked in a childish tone. I turned off the faucet and made my way upstairs. After running through the shower to rid myself of the paint, wishing I could wash the bruises off my skin as easily, I dressed in a fresh blouse and jeans while contemplating what to do with my face. I didn't own concealer or foundation. My cosmetic collection only consisted of a small eye shadow palette, lip gloss, and a tube of mascara.

Wrapping a towel around my wet hair, I decided to go see what my grandmother had in her vanity. I stood by Olla's door for a moment, then slowly walked in while keeping my focus on her dressing table since there wasn't enough time to take in what would surely feel like a shrine of her belongings. I picked up the glass bottle of her favorite Estée Lauder foundation and examined it, only to find it dried out. I leaned close to the mirror and scrutinized the damage. The scab on my lip still looked gnarly and the bruising had faded to zombie green and yellow, but at least I didn't look like I had a chaw of tobacco in my mouth any longer. I unscrewed the cap off the Olay lotion and sniffed it. The light scent of almonds and flowers smelled like my grandmother when she leaned in to kiss my cheek. I squirted some in my palm and smoothed it over my face.

Close to falling into my grief, I hurried out of Olla's room and rushed through drying my hair.

Now in a terrible mood and missing my grandmother, I stomped downstairs. "Let's go get this over with."

"Sheesh, what a great attitude." Gilbert held the door open for me. "Would it kill you to try making the best of this?"

"Probably." Shoulders slumped, I shuffled past him.

"This meeting is nearby. Just off the island at the Methodist church, so it's convenient."

"Okay."

"Okay," Gilbert mimicked me in a whiny tone. Guess I deserved it.

Not even fifteen minutes later, we walked into the small fellowship hall of a quaint, redbrick church and it smelled like an all-you-can-eat Sunday buffet, making my mouth water. I hadn't just lost days while painting, but also mealtimes.

"Is this AA or a church potluck?" I muttered, zeroing in on the various covered dishes taking up the entire surface of the counter.

"They always provide a meal at this meeting. Be grateful," Gilbert muttered back as we joined the short line.

Three older ladies with wide smiles served up the food, each one wanting to know how I was doing. I wanted to point out the obvious, *I'm attending an AA meeting with a bruised face and busted lip, how do you think I'm doing?* Instead, I gave the typical response. "I'm fine. How 'bout you?"

One with red hair stopped me before I veered away. "My name is Betty. Let me know if you need anything at all."

"Yes, ma'am." I offered a faint smile and turned to find a place to sit. The group only took up two tables. A quick head count came to a total of thirteen people.

Gilbert caught my attention and waved me to join him at the second table.

After everyone had their plate and someone said grace, we dug in. Another perk to this meeting was the freshly brewed tea. You had to give it to the little Southern church ladies, they knew how to make a dang good glass of sweet tea. The crispy fried chicken and mashed potatoes were on point too.

Once plates were mostly empty, a man stood at the small podium in front of us and introduced himself as Reggie.

"Let us stand and recite the Serenity Prayer." Reggie waited until we were all on our feet, then began leading us. *"God grant me the serenity to accept the things I cannot change, the courage to change the things I can, and the wisdom to know the difference."*

As we settled in our seats again, the church ladies went to work, walking around and passing out little plates of pound cake, followed by coffee. I ate the cake but pushed the cup of coffee over to Gilbert.

This meeting didn't have raised voices or wayward elbows to the face, but it seemed a bit saccharine for my taste. It was like everyone was on their best behavior, for fear of being scolded by God himself if they stepped out of line in any way.

"This is making me uncomfortable," I whispered, but Gilbert shushed me as a woman joined Reggie at the podium. Between her limp ponytail and baggy clothes, she looked awfully tired.

"Hello. My name is Maren and I've been sober for five months."

The short amount of time into her sobriety caught my attention but then she proceeded to tell us her heartbreaking story.

"I've struggled with alcohol a lot in the last three years since my divorce and well, I hit rock bottom a year ago." She sniffed, wiping under her nose. One of those sweet church ladies hurried over with a tissue. Maren thanked her. Instead of using it, she began folding and unfolding it while speaking. "I'd found out my hus—ex-husband got engaged to his mistress." She sniffled a watery laugh. "Not very original, I know. So, anyway, I'd polished off two bottles of wine before I knew it and midway through making dinner, I ended up on the couch. Blacked-out drunk. I woke up to screams and smoke. My twelve-year-old got the fire out but not before she burned her arm. I was so wasted that I had to have my fourteen-year-old son drive us to the ER. I was arrested for child endangerment and haven't seen my children since the hearing."

As tears streamed down Maren's face, I found myself crying right along with her. Gilbert patted my shoulder, knowingly.

"I miss my children so much, but I know I have to fix me before I can be the mother they need." Maren sat down and the group quietly clapped.

Reggie returned to the podium. "Maren, we're all here to support you in this. Thank you for sharing with us tonight."

A few others stood and shared but I was stuck on Maren's story and how similar it was to mine. One of the things my counselor shared with me in rehab on one of my lowest days came to mind. *Junie, you have to put your oxygen mask on first before you can help your child.* I'd heard something like that before but it never really resonated with me until then. Even though it felt incredibly selfish, she explained otherwise. Putting yourself first when you're unhealthy must be a priority. You want those you love to have the healthiest version of yourself.

The meeting concluded and I was first to leave the table and make a beeline for the door.

"Sweetie, don't forget your to-go plate." Betty shoved a weighty Styrofoam box into my hands and gave me a hug.

"Thank you." I held the container in front of me to ward off any more hugs and fast-walked to Gilbert's car.

He drove us out of the lot and turned the radio down. "You okay?"

"Yes, sir. Maren sharing her story . . . That gave me a lot to think about. My counselor told me that making your needs a priority is necessary in order to be a healthy parent."

"Your counselor is right. And I'm proud of the steps you're taking to do just that." Gilbert reached over and patted my shoulder like he did earlier. I'd begun to wonder if he'd let me adopt him as my grandfather after my probation was up. "What did you think of the group?"

"It's an AA meeting, what do you think?" I stared out the window. "Those church ladies were nice, but I didn't care for them staying for the meeting."

"This is an open meeting group. They can observe but not participate."

My nose scrunched up. "Why would they want to?"

"Maybe to understand addiction and recovery better. Those who educate themselves tend to have more empathy." He changed lanes, allowing a speeding truck to get around us. "Give this one a chance, please. You should even consider attending a service on Sunday."

"Yeah. Like that wouldn't be uncomfortable. *Oh look. It's that young alcoholic from the AA meeting.*"

"It wouldn't be like that and you know it. You're so worried about someone judging you that you've become the judge. Already condemning that entire church group before giving them a chance."

Properly scolded, my face heated. "Now I feel like a jerk."

"As you should." A prickly silence filled the car for a few miles before Gilbert spoke in a softer tone, low and serious. "Just give it some time. I promise you'll get more comfortable. It took me a while to settle in with the support group I attend, so don't get discouraged."

"Your group?" I angled in my seat and lightly swatted his arm. "Why haven't you taken me to that one? You ashamed of me, Gilly?"

Gilbert turned on his blinker and took a left onto Ben Sawyer Boulevard. "It's a little different than traditional AA meetings."

"I like it already."

Gilbert rolled his eyes and shook his head. "No, you won't. It's still folks supporting one another in our sobriety. Besides, it's private, invitation only."

"I bet you could get me in."

"How about this. If you commit to the group meeting at the church, I'll see about getting you an invite to mine."

"Fine. I really don't have a choice anyway."

Gilbert downshifted as we began crossing the bridge. "True. But you have a choice on how you handle it. Stop looking at all this as punishment."

"How else is there to look at it?"

"Grow up, Junie."

I gawked at him. "Wow. You're just all kinds of nice tonight."

He cut me a quick glare, then refocused on the road. "You know I'm a straight shooter, so don't get all bent out of shape."

"That you are."

"What about a job? You made any progress?"

"I'm still working on it," I muttered, keeping my eyes averted.

"Well, keep me updated, so I can add it to my report."

After Gilbert dropped me off, I went inside and settled at the kitchen island with my laptop. I was part owner of a million-dollar property yet totally broke. I had to fix that—fast—so I started searching for a job. The requirements for anything appealing knocked me out of the running. College degree? Nope. Experience? Not much. Background check? Best not to go there . . .

Every option dried up faster than a tidal pool at low tide, so I gave up on that and decided to touch base with my brother.

I moved to the couch, took a deep breath, and hit the call button.

"Hey." Cy answered on the second ring but sounded distracted. "Everything okay?"

"Yeah. Just checking in."

"Mm-hmm."

"I just got home from an AA meeting. Oh, and I took a drug test." I told him this to see if he was even listening.

"Did you pass it?" His question stung, but I guess I deserved it. At least he was paying attention.

"I'm not calling you from jail, am I?" We both grew quiet and I instantly regretted snapping at him. "Look, I just wanted to call and say hey. Not to bicker. How's everyone doing?"

"Everyone is fine." He didn't elaborate, as if intentionally torturing me with his vagueness. "Have you spoken with Mom and Dad?"

"The time difference makes it hard to call, but we've exchanged a few texts." I propped a pillow in my lap and smoothed my fingers over the soft material. "I'd love to see Fern." Even though I already knew the answer, I held my breath.

He sighed with a good bit of aggression. "That's being selfish, Junie."

"Selfish? She's my daughter."

"Yes, but I have custody of her because of your arrest." Oh, he just loved twisting that knife at every chance.

"But . . ." I looked around the living room, landing on a picture of Olla standing on the front porch. Cy on one side and me on the other with her arms draped around us. "I'm doing everything I'm supposed to in order to get her back. Come on, Cy, give me a second chance."

"You've already been given a second chance and failed. Think about your daughter for once. It wouldn't be fair to Fern to insert yourself back into her life only to mess things up again. She needs stability." There was some rustling in the background. "I have to go."

I started to plead with him but he'd already hung up. There were eleven years between us but a lifetime of guilt reinforced the barrier. Clutching the pillow to my chest, I stared up at the shiplap ceiling. Somehow, I had to secure a third chance, to show my brother I had earned it this time instead of him giving it over begrudgingly as a gift.

8

Finding yourself in a fine pickle. I liked pickles, so I never got on board with this saying, but today I supposed the meaning of it applied. I needed to open a bank account, sell my car, and renew my license—a fine pickle indeed. I figured the bank and car dealership would require a license, so I needed to start the day at the unhappiest place on earth.

I checked my outfit one last time before heading out. I recalled someone saying one time that you should dress for the day you wanted. In a teal floral maxi skirt and a bright-white T-shirt with a few well-placed curls in my hair, I dressed for a fresh, optimistic day.

"Here goes nothing." I gave my reflection a determined nod and left.

I pulled up to the Department of Motor Vehicles and grimaced. A line at least twenty deep had already formed by the door. They all had the same idea as me to arrive before it opened.

I gathered my bag, the paperwork, my resolve, and took it all with me to my place in line.

Forty minutes later, someone called my number. Not terrible but not great either. I stepped up to the tall counter and said good morning, to which I received no reply.

The frowning woman with zero personality barely spared me a glance. "How may I help you?" The name tag pinned to her blouse only held two initials. L. J. I wondered if they stood for Least Joyful.

"I need to renew my driver's license." I handed her the paperwork from rehab and the form I had filled out while waiting in line.

I know DMV workers are not known for their sunny dispositions, but I stood there and witnessed this one's cool attitude turn downright frosty. Without saying a word, she attacked her keyboard, punishing it for her grievances with me, apparently.

"The reinstatement fee for a suspended license is one hundred dollars." *Did she just say that louder than necessary?*

"Oh, uh, okay." It pained me to part with most of my cash supply, but I had no other choice. I fished out two twenties, five tens, four fives, and held them out to her. By L. J.'s sour face you would have thought I'd handed her a used tissue.

With just her fingertips, the peeved woman recounted the money. She tossed two fives back to my side of the counter. "You counted wrong."

Why don't you keep it and try buying yourself a personality? "Oops. Sorry about that." I managed a smile.

Did L. J. reply? Of course not. She turned and walked over to a clerk's desk right behind the counter.

"Cash?" the colleague quipped.

"She just got out of rehab. Who knows where she got it from." L. J. showed off my paperwork. They whispered something, then glanced up and met my eyes, showing no shame at all in judging me.

"Do you ladies have a question? I'm a natural blonde if you're wondering."

They looked away and got back to work. L. J. took her sweet time returning with the receipt, Frisbeeing it across the counter. I slapped a palm on top of it to prevent it from flying away.

"Read line five." She pointed to the vision exam machine.

"Can I get a cleansing wipe first?"

Sighing, she tossed the little packet to my side of the counter. Who did this heifer think she was?

With trembling hands, I cleaned the front of the machine, rested my forehead on the right spot and rattled off the letters.

"Go to the end for your picture." L. J. walked off with no other instructions.

I met her at the photo-taking station and stood on the *X* on the floor.

"Sign your full name on this screen." L. J. tapped the name pad with a pen.

I stepped forward and used the attached pen to write my name. Then I returned to the *X*, hoping to get this over with already.

"Look straight ahead. Okay, you're done."

I blinked. "Wait. What? I wasn't ready." I gazed at the lens, wondering why it didn't flash or anything. "Couldn't you have given me some kind of warning?"

She typed something on the computer behind the camera. "We'll call you when it's done."

"But . . . can we take it again?" I asked with no response.

L. J. returned to her spot at the long counter of misery and called for the next in line.

Fuming, I sat in one of the plastic chairs. Over the next twenty minutes my fuming grew to boiling. I waited as four more people got their photos, being allowed time to prepare. I waited some more as all four received their licenses and went on their merry ways. Shoot, one woman was permitted to retake her photo because she wanted her hair over her shoulder.

Fed up, I crossed the room and cut in line. "Sorry, sir. This shouldn't take but a second." I gave the man an apologetic smile, then directed a frown at L. J. "I just need my license."

"Didn't I say we'd call you when it's ready?"

"I believe you forgot me. Four other people got theirs and they were behind me."

Her eyes narrowed. "Your name?"

"Juniper Wilder." I had to say it through clenched teeth to keep from yelling it.

"I'll check once I finish with this gentleman you jumped."

With no other choice, I returned to the plastic chair. Fifteen minutes passed by before L. J. finally called my name.

"I was wondering . . ." I snatched the license from her hand. "Does L. J. stand for Lousy Jerk?"

She glared. *"What?"*

"Seriously, *Lousy Jerk*, I hope you never make a mistake of any kind and have someone treat you the way you've treated me while working on righting your wrongs." I turned on my heel and stormed out.

I reached the car and braved checking the license. Red-faced with squinted eyes and a harsh frown. I'd never be able to look at this photo and not see and feel the humiliation.

*

Grinning like a possum eating a sweet potato. Another familiar saying popped into my head as I squinted at the smarmy car salesman. Pickles, now potatoes. I feared what was next.

I motioned toward my car. "But it has less than ninety thousand miles on it."

Howey played with the top button of his green polo shirt, never losing his flashy smile. "But there's a dent on the side and it needs new tires."

Frowning, I crossed my arms. "We're still talking about a three-year-old *Mercedes*."

"I bought one just like it at the sale last week for less than what I'm offering you. Fifteen is my final offer, sweetheart." Patronizing possum, acting like he was doing me a favor.

Arlo paid almost triple that after winning a hundred and twenty-five grand on a scratch-off ticket. He bought us both new vehicles, me a proper wedding ring set, and blew through the rest of the money within a week. The rings, my car, and his motorcycle were all we had to show for his winnings. Then he wrecked the motorcycle. Now only the rings and car remained. I needed the money too much to hold on to it any longer.

My eyes and nose began to sting.

"Aww, don't cry . . ." Howey ran a hand over his receding brown hair. "Tell ya what. I'll give you sixteen for it and I'll even give you a ride home." He grinned wide, flashing bright-white teeth.

"Fine." I stomped past him, ignoring his outreached hand. No way was I shaking on this offer. We both knew he was ripping me off and I was desperate enough to let him.

After signing the paperwork and receiving my check, Howey brought me home like he promised. I went inside and retrieved the keys to Olla's car, then backtracked outside. The crushed seashells crunched underfoot as I picked my way across the path leading to the detached garage. I punched in the code and the door whirled up, revealing Olla's baby. An older model Cadillac Escalade, in pristine condition other than a thin layer of dust muting the champagne paint job.

I slid behind the wheel, taking a moment to adjust the mirrors and seat. Even though this was a nice SUV, it seemed prehistoric to have to use an actual key instead of pressing a start button.

"Please, please, please," I chanted, twisting the key in the ignition. It hesitated for a moment before firing up. "Thank you, thank you, thank you." Carefully, I backed out onto the narrow road and took off down Middle Street. It felt like driving a tank compared to my small sedan.

As I recrossed the bridge, it started to drizzle. I fiddled with the controls until figuring out how to turn on the windshield wipers. Instead of swiping the rain away, the blades tripped over the glass. Apparently dry rot had gotten the better of them. Shreds of black dangled in the wind like pull-and-peel licorice.

"Figures." Not too keen on hanging my head out the window, I swung by an automotive store to get new wipers. Thankfully that was a pretty cheap fix.

After the store clerk helped me change the blades, I loaded back up and twisted the key in the ignition. This time nothing happened. "No, girl. You can't do this to me."

I tried again. Nothing.

I gathered my bag and went inside the store once again.

"Back so soon, young lady?"

I took the time to read his name badge this time. "Hi, Greg. Yes." I hitched a thumb over my shoulder. "The darn thing won't crank now."

"Let's test the battery." He grabbed a doohickey and led me outside. "Pop the hood for me."

It took thirty minutes to figure out it needed an alternator and I would be out six hundred and fifty more dollars. I wanted to cry, to call Cy and have him fix this, to just walk away, but none of those were options I could afford. I had to learn to do all these things on my own.

"We have a garage on the back of the store for easy fixes, like this." Greg tapped the small box holding the part needed to get me on my way.

"How fast can it be done?"

Greg checked his computer. "Maybe a few hours. Our mechanic only has two other vehicles ahead of yours. You might want to get someone to pick you up."

I swallowed with difficulty. I had no one I could call on a whim to pick me up.

As if sensing my distress, Greg spoke up. "We have a waiting area. It has a coffee station and a snack machine. You're welcome to hang out there."

"Okay. I . . . I need to go to the bank just up the road and . . ." I sighed. "I'll be back later."

I walked two blocks to the bank and set up an account. I deposited the check from the dealership, then purchased a cashier's check to send to Cy for what I owed him in lawyer fees and the fine he paid to get my car out of impound, plus the new phone. That left me very little in the account. Especially after making a withdrawal for the car repair.

On the way back to the parts store, I stopped in at two clothing boutiques to see if they were hiring. They were not. Then I tried at a deli, who also said no. At least it killed some time and I only ended up waiting in the store for about an hour.

With the day still fairly young and me still fairly broke, I riffled through my bag for the list I'd made last night of places hiring and started with the closest. Waiting tables was not my dream job, but beggars can't be choosers. The Caddy fired right up this time, and I was able to get on with my task at hand without any more vehicle incidents.

Straightening my long skirt, I made my way into a bistro on the water near Shem Creek. The interior was dim and cool, blocking out the humid day just outside, and the air hung heavy with the savory scent of smoked brisket. Workers were busy setting up for lunch but in no time I was sitting in a back booth, filling out a pretty straightforward application. Name and address, level of education completed, but then it got tricky with wanting employment history. I hadn't worked since before Fern was born. Finally, I wrote down my brief job history: convenience store cashier and tattoo parlor receptionist.

Both jobs were in the customer service industry, so maybe that would work in my favor. I flipped the paper over and my eyes landed on the dreaded question. *Do you have any felony convictions?* The answer to that question would definitely not work in my favor.

Smoothing my thumb along the top of each fingernail, I glanced around at the mostly-twenty-somethings who made up the waitstaff. On paper, I fit the aesthetic. Except for that one question.

The rehab center had a workshop where professionals came in to educate us on how to live productive lives after being released back into the world. Job applications were covered and one volunteer advised us to put "will discuss during the interview," but in my mind that only drew out the inevitable. Tapping the pen on the paper, I debated until simply writing *yes*.

In less than twenty minutes, I was back in the Caddy after the manager gave me a simple *no*.

I placed my head against the steering wheel and groaned. "I just want to go back to bed."

After a few minutes of going back and forth about whether to go home or to keep searching, I straightened in the seat and checked my list for the name of the next restaurant.

The afternoon turned into a repeated pattern of *no* as I zigzagged up and down Coleman Boulevard to no avail, but who could blame them for not wanting to hire a felon?

With very little gumption, I pulled into the parking lot of the last restaurant on my list. I tried smoothing the wrinkles from my skirt, but it was no use. It was as if all that fresh optimism from this morning had gotten lost in those wrinkles.

A woman wrapping silverware greeted me. "Sorry, but we don't open for another hour."

"I'm actually here to apply for a job."

"Oh. Okay. Let me get the manager." She dropped the bundle of silverware and crossed to the back. She returned moments later with another woman around the same age.

"Hi. Dee said you're looking for a job?"

"Yes."

"We have a few openings with the waitstaff." She handed me an application and led me to the bar to fill it out. "I'll be back by shortly." She hurried off without even telling me her name, but it didn't matter. I already knew this was a bad idea.

Instead of starting on the application right away, I read over the frozen cocktail specials written on a blackboard.

Drink of the Day. Lowcountry Lemonade: vodka, triple sec, lemon juice, strawberry puree, and simple syrup. Served over crushed ice.

Suddenly parched, I tore my eyes away from the sign only to latch onto the whirl of vibrantly colored slushies as the machines churned them. *Blue Lagoon. Pineapple Paradise. Margarita. Planter's Punch.*

"Hey, beautiful. Can I get you a glass?" The bartender came into view and motioned toward the row of slushies.

"Oh, uh." Frazzled and closer to saying *yes* than I should be, I smiled half-heartedly. "No thanks."

"Let me know if you change your mind. Name's Chance."

Goodness gracious. Today, I'd set out looking for a chance, just not one in the form of a handsome bartender. Shaking my head, I refocused on the job application.

Or I tried, because that frozen cocktail machine had consumed me. I could all but taste the icy sweet beverage slipping down my throat, the slight bite of alcohol warming behind the cool.

Painfully tempted, to the point my jaw ached from clenching it, I silently prayed, *Please, God, take away my taste for unhealthy things.* I started each day with this prayer and at the moment I needed a second helping of it. Overwhelmed and with a headache pounding behind my eyeballs, I left the form incomplete on the bar and snuck out when the bartender turned his back to me.

Overwhelmed and beyond frustrated, I eased into traffic and came to a stop at a red light. Staring at the blue-and-white South Carolina license plate in front of me, I read my state's motto.

While I breathe, I hope.

Some days, I felt like I could barely breathe, much less hope.

White-knuckling the steering wheel, I glared at the license plate and yelled, "Is a job too much to hope for?"

Apparently so.

With all my cares to give gone, I returned to Sullivan's Island.

In a last-ditch effort, I decided to stop by the community message board to see if anyone was looking for a housekeeper or something, anything. The large board didn't have a blank space on it, filled with flyers for festivals and such. I perused them until my eyes landed on one with the cutest puppy on it. Figuring it was for a lost dog, I moved the paper beside it out of the way and read over the details. *Seeking dog walker.* I liked dogs okay and had always wanted one as a child but my parents were never in one place long enough to get me one.

Rereading the details on the flyer, an idea came to me. A humbling one, but an idea, nevertheless.

9

My favorite pastime used to be daydreaming with Arlo. I thought he was just the dreamiest thing ever, an unkempt version of Ryan Gosling with long hair. Arlo painted us a pretty picture for the future.

NYC is where we should be, babe. We can backpack around like they do in Europe until we find a loft. We'll paint and sell out art shows.

He made it sound so romantic and extravagant. My reality looked nothing like our daydreams, I thought begrudgingly, as I stood in this crotchety lady's yard with a bag of poop in one hand while wrangling a yappy dog in the other.

"Get still," I ordered, but Poe didn't listen. Probably because he couldn't hear me over all his dang yapping.

"Stop riling my baby up like that," Mrs. Arnold snapped. "Just put him in his stroller."

I hadn't even gotten out of her yard yet for the hour-long walk, and by *walk* I mean pushing this rat of a dog in a stroller, because this was her way of getting out of paying for a leash permit. At least he'd done his business before we got started. No way was I going to get stuck paying the three-hundred-dollar fine for no leash.

A few Internet searches and YouTube videos was all it took to figure out what all I needed to become a dog walker extraordinaire. Luckily, this job didn't require a resume or background check. Just two abled legs.

Within days after posting a flyer, I had a full schedule of fun dogs and nice owners. Well, except for Mrs. Arnold, who claimed to be a relative of the late poet Edgar Allan Poe. I knew all about the Poe history on Sullivan's Island. It's been said that the famed poet didn't too much care for his time here, but that didn't deter locals from sprinkling tributes to him all over the island. Street names, a library, a restaurant.

"Are you listening to me?"

I gave her a bored look. "What was that?"

"I said don't take Little Poe on the beach. The sand is the devil to get out of his hair." She flicked her liver-spotted hand. "Just keep him in his stroller."

"Yes, ma'am." I used my elbow to open the trash bin at the end of her driveway and slung the little blue bag inside. I didn't take into consideration how crappy this job was going to be.

"But take him on the nature trail. He likes that."

"Sure thing." I placed Poe in the stroller and zipped the covering. He immediately started yapping again, sounding like one of those clown horns, honking over and over again. "Let's go, Little Poo."

"Poe, dear. His name is Poe. After my cousin. The famous poet." She nodded her head in a way that had me nodding along with her.

"Yes, ma'am. That's what I said."

Frowning, Mrs. Arnold lifted her hand to her ear and fiddled with her hearing aid.

Messing with the old bat was quickly becoming my favorite thing. That's what she got for trying to lowball my fee, saying twenty an hour was highway robbery. I'd like to see her survive on my wage. She lived in one of the grandest homes on the island. With rich yellow paint and dark-gray shutters, there was no missing the grandeur of The Gold-Bug. Fittingly named, I supposed, since the woman was clearly obsessed with the works of her famous poet cousin.

"We'll be back in an hour." Forcing a smile, I turned the fancy dog stroller and started down the sidewalk.

"With how much you're charging me, he could stand for a longer walk than that!"

I ignored her and kept trucking it. I didn't mind the dog walking. The exercise and fresh ocean air had been good for me. Plus, the dogs made me laugh, something I hadn't done genuinely in a long time. Yesterday, Beau, a French bulldog who wore a blue bucket hat, had a bad case of gas. Each time he let one rip, it startled him. The stout dog would look up at me like it was my fault, making me crack up. And then there was Jazzy, the giant gray-and-white Bernedoodle with ice-blue eyes. Scared of her own shadow, she insisted on walking behind me on our morning walks. They all seemed to be genuinely happy to see me each time I showed up and that did wonders for my low self-esteem. It had been a long time since I'd received a welcoming reaction from anyone.

After carting Poe around the island, I dropped him off and picked up Winston. Goofy and affectionate, the golden retriever weaseled his way into becoming my favorite rather quickly. Winston's owners were adamant about him being a goldendoodle, but I saw no doodle in him.

Winston led me to the beach and the big lug splashed us both while trotting along the edge of the water.

Laughing, I put a little tension on the leash. "Slow down, silly."

Winston did a little shimmy and bit at the receding water.

Even though in only a short hour or so the beach would be swarming with vacationers, we basically had the beach to ourselves. I angled my head and listened to the melody of rolling waves, tinkling of seashells and hermit crabs in the surf, chirping seagulls, and the wind humming all around.

"You hear that, Winston? Olla used to say this is the original beach music soundtrack."

"Ruff!" Winston darted toward a seagull, yanking me along with him.

"Whoa, you goofball!" I laughed, pulling back on the leash to slow him down.

Where my stroller duty with Poe was more of a lazy stroll, Winston gave us both a good workout and by the time we started back up the path that led to the road, I was right winded.

I patted him on the back. "I wonder if your people will miss you if I happen to take you home with me."

Winston shook, sending bits of sand and water in every direction, and looked up at me with a goofy grin on his cute face, as if daring me to kidnap him.

I laughed. "Don't tempt me. They would miss you and probably send my butt back to jail." I gave him one more pat, straightened, and continued along the path. "Let's go."

The always-cheery dog let out a low rumble.

"What is it, boy?" I looked around to see what had his hackles raised just as a lanky guy stepped onto the path in front of us.

"Sassy? Is that you?"

Wearing Grandma's oversized straw hat and giant sunglasses, I was half tempted to pretend to be someone else.

Winston released another growl, so I cautiously tightened my grip on his leash.

Ignoring the dog's warning, Deaton stepped closer and angled his head to get a better look at me from underneath the hat. "It is you!"

"What are you doing here?" Laughing nervously, I tugged on the leash to move Winston behind me, but he wouldn't budge.

"My old man's buddy owns a house on the island, down by the point." He jabbed a thumb over his shoulder. "He needed a house sitter. I knew you were here, so I thought it would be fun to hang out with you for the summer." Deaton shrugged. "Say, why didn't you ever call me?"

I studied him for a moment. In the month since I'd last seen him, Deaton had gotten a haircut and had put on a little bit of weight. His hollow cheeks were no longer so hollow and the dark circles underneath his eyes were gone. He looked good, healthy. "Uhh . . . I lost your number."

Deaton's lips turned into his signature devilish smile. "Sounds like a line from a song. Here, let me see your phone." He held his hand out.

"I left it at the house. Sorry."

"Okay. Well, the house I'm at is that giant orange one, can't miss it. Come by and see me." He reached to pet Winston but quickly recoiled when Winston growled.

"I better get this one home." I began walking forward, making it clear our little run-in was over.

"Why are you acting so weird? It's just me." Deaton motioned toward himself. "Didn't you miss me at all?"

I huffed a faint chuckle and shook my head. "I'm sorry. It's just . . . seeing you like this out of the blue surprised me."

"I hope it's a good surprise." His lips pouted out.

"Oh, most definitely," I teased. "Seriously though, I have to get going."

Deaton gave me and Winston a wide berth as we passed him, nearly stepping on the sea oats lining the sandy path. "We should get together for a drink or something."

"Can't. I'm an alcoholic," I answered without slowing down.

He laughed, as if that were funny. "I meant coffee. Or we could get a bite to eat."

"I'm really busy right now. Sorry!" I skedaddled before Deaton could respond. I frowned down at my hairy companion as we reached the sidewalk. "It's going to be a long summer."

Winston ruffed in agreement.

I dropped Winston off and headed home a little worse for wear. I would probably have a sore neck tomorrow from continuously looking over my shoulder the entire way home. I didn't consider Deaton bad, just trouble, and I couldn't afford to invite that around me.

As I approached my yard, I heard the newly familiar taps of a keyboard from next door. Well, more like pounding. The guy assaulted his laptop daily. That rapid-fire TAP, TAP, TAP! Henry had a desk set up under his covered patio and hadn't moved from that spot very much in the last few weeks. We pretended not to notice each other most days since our botched coffee date, so I hurried inside to keep it that way.

I went to the kitchen and checked my to-do list for the day. I marked off dog walking and tapped the pen against the second chore. *Supplies scavenger hunt.* I knew Olla had all sorts of useful material I could use, so after getting myself cleaned up, I started in her sewing room.

My grandmother was a seamstress by trade, so she left me a treasure trove of fabric, ribbon, rhinestones, and such that would be great for the hats I was customizing. Sitting cross-legged on the floor, I opened a plastic bin and found it filled to the brim with precut quilt squares, triggering a memory of one of Olla's quilt projects. She had discovered a tear in one of the middle squares after she finished the quilt. The flaw was big enough that she had to take the entire quilt apart and then work on putting it back together.

I picked up a green-and-pink striped square, feeling its soft fabric. Reflecting on the flawed piece from Olla's quilt, I saw myself in it. As the flawed Wilder who tore my family apart, I now had to take responsibility for mending it.

I replaced the lid to the bin and moved to the next one. "Oh my gosh. How could I have forgotten about this?" I pulled out a strip of fuchsia-and-coral quilt squares already sewn together. "Oh, Olla, you never got to finish it."

The baby-blanket time is so short, I want to make something Fern can use for a long time. This will be her big-girl blanket.

My grandmother had taught me how to sew by the time I was eight, so I felt confident I could finish this gift she started. I moved the container over to the sewing table. Thankfully, Olla had a hand-drawn diagram of the quilt pattern. She'd even colored it in so I could see the coral pinwheels with pink backgrounds.

An hour passed easily as I pinned pieces together. I'd forgotten how fun projects like this could be. Stopping mid-pin, I decided this should be a treat for after finishing other tasks, so I finished pinning the piece, then went back to my original job at hand.

"Focus, Junie."

I gathered my findings and moved up to the workroom. I settled down at the table and lost myself for a while with drawing out a sunflower design on a floppy boho hat. I used fabric paint to color the design. While it dried, I flipped through a box filled with vintage bookmarks until finding one with a sunflower. I cut it in half and tucked it along the decorative band. I'd seen examples of artists using playing cards, so I figured the bookmarks could work too.

Once the hat was complete, I switched my focus to setting up social media accounts for Fernie's Fancifuls: Custom Hats and Accessories. I loaded pictures of the pieces I'd already finished—several pairs of earrings made from felt, suede, and copper wire; two cowboy hats with patchwork sections and hand-painted designs. The pyrography pen I'd ordered was due to arrive this week. I couldn't wait to try my hand at burning designs on hats and other pieces.

Feeling quite accomplished, I moved downstairs to cross off the last item on today's list, calling my brother. Even though there was still a good bit of ice in his tone and he had the attitude of a man paying penance for a crime he didn't commit, he kept accepting my calls. I made sure to check in with him quite often to prove I wasn't going anywhere, that I would continue to show up from now on. Not in the physical sense right now, but eventually.

Last week, I'd been hopeful that things were turning around when I noticed he actually texted me. But as soon as I read it, that hope went out the window.

Where'd you get that money?

Instead of thanking me for the check I'd sent him, he attacked with accusations. I was half tempted to text some smart-aleck reply—*I had a great weekend moving some merchandise for my dealer*—but I didn't. Cy had never appreciated my snarky humor. I simply told him the truth, that I sold my car. His reply was just as simple. **Oh.**

Taking a deep breath now, I called Cy and he answered on the third ring.

"Hey."

"Hey. How's it going?" I leaned against the sink and looked out the window, finding Henry with his head bent toward his laptop on the back patio.

Cy cleared his throat. "I've been pretty busy."

I waited a beat for him to elaborate, but of course, he didn't. "Have you finished up with school for the summer?"

"Mostly."

Henry looked up from his laptop and our eyes met. Offering him a brief smile, I moved away from the window and started rummaging in the pantry for a snack. "That's great. Y'all should head to the island." I stopped plundering when I heard his pensive sigh, already accepting his rejection. "Sometime soon then. So . . . The dog walking is going well and I got a lot done on my website today. Boy, I sure am glad for YouTube." I laughed but turned it into a cough when he didn't join in. I wanted to scream and demand to know why he had to make this so hard. Did I deserve this? Maybe, but darned if it wasn't getting old.

"You're still making time for AA meetings, right?"

I glared at the shelf of canned soups. "Yes. I join a few virtual meetings each week. I downloaded this app that helps me locate meetings. It's quite helpful. And I attended one in person last night. The church ladies fed us barbeque pork chops. Yum. Yum."

"I hope you're getting more out of it than just food."

My brother's sharp tone nearly set me off, but I managed to rein it in. "We do a devotion and then they open it up to anyone who'd like to share. Some give their testimony. Others are just having a bad day and need to vent. The group is super supportive and encouraging. It's nice to have people be so kind to you even if you're a loser like me."

Cy breathed a haughty chuckle. "Poor Junie. I bet you love playing your little victim role with them."

I slammed the pantry door and pretended to punch it. "What are you talking about?"

"What was it that Olla used to say, *The squeaky wheel gets the grease*?" The familiar idiom hit its mark. "It's always something with you, and then you go whining about it like you're the only person with problems."

I placed my forehead against the door. "I'm so tired of this."

"You're not the only one."

Straightening, I spun around. "Well then, we best call it a night." I ended the call for a change but found no satisfaction in beating him to it.

10

It was peculiar that an object possessed the ability to resurrect the dead. Well, more like the ghost. Standing before the box marked *Arlo* in bold Sharpie, the hairs along my neck rose and my heart sped up. With shaky hands, I pried the flaps open and moved the container of paintbrushes to the side. Underneath it was an unfinished drawing of a woodland fairy. Maybe one day I'd finish it and give it to Fern, but today I just wanted a part of him I could carry closely. I lifted his blue trucker hat from the box and brought it to my nose, breathing in the satisfying combination of earthy acrylic paint and apple-scented shampoo.

"Happy birthday, Arlo." He would have turned twenty-seven today. It seemed so cruel that he didn't get to.

No matter how bad our last years together were, his escalating drug problem and our financial difficulties, I truly loved him and I had no doubt he loved me. He always had my back, that I could depend on.

One of the last times I remembered Arlo wearing this hat, he was taking up for me. Some random guy at a bar said I looked like a Lainey Wilson reject, with my bell-bottoms and cropped top. Arlo didn't take kindly to it, shoving him against the wall. We ended up being kicked out after he threw a few punches. That was Arlo, a mess of a man, but he'd been mine.

Now that he was gone . . . alone in this, I'd have to take care of myself.

Sometimes my grief snuck up and expanded like a deep breath, filling my chest with sharp pain instead of oxygen. I held the hat to my face and allowed myself a moment to mourn.

"Get it together, girl." Adjusting the strap, I situated the hat on my head and slid my long braid over my shoulder. Dressed for work in an oversized T-shirt and leggings, I fastened the pack around my waist and got on with it.

I picked up Poe, situated him in his little stroller, and began walking down the street. We made it about a half mile when I noticed a black Corvette coming down the road. It came to a stop and then the driver's window silently rolled down.

"Not now, Gilly. I'm working." I lifted a hand from the handle and waved goodbye. "You'll have to come back and test me later."

The window rolled up and the car accelerated. A few minutes passed and then I heard someone walking up behind me in a clipped pace. Steeling myself, I peeked over my shoulder and caught sight of my probation officer trucking it. I stopped until he caught up.

"I thought you were walking dogs, not babysitting."

Poe yapped, as if offended for being mistaken for something cute and cuddly.

Gilbert leaned close to the mesh covering and narrowed his eyes. "That's one ugly dog."

"Don't be rude, Gil. We don't want to hurt his feelings," I joked. "It's always a pleasure to see you, but I'm on the clock."

"Lead the way." Gilbert motioned for me to move.

I side-eyed his leather dress shoes. The first day I walked dogs I made the mistake of wearing my Birkenstocks, thinking for sure a ten-year-old pair of sandals had to be broken in plenty enough. My beloved shoes failed me, but my sneakers got the job done. I figured it was only polite to warn him. "Your feet are going to hurt."

"No they won't. These are orthopedics."

I slowed the stroller and squinted at his fancy shoes. "I've never seen old man shoes look that nice."

He dismissed my silly comment with a wave of his hand. It was getting harder and harder to rile him up. "How's it been going?"

"Okay, but man, am I so ready to get Fern back."

"When do you plan on trying to regain custody?"

"I'd go pick her up today if Cy would agree to it."

"Can you afford to take care of her if he did agree?"

"Money is pretty tight, but with some time and effort, I think I can grow my hat and jewelry business to make enough to support Fern and myself." I huffed, nearly growling. "I just want to *see* her, but Cy is all about keeping her away from me until I can prove I can stay clean."

"I know it's tough, kid, but maybe you should try changing your perspective. You've been given a chance to get your life straightened out while your daughter is being well taken care of."

"I'm not trying to sound like an ungrateful brat, it's just . . ." I adjusted Arlo's hat, pulling the bill further down to hide the tears filling my eyes. I wanted to cry out and tell Gilbert I was lonely, that today was my dead husband's birthday, and a drink sure sounded good at the moment, but I didn't want to sound like that brat nor did I want to worry him. "It's just hard, ya know?"

"I do know, to an extent. You want to talk about it?"

"Nah. There's no fun in it."

We moved along the sidewalk for a small stretch, sidestepping other pedestrians every so often.

"What have your days been looking like?" Gilbert asked, breaking the silence.

Him changing the subject felt much like a gift, so I happily filled him in. "Mornings are busy with walking the dogs. I've attended a few online AA meetings. When I'm not doing either of those, I'm making custom hats and jewelry." I veered around a sectioned-off area of the sidewalk under repair. "I'm looking at renting a booth at the farmer's market. It's every Thursday until the end of June. I know I only have a month to participate, but if that goes well, I'll look at booth spaces at other local markets and festivals."

Gilbert grunted. "Okay. And what are you doing for fun?"

I laughed but with a quick glance at his flat expression, I realized he was serious. "What?"

"*Fun.* You just said there's no fun in talking about your situation, so what *is* fun for you?"

I slowed, checking for traffic, then crossed the street. "I don't think fun fits into the equation at the moment."

"Fun is a part of life and last I checked you're still living."

Arlo popped into my head. The birthday boy no longer living who lived to have fun. My throat tightened.

"What's wrong?"

"Nothing."

Poe let out a string of high-pitched yaps. I stopped the stroller and placed a small amount of water in his portable water bowl.

"That rat is spoiled rotten. You his personal servant?"

"For one hour, three days a week, I am." I placed the bottle into the cupholder and started walking again. I'd hoped the little yapper's interruption had distracted Gilbert from the conversation. I didn't want to share Arlo's birthday with anyone, just wanted to keep it to myself.

"You remember what Maren talked about at the meeting, right? About taking care of herself so she could take better care of her children?"

"Please don't start with me today." I rolled my neck and looked heavenward.

"It's my job. Sorry." Gilbert reached over and took the stroller, popping it on the back two wheels, as if Poe was the kind for excitement. The little thing yapped a happy yap, so maybe he was. "Your assignment this afternoon is to take a fun break."

I shoved my hat lower and snorted. "What exactly is a fun break?"

"Have you enjoyed the beach since arriving?" He set the front wheels back on the sidewalk and continued pushing.

"I take some of the dogs for walks there, yes."

Gilbert shook his head. "You mean to tell me in the five weeks you've been here you ain't sunbathed or took a dip in the surf just for fun?"

I studied my shoes, letting my silence be the answer.

"Okay, here's your homework assignment. Once you're finished with the dogs, you're to spend the rest of the day relaxing on the beach. Take a book if you want, or meditate, or sleep. But remember sunblock."

The thirty-minute timer on my phone went off, so I took over the stroller and turned around to head back in the other direction. "I get antsy. Not sure I can manage the whole afternoon."

"Just do your best. You need more time out of the house." Gilbert gave me another grandfatherly shoulder pat. "We both know isolation doesn't play well with alcoholism. It's triggering."

"Oh, the triggers . . ." I groused. "My life will never be free of those, will they?"

"Probably not, but if you keep focused on HALT, it'll get easier to manage them." Gilbert checked his phone, then returned it to his pocket.

"Hungry. Angry. Lonely. Tired." I rattled off the acronym like a good student. "Okay, Gilly. I'll do my best."

"That's all I ask. You're doing great, kid. Just gotta keep it that way."

We parted ways once we reached his car and then I dropped off Poe. Next, I walked Winston and Jazzy. The day had heated up to uncomfortable. Drenched in sweat and sand, a dip in the ocean started sounding rather appealing.

I handed Jazzy off to her owners and walked the block to Winston's home. I knocked on the door and a moment later, Alden opened it.

"Hi, Junie. How'd it go?"

"Great. I gave him water but with this heat, he may need some more."

Winston barked in agreement and offered Alden his paw as if he'd been asked to perform the cute trick.

Alden laughed, holding his palm up to receive the sweet gesture. "It's going to be hard to give him back at the end of the summer."

"What do you mean?" Did he share custody with an ex?

"My sister works at an animal shelter. She kept on until I agreed to foster Winston for the summer. My wife and I travel so much for work, it's not feasible to be full-time dog owners." Alden shrugged.

I glanced at the happy pooch, feeling right sorry for him. I knew how it felt to not have anyone claim you. Too bad I was in no place to claim him.

"Here." Alden turned toward the entry table and picked up a stack of cash. He held it out to me. "Thanks for walking him."

I stared at the money, knowing from other paydays it would be my fee plus a twenty-dollar tip. "No . . . If you're fostering Winston, then the least I could do is walk him for you."

"But this is your job, right?" Alden held the money a little closer, still trying to get me to take it.

"Please let me do this . . . I . . ." For some reason, my eyes began to water. "I want to do this for Winston."

Alden reversed a step, his face furrowed. "If you're sure."

"I am." I gave Winston a big hug, feeling a newfound kinship with him. "See you later, big boy."

Making it back home, I rummaged through my room for a bathing suit so I could get my assignment from Gilbert out of the way. In the dresser's bottom drawer, I found a floral halter-top bikini I hadn't worn since high school and tried it on. A little snug, but it would do. I plucked my dog-haired shirt off the floor, gave it a shake, and added it to my canvas bag.

After dousing myself in some Banana Boat SPF 50 that was out-of-date but better than nothing and putting Arlo's hat back on, I grabbed a bottle of water and a beach towel and tossed both in the bag on my way out the back door.

Crossing the gentle incline of my small yard until meeting up with the shore, I settled onto the warm sand and looped my arms around my knees. It felt so wrong to indulge in the beauty of the beach. My daughter should be here, building sandcastles and frolicking in the surf. Thinking of Fernie and unable to sit still, I began collecting seashells and tried figuring out something I could make with them for her. Perhaps a seashell mobile to hang over her bed. Would that be safe?

Just off to my right, a group of middle-aged women let loose a chorus of laughter. One lady with a straw hat poured what appeared to be red fruit punch into plastic cups, another friend helped her pass the cups out. The sweet, overly ripe scent of booze wafted through the breeze, making my mouth water.

Sometimes, like now, the cravings came out of nowhere, so fierce it made not just my knees weak but my entire body.

Swallowing with difficultly, I pinched my eyes shut and tried to come up with a distraction. Fast. Before I did something stupid, like joining the group and asking for a cup of fun too.

A few drinks would go a long way to help me forget the significance of the day.

"No it wouldn't," I mumbled to myself. "That's a lie and you know it."

Spinning around, I opened my eyes and noticed Henry on his back patio. He looked like a good-enough distraction, so I grabbed my belongings and hightailed it away from the women and their tempting beverages.

I walked around the sparkling pool and stopped in front of his table. "Hi, Henry."

He looked up and waved with his spoon, then used the back of his hand to adjust his glasses. "Hi." A confetti of Fruity Pebbles decorated the front of his shirt. Did an entire spoonful miss his mouth?

"Got a little on your shirt." I pointed.

Chin tucked, Henry surveyed his shirt. He collected a rainbow of cereal and popped it into his mouth. "You want some?"

I shook my head. "No thanks. Not much of a fan of Fruity Pebbles."

Henry dropped his spoon and gasped in absolute seriousness. "You're joking? What would Fred think?"

"Yabba Dabba Do?" I lifted my shoulders. "I'm more of a Raisin Bran kinda girl."

"Ohhh." Henry picked up his spoon and used his shirttail to wipe it off. "Boring then."

I didn't dare tell him my grandmother got me hooked on it due to its being high in fiber. Seriously, that was just a joke waiting to happen.

"Is this another challenge from Gilbert the Life Coach?" Henry shoveled another spoonful into his mouth.

"No." I hitched my thumb over my shoulder. "Today's challenge was for me to enjoy the beach." *Which I failed.* "But I stopped by here out of concern for your poor laptop."

He glanced at his laptop. "Yeah? Why's that?"

I crossed my arms but dropped them after remembering my attire. "I fear for its safety."

"I assure you it's tough enough to handle me."

"What is it you're doing this summer that requires regular keyboard attacks?" I remembered him saying he was a math professor, but that didn't seem like a job that needed so much typing.

Henry's face grew from nicely bronze to red in a flash. He looked off to the side, avoiding my eyes. "I'm a . . . uh . . . I write books in the summer when I'm not teaching."

I helped myself to the seat across from him and placed my bag beside it. The shells jingled inside as if to remind me I had better things to be doing than being a nosy neighbor. "Ohhh . . . like math textbooks?"

He stared into the bowl of cereal. "Not exactly. I, uh . . ."

"Sorry. It's none of my business." I started to rise from the chair, but Henry shook a hand to stop me.

"It's nothing weird. Just something I keep to myself." He flipped through the stack of papers, notepads, and books beside his laptop until selecting a hardback with a familiar cover. "I write fiction."

I took the book he offered. "Oh, okay. Like H. M. Rossi. I love his work!"

His face scrunched. "You do?"

"Yeah." I flipped open the book and was blinded by bright-yellow highlighted sections and lots of scribbled notes in the margins.

"But you said you didn't like *Too Far Gone*."

"I never said that. I only said it wasn't his best."

Henry stood and went inside.

Thinking I'd offended him somehow, I gathered my bag to leave but he returned with an armful of books. At closer inspection, I realized they were all H. M. Rossi books. "Are you like obsessed with this writer?" I asked as he piled them all onto the table in front of me.

Sitting down, he turned the laptop so I could glimpse the screen and pointed to the header at the top of the Word document. *Gone Too Far by H. M. Rossi.*

I gawked at the screen, not believing what was right there before me. "No. Way!"

"I agreed with your critique on part one. Not enough romance. And it needed better pacing. This is my attempt at redeeming the story."

I blinked at the screen, taking in the words of the master storyteller, then looked at the man himself. "No. Way." I couldn't wrap my mind around it. "You're a math professor who writes bestselling romance novels?"

"Romantic *suspense*." He adjusted his glasses, evidently serious about the suspense part.

I tilted my head and absently licked the now-healed part of my bottom lip. "That math ain't mathin'."

"It's the perfect cover."

"I can't believe you didn't say anything that day on your porch. Why were you reading your own book anyway?"

"I had an interview and wanted to refresh my memory on a key scene."

I remembered my flippant comment. "Oh my gosh! I . . . I didn't mean to insult your work!"

His lips twitched. "You were being honest and, as I've already stated, I agree with you." His face grew somber. "I was going through a difficult time while I was writing that story."

"What happened?" I asked before thinking it through. "Wait. You don't have to answer that."

"I lost my father while in the middle of writing *Too Far Gone*. And well . . . it's hard to create a romantic story when your real world is anything but romantic."

"I'm really sorry, Henry."

"You didn't know. It's okay." His tone was flat, like the line he'd just spewed had been one he'd said on repeat lately. "As cliché as it sounds, life does go on and that's what I'm trying to do."

"Yeah . . ." I frowned. "Why don't you have your photograph on the back of your books? That could have saved me from putting my foot in my mouth."

"It's in my contract that they don't use my photo."

"Why?"

"I'm selling a work of fiction. Not my face."

I didn't have a comeback for that, nothing I'd say out loud anyway. This man had a face that would sell just about anything. Blushing from that thought, I averted my eyes and refocused on his computer screen without thinking. He quickly turned it away, but not before I noticed an orange square of paper. "What's that Post-it note for?"

"Oh." Henry plucked it off of the side of the keyboard. "It's the day and time I sat down to write. I tend to lose track when I'm writing and if I don't do this . . ." He studied the piece of paper. "I won't know how long it's been since I left reality." Then his gaze shifted to the screen and I knew he was slipping away.

Starstruck and struggling not to fangirl, I collected my bag. "Welp, I guess I'll let you get back to your other world."

Henry mumbled a goodbye, his fingers already pounding away.

This scoop was too juicy not to share. I mean, seriously, a famous author was living right underneath Sullivan's Island's nose! I closed the front door and pulled up the contacts list on my phone. Five. I had five contacts. Mom, Dad, Cy, Lana, and Gilbert. Feeling right pathetic, I exited the contacts and figured it was probably best to keep Henry's secret to myself.

11

I stepped onto Henry's patio four days ago on a mission to find a distraction and boy did I ever find one. Any free moment since, I used it to do some online investigating. Not that I was stalking the man or anything, just curious as to how he'd managed to become an international bestselling author while keeping his identity under wraps. Reddit forums and TikTok videos had gone nuts over conspiracy theories about who the elusive H. M. Rossi could be. More than a few theorized that another famous female author was behind the pen name. Several actors' names had also been tossed into the ever-growing pool of speculation. An article in *Publishers Weekly* focused on the mystery of the author's identity and how it seemed to be a driving force behind the astronomical book sales.

Why in the world was Henry still teaching? Better yet, why had he shared such an epic secret with the likes of me, an alcoholic who came home from an AA meeting with a busted mouth? I sure wouldn't trust me.

Lana was a huge fan and I picked up the phone several times to call her, but my estrangement with Cy extended to his wife, so I left her alone. Seemed that was the best thing I could do for my family. Just leave them alone.

Besides that, for some reason I couldn't quite pinpoint, I wanted to help protect Henry.

With Henry's secret fresh on my mind, I was barely paying attention during tonight's AA meeting at the Methodist church, where a young guy named Kason blamed his parents for his addiction. His whining reminded me too much of myself. Especially after that first stint in rehab years ago.

I hadn't seen it then, but I did now. The denial. The blame game. *It's everyone else's fault, not mine.* The victimizing. I blamed it all on my parents too. All the way back to my first stolen taste of alcohol at some fundraiser my parents were hosting to save the trees. They didn't even notice that I got drunk that night, later getting sick from it. But this time around, I knew that, sure, some of my problems stemmed from not getting what I needed from my parents emotionally, but I couldn't blame them for my choices. That was on me.

"My dad said I can't come back home if I don't attend these stupid meetings." Kason peppered his complaint with colorful words. Shocked, I scanned the room but didn't find Betty or the two other church ladies clutching their pearls. They just looked concerned. Listening to Kason drone on about how no one understood him, it was clear he wasn't ready for help. I just hoped he lived long enough to change his mind.

Between Kason's whining and me stewing over Henry's secret, my agitation level was through the roof by the time I arrived home. Instead of going inside, I stomped next door and found the famous author in his usual spot on the patio. I placed the Styrofoam container beside Henry's empty cereal bowl and crossed my arms, waiting for him to finish typing.

His fingers stilled and he glanced up. "Is everything okay?"

"Yes." Huffing, I flicked a wrist toward the to-go plate. "I brought you some supper."

"Thank you?" He eyed me suspiciously as he slid the laptop out of the way and replaced it with the plate. He flipped open the lid and inspected the contents as if it might be poisonous. "I haven't had chicken bog in forever."

"The church ladies like to feed us alcoholics at our AA meeting." I took the seat across from him and continued to glare.

"That's really nice of them." Henry swiped the spoon from his bowl and shoveled it into the mound of chicken, sausage, and rice. He completely ignored the flippant tone of my comment, like he knew me so well, but he didn't.

"What do you know about me?"

The spoon was halfway to his mouth. It hung midair as he narrowed his eyes, looking like a man fearful his next step could possibly cause something to blow up. "What do you mean?"

"The facts, sir. What do you know about me?" I smoothed my thumb over my fingernails.

"Why?"

I jabbed a finger at him. "Stop answering my questions with more questions."

Henry dropped the spoon into the plate without eating any and rubbed his forehead. "Clearly, I've messed up somehow and I'd rather you just be straight with me about it."

"We've known each other for less than two months. We're neighbors." I slashed my hand through the air. "Not even friends. The only thing you know about me is that I'm unemployed and a recovering addict."

Henry shook his head. "You're not unemployed. You have a dog walking business."

That surprised me, him knowing about the dogs, but this was a small island. "The point is you hardly know me, so I don't understand why you felt it was safe to tell me your secret."

Henry chuckled, looking relieved, which only confused me. He picked up the spoon and took a big bite.

"It's not funny. I could expose you in an interview with a gossip magazine for a pretty penny." I straightened in the chair. "Or secretly film you typing and post it on social media. It would go viral and I'd make bank."

He frowned. "Wait. Are you here to blackmail me?"

I snorted. "No, but you're lucky I don't. Seriously, you shouldn't dump a secret like that all willy-nilly. That's a lot of pressure on me."

"I didn't think about it like that. I'm sorry."

I held a palm up. "Just eat. Your secret is safe with me, but you need to be aware that I'm good and well ticked about it."

"That's fair." Henry loaded his spoon with green beans. "But you should be aware that we are, in fact, friends."

Another snort. "I don't think so."

"Well, I do. My friend made me coffee. My friend shares her food with me. My friend is keeping my very important secret."

I crossed my arms and scoffed. "Seems like a really lopsided friendship. No thanks."

Unperturbed, Henry lifted a shoulder, then dove back into the chicken bog.

Our exchange seemed to be bordering on the lines of flirting. I needed to leave well enough alone and go home, but my body wouldn't budge from the chair.

I angled toward the pool and watched the water sparkle underneath the patio lights while listening to the hushed roar of the ocean waves.

I loved how the ocean sounded so different in the dark. Without the sense of sight, the sense of hearing intensified and allowed me to fully focus on the lullaby. No wonder so many sleep apps included ocean waves.

The Styrofoam squeaked as Henry shut it, breaking the quiet spell. Still not ready to call it a night, I reached into my bag and produced the Ziploc bag of brownies. "They gave me these too. It's not cereal but still has plenty of sugar."

Henry took one, re-zipped the plastic bag, then tried giving it back.

Yawning, I shook my head. "No. You can't live on cereal alone. Keep it."

"Thanks." He scarfed the brownie in two bites and swiped another. "How'd your meeting go?"

"Fine."

"Does attending a support group seem to be helping you with your sobriety?"

"Sure."

"*Fine* and *sure* . . ." Henry sat back and shook his head. "You've read my stories, right?"

"Yes. All of them."

"It's only fair that you'd let me read yours."

I wrinkled my nose. "It's not a fun read."

He took a long pull from his refillable water bottle. "Not all stories have to be fun to be intriguing. And you, you intrigue me."

"Of course. Train wrecks are intriguing," I said quickly, brushing off his comment.

Henry opened his mouth, then closed it before anything escaped.

"Just go ahead and ask."

His eyes cut toward the shore past my shoulder, then back to me. "How . . . When did you realize you had a problem with alcohol?"

"I guess in my late teens." I took the clip out of my hair and massaged my scalp. "You know how when you're filling a glass, you know to stop when reaching the rim?"

"Yeah."

"When I drink, I can't see the rim. I just keep filling until it's way past full. Pouring over and making an absolute gaum. I've been clean for a little over six months, but staying clean is a slippery slope. I ask God every day to take the taste of unhealthy out of my mouth. I'm scared I'm gonna forget to ask one day and end up failing again."

"Then I'll pray too."

I rolled my eyes. "Yeah. Okay." It was a nice thought, but I seriously doubted he had any real intentions on following through.

Henry leaned to the side and plucked his phone from his pocket. "I know we're not *friends* or anything, but whattaya say we exchange numbers."

My face scrunched. "What for?"

"In case of emergencies or something."

I couldn't think of a good reason not to, so I took out my phone and created a new contact under the name of Mr. Mystery. Once I saved my sixth contact, I pushed the chair back and stood. "Goodnight, Mr. Mystery."

Henry chuckled. "Goodnight, Junie."

Sharing that little part of my struggle with sobriety with Henry actually made me feel lighter, like I'd been lugging around a bulky bag of stones and was finally relieved to be able to put it down. Maybe those counselors and Gilbert knew what they were talking about after all.

12

The next morning, while waiting for Beau to finish his business, I picked up my phone and found a text message from Mr. Mystery.

God, please keep the taste of unhealthy out of Junie's mouth today. Please show her she is strong enough. Please also help her to always remember her nice neighbor when she has leftovers.

This felt like I had someone else in my corner who wasn't being paid or obligated in any way to be there. I'd just have to make sure to keep Henry and his kindness in the right perspective. Friend. Maybe we could make that work.

I read it twice before putting the phone away and fishing a poop bag from my pack. "Beau, I think I have a new friend."

The stout dog peeped up at me from underneath the brim of his hat as if to say, *you talking about me, right?*

I finished dog walking duties and decided to set up shop on the back patio to work on some pieces for tomorrow's farmer's market. Using the handheld torch to add singed details along the edges of the hats made me a bit nervous, and I certainly didn't want to burn Olla's house down, so outside seemed safer.

An hour or so in, Henry huffed from next door.

I looked over and saw him circle his patio table. He stopped, rubbed the back of his neck, and glared at his laptop. It was as if he were suspicious of it for some reason.

"Are you having a lover's quarrel with your laptop?"

Henry's head turned my way. The poor guy seemed a bit out of sorts, his dark curls sticking on end, glasses lopsided as per usual, T-shirt and board shorts looking like he had slept in them before taking a whirl through a wind tunnel. "I painted my hero into a corner." He scratched his temple. "Can't figure out how to get him out of it."

"Have you asked him?" At my question, his eyes shot up and met mine. "What?" I said.

Instead of responding, Henry paced back to his laptop, scooped it up along with his water bottle, and started my way.

I clicked off the mini torch and put the hat down. "What are you doing?"

"I need to see if this deck is holding the answer to my dilemma." Across from me, he stacked spools of jute and leather and moved them to the side to make room on my table for his laptop. He pulled the chair out and jumped when a boisterous bark came from underneath the table. He crouched down and came nose-to-nose with my company. "Do you realize there's a dog under here?"

"Yep." Tilting to the side, I reached to run my fingers over the soft hair on the dog's back. "This is Winston. I'm dog sitting while his people are out of town for the day."

Henry let Winston sniff the back of his hand, then he scratched behind his ears. "Good-looking dog."

"He's the sweetest and goofiest dog ever. I thought about kidnapping him, but I'm over it now." I righted myself in the chair.

Henry took a seat. "Why's that?"

"The stinker destroyed one of my sandals, the TV remote, and tore my favorite bra slap-up. All within an hour." I wagged a finger at Winston and he managed to grin at me between panting, his big ole pink tongue lolled out the side of his mouth. I slid his iced water bowl closer to him with my bare foot. He started playing in it as if the bowl was a splash pad. Rolling my eyes, I scooted out of the way of his mess.

"Yeah. I'd give him back too." Henry situated his laptop and squinted at the screen.

I opened my mouth to make small talk or offer Henry a pack of crackers because that was all I had to offer—you know, Southern hospitality—but his fingers were already flying over his keyboard at a brutal speed. Clearly, he'd figured out how to get the hero out of the painted corner, so I picked up the unfinished hat and went back to torching the edges and along the top of the crown. Wildly, working together in silence seemed as natural as breathing, and in no time a few hours had slid by.

I finished a second hat and thought about starting another, but car doors slammed out front.

"It sounds like Winston's people are here for him. I'll be right back." I stood and patted my leg and the dog followed me inside. I handed him off to Alden and returned outside.

"What's that on the very top of the house?" Henry pointed toward the crow's nest.

"Oh, that's one of my favorite hiding places. Want to go check it out?"

A slow smile spread along his lips as he rose to his feet. "Sure."

I led us upstairs and through my workroom that led to the small staircase to the crow's nest.

"Oh wow."

I stopped by the door to the stairs and turned to see what had caught his attention.

Henry gestured toward the colorful wall. "Did you grow this garden?"

I tried to hold back a smile but liked how he said that, so it slipped out. "Yes. This is my workroom."

He stepped closer to the wall, studying the image like a serious art dealer. "I get why you'd want to work outside with the coastal views but this room is inspiring all on its own."

"Thank you." I fidgeted from foot to foot while he took his time checking out the mural. No one had studied anything of mine like this since Arlo.

"You're very talented, Junie." He looked over and held my gaze.

"I only know how to draw flowers and plants and that's from years of tracing them." I knew my drawing talent had pretty substantial limitations.

"Don't downplay this. I paid you a compliment. Just say thank you."

Face warming, I mumbled, "Thanks," and darted up the stairs to the roof. I crossed to the railing and spotted two dolphins frolicking in the surf. Several moments passed before Henry joined me.

He let out a pensive sigh. "I thought this would be impressive, but it's not."

Face scrunched, I looked over at him. "Not impressive?" I waved a hand toward the ocean. "Seriously? We have a bird's-eye view."

Henry shrugged. "Still doesn't beat that garden I just walked through."

"I have something even better to show you." I shoved off the railing. "Come on. You'll like this." I made my way to the first floor and stopped in front of the gilded six-foot-tall mirror on the wall under the staircase. "Only three people know about this and only two are still alive to tell it."

Henry shook his head. "I'm not sure I need that kind of pressure in my life."

"It'll be worth it. Promise."

He straightened his glasses. "If you say so."

I skimmed my fingers along the right edge of the frame until finding the small groove. With a swift pull, the mirror swung open like a door and revealed a hidden room underneath the staircase. "Welcome to the book nook. Watch your head." I stepped inside and flipped on the light, illuminating built-in bookcases lining all four walls.

"It's deeper than the stair width," Henry commented as he craned his neck to take it all in.

"Olla opened the wall to a storage closet on the other side to make it larger."

Henry bent forward and gasped. "These are first editions."

"Yes. My grandmother was a collector, but she wasn't too precious about them. She let me and Cy read them." I moved to the left wall and selected a first American edition of *Mary Poppins*. "I almost got my privileges revoked for this though." I opened the book to the very back and showed him the crayon scribbles.

Shaking his head, he *tsk*ed. "I don't believe I can be your friend anymore. Give me that." He reverently took the book from me and put it back on the shelf, then perused the shelves until picking one.

"This makes us even," I said.

He glanced up from the book in his hands. "What do you mean?"

"I know you're a famous author and you know about my hidden book nook. We both have secrets to keep now."

Henry gave me a funny look as his face flushed.

"What's wrong?"

He opened his mouth, then shut it, then started again. "What if I have another secret to—"

"No." I shook my head and waved a hand. "Nope. I don't want any more of your secrets, buddy, so save it."

"That might not be a good idea." He closed the book and put it away, then stepped closer.

I crossed my arms and raised my chin. "Don't care. I don't like keeping secrets, so don't burden me with more of yours," I joked, but Henry remained serious.

"You're not what I expected." He stepped closer and brushed my hair off my shoulder.

"Why would you expect me at all?" I whispered.

Henry straightened his glasses and studied me like no one had ever done before. "Your eyes are mesmerizing. They remind me of emerald starbursts." His intense stare and words made me shiver as the small space grew warm. I'd not felt anything like this since Arlo, and it made me mad to be feeling it now.

"You can't kiss me," I whispered, breaking the spell.

Henry slowly blinked, then his eyes dropped to my lips. "I know . . . but I can almost taste it." He backed out of the room but I stayed rooted in place until I heard the back door closing.

I dropped onto one of the floor cushions, drew my knees up and rested my head on them. I had no business even thinking about kissing a man.

"Good grief, I hardly know him!"

When the room didn't respond, I lifted my head and forced myself to focus on something more important than that man's pouty lips. I scanned the bookshelves until finding a copy of *Alice's Adventures in Wonderland*. I plucked it from the shelf and flipped through it. This would be a good book to read to Fern when she came to live with me. Thinking about my daughter did the trick, placing my thoughts squarely where they belonged, but that only made me lonely.

Leaving the book nook and thoughts of that almost kiss, I turned on some music and busied myself with sweeping and mopping the kitchen. But no matter how busy I kept, loneliness hovered close by. I picked up the phone and scrolled through my contacts. Not even a full swipe up was needed to display my options. I debated calling Gilbert to see if he wanted to grab a bite to eat at that BBQ joint we'd talked about. Then I remembered Wednesday nights were his family night with his son and grandson. I stared down at Cy's name but had no desire to go a round or two of belittling with him. Lana's name was right underneath his and in a moment of weakness I tapped it.

On the second ring she picked up. "Junie?" The whispered hesitation in her voice told me this was probably a mistake, to hang up and leave her alone, but I decided to give it a go anyway.

"Lana. Hey!" I took a seat at the kitchen island. "How are you doing?"

"Good."

One-word answers. Just like her husband. And that made it clear this was definitely a mistake. "And the children? Alex? Fernie? I mean Fern?"

"They're fine. You?"

Lonely. Depressed. Miserable. "Fine." I shooed a fruit fly hovering over my two bananas. "I'm working on some custom hats and some jewelry." When she didn't comment, I rambled a little more. "It's for an online boutique. I'm calling it Fernie's Fancifuls."

"That's . . . cute."

I dabbed at my sweaty upper lip. "Could I . . . maybe speak to Fernie?"

"I love you, Junie. I really do, and I'm rooting for you." She sighed. "But please don't put me in the middle of this between you and Cy."

A tense silence ensued. Not ready to give up just yet, I opened my mouth and asked, "Could you at least send me a picture of her?" Tears welled and splashed down my twitching cheeks. "I miss her so much."

A deep voice in the background announced he'd made it home. "Listen, just keep doing what you're doing and prove yourself." She hung up.

I pulled the phone away from my ear and stared through a blur of tears. Sniffing, I dropped it on the counter and placed my forehead against the cold marble. The sensation was a shock against my fevered skin. Everything hurt and I needed something, anything, to soothe it. A simple light-blue disc, no bigger than the end of an eraser could erase so much. Lifting my head, my gaze shifted to the back windows, to the sea swelling just feet away. How easy it would be to just drift with the outgoing tide while one or two of those pills dissolved the pain and defeat away.

No one would care or notice, so why not?

"No." I turned my back to the ocean view, blinking, spilling more tears. "Pills are bad. No pills." But then the whisper shifted again. *Why not a crisp glass of wine? It's legal. Why not?*

Shoving my fingers through the tangles of my hair, I pulled, growling in frustration. In pain. "No!"

Needing to focus on anything else but this craving, I stomped upstairs and studied the list on my dresser mirror. The easy tasks—*sell car, get a job*—were checked off, but the major ones remained incomplete. I'd already cleared out the guest room beside mine, but that had been as far as I'd gotten with transforming it into Fern's room. I went into the workroom and inventoried the leftover paint. I carried the red, pink, orange, yellow, and white cans into the garage and mixed them in a clean five-gallon bucket. I stirred with a broom handle until my arms burned and the paint turned into a pretty shade of coral.

"Perfect."

Lugging the bucket upstairs, I began painting. My mind spun with new ideas on how to decorate Fern's room as the roller glided over the white walls, transforming them into a tropical pink. "The quilt will go so well with this, Olla. You wouldn't mind if I moved your flower lamp in here, right?"

Hours passed with me painting and talking to my dead grandmother. Then I started talking to my dead husband.

"I'm going to draw a peony flower and have it holding a bouquet of baby's breath over the door. Remember the one I drew you? It'll be a little token of that day in here for our daughter. Maybe I'll get the original one framed for her too . . ."

Talking to Arlo set off the tears again. I rolled my stiff shoulders and tried getting my act together. Finishing up the first coat in a blur, I cleaned up and stumbled to the shower.

Exhausted, overheated, and my heart pounding, I shuffled into the bedroom and crashed on the unmade bed. With the fan rotating full blast overhead I sunk into a fitful sleep. One full of disjointed what-ifs and how-comes.

Surely, this wasn't the satisfaction of living on the straight and narrow, because nothing about it was satisfying.

13

The locals used to call my grandmother the sewing lady. If you needed a pair of britches hemmed, a new zipper added to your dress, or a certain Halloween costume created, you went to Olla Wilder. But before becoming the sewing lady, Olla had aspirations to create costumes for Broadway. All it took was a family vacation to Charleston, South Carolina, and meeting a sweet-talking young man for the Connecticut native to change that glitz-and-glam dream into one that found her living on a barrier island, several hundred miles away from home, piddling with folks' clothes. Or so she used to say, all the while wearing a big ole grin. She told me she never regretted her choice to fall in love, but I knew she missed the idea of that dream. It worked in my favor, because she created the most fun dress-up clothes for me and Cy until my brother decided he was too old for such. I used to love parading around in the hooped skirt dress, pretending to be a princess, or the pirate getup I swiped after Cy gave up having fun.

Now, dressed in a creamy-white-and-turquoise boho dress and a pair of tan cowboy boots, I wondered if I could pull off pretending to look like a woman with her act together.

"Good luck with that," I told my reflection in the bathroom mirror as I finished plaiting my hair in a long braid. I secured it with a leftover strip of leather twine and tried smiling at myself. "Now that's definitely pretending." Sighing, I picked up the Western hat and smoothed my finger over the sunflower seared into the tan fabric. I straightened the turquoise brooch pinned to the lace around the crown and then settled it on top of my head.

My phone dinged in the bedroom. I finished putting on a pair of leather beaded earrings and left the bathroom to go check it, finding two messages. The first was from Henry. I expected it, considering he hadn't missed one morning since making that promise to me.

God, please keep the taste of unhealthy out of Junie's mouth today. Please show her she is strong enough. Please also help her to understand how tasty Fruity Pebbles are.

But the message notification from Lana shocked me. Bracing myself, I tapped on the icon and my pretending to be a cool and collected woman crumbled. I sat on the edge of the bed and stared at the photo of my child. Her hair had grown past her shoulders and was now a little lighter than the dark-blonde shade I'd remembered, but she was still so familiar.

I stared at the picture until tears blurred my vision. I wished I could find the off switch for my darn tear ducts. This crying all the time was really starting to get on my last nerve and I sure didn't have time for it today. I returned to the bathroom and washed my face but it did little good, so I went into the kitchen for an ice pack to run over my eyes.

A bit frazzled but present, I made it to Stith Park in time to set up the booth at the farmer's market. With ten minutes left before opening, I placed Olla's antique gold makeup mirror on the end of the table I'd dressed in a rust-colored velvet tablecloth with ruffled edge. I took a step back to admire the retro farmhouse vibe for Fernie's Fancifuls.

Olla's collection of antique cake stands served as hat stands, and a few serving trays displayed my handmade earrings and bracelets.

"Love your booth," a woman said in passing, wearing a denim jumper and a red bandana holding her hair off her friendly face.

"Thanks! Oh, would you mind taking a picture of me in front of my display?"

"Not at all." She U-turned and accepted my phone. "You match the vibe of your display."

"That's what I was going for." Smiling, I adjusted the leather bracelets on my wrists to make sure they showed off the turquoise stones.

The lady snapped several pictures before handing me the phone back. "I'm at tent number thirteen, selling homemade soaps and essential oils. If that set of braided earrings with the blue stones are still here at the end, I'd like to buy them."

"I'll hold them for you."

She waved off my offer. "No. Sell all you can. That's the name of this kinda business." She walked away before I could even ask her name.

A little old lady shuffled up and wanted to try on the green hat so I gave her all my attention. In the end, she passed on the hat but I didn't let that dampen my spirits.

I took a moment to post the booth pictures to social media, tagging the farmer's market. It made me feel official, even with only two hundred followers.

Within the first hour, I sold the pink fedora with branded roses and the black hat with lots of leather and lace ribbons around the crown, as well as a few sets of earrings and bracelets. At least I made back the money I'd used for booth rent and materials. During the lulls, I worked on a creamy-white hat with a bridal theme in mind, dressing it with lots of lace and dusty hues of pink and mint.

"I'm loving that hat." A woman spoke, drawing me out of my creative zone.

I looked up and narrowed my eyes. "I know you."

She gasped. "Junie Wilder!"

I set the hat down and rounded the table to give her a hug. "Bekah Chaney!"

"Soon to be Greene." She released me to show off a gigantic diamond ring.

"Congratulations," I said in wonder, looking at my childhood friend. "It seems like forever since I've seen you."

Bekah shook her head. "It's been, what, seven years?"

I bobbed my head left to right. "About that long. You live on Sullivan's?"

"Just moved back. I took over my mom's boutique." Her attention moved to my table. "Did you create all this?"

"Yes. It's a new venture, but I'm really loving it."

Bekah inventoried the collection. "I can tell. I remember you were into drawing when we used to hang out."

"Yes." I shifted foot to foot and played with the bracelets on my wrist.

"Are you back on the island too? How's Olla?"

More feet shifting, I cleared my throat. "She passed away a few years ago . . . I'm here for the summer. Maybe longer."

Her smile fell from her face. "Oh shoot. I'm so sorry, Junie!"

"It's okay." Flushed, I pulled the brim of my hat down a little lower.

"Well, I'm looking to expand what the boutique carries. Why don't you stop by sometime next week and let's talk about maybe placing some of your hats and accessories on consignment."

"Really? That would be great!" I pulled her to me for another hug. "Thank you!"

Bekah giggled at my enthusiasm, having no clue how much I needed this chance. "And I want that hat you're working on. I think it'll be fun to wear something like that for my upcoming bridal events."

I looked over my shoulder at the unfinished work. "Sure. I can customize it any way you want. I have this pyrography pen I use to brand designs." I'd just gotten it delivered last week and only ruined two hats so far. Besides those, this new art medium had quickly become my favorite.

"I'm not sure what that is, but okay."

Before Bekah left, we exchanged numbers. Now I had a whopping seven contacts in my phone. Seven that counted. That meant something. Not random. Not frivolous.

With only thirty minutes left, I began to clean up and make note of the best sellers so I'd know what to focus on making for next Thursday. With hardly anything left over, I guess that meant more of it all. Man, did I feel accomplished. And proud. Something I hadn't felt in quite a while.

As I stacked the tray of earrings into a bin, a guy wandered up and tried on a dark gray fedora with a collection of long pheasant feathers tucked into the metal and leather band.

"What do you think?" he asked, his voice raspy and familiar.

I glanced over and found Deaton grinning at me, adjusting the hat to sit at a slanted angle on his head. *Dapper,* I thought, but refused to say it out loud. He looked even healthier than the last run-in several weeks ago. Tanned and not so scrawny. Eyes focused and playful. *Arlo.* He looked so much like Arlo that it pierced me in the chest and made my stomach flip.

Deaton picked up the antique mirror and admired his reflection. "Did you make this hat, Sassy?"

"Junie. I'm Junie. Not Sassy." *And you. Are. Not. Arlo.* I blinked away from his impish smile. "I decorated the hat, yes."

"Impressive. I'll take it." He returned the mirror to the table, withdrew his wallet, and handed over a sleek black credit card.

I swiped his card through the handheld reader and gave it back. "Thank you, sir."

"Sir?" Chuckling, Deaton returned the card to his wallet. "This thing is closing down. Let's go grab some dinner. My treat."

My phone dinged in the pocket of my dress. I took it out and read the message. "Can't. Sorry. I have a meeting with my probation officer." Even though I didn't have to, I turned the screen so he could read it. **Be ready in thirty minutes. Test time.**

"He warns you about tests?"

"Not always." I thumbed out a reply. **Wrapping up at the farmer's market. May take a little longer.** I attached one of the pictures of me and my booth the nice lady had taken earlier.

OK. See you at the house.

I sent a thumbs-up emoji.

Deaton swiped my phone right out of my hand.

"Hey!" I poked him in the side. "Give that back."

He dodged away from me while his thumbs flew across the screen. "There. Now we have each other's contact."

"Alright, you spoiled brat. You got your way." I snatched my phone back. "Now leave me alone."

"Another time then. I need the opportunity to beat you at King's Corners. I think you used to cheat." Deaton flicked the end of my braid hanging over my shoulder and winked.

"You know good and well you just stink at that game." Retreating a step out of his reach, I busied myself with packing up. "Stop distracting me. I have stuff to do."

"Later, Sassy." He strolled away with his hands casually in the front pockets of his designer jeans. He'd mentioned one time that he came from an influential family, something in the political world, and you could tell it by the way he carried himself with lots of inherited confidence.

There was no denying his appeal, why people gravitated toward him. Fun in a wild, careless way. I almost called out to him, to agree to meet up later tonight for that card game, but held my tongue. It would only lead me to places I had no business going. Deaton fell firmly in the category of unhealthy friendships, and if I didn't keep away from him, I knew I'd end right back where all this probation and custody battle began.

Pulling up the contacts on my phone, I deleted Deaton and the temptation to ever reach out to him.

14

By the time I made it home, Gilbert's car was already parked in my driveway.

"Here. Let me get that." He took the bin out of my arms and started up the steps.

"Thanks." I grabbed the other one and we went inside.

Gilbert let me change clothes before handing over the brown bag that I'd begun referring to as the *pee pack.* Another clean test, then we were heading out.

"Where are we going this late?"

"It's not even eight yet."

"Feels late to me." Especially after working the farmer's market on very little sleep.

"My support group likes to meet outside so we hold evening meetings."

At the mention of his mysterious private group, I dropped my attitude. "You got me an invite?"

"Yes, ma'am. Don't blow it."

"How could I possibly blow it? Is there a secret word I need to know for entry?"

"No."

I asked Gilbert a million questions on our drive to Downtown Charleston, and he mostly grunted instead of answering.

"Knock it off, kid. You'll see when we get there." Gilbert gave me a quick, terse look. "Calm down."

"I am calm."

"If your knee bounces any higher it's going through the glove box."

"Sorry."

Gilbert parked on East Bay Street and we walked down the sidewalk a few blocks. Jazz music entwined with the clip-clop of horse hooves on the pavement, adding to the ambiance of the early evening. A tour guide spoke about the great earthquake of 1886 as the carriage moved along at a slow pace.

Gilbert came to a stop in front of one of the famous Rainbow Row homes.

I reclined my head and took in the light-blue three-story historic house. "Wow."

"You ain't seen nothin' yet." Gilbert opened a giant wrought iron and wood gate and motioned me forward.

I stepped off the busy sidewalk and smack-dab into the most enchanting garden I'd ever seen. Palmetto trees mingled with all sorts of lush landscaping, and in the middle of the garden stood a slightly smaller replica of Charleston's famous pineapple fountain. A magical oasis tucked away just past the facade of stone and stucco.

"Wow . . ." Inhaling the pleasant aroma of freshly cut grass and salty air, I regarded the table off to the right in the shade. Fancy yet whimsical enough to be straight from the Mad Hatter's tea party. Fine china with patterned bands of soft pink and platinum accents. Flower arrangements filled vases in the same pattern. The spread included petite sandwiches, mini cupcakes topped with edible flowers, a punch bowl filled with a soft-yellow slushy surrounded by crystal cups.

In bell-bottom jeans and an off-the-shoulder blouse, I would have felt way underdressed had it not been for the other seven people milling around the table, who were all casually dressed too. One woman stuck out from the small group. With curly sandy-blonde hair styled in an unruly bob and wearing a colorfully patterned caftan that screamed tropics, she reminded me of Olla's favorite TV character Mrs. Roper from *Three's Company*. She fluttered among the group but as soon as she spotted me and Gilbert, she rushed over with her arms stretched wide.

"There you are!"

I reversed a step, thinking she was going in for a hug with Gilbert, but the next thing I knew I was in the cocoon of silky soft fabric that smelled like an expensive perfume counter.

"You must be Junie!" The lady put some space between us and placed her hands on my shoulders. "You are so, so lovely, dear!" Her enthusiasm was close to sensory overload. If she was like this when she was sober . . . "I'm Patsy Dupree. Welcome to my home."

"Thank you for including me."

"Gilbert insisted, and I tend to listen when he speaks." Patsy winked at Gilbert, then gave me a motherly look. "I hope you're wise enough to do the same."

I refrained from rolling my eyes. "What other choice do I have?"

Her burst of laughter sounded very similar to the tinkling of her bracelets as she slung an arm over my shoulder and led me to the fancy table. "My friends, we have a new friend. This is Junie."

Everyone turned toward us as a chorus of "Hey Junie," rang out.

Patsy squeezed my shoulder. "Welcome to the Magnolia Nephalist Society."

Having no clue what *nephalist* meant, I shot a quick questioning look toward Gilbert. He replied with a smirk.

"Everyone, please introduce yourself and share a little bit of your story with Junie."

A thin man with warm brown skin raised his hand. "I'm Chris Evans. Not Captain America, obviously." He motioned toward his lanky body. "I was a sommelier for twenty-eight years and excelled in being a functioning alcoholic. No one would know if it weren't for the times I pushed past my high tolerance and right into a blackout. It finally got out of hand a few years ago, so I switched to bread making."

An older lady stood from her chair with the support of her cane. She wore cartoonish glasses, oversized and bright purple, that took up most of her wrinkled face. "Hiya. I'm Pearl," she began with a thick Northern accent. "I lost my mind but I don't miss it so much." That was the first thing she said, I kid you not. She tucked her dyed jet-black hair behind her ear, showing off the biggest pair of pearl earrings I'd ever seen. I'm talking giant gumball size. "I'm a retired subway train operator from Queens, New York. But I picked up an excessive gin martini habit before calling it quits. I've made more mistakes than I have teeth. Teeth!"

Before she could go off on a tangent, which clearly she could, a young woman, perhaps only in her late teens, spoke. "My name is Mei. A classically trained violinist. Been playing since I was three. Some call me a prodigy." She shrugged her thin shoulder, as if wanting to dismiss that claim. "I learned under the top instructor in the United States. Sounds like a dream, right? Well, he was Satan himself and the pressure of performing became too much. To cope, I snuck liquor from my parents and it got so out of hand that I started stealing it at orchestra after-parties. And well, here I am." She shrugged again and offered a sad smile.

After her, the rest introduced themselves. Bruno, a youth pastor from Peru who helped build a church in Guatemala last summer. His missionary work had taken a toll on him and he coped by drinking himself into a stupor every night. Jackée, a single mom from Alabama who had battled addiction since her youth. Axil, just Axil, no other information came from the bald brute of a man.

"I'm Gilbert. Y'all already know that and Junie does too." Gilbert placed his arm around my shoulder, such a fatherly gesture. Or so I thought until he used his grasp on me to shove me forward. "Junie, tell these folks who you are."

"I'm *Junie*." I paused to glare at Gilbert, and a few laughed. "Been to rehab twice. Apparently, the first trip didn't stick. Here's hoping it does this time around." I thought about stopping there but in the next breath, more spilled from my lips. "I was sixteen when I met my first love and he introduced me to my second—alcohol and drugs. Pills to pours, that became our routine. He made me a widow and a single mom by the time I turned twenty-three. And I've done everything I could to ruin my life ever since." I finally hushed after that when everyone looked at me with pity. I hated pity.

Thankfully, Patsy spoke up. "My name is Patsy Dupree. I'm an alcoholic. Coming from a wealthy family, I used to think I was invincible and above the law, the rules. I woke up from that nonsensical thinking twenty-two years ago. Driving three sheets to the wind, I hit a pedestrian right down the road here near the Battery. Almost killed the young man. He recovered, praise the Lord, but I'm not sure I'll ever get over it. I've been sober ever since." She gave the group a meaningful look. "Our stories aren't pretty, but that doesn't mean we stop living. We should celebrate that we've been through hell and back and are still standing. We are from all walks of life but have one main commonality, to overcome our addictions. We support each other in our sobriety and help lift one another up on the hard days, because there will always be those pesky days."

A few agreed quietly and then Patsy dusted her hands together. "Okay. So I splurged and got us some yummy treats from Carmella's.

Mini cakes. The key lime tart is my favorite. Plus there's some chicken salad sandwiches, Lowcountry dip, and pickled veggies. So please help yourself."

Gilbert, clearly hungry, made it to the table first, picking up a delicate plate and filling it with all sorts of treats. "Come on, Junie."

The pack of crackers I had for lunch was long gone, so he didn't have to tell me twice.

This unorthodox meeting was more like a garden party or a cocktail hour without the booze than an AA meeting, but I was here for it.

I filled a punch cup and took a sip, enjoying the sugary slush of pineapple juice and the fizz of ginger ale. "Mmm. This is what my grandmother called shower punch."

"Mine too!" Patsy raised her crystal cup and clinked it to mine. "This is actually my grandmother's recipe." She leaned in and whispered, "The secret ingredient is pureed pineapple. Gives it more tang than just the juice."

After everyone was seated with their fancy plates, I expected Patsy or a leader to stand up and call order to the meeting, maybe start with the Serenity Prayer, but nothing. Everyone just ate and chatted. Jackée sat beside me and with great pride in her voice, she told me all about her two sons, Najee and Omar. How the preteen boys were big into baseball, one the star pitcher, the other known for his batting skills.

Don't get me wrong, I wasn't mad about it, just not what I expected. After years of these types of meetings, a garden social was not the norm.

After we finished up, Patsy waved us over to the pineapple fountain, where I saw a little table with a pile of plastic sunglasses on it. "Everyone take a pair of glasses, please."

"Somethin's wrong with mine," Jackée mumbled from beside me. "They're greasy."

"Mine too," I agreed quietly, not wanting to complain too loudly.

"They're supposed to be, honey. Just trust me." Patsy nodded her head.

"They smell good. Sweet," Chris Evans spoke up.

"I used coconut oil." Patsy clapped. "Okay, y'all stay right here and I'm going to move over to the gate."

"Why?" asked Pearl.

"We're going to play Red Light, Green Light. When I say *green light* you start moving toward me. When I say *red light* you stop. If you don't stop immediately, you have to go back to the fountain and start over. First one to give me a high-five wins."

I put on my smeared glasses and could barely make out the hand I held up before me.

Patsy yelled, "Green light!"

Blindly, I took off and bumped into someone almost instantly. By the time we righted each other, Patsy yelled, "Red light." Then in quick succession, "Green light."

Like zombies on a warm Lowcountry night, arms stretched forward and gait a bit wobbly, we meandered across the garden.

Bruno whooped. "I won!"

We all ripped off the glasses and sure enough, he stood beside Patsy. I hadn't made much progress away from the fountain. I'd never been all that good at these sorts of games.

"Okay," Pearl started. "What's our lesson for the night, Madame Yoda?"

Patsy smiled, fixing her caftan where it had slipped off her shoulder, probably from Bruno barreling into her. "Just like these greasy glasses, being impaired causes us to not see clearly."

"Clearly," Pearl said with much exaggeration.

"We've all come to this place because of struggles that impair us. Tonight, it was me who gave you the smeared glasses and told you to find me. That may be the same case with your circumstances. Someone else may have been responsible for what led you to this point, but it is your responsibility to move on to a better place." She swiped Bruno's glasses and snapped them in two. "We must take charge of our choices. We choose to stay sober and vigilant."

I swiped my thumb through the coconut oil, doing nothing but making a bigger mess on the lens.

"It's difficult to do this on our own. If that weren't the case, we certainly wouldn't be standing in my yard, now would we?" Patsy gave us a studious nod. "But with the support of one another, we can and we will."

With the lesson received, the small group wandered back to the table to collect their belongings and chat for a while. No one seemed in a hurry to leave.

"Don't forget to take a loaf or two!" Chris Evans called out, producing a bountiful basket of wrapped bread. Everyone took at least two loaves but me. They apparently had people. I had no one.

I turned to leave only to find Patsy right behind me, holding a fancy floral gift bag. "Oh, hi. Uh . . . thank you for allowing me to attend tonight."

"My pleasure, honey." She held the bag out to me. "I'm sure you went through the twelve steps in rehab."

"Yes." I accepted the heavy bag and peered inside, finding two books, one slim and one quite thick.

"Good, good. Well, this is my favorite Bible study accompaniment for the twelve steps."

"Oh, uh, thank you."

Patsy shifted, draping an arm over my shoulder and engulfing me in her designer perfume. "Junie, I want you to understand that attending the Magnolia Nephalist Society meetings is optional, but if you'd like to become a member of our group there will be requirements."

My shoulders stiffened under her embrace. "What are they?"

"If you want to attend our meetings, you must also attend church services every Sunday with me and the other members."

"Oh." My Grandma Olla never required me to attend church with her, but out of respect, I always did. The two years I lived with Cy and his family, he made it clear that as long as I was under his roof, I would attend each and every service with him and his family. I had nothing against church per se, just that my lifestyle didn't really line up with the messages.

"Just think about it. If you're at church Sunday, that will be our answer. No pressure." Patsy smiled widely and I wondered how on earth her shiny apricot lipstick still stuck to her friendly lips.

"Okay." I smiled, doubting any of my ninety-nine-cent cherry-flavored Chapstick remained on my own lips.

Everyone, with freshly baked sourdough bread in hand, said their goodbyes and parted ways for the night.

I buckled my seat belt before asking Gilbert, "Is that even considered an AA meeting?"

"Maybe not in the traditional sense, but all you really need to establish a group is a meeting place, literature about substance abuse, and a coffeepot."

I snickered. "More like a punch bowl."

"Nothing wrong with punch, especially on a hot humid night."

"No doubt. That punch hit the spot." I adjusted an air vent. "What does that nepha word mean?"

"*Nephalist* is a person who doesn't drink alcohol."

"Oh. Now it makes sense."

"What did Patsy give you?"

I pulled the heavy Bible and workbook out of the gift bag. "Do you have this version of the twelve steps?"

Gilbert glanced over. "Yes. It's one of my favorites." He checked his mirrors, then pulled onto the narrow street.

I smoothed my hand over the glossy green cover. "I can't believe Patsy said I couldn't come back unless I went to church with her."

Gilbert veered onto the Ravenel Bridge. "You know that's not how she put it."

"Yeah. But that's the gist of it. In order to be a member, I must attend church on Sunday."

The old man started wailing like a baby, putting on a show. "Poor Junie! She has to leave the house for an entire hour or two on Sunday. Poor, poor thing!" He picked back up on the faux crying, that *waah, waah* sound.

I playfully popped him in the arm. "Oh hush! I'll go as long as it's not some weird denomination that requires women to wear dresses down to their ankles and no makeup." I added for good measure and sass, "And no animal sacrifices!"

"Hmm . . ." Gilbert cocked his head. "It's the third Sunday, so you should be good."

"You know going to church isn't the be-all and end-all. Going didn't keep me sober in the past. Heck, I've attended church smashed more times than I care to admit."

"Better than not going." He shrugged, as if it were no big deal, but I wasn't fooled. Nothing about going to church intoxicated was okay. "Are you against church?"

"No." I stared out the window, taking in the lights sparkling in the dark. "I just don't think someone like me, an alcoholic, should be in church."

"You ever heard of that verse from Matthew? The one that came straight from Jesus' mouth?" Gilbert sent a sidelong glance my way.

"Which one?"

"*Come to me, all of you who are weary and carry heavy burdens, and I will give you rest.* I think addiction is a pretty darn heavy burden. Church is exactly where we should be. The support that comes from such a community is what we need to help us in our struggles." Gilbert, knowing he'd said all he needed to say, turned up the radio slightly and hummed along the rest of the way to my house.

With my hand on the door handle, I said, "Thank you for getting me an invite to this group."

"Oh wow. The kid has manners!" Gilbert laughed.

"Don't get used to it!" I got out of the car and closed the door, pausing long enough to stick my tongue at him before walking away.

I sat at the kitchen island and riffled through the two books Patsy had given me, finding a handwritten note on some really fancy card stock with her initials embossed at the top.

Junie,

God has placed you in our little group for a reason. I want us both to commit to seeing what that reason is. I hope to see you Sunday.

Warmly,
Patsy

Rereading the note, feeling like someone actually cared, I knew I'd commit to the Magnolia Nephalist Society, as quirky as they might be.

15

I heard somewhere one time that if you can't have the big happies in life, at least try enjoying the small ones. While walking the last dog of the day, I focused on a small happy waiting at the house. The sourdough bread Chris Evans gave me last night.

Putting away the leashes and my fanny pack, I sorted through my options. Fresh slice with butter or peanut butter. Or toast with butter or peanut butter.

"Both, definitely both." Some days my appetite was a no-show, then others, like today, it showed up like a monster. I took the bread out of the pantry and placed it on the counter. Reaching for a knife, I heard the doorbell.

Wiping my hands on my jeans, I went and answered the door, finding a rumpled Henry wearing a faded blue T-shirt and equally faded red swim trunks, with a shot glass in his hand. "Umm . . . No thanks."

"It's not what you think. I know we already established that we wouldn't be asking for sugar, but here I am." He held up the shot glass.

Eying the glass, my brow arched. "So, you're skipping the cereal and just doing straight shots of sugar now?"

Remaining serious, he shook his head. "Actually, I need salt."

"A shot of salt?"

Henry scratched his temple and eyed the tiny glass. "I don't need a lot of salt. Just maybe a half a shot. My other neighbor, Mrs. Frank, gave me some tomatoes, so I figured I'd eat them for lunch instead of Cocoa Puffs."

"What? You're not cuckoo for Cocoa Puffs?" I smirked.

His blue eyes twinkled behind his glasses. "I'm absolutely cuckoo for Cocoa Puffs. They're magically delicious."

I barely suppressed a full-on laugh at that and waved him inside. "I think you have the wrong cereal."

"You have a cough?"

"No." I crossed the kitchen, opened the spice cabinet, and pulled down the container of salt.

"Then what was that?" He placed the little glass on the counter.

I flipped open the spout and carefully filled the shot glass about three-fourths full. "Me saving you from my laugh."

"Come again?"

"My laugh. It sounds like a hyena dying, so I try to suppress it for mankind's sake."

"Well. That's just sad."

"Why?"

"Laughter is a freeing expression. It shouldn't ever be suppressed. No expression should be for that matter."

"I suppose you're an expression expert." I put away the salt and closed the cabinet door.

"Of course. I have to be in my line of work." He leaned a hip on the counter and adjusted his glasses. "Do you know why your lip quivers?"

"Nope." I swept a few loose granules of salt off the counter and into the palm of my hand, then dusted my hands together over the sink. "Why's that?"

"The science of a lip quiver is when your brain demands you not to react but your soul rebels in that small quiver anyway."

"You made that up."

"I get paid to make things up."

"Henry, you're too charming for your own good."

He held his hands up. "I don't mean to."

"It's okay. You can't help yourself."

We shared a moment that felt wildly similar to the one that day in the book nook.

This time, Henry broke it by taking a step away from me. "Well. I better spare you from any more of my charm." He turned and started toward the door.

"Wait. What about the salt?"

Absently, he looked around the kitchen. "Salt?"

"That's why you're here, remember?"

He blinked and the confusion cleared as he circled back for the shot glass. "Oh yeah. That's right."

"Are you making a sandwich?"

"That would require bread. Mine had mold on it."

I reached for the fresh loaf on the kitchen island. "Well, you're in luck. Chris Evans gave me a loaf of his homemade sourdough. I'll share."

"Captain America?"

"Same name, but I think that's where the similarities end. I met him last night at a group meeting." As I unwrapped the bread, the entire room filled with delicious notes of yeast and tangy sweetness. I grabbed a serrated knife. "Bread making is his new way of dealing with stress."

"What's your new way of dealing with stress?"

"I learned yoga and meditation in rehab, but to be honest, walking dogs has really helped. Brisk exercise and their goofiness seem to be a winning combination. How about you? What's your stress relief?" I was impressed by how easy making conversation with him was becoming.

"I used to swim competitively in high school and college. Now I swim to keep in shape and it works fairly well for stress relief too." His stomach growled loudly. With his glass of salt, Henry began to leave once again.

Laughing, I called out, "Wait. Now you're forgetting the bread."

He didn't slow down. "If you're sharing bread with me, then I'll share the tomatoes with you. Be right back."

Shaking my head, I cut the loaf into thick slices, stealing the end piece as a quick snack. Oh my, did Chris Evans know how to make delicious sourdough.

Henry returned with a plate of sliced tomatoes and placed it beside the bread. I eyed the mound of perfectly ripe circles. "Did you keep some for yourself?"

He straightened his glasses and gave me a sheepish smile. "Do you have some mayonnaise I could borrow?"

I laughed again and dug the jar of Duke's from the fridge.

"Just so you know, I hear nothing wrong with that laugh."

"If you say so." I turned and caught him swiping the other small heel of bread. "Good stuff, am I right?"

"So right," Henry garbled out, his cheeks full of bread.

I opened the cabinet and a Land O'Lakes butter tub fell out.

Henry picked up the tub and handed it to me. "This reminds me of my mom. She won't toss these types of containers, says they're great for storage. If you find one of these containers in her fridge, you cannot assume butter is what is inside of it. It's like a game of chance."

"That was so Grandma Olla. One time I grabbed a Cool Whip container and dug my spoon into the white fluff but as soon as I put it in my mouth, I discovered it was solidified bacon grease and not Cool Whip."

Henry made a face, twisting his lips. "Yikes."

I stuffed the bowl to the side in the cabinet and collected two plates.

Standing side by side, we assembled our tomato sandwiches. Then I poured us each a glass of Country Time lemonade. "Want to sit out on the back deck?"

"Sure." Henry stacked my plate on top of his and picked up a glass.

We settled at the patio table. "So, tell me what's happening in H. M. Rossi's world today."

Henry bit into his sandwich, taking his time to savor it. "What do you want to know?"

I shrugged. "What scene are you working on?"

"Oh. You're not going to believe this . . ."

With tomato juice dripping down our chins and wrists, Henry talked about a scene where the heroine was trapped in a cement hopper and he was debating on how to get her out of it. He paused long enough to go inside and make himself another sandwich. "I need a last name for my villain," he declared, rejoining me outside.

I thought it over while finishing the last of my sandwich. "How about Monkshood or . . . Larkspur."

"What kind of names are those?"

"Poisonous plants."

Henry put his half-eaten sandwich down. "Should I be concerned?"

"Not really. When I was a teenager I started drawing poisonous plants from my mom's plant guidebooks, kind of as a joke to her. I memorized the names of a lot of them." The joke was on me because Mom barely commented.

"Oh. Okay, but those sound more like fantasy villain names. I'll keep them in mind if I ever switch genres."

I leaned back in my chair and stared at the ocean. "Tell me about this villain?"

"He's seeking vengeance for a friend done dirty. He has an obsession with collecting farming properties with underground shelters."

"That's creepy. Maybe look up farm equipment names and come up with his name from that."

"I like the way you think. His name will be a connection, but readers won't necessarily pick up on it."

"Exactly."

Henry sprawled in his chair and placed his hands behind his head. Face tilted toward the sun, he said, "I've shared more of my story with you, now it's your turn."

I took a sip of lemonade. "You told me fiction."

"But my secret is nonfiction." He propped his legs on top of the deck railing and crossed his ankles, drawing attention to his mismatched Crocs. One dark blue. The other army green. Did he even realize he had on two different shoes? Probably not.

The shoes reminded me of Fern's tiny pair of Crocs that were sparkly pink. The very ones she wore the day I got arrested. She probably couldn't even fit in them anymore.

"I have a two-year-old daughter," I blurted. "She'll be three in September. Her name is Fern but I call her Fernie."

The rustling of the palmetto trees and the hum of the ocean followed my confession until Henry cleared his throat. "That's a nice name."

"Thanks. My parents are all about trees and plants so they named my brother Cypress and me Juniper. I thought it would be fun to carry on that tradition." The wind picked up my hair and blew it in my face. Gathering it in one fist, I pulled the tie off my wrist and secured it in a topknot.

"Junie, where's Fernie?"

"My brother now has custody of her, but I'm working on getting her back." I stole a glance to gauge his reaction, but he wore a neutral expression, making it difficult to get a proper read on him. "I was arrested for driving under the influence last fall. She was in the car with me."

Henry didn't respond and I didn't know what else to say, so we both sat in silence for a while. A few seagulls squawked as they flew overhead. One swooped down and swiped something from the shore, then flew away.

"Tell me about Fernie," Henry said softly with a nonchalance that I knew was put on, considering what I'd just confessed.

"She's so funny and silly and you just can't help but smile around her." I laughed quietly. "This one time, my brother burped really loudly after chugging a can of soda. Fernie took a drink from her sippy cup and mimicked him. Her burp sounded more like a growl, but we all cracked up. That's Fernie for ya, silly little thing . . ." Or that's how she was last fall. I hoped the nightmare I'd brought on us hadn't snuffed out her sense of humor.

"Does she look like you?"

"I'll be right back." I grabbed my phone from the kitchen counter and returned to the deck. I pulled up the picture Lana sent me and held it out to Henry. He wiped his hands on his shorts, then accepted it.

"She has your green eyes." He grinned up at me.

"Yeah, but she has her daddy's nose and chin, and when she smiles . . . those dimples are all Arlo." I took a seat and blinked back the stinging in my eyes. "Arlo had this look he'd give me when he was trying to concentrate. His nose would scrunch up and he'd squint only his left eye. Fern makes the same face." It would knock the air from my lungs, like a sucker punch, every time she'd make that face.

Henry placed my phone on the table in front of me. "The dad . . . is he not in the picture?"

"Dad and husband. No. Not anymore. He died in a motorcycle accident three years ago. I was seven months pregnant."

"Junie . . . I didn't know."

I sniffed and cleared my throat. "How would you?"

A little crease formed between his eyebrows. He opened his mouth but closed it, then opened it again. "I'm really sorry you've had to go through so much at such a young age."

Batting a stray tear away, I huffed. "You talk like I'm a child."

"No. Not a child. Just young. It doesn't seem right to lose a spouse in your twenties."

"Yeah, well, most of life doesn't seem right." I gathered Henry's empty plate and stacked it with mine. "Lunch break is over. Time to get back to work."

"Let me help." He tried taking the stack of dishes as we both stood, but I moved out of reach.

"I've got it." I gave him a half-hearted smile. "I'll see you around. Thanks for the tomatoes."

He frowned. "Sure. Okay."

Ruining a tasty lunch with my unsavory confession, I grabbed the napkins, tossed them on top of the plates, and beat a path inside, leaving Henry and another botched attempt at socializing behind.

I decided to work upstairs instead of on the deck to avoid another run-in with Henry. Hours went by with Arlo and Fern heavy on my mind. As I strung wooden beads onto a leather bracelet, the ache of grief crept over me like a nasty summer cold. Olla told me once that the passing of time didn't necessarily make the hard parts disappear but it dulled the sharp edges enough that they didn't cut as deeply anymore. Maybe, but today the edges had been drastically resharpened.

I wanted to remember Arlo in a good light, not the dark parts before his life completely snuffed out. I flipped through the pages of my short past until landing on the moment I told him I was pregnant. We were both stretched out on the grass outside our small apartment, drawing in sketchbooks. Something we did often, losing ourselves in the art for hours at a time. I remembered looking over, admiring the black smudges of charcoal on his hand as he used his fingertips to blend a shadow on a gnarly tree that was actually an old man. My own drawing that day was of a lush peony cradling a bundle of baby's breath. When I had finished the flowers, I selected a stick of dark-pink chalk and wrote *I'm pregnant* at the bottom, then slipped it on top of his drawing. Arlo stared down at the drawing, slack-jawed for a heavy minute before a smile bloomed on his face wide enough to bring out his dimples and the sparkle in his brown eyes. It was the mischievous look that always gave me a heads-up that we were about to get in over our heads but danged if it weren't gonna be fun anyway.

Vision blurring and hands shaking, I put the bracelet down. A sob worked its way up my burning throat and tore its way to freedom. I cried. Loud and messy. Sweating, nose-running messy.

I scooted out of the chair and stumbled my way down the stairs, sneaking inside the book nook underneath the stairs. I secured the door behind me without turning on the light and curled up in a ball on the floor, staying there until the cries decreased to whimpers, then to silence.

Overcome with exhaustion and a sense of defeat, I dozed off briefly and woke up confused about my location. My hand reached out and bumped into a row of books. Remembering, I slowly sat up, only to be met with a wave of vertigo, followed by an intense pounding at my temples. Clutching my head, I breathed through the dizziness and pain. When it ebbed, I crawled out from under the stairs, climbed to my feet, then went to my bathroom for a long, hot shower.

Night had totally descended by the time I reemerged and made my way downstairs. Feeling parched, I chugged a glass of water, refilled it, and drank that too. Knowing I needed to keep on my self-imposed schedule, I gave Cy a call while rummaging the pantry for something for supper.

He answered on the fourth ring. "Hello?"

"Hey, Cy. It's Junie. Just checking in."

After the expected pause and barely audible sigh, he finally acknowledged me. "Hey. You sound like you have a cold or something."

I cleared my throat. "I think it's just some sinus congestion. I'm okay."

"What are you up to?"

"Nothing much. I rented a booth at the farmer's market yesterday. You remember we used to go to it with Olla?"

"Yes. Did you sell anything?"

During our last phone call, I told Cy about the hats and accessories and he had voiced his doubt that there would be any market for that around Charleston. I was happy to share with him that there was, in fact, a really good market for my creations. "I sold almost everything I brought. And I ended up with three custom orders."

"That's good."

"I also created an Etsy shop. No sales yet, but it's brand-new. I think I can make a good profit if I keep it up."

Cy huffed. "That's the problem with you though. You never seem to keep things up."

"I didn't mean it like that. I will keep it up, I just—"

"You've never been able to stick to anything."

Face growing hot, I felt on the verge of tears again. "Then I'll just have to prove you wrong."

"Nothing would make me happier than being wrong about you for a change."

"Awesome. I'll work on that. Sorry I bothered you. Good night." I ended the call and tossed the phone onto the counter. Needing some air, I went outside and sat on the deck steps.

Off in the distance, a cargo ship slowly approached the harbor. It was probably carrying another load of Amazon finds. How wonderful would it be if God was more like Amazon. Just one-click your prayer request and have it delivered within one to two business days. I'd prayed and prayed lately, asking God to help me fix this rift with Cy and ultimately get my little girl back, but he hadn't delivered yet. Maybe my selection had some kind of error or it was on back order. I just didn't know.

16

Look, but don't touch. Look, but don't touch. I should have been ashamed, but I couldn't pull myself away from the kitchen window. Olla's stilted house practically gave me a bird's-eye view into Henry's pool. Enthralled, I watched his long, lean arms slice through the water. Lap after lap. *Look, but don't touch.* My elbow slipped, plunging me into the warm dishwater, effectively snapping me out of my gawking.

"Serves me right." Shaking my head, I finished washing the last bowl in the sink and placed it in the dish rack. I grabbed a towel and tried drying off my sleeve but it was saturated. Giving up, I darted upstairs, swapped shirts, and hustled to the front door.

I searched my bag for lip balm while slipping my feet into my Birkenstock sandals. My hand hit against the side pocket, making the contents inside rattle. Taking a moment, I unzipped it and fingered through my brightly colored AA sobriety chips. Eight in total so far. My counselor told me to keep them close to help remind me of how far I've come. Tucked away in a side pocket wasn't doing me much good.

An idea came to me but I was already running behind to meet Bekah, so that would have to wait until later.

I wrapped the strap of my bag across my chest, picked up the hatbox by the door, and headed outside. Today I would only be bringing one hat and a dozen sets of earrings and an assortment of bracelets. All the items fit easily enough in one hatbox, which could be placed in the oversized basket on the front of my sixteen-year-old mint-green beach bicycle. No need to take the Caddy out for such a short trip.

After stowing my bike between the building and a big palmetto tree, I grabbed the hatbox and made my way inside. Notes of fresh citrus mingled with the salty scent. The designated perfume of all old buildings near the coast. How could any building sit this close to the ocean and not absorb its briny aroma?

Bekah waved, acknowledging me, but she was busy with a customer at the register, so I walked around and explored. The boutique looked much the same as it did when I was a kid. Coastal shabby chic aged well. The walls were still the faintest robin's-egg blue and the windows were dressed in light-pink shutters, as if the sun had poured in and bleached away most of the color. Bleached wood floors and driftwood chandeliers lent to the coastal theme without being so obvious.

"Aren't you Olla's granddaughter?"

I jolted, spinning around to find an elderly lady staring up at me. "Uh . . . yes, ma'am."

"I'm Winona. Olla and I used to play bunco together over at Essie's house at the end of Poe Avenue." She placed a hand on her chest. "I sure miss the ole girl."

"I do too." I vaguely remembered Winona, mostly that she liked to talk nonstop.

"It's a shame you lost your husband and her so close together like that." She clucked her tongue. "Such a shame. But at least you have that baby girl, right? How old is she now?"

"Umm . . ." In my peripheral vision, I noticed Bekah come to stand beside us. "She'll be three soon."

"Aww, that's just something. What'd ya name her? After Olla, I hope. That woman was so excited about becoming a great-grandmother again."

"Her name is Fern Olla Wilder."

Winona gripped my forearm with her tiny, wrinkled hand. "I love it! And I know your grandmother would have too." Her cloudy blue eyes narrowed. "Why doesn't she have her father's last name?"

"He loved the name Wilder, so he changed his instead when we got married."

"What was his last name?"

"Smith." I shrugged, trying to keep the mood light when I felt far from it. Arlo's personality was too big for Smith. Wilder fit that wild man perfectly, and just talking about him struck me with a profound sadness.

"Smith isn't bad, but I like Wilder better too." Winona squeezed my arm one last time and let go. "Bekah, dear, did you get my blue seersucker dress in for the Fourth?"

Bekah gave me a sad smile, then turned toward Winona. "Yes, ma'am. Would you like to try it on?"

The holiday was still three weeks away, but I guess some folks liked to be prepared well in advance.

"Nah. Just ring me up, honey." Winona made her way to the register and said over her shoulder, "Junie, come see me sometime."

"Yes, ma'am." I didn't have a clue where she lived and didn't feel like asking. I had more important things on my mind. I was pretty sure as soon as Winona left, Bekah would have lots of questions about what she'd just overheard and my answers would probably lead to this opportunity being snatched away.

Once Winona left, Bekah led me to a small round table with an empty hat display. "I think we should set you up here for a test run.

See how the pieces sell. We can do it on consignment to begin with and I'll keep twenty percent commission. I looked it up and that's the going rate. If you're good with it."

"Sounds good to me."

We made quick work of arranging my items on the table. Bekah added a vase of creamy white flowers and placed a few lace napkins underneath the sets of earrings to add texture to the table.

I straightened a bracelet. "I suppose you want to ask me about my husband and daughter."

"I told my mother I ran into you and she filled me in a little bit. She said your husband died in an accident shortly before Miss Olla passed. I remember Arlo, sort of . . . I met him at that bonfire a long time ago. I'm really sorry, Junie." Bekah gave me a pitying look, one I didn't want, especially if she didn't know the part of my story that landed me in jail and rehab. "Momma said you have a small child but didn't know any more details than that."

"I . . . She's staying the summer with my brother and . . ."

"We don't have to talk about it unless you want to."

"I . . ." I started again, but a group of young women walked over to the table. They were a garden of Lilly Pulitzer patterns with shiny sandals on their feet. Their oversized Kate Spade bags seemed to emphasize their shopping mission.

A very tall brunette plucked the hat off the stand and tried it on. "Oh my gosh. I need this hat!"

The others *ooh*ed and *aah*ed as she modeled it. Then they each took turns wearing it and I feared they were getting makeup on the inner part. Surely, one of them would buy it.

"This is the designer, Junie Wilder." Bekah placed her hand on my shoulder.

A redhead gasped as she took her turn modeling my hat. "The designer! What a treat!"

"Let us know if you have any questions." Bekah motioned for me to follow her to the counter to give them some space to explore, but it was hard for me to look away. They were practically manhandling my poor defenseless hat.

In a tornado of giggles and loud chatter about lunch reservations, the women left the displays in disarray without buying a darn thing.

I hustled to the table and put my items back to order, checking for makeup on the hat. I sighed in relief. "They must have been wearing magical setting spray over their makeup. At least they didn't dirty the hat."

Bekah rehung a few sundresses they'd left on the hangers haphazardly. "Same with these dresses."

I noticed one of the earrings had a bend in it and tried to straighten it. Those women had just manhandled my livelihood like it meant nothing, but it meant everything to me. Each piece I sold was one step closer to being able to take care of my child. They'd just cost me a step, and I wanted to chase them down and scream at them for it.

I held up the ruined earring for Bekah to see. "I'll have to take this home to repair it. How do you not blow a gasket when people treat your stuff so poorly, then don't even buy anything?"

"It's part of the business." She picked up a coin purse from the floor and returned it to a display. "More times than not, customers buy something. And who knows, they may come back and make some purchases after their lunch."

"I guess you're right." I moved toward the door and stopped before pushing it open. "Thank you, Bekah, for this opportunity. Really. Thank you."

Her smile blossomed, spreading to her eyes. "You're welcome. See you soon."

I pedaled home and took my phone out to the deck while trying to calculate the time in the UK. My parents should be home from work, so I pulled up my mother's contact and FaceTimed her.

Mom's face filled the screen. "Junie! How are you?"

"Good."

Dad joined her. "There's my girl."

"Yep. Here I am."

"Anything new?"

"Actually, yes. Remember my childhood friend Bekah Chaney?"

They both nodded, but I could tell by their cloudy expressions they didn't.

"We hung out a lot when I stayed with Olla in the summers."

"Oh . . ." Mom nodded but still the cloudiness remained.

My parents tended to get so absorbed in their own bubble of life that they hardly registered anything outside of it. I'm sure the thousands of miles they put between them and family made that all the easier.

I often wondered if the right amount of attention on me instead of on their adventures would have made a difference. I tried to picture my father as the stern type, ready to scare off any boy who came sniffing around his daughter. Cy filled in for my father the best he knew how, but Arlo used to take Cy's threats as challenges. He'd figured out my brother's buttons early on and pressed them at any opportunity, but I had a feeling Arlo wouldn't have done that with my father.

"Well anyway, she took over her mom's boutique here on the island and she's carrying my hats and accessories."

"That's great, sweetheart." Mom beamed. Cy had her smile. Their lips almost disappeared when they smiled, showing off what seemed like too many teeth. "What kind of hats?"

I'd texted her pictures of my booth from the farmer's market. Would it have killed her to take the time to pay attention to a simple text from her own daughter? "Western."

"That sounds fun," Dad commented.

"Yep." I wanted to end this uncomfortable conversation but I had to ask an uncomfortable question first. "Dad, did . . . uh . . . did Olla happen to leave an inheritance for me?"

Dad shrugged. "I'm not sure. I think it's all tied up in the house. You'll have to ask your brother."

Everything my parents said rubbed me wrong today, so before I could rein it in, I fired back. "But she was your mother. Isn't this something you should know?"

Dad finally focused. "Well, I'm sorry, but Cy is the executor of Mom's estate. She made that choice. Not me."

No wonder my brother was so bitter. The weight of this family had always landed on his shoulders.

"Do you need money?" Mom piped in, playing peacemaker.

"No ma'am. Just curious." Of course I needed money. New tires for the Caddy set me way back and I still needed to get Fern a proper bed. "Well, I just wanted to say hey. I'll let y'all go."

"Oh wait. How about flipping the screen so we can see the beach? I really miss the ocean!"

She really missed the ocean? Not me? Not my brother? Not her grandchildren? Just the ocean.

"We're not that far from an ocean here," Dad spoke.

"Yes, but we're too busy to get near it," Mom told him.

I flipped the screen and angled it to show them the ocean sparkling from the sun overhead. Beyond our yard, set up on the beach, parents were lounging in chairs while children ran around squealing with beach pails and shovels in hand. A good-humored buzz of conversation could be heard above the roar of the incoming waves.

"Ahhh . . ." Mom sighed. "It's breathtaking, isn't it, Rupert?"

"Yes, dear."

Mom clucked her tongue. "Junie, that *Rosa setigera* is in serious need of deadheading."

My eyes moved over to the orangey-pink roses peeping over the railing. Completely covering the trellis below the deck, that climbing rosebush had to be at least twelve feet tall. Why she couldn't just call it the prairie rose or simply the pink rosebush was beyond me. "I'll take care of it."

"You should tend to it at least two times this summer. It helps to encourage growth."

I nodded, clamping my lips together instead of saying something I'd regret. Like, *if you tended to your children the way you do plants then perhaps that would encourage their growth as well.*

"The rich salmon color is so gorgeous. It really pops with the ocean as the backdrop." Mom continued mooning over the plant as my arm tired of holding up the phone.

"Okay, guys, I really do need to get to work."

We said our goodbyes. After ending the call, I shot Cy a quick text.

Hey. Did Olla leave us an inheritance?

Surprisingly, Cy responded right away. **Lady Indigo.**

I rolled my eyes. **Besides the house.**

She put the money in a trust to maintain the house. Taxes, insurance, upkeep. Stuff like that.

OK.

I'm not giving you money.

I fired back. **I'm not asking for any!**

Fed up with my entire family, I stormed into my room and inventoried my jewelry box. The only pieces of any value were my wedding ring set and a double-strand pearl necklace my parents gave me on my sixteenth birthday.

I slid the rings on my finger and took a moment to admire the glittering diamonds until tears distorted my view. I intended to pass this down to my daughter in the future, but her needs now outweighed the sentiment. Besides, the rings or the necklace had no practical purpose. The rings couldn't bring Arlo back, any more than the pearls could bridge the gap between me and my parents.

After googling local pawnshops, I picked the one with the best reviews. Not giving myself time to dwell on it for fear of changing my mind, I grabbed the jewelry and set out.

It's wild how something intended to last a lifetime was gone in minutes. The pawnshop guy did me as dirty as the car dealer, but I left with enough to get my daughter a bed and that was all that mattered.

Needing to do something to right this awful mood besides going on a bender, I returned home and decided to work on a personal project. Something just for me. I rummaged around the storage room and found one of my old paintings. Just a simple beach scene that wasn't all that good. I brought it to the workroom, along with my AA chips, to work on a proper reminder of how far I'd come.

17

Why is it when someone tells you to do something it makes you not want to do it? I found myself wrestling with this as I drove away from Sullivan's Island and toward said thing that I was told I had to do. Gilbert had offered me a ride, but I declined, wanting the freedom to skip out if I changed my mind.

Like I said, I had nothing against church, I just didn't want religion shoved down my throat. But I really liked the Magnolia Nephalist Society and Patsy, and I thought I could really find my place in this group. So, with a good bit of apprehension, I set out to Seacoast Church. Only a thirty-minute drive, but long enough I talked myself into and out of attending a half dozen times until it was too late and I was in the thick traffic on Long Point Road.

Seacoast Church looked more like a college campus than a church. A police officer directed the traffic, making it a little easier to turn into the entrance. With the help of parking attendants, it didn't take too long to find a spot.

I fell into step with a large group of people, hoping if I followed, they'd lead me to the right place. I was used to attending church services with no more than a hundred, this had at least a thousand. Finding Patsy would probably be about as easy as finding a lost earring on the beach.

The sanctuary with its large screens, an impressive stage, and cushioned stadium seating looked more like a theater than a typical church with wood pews and a small pulpit. I stood at the back, pushing against the wall to keep out of the way of people flooding in, and scanned the crowd, trying to spot Gilbert's white head or Patsy's curly one or Jackée's twists. After five minutes of searching, I became disheartened. What if Patsy didn't see me? How would I be able to prove to her I attended?

"There you are, suga'!" Patsy suddenly appeared next to me, locked her arm with mine, and led me to the middle of the section and almost smack-dab in the middle of the room, scooting us around people already sitting.

Seeing the row of familiar faces, I immediately thought, *There's my people!*

"Hey." As I settled into my impressively comfortable seat beside Gilbert, I glanced around. A preconcert vibe crackled the air, an energy of anticipation and giddy chatter. "This place is huge."

Gilbert nodded. "They have great services. You'll see."

Looking to the left toward the front, my eyes snagged on the back of a head that looked familiar. The guy turned his head and spoke to a young boy on his right, and the sight of those black glasses helped to confirm my suspicion. What were the odds of running into Henry at a random church in the Charleston area? Some say in jest that there is a church on every corner in the South, but it's close to being true.

Henry laughed at something the boy said, then looked to his left and spoke to a woman who looked close to his age. Did Henry have a secret family he hadn't mentioned?

The strum of a guitar drew my attention away from Henry and his maybe wife and child. I looked toward the stage and focused on the praise band as they asked us to rise and sing along. It was all high-energy and quite uplifting.

Rehab offered a weekly service, put together by a local church. Nothing wrong with those services, though they were mainly geared toward our recovery. This was different. Instead of being an alcoholic, here, I was just another soul wanting to draw closer to God. I liked it. I felt normal for once in a very long time.

The music came to a close and we took our seats as a youngish guy in a white hoodie and charcoal dress pants took the stage with a large iPad. I figured he was going to do the prayer and turn it over to the pastor but was pleasantly surprised when he instructed us to turn to Genesis 32. Within twenty minutes, he'd delivered a message about knowing who we are by knowing who God is. I liked it enough that I made some notes on my phone.

The service was over before I was ready, a problem I never thought I'd have to endure. With everyone rising and meandering out, I didn't see Henry again and maybe that was for the best.

"Let's go eat," Patsy suggested once we made it outside.

"I'm game," Chris Evans said. "There's this brunch spot I've been wanting to try out. Not a mimosa or Bloody Mary in sight. We're safe!"

My cash didn't flow freely enough for fancy brunch splurges, so I started toward my car. "I can't, but I'll see y'all Thursday."

Gilbert placed his arm over my shoulder. "Let me treat you."

I tried shrugging out of his hold but the old man wasn't having it, as always. Too bad. I didn't feel like being his charity case today. "Seriously, I can't go. Maybe next Sunday." I smiled, hoping it would encourage him to leave it at that. Thankfully, he did.

Traffic was a bit of a challenge to maneuver, typical for the summer season. I ended up behind Henry's Jeep just before making it back to the island. I debated sitting in my vehicle until he made it inside his house but that seemed silly, so I got out and chanced it. Of course we met up in our front yards.

"Nice shirt." I waved toward him.

Tucking his chin, Henry stared down at the pale-green button-down shirt as if having no idea where it came from or how he came about wearing it. His shirt and the khaki chinos were wrinkle-free, making him look like Professor Morrison, not rumpled Henry the neighbor. "Oh . . . ah thanks. I just came from church."

"Yeah? Me too." I readjusted the strap of my bag onto my shoulder. "I actually think I saw you."

He squinted. "You did?"

"At Seacoast. With a woman and young boy."

"That was my sister and nephew." He fiddled with his set of keys. "Why didn't you say something?"

I waved off the notion. "I was near the back."

"Oh." He looked toward his house, and I took the hint.

"Well, I'll catch ya later." I scurried up the steps and went inside. After telling Henry about Arlo and Fern two days ago, I didn't know if it was possible to revert to the lighter rapport we'd finally established before. That part of my story held too much weight.

Locking the door behind me, I made my way to the kitchen island. My phone chimed. I dug it out of my bag and found that I'd been added to the MNS group text.

Hi Junie. This is Patsy. Save my number. Everyone else, please identify yourself so Junie can save your contact as well. See y'all Thursday!

My phone began vibrating in quick succession as others replied.

Chris Evans

Pearl Anzalone

Jackée Davis

Bruno Castillo

Mei Lee

Axil Nelson

Gilbert Gordan. I'd already saved his number under *Gilly*, so I didn't bother changing it.

In a matter of seconds, my contact list had doubled. Thirteen contacts might be a paltry amount to some, but to me, quality far surpassed quantity in this case. Those thirteen people mattered most to me.

I placed the phone on the counter and glanced at the clock. Noon and some change, which meant a whole lot of hours left in the day. The silence of the house felt louder than the praise and worship band from earlier. A swift, antsy sensation came over me, one that made me thirsty, which really ticked me off. I'd just attended a great service, yet the struggles simply magnified out of the blue to torture me.

I recited HALT. "Hungry. Angry. Lonely. Tired. What is triggering you?"

Somewhere in all those knots in my stomach a hunger pang made itself known. I knew I needed to eat something. I wasn't angry, but I was agitated. Definitely lonely. Always lonely. As well as tired.

The idea of a nap came and went. I was too keyed up to sleep. I toyed with going upstairs to work on a hat or two, but the house seemed to be closing in on me. Kicking off my sandals, I swiped a peach from the fruit bowl and headed out to the back deck. I took a bite of the ripe fruit, enjoying the hints of tartness amidst the sweet. Peaches, the official taste of a Southern summer. Not sure if it was actually official but it should be, if you ask me. I leaned on the railing and stared at the waves rolling in, then out. Laughter and chatter from nearby beachgoers carried on the breeze and made me feel not so lonely. This was good, me recognizing the triggers and doing something productive about it.

In no time, I finished off the peach and contemplated going back inside for another, but the gritty slide of my neighbor's patio door had me changing course. I didn't feel up for chatting with Henry—I'd probably drop more of my burden on him and he'd held enough of it already—so I tossed the peach pit into a garbage bin and followed the coastline.

Reaching the jetties, I climbed onto a rock, out of the way, and watched two older men cast their fishing lines.

"What do you call bad bait?" one friend asked the other. The lures on his bucket hat shimmered when he moved his head.

"Dunno. What?"

"A fail-*lure*." He guffawed, sending his hat décor to jingle. "Get it? Fail. *Lure.* Failure."

"I get it, Don." The other guy shook his head, apparently above corny jokes. "Why did the fish blush?" Maybe not above it after all.

"Why?"

"Because it saw the ocean's bottom."

They snickered like silly boys.

I couldn't help but pipe in with a lame joke of my own. "How many fishermen does it take to change a lightbulb?"

Both men craned their necks until finding me sitting off to the side. "How many?" Don asked.

"Just one. But you should have seen the size of that lightbulb. It was this big." I held my hands far apart and made an exaggerated face.

They laughed.

The taller one opened his mouth to say something, but his fishing pole came alive, and the line started making a whining noise. "Holy moly. I got me somethin'!" He grabbed the pole and began reeling with all his might.

Enthralled, I stood to get a better look. A small fin popped up out of the water. "I think you hooked a shark!"

In a blink, a group gathered around, and we all waited with bated breath. It felt like hours passed with the old guy huffing, reeling, swearing under his breath, and huffing some more. With the help of his buddy, he was finally able to bring in a juvenile shark.

We all cheered, taking in the beast thrashing on the shore.

A teenage boy tiptoed closer. "You keeping it?"

"Nah. It's a beauty but I ain't got no use for it." The fisherman allowed everyone a good look, some snapping pictures. "Alrighty, we need to let him get on home. Help me, Don." The men hoisted the shark into their arms and returned it to the water.

Most of the onlookers lost interest and wandered off, but I stayed a little longer, listening as Don talked about a bigger shark he'd snagged during an offshore boating excursion.

I huffed. "Well. That was nothing to snuff at. How big you reckon it was?"

"It was about four feet long. Maybe forty, fifty pounds." Don popped open his cooler and pulled out two icy bottles of beer. "You gonna help us celebrate our catch, little lady?"

My throat went dry just thinking about how that beer would quench my thirst. "No thanks. But let me ask you this . . ." I wrangled on a smile I wasn't feeling. "What do you get from a bad-tempered shark?"

Don smirked underneath a burly mustache. "Dunno. What?"

"You *get* as far away as possible." I eased down the rocks, careful to not lose my balance. "You guys take care."

One of the men called out, "Ah, come on, sweetheart. Just one beer!"

I waved over my shoulder and kept on moving. Not gonna lie, I was proud of myself for resisting the temptation. But that light feeling didn't last long. Loneliness crept back in, and a voice joined it. *One beer wouldn't have hurt you.*

Moving fast to dodge the voice, I trekked home and decided to hunker down and binge-watch *Golden Girls*, another one of Olla's favorite shows.

Day turned into night while I devoured mouthfuls of microwave popcorn and watched the other women try their darndest to keep Rose straight.

In the last episode I watched before calling it a night, Dorothy told Rose, "Go to bed, sweetheart. Pray for brains."

I had brains, I felt sure, but I needed those brains to function clearly. Leaving my couch-potato state downstairs, I went to bed and prayed for a good night's rest.

Instead, a nightmare of shark wrangling and beach beers ensued.

18

"You're too purty to be embarrassing yourself like this, young lady." I clucked my tongue and motioned toward a guy doing all sorts of tricks with his dog by the park swings. "Look at that dog over there, listening to his owner." I gasped. "He just did a backflip! Seriously, Jazzy, the least you could do is get up and walk."

Jazzy responded by rolling away from the talented canine. Her fluffy gray-and-white coat was getting dirty, but I couldn't muster enough energy to care. This oppressive heat had wrung the life out of the both of us.

I lifted the collar of my T-shirt and used it to mop the sweat off my face. "I'm gonna have to look into walking you and the others earlier in the morning."

Jazzy lifted her head and glanced my way.

"What, little girl?" I caught myself baby talking to her, something I did without realizing it most of the time. "What's Miss Jazzy need?"

She rolled onto her back and let out a playful bark.

"I'm not rubbing your belly. No rewards for bad behavior, missy."

That stinker shimmied like an inchworm until she was close enough to nudge my leg. Giving in, I plopped onto the ground and rubbed her belly. I fished out a bottle of water and the collapsible bowl from my pack and shared it with her. We remained in the shade until the water was gone and she seemed to find enough energy to make it back to her home.

After dropping Jazzy off, I started toward my house, but stopped to check my vibrating phone. Cy's name flashed on the screen, sending me into a tizzy.

"Cy? Everything okay?"

"Yes. Just calling to check in. How's it going?"

Relieved, I pressed the phone between my ear and shoulder and rolled up the leash. "Good. Just finished dog-walking duties for the day. I'm gonna grab a quick shower, then get started on a hat project. I'm using some of Olla's quilt squares underneath the brim. It's going to be so cute."

"Hmph . . . You're still attending meetings, right?"

Rolling my eyes, I tucked the leash into my pack. "*Yes.* Two a week in person. Tuesday and Thursday. I'm catching online meetings and I'm going to church on Sunday like a good girl."

"Listen, I uh . . . I have something important to tell you."

I stopped fiddling in the pack and clutched the phone in my hand. "Is it Fern?"

"No. Well, in a way, yes."

"Just spit it out already, Cy." I sidestepped a jogger. In her own little world, I doubted she even saw me.

"Don't freak out, but . . . I've been offered a position at Vanderbilt in the fall."

"Where's that?"

"In Nashville." He cleared his throat. "They want me there by mid-August. Lana has already started packing. We have a lot to get done."

"Oh . . ." I took my own emotions out of the equation and focused on my brother. "Cy, I'm excited for you! I can come up this weekend to help. Then Fern can come home with me." I picked up my pace, happy to have a mission to focus on.

"No. Fern is coming with us."

My shoe caught the lip of the sidewalk and I almost tripped but righted myself in the nick of time. Between the near miss and Cy's declaration, my world slanted, making me dizzy. "But you know I can't leave South Carolina. I'm on probation for another ten months."

"So you expect me and my family to just put our lives on hold until you get your life straight?"

Knees weak, I veered off the sidewalk and leaned against a street marker. "You're talking about my family too. My *daughter* more specifically."

"You mean the daughter I have custody of because you got arrested?"

I rubbed my chest, but it did nothing to relieve Cy's blow. "But I've been working so hard to fix this! Please don't take her that far away from me. Two hours away is already unbearable as it is."

"Listen, we both know she's better off staying with me and Lana. So, cool down and we'll talk some more about this soon." Cy hung up.

Panting, I placed my hands on my stomach, worried all my innards were seconds away from spilling all over the place. Pressure under my ribs made it impossible to take a decent breath as my composure began unraveling, fraying like a dry-rotted rope ready to snap. I couldn't even inhale enough to sob, only able to push out a wheeze as my entire body shook.

"Are you okay, sweetie?"

I blinked to fight against the blur of my vision and caught sight of an elderly man standing in front of me. Nodding, I coughed and wheezed.

"I'm not so sure . . . I can call the 911."

Waving him off and sucking for air.

"But it could be a heat stroke or something."

I pushed to standing. "No . . . Thanks . . . though." I started down the street as quickly as my weak legs would carry me. *I need Gilbert.*

*

"They can't take my baby to Tennessee!" I paced the living room, dodging the wingback chair, nearly stumping my toe on the leg.

Sitting on the couch, Gilbert sighed. "Then you probably need to talk to a lawyer."

I stopped mid-lap and gripped the back of the chair. "I can't afford a lawyer!"

"Stop yelling!"

"Sorry!"

"You're still yelling." Gilbert wagged a finger at me. "Don't get yourself worked up in such a lather."

I glared. "You say that and all I can picture are soap bubbles."

He glared back. "Then use them to wash away your attitude."

I inhaled deeply to regain my composure. "Again, I'm sorry. I just don't know what to do."

"There are legal aid services to help those who can't afford to pay. Start there and also call your caseworker." He checked his watch and rose from the couch. "I need to head out."

"Why? You just got here. And hello!" I motioned at myself, arms flapping like a loony bird. "I'm having a crisis!"

"And you're yelling again. Stop it." He continued toward the front door. "I have an appointment to get to."

I hurried out behind him and stood at the edge of the yard as he got into his shiny Corvette, my panic barely ebbing. "I could really use some advice, Gilbert."

With his hand on the door, he stared off for a beat before saying, "If you see a toilet seat in your dreams, don't sit on it." In the span of time it took him to close the door, crank the car, and start backing out of the driveway, I finally made sense of his words.

"Huh? Oh . . ." I ran, waving my arms. "Hey! Wait!"

He rolled to a stop and the passenger window whirled down.

"Now's not the time for lame jokes! I'm serious. Please! I can't handle this on my own. I can't lose Fernie for good!"

Gilbert tapped a thumb against the steering wheel. "Junie, if you keep saying you can't then you won't. Start saying you can, and you will. And instead of making a scene, make a plan. You're grown, so act like it."

I finally gave up and let him go. I knew he wanted me to be an adult and handle this problem myself. I'd have to start with the caseworker like he said, even though it felt like too big of a responsibility. But that's what mothers had to do, right? Adult even when it's hard.

In a dejected slump, one I seemed to have mastered, I started toward the front door. As I reached the porch steps, Gilbert's car stopped and began reversing until coming to a stop by the mailbox. His window lowered once again.

Feeling guilty for holding him up, I waved for him to go ahead. "You don't want to be late for your appointment."

Gilbert flipped his sunglasses onto his forehead and frowned. "Get in."

"Huh?"

"Hurry up!"

Let the poor man go. That would be the decent thing to do, but I was too keyed up to do the decent thing, so I made quick work of locking the house and loading up into the passenger's seat. Gilbert had done me a favor, extended with a great deal of trepidation, so I kept my mouth shut the entire drive. My silence lasted until reaching the check-in counter at Topgolf.

"This is your important appointment?" I asked as we waited for the employee to confirm Gilbert's time slot. Sure, Gilbert deserved retirement fun such as golfing, especially since he had to put up with my sorry behind, but I couldn't help but razz him a little.

"It is, in my book."

The young woman keyed in something on her computer screen. "You're in Bay Seven today, Mr. Gilbert."

"Thanks, Caitlyn." Gilbert walked off and left me no choice but to follow.

"Y'all on a first-name basis? Wow."

"This is my happy place." He started up a set of steps. "Let me be happy."

"Absolutely. Go. Be happy, my friend." I made a sweeping motion.

We made it to our designated area and Gilbert held out a golf stick. "Here."

"That's okay. I'll just watch." I sat on the small couch in our lane. I'm calling it a lane, because it reminded me of a bowling lane set up, except this was partially outside. And instead of bowling, I supposed the object of the game was to smack the heck out of a golf ball and try aiming it at certain targets set out on an Astroturf field that was surrounded by a tall, humongous net.

"No. You're playing. This'll be a good stress relief." He shoved the golf stick into my hand, then turned to the touch screen to set up our game—again, a lot like bowling, but not. He typed his name, then on the next line he typed what I guessed was supposed to be me. *Pain in the Butt.*

"I don't know a thing about golf, Gilly." I poked him in the side. "And that's not my name, sir."

He flinched away from me. "It is today. And it's not hard. Just hit the ball with the club. Easy enough, yeah?"

"Sure."

FYI, it was not easy enough.

The first round, I barely got the ball off the tee thingy. I'd be the first to admit God hadn't divvied out any athleticism to me, frustratingly so.

"You're overthinking it. Just whack the danged thing!" Gilbert huffed.

I placed my hands on my hips and glared in his direction. "Look who's yelling now."

He stood from the couch and grabbed his own golf stick—or whatever it's called—and demonstrated for the hundredth time. With little effort, his ball sailed to the back of the net.

"Show-off," I muttered.

A server came by and checked on us. "Can I get y'all something besides the waters?"

"No thanks," I said, politely. Water was free, so I'd be sticking with that.

"You ain't hungry?" Gilbert asked, motioning toward the menu on the table in our lounge area. "They've got some good choices."

"I'm good. Thanks," I repeated. Even though I'd not eaten since yesterday, my stomach was tied in too many knots to eat. Most of the knots were made up of concerns about how to stop Cy from doing what he had planned to do. The rest were made up of worry about how me going against him would most likely finish ruining our relationship. I loved my brother, but I sure didn't like him all that much at the moment.

I had a newfound determination with the next game. I stepped up to the tee and imagined the ball as my stubborn brother's face.

Gripping the golf stick tightly, I rotated and whacked the tar out of that ball, sending it far enough to reach the midway target. The more into it I got, the looser the knots in my body became, and soon I was actually enjoying myself—and enjoying just hanging out with the old guy.

Humble brag here, I beat Gilbert's score the second round by 225 points. Come to find out, I wasn't too shabby of a player.

"Beginner's luck," Gilbert grumbled on our way out.

"Thank you, Gilbert. I feel much better now."

"Good." He wrapped an arm around my shoulders and I was pretty sure this was what fathers did, offering comfort, protection. My own father was always distracted around me or overtalking me about something awesome and wonderful happening with his work. As if sensing my thoughts, Gilbert added, "I'm always here for ya, kid."

To stop the emotions wanting to bubble up and out of my eyes, I cracked a joke. "Even if I whoop your butt at golf?"

He snorted. "Like I said, beginner's luck."

I *was* lucky. Lucky to have Gilbert in my corner.

19

"Your heart's still ticking, but, if you don't mind, I'm gonna tweak it a bit." I reached inside her chest and pulled the chain until the weight was repositioned at the top. I repeated this with the other two weights. "There ya go, ma'am." I closed the front of the clock and used a clean rag to wipe her down. Sighing, I stepped back and checked the time, which showed I still had too much time to dwell on the awful news Cy dumped on me yesterday.

Wandering into the kitchen, I picked up my phone and stared at the screen. I could call my parents and demand they parent up and get my brother off my back. I could hear that conversation playing out in my head.

Cy is being a meanie. Make him stop. Make him share my daughter with me!

I'm sorry, sweetheart, but we are in the middle of saving a tree!

I pocketed the phone and rubbed my forehead, then looked up and my gaze connected with the delicate stemware on display in Olla's hutch. Images of women in movies or TV shows sipping on a glass of wine to relax came to mind. I wished I could do that, just one glass to calm myself, but I never stopped at one glass.

What if you make yourself one glass then pour the rest down the sink. No temptation!

"No!" I spun in a circle and growled, trying to shake the inner voices.

Not trusting myself to be alone, I fled the cravings and made my way over to Henry's, but he was on his way out.

He came to an abrupt stop, nearly plowing into me at his front door. "Oh! Hi!"

"Hi," I parroted, watching him shove keys and a wallet into his pockets. "Where're you off to?"

"Book research." He didn't elaborate, making it clear it was none of my business.

"Oh." I shuffled back and forth, eyes trained on the weathered floorboards of the porch. "I'll uh . . . see you around then." I turned to leave.

"Would you like to go with me?"

I slowed, looking over my shoulder. "I don't want to get in the way."

Henry shook his head and motioned for me to follow him. "You won't. Come on."

I should have let the guy do what he needed to do in peace, but I desperately needed a distraction. One that would snag my mind away from my problems and the cravings, so I climbed into his blue Jeep without questioning our destination.

For the second time in two days, the destination ended up surprising me. "A tattoo parlor?"

"Yes," Henry replied, holding the door open to the shop, and the exotic aroma of incense pulled us inside.

"Patchouli?" I mumbled and a guy covered in intricate ink agreed.

"Good nose. Patchouli and rosewood." He grinned, brushing a dreadlock out of his face with a tattooed hand.

"Hey, Zee." Henry did some complicated fist bump with the guy.

"This is my friend Junie. You cool with her hanging out with us while you ink me?"

I gasped. "You're getting a tattoo?"

"Why else would he be in my shop?" Zee chuckled as he led Henry to an iPad mounted on the counter. "Fill this out while I set up, man." He walked toward the back of the shop where the low hum of tattoo guns sounded busy and steady, mingling with the laid-back melody of reggae music coming from the overhead speakers.

"This is for book research? A tattoo?" I whispered.

Henry filled out the section wanting to know what placement he wanted. Thankfully, he scrolled over the genitalia option and tapped the box for his left inner arm. "Yeah. Don't tell Zee, but I'm a little scared."

Bob Marley began crooning the lyrics of "Could You Be Loved" as Henry finished up the consent form, signing his name with an H and then a squiggly line.

"By the way, how'd you come up with your pen name?"

Henry looked over his shoulder as he hit the submit button. "H. M. is my initials, Henry Morrison. And my nonna's maiden name is Rossi."

"Ah. Makes sense now." I swiped a tattoo book and moved to the leather couch, preparing to get settled for a while.

"Come back with me." Henry motioned toward Zee's station.

Running my thumb over my fingernails, I glanced around, then met his gaze. "You sure?"

"Sure." Henry gave me a lopsided, boyish smile. One that talked me into following immediately.

Zee got down to work rather quickly and efficiently, the gun humming away. About twenty minutes in, an ache settled into my arm. I rotated it a few times, then rubbed my shoulder.

"You having sympathy pains?" Henry chuckled.

"No." I made a face and kneaded my arm. "I went to Topgolf with Gilbert yesterday. It's got my arm sore."

"Ah. So he's back to being your personal trainer?" Henry's blue eyes sparkled, as if we were sharing an inside joke. I guess we were, because he knew darn well Gilbert was no such thing.

"For now, yes."

Henry nodded, seemingly not in any pain as the needle continuously dug into his arm. "Gilbert is a nice guy."

"Yep." I wanted to come clean and admit what Gilbert was to me, probation officer/sponsor, but the old man was so much more than that, and a tattoo shop wasn't the right place for that conversation.

Less than an hour later, Zee slapped a piece of clear wrap around Henry's bicep. "Keep it covered for the next hour. Clean with plain antibacterial soap and only put some unscented lotion like CeraVe on it. No sun and no pool for at least the next week."

I could easily see the bold *#15* inked along his toned inner arm. "Hashtag fifteen? What's it stand for?"

"It's . . . my lucky number." Henry's tone said there was more behind it than that.

I waited until we made it outside to pick back up on the conversation. "What's the number really about?"

Henry straightened his glasses and peered around. No one was in earshot, I'd already checked. "Fifteen is where my third book hit the *New York Times* Best Seller list. Stayed there for three weeks too."

"Yeah, but you've had several to hit number one since then."

"The goal was to hit the list." Henry unlocked my door, then held it open for me. "I didn't care where."

I climbed in the seat and gave him a dubious look. "I'm not buying that."

"Then you're not an author." Henry winked at me and closed the door. He rounded to the driver's side and climbed in. He drove out of the parking lot and down the road a ways before adding, "Authors say they don't care about the list, that it's about the writing first and foremost, and it is, but don't let any of us fool you. We all want on that list."

I gave that some thought. "Why not put number one on your arm instead of number fifteen?"

He made a right. "It's like this box was checked after I hit number fifteen, and it never really mattered to me after that. I proved I was a legit writer to myself and that's all that mattered."

I considered what number I would have tattooed on my arm, if I was into tattoos. Fern's birthday? No, that was the best day. I needed a hashtag-fifteen day. Maybe forty-five. That was the number of days I stayed sober after my first stint in rehab. It proved I could do it, and I was determined to make it an infinite number this second time around.

"What if you wrote those books . . . all thirteen of them . . . and none of them ever hit a bestsellers list? Those same stories? Aren't they just as good even without the NYT title beside them?"

Henry glanced over before refocusing on the busy road. "You ever set a goal and once you achieve it, realize it wasn't as grand as you had expected?"

I stared out the window, chagrined. "I've never achieved any goal I've made, so I don't know."

Henry changed lanes and for a few miles all I heard was the roar of the engine. Finally, he said, "You're young, Junie. You have plenty of time to make goals and then see them happen."

I shrugged, not feeling so optimistic. "If you say so."

"What are some goals you have?"

"Let's see. Maybe not get arrested again. Oh! And I would really like to never go back to rehab. It wasn't my scene."

"Stop being facetious."

"What do you mean?"

"You have significant goals you're working toward." He side-eyed me. "Your sobriety. Regaining custody of Fernie. Your hat and accessory business."

"I want my daughter back more than anything, but I'm so . . . I'm overwhelmed. The cravings, the body aches when I deny the cravings. And the stress of trying to eke out a living so I can support myself and Fernie. Each day I wake up knowing I have to do all the hard things, to prove to my family and to the court I can be a decent parent."

Henry said nothing until he pulled into his driveway and shut off the engine. "Junie . . . Those goals are hefty—"

"I know it."

He turned in the seat and looked at me head-on as his hand found mine. "But from what I've learned about you this summer, you're more than capable. Don't give up, no matter how hard it gets."

"I won't." My eyes pricked and my throat tightened. "Thanks for today. The distraction and for this talk. I really needed it."

"Any time." He squeezed my hand, then let go.

I climbed out of the Jeep and made my way inside my house. I started up the stairs, but a knock at the door had me reversing to answer it.

"So . . . I found this on my porch." Henry held the basket of tomatoes a little higher. "You wouldn't happen to have any more of that good bread, would ya?"

I shook my head. "Sorry."

He looked over the plump tomatoes. "It's okay. We can just slice them up and eat as is."

For a second, I considered telling him no thanks and ending things where we left them in the driveway, but he didn't seem put off by my disastrous life, and those tomatoes sure did look good, considering I'd spent most of the day too upset to eat anything. "You ever had tomato cracker salad?"

He shrugged. "Can't say that I have."

"Well, you're in for a treat then. I'm gonna make you my Grandma Olla's tomato cracker salad." I waved him inside and closed the door. Entering the kitchen, I grabbed the mayonnaise and a sleeve of saltine crackers.

"This is new."

I looked over my shoulder and found Henry standing before my painting. "I just finished it last night."

He leaned in closer. "What are those raised circles in the center of the flowers?"

I joined him and smoothed my fingertip over the center of the purple chrysanthemum. "My AA chips. If you look closely you can see this one says *start*. I received it at my first meeting in rehab. The flower is a chrysanthemum. It symbolizes a fresh start."

"Hmph." Henry tapped the center of a red-and-orange flower. "This one says twenty-four hours."

"That's a blanketflower. It can grow in extreme environments. It represents surviving. I was barely surviving at that point, but still." I shrugged, focusing on the yellow flower beside it. "The daffodil is associated with overcoming challenges. Its center is my six-month chip."

"And the sunflower?" Henry traced the brown center.

"My four-month chip. Represents healing and resilience. About that time, I felt like I was finally turning a corner in treatment." I pointed to the deep fuchsia flower near the top of the painting. "Echinacea symbolizes strength and health. I'll add more chips as I earn them. I'm due my seven-month one."

Henry turned to me, his eyes soft. "This is . . . I love it, Junie. It's clever, chock-full of private meaning . . ." He shook his head. "How do you know so much about flowers?"

"I think I already told you. Plants and trees are my parents' world. I tried to learn all I could about them, hoping to be a part of it. But it was all for nothing. They still didn't let me in." Moving away from the painting, I returned to the counter and slammed my fist down against the pack of saltines. It felt so good I did it again.

"What did those poor crackers do to you?" Henry laughed nervously, probably thinking I was about to have a come apart.

"You have to crush them for the salad," I explained, giving the pack another firm whack. "How about dicing up those tomatoes. There's a cutting board beside the knife block." Keeping my watery eyes turned away from his, I finished crushing the crackers and poured them into a bowl.

Henry cleared his throat. "I know how it feels, wanting to fit into your parents' world. That's why I became a professor, to fit into my father's academia world."

I looked up and regarded Henry as he carefully chopped a tomato. "How'd that work out for you?"

Henry focused on the tomato. "Okay, I guess, until I told him I wanted to be a writer." He huffed. "I had my first manuscript printed out and bound at the Office Depot especially for my dad to read. It took a month for him to get back to me. He said it was silly, girlie fluff. Said I needed to stick to teaching math." The knife stilled as Henry glanced up at me. "That's why I've continued teaching and kept the books secret, so I wouldn't embarrass him."

I gasped. "Henry, that's . . . Your books aren't silly or fluff reads. But even if they were and that's what you're passionate about, you have nothing to be ashamed of. You do you and be proud of it."

Henry finished the last tomato, walked the knife to the sink, then leaned on the counter beside me. "Same goes for you, Junie. Take your own advice and stop worrying about fitting into your parents' or your brother's world. You're remarkable as you are."

"You don't know me well enough to say that, but thank you for saying it," I muttered, adding two dollops of mayonnaise to the bowl and the tomatoes, then a sprinkling of salt and pepper. "Salad is ready."

Henry adjusted his glasses and peered into the bowl. "This is salad?"

"Yep. Normally, Grandma would add green onions and a boiled egg, maybe bacon, but I don't have any of that, so it is what it is, which is delicious."

I halved the salad into two bowls and handed Henry one with a fork. "You'll like it, trust me."

He took a tentative bite, and his eyes lit up. "That is oddly good." He shoveled in another forkful.

"Told you." I took a bite too and tasted the tangy flavor of the mayo mixing with sweet memories of sunshine and laughter, also known as a summer-ripe tomato.

We stood by the sink and, like magicians, made our makeshift meal disappear.

"Why did you need a distraction today?" Henry said as I turned on the faucet. "You never said."

The deep pinch in my stomach came back with a vengeance. I squirted dish soap into the stream of hot water. "My brother dropped a bomb on me yesterday."

"Yeah? What kind?"

"He got a job in Tennessee and plans on taking my daughter with them." I placed the dishes into the soapy water and grabbed a dishcloth. "My probation won't allow me to leave the state for several more months. So I'll be stuck here and they'll be all the way in Tennessee."

"He's only now telling you this?"

Henry's question and the sharp tone of his voice gave me pause. I turned from the sink and met his stern gaze. "What do you mean by that? Should he have told me earlier?"

"Yes. He's . . ." Henry closed his mouth, then started again. "Taking a position at a university isn't like applying to McDonald's and starting the very same week. It's a much longer process."

I finished washing a bowl and Henry took it and began rinsing it. "So you think he's known for a while?"

"Yes," Henry said adamantly, placing the clean bowl in the rack.

"Maybe he didn't want to tell me until he was certain, I don't know. But I can't let him take her out of state. If that happens I'm scared I'll never get her back."

"I really wish there was something I could do to help you. I'm sorry."

"You have nothing to apologize for. This is my fault . . ." I fished the two forks out and washed them before handing them to Henry. Our sudsy hands brushed. If I were a normal woman in my mid-twenties, this could have easily led in a different direction than the uncomfortable path we were currently on. "I've looked into getting a lawyer."

"A lawyer. You think that's necessary?"

I unplugged the sink and dried my hands. "At this point, I do. I'm not saying I don't deserve this crappy hand dealt to me, I'm just saying I deserve another chance. If I didn't think I could do right by Fern, I'd hand her over with no protest, but I feel in my heart I can be the mother she deserves. I just need the opportunity to prove it."

"Then get the lawyer and fight for her."

I sniffed away the tears and nodded.

Henry pulled me into an embrace and I allowed it, sinking against his chest. The steady in and out of his breaths helped to slow mine after a while. This warm, gentle place, I could get lost in it. Stay right here and let him make me forget all the awfulness life was currently dishing out to me. But real life called, so I stepped out of his arms and pointed to his wrapped tattoo. "Enough about me. You, sir, need to go write now that you've done your research."

He didn't move, as if ready to stay rooted in my troubles.

"Seriously, Henry, go. I have to head out to my AA meeting soon, anyways."

Henry left as quietly as that day I made him coffee. I had to give it to the guy, he knew when someone needed space.

I sat down on a stool and placed my head on the counter.

Even though all I wanted to do was to hide and bawl my eyes out, I knew I had to pull it together and attend my meeting. At least among the broken I could be openly broken too.

20

I arrived early at the Methodist church, still thinking about Henry's words—*fight for your daughter*—and still feeling that hug. I liked both too much, but only one of those had any business taking up space in my mind.

The fellowship hall door opened just as I reached for it.

Betty popped her head out. "I thought that was you, Junie."

"Hi, Betty. Could you use a dishwasher?" I held my palm up, volunteering.

"You're so sweet. Come on." Betty strode into the kitchen with the ever-present pep in her step. I hoped I aged as well as this one. "I'm making deli sandwiches and I made a cookie platter earlier. So not too much of a mess."

I went straight to the sink and started the dishwater just like I did earlier at Olla's. Only a few mixing bowls and a cutting board. This mindless task wouldn't take long. "Feel free to make a bigger mess. I'm in need of a distraction today."

"Aww. You poor thing. Having a bad day?"

"Most days." I shrugged. "Can I ask you something?"

She held a small watermelon in place and sliced into it. "Sure, sweetie."

I rinsed a serving spoon and placed it in the dish rack. "Why do you prepare us a meal every week? Isn't that a lot on you?"

"There's no more than fifteen people most meetings. That's not very large." Betty used the back of her hand to brush a lock of red hair off her cheek.

That sounded like a lot to me. "But why do you do it?"

Her warm smile faded, and I wished I could backtrack and keep my mouth shut. "My husband Ernest . . . he struggled with the bottle. Drank himself to death. I never understood why he couldn't just stop, so after his death I came to this open meeting to try figuring it out." She emptied a colander of strawberries onto a glass platter and handed it to me.

I plunged the colander into the soapy water and started scrubbing even though a rinse was all it needed. Betty's words reminded me of what Gilbert told me that first night here when I griped about Betty and her two friends being at the meeting, how he explained they wanted to understand. I'd been so insensitive that night and almost blurted an apology to Betty, but she continued before I worked up enough nerve to do it. She didn't know I owed her an apology, anyway. Maybe my helping her and thanking her was apology enough.

"That first meeting Reggie talked about cell phones. Asked us how many times a day we picked ours up." She plucked green grapes off the stem and added them to the strawberries. "Do you have any idea how many times you pick yours up in a day?"

I shook my head. "It's probably embarrassingly high. I check for texts before I even get out of bed. I check the weather app before taking the dogs for walks. I check emails and social media. My Etsy page. I'm constantly looking something up on the Internet . . ." I shrugged again.

"Same. I text back and forth with my daughters all day. I catch up with friends on the Facebook. It's basically always within reach. Reggie said one website listed that the average American picks up their phone nearly a hundred and fifty times a day!"

I did a double take. "One hundred and fifty times? You think that's right?"

"Wouldn't surprise me. I tried counting one day. Since I was more aware, I probably didn't do it as much, but I reached eighty times before bed."

"Wow. That's . . . wow." I shook my head. "Why was Reggie telling y'all about this?"

"He asked us to imagine being told we could never pick our phones up ever again. I couldn't even imagine it. Then he said that's what it feels like for an alcoholic who can never pick up a drink ever again. They will always have that desire to drink, just like we always have the constant need to check our phones."

I thought about earlier. How I craved picking up a fancy glass of wine. "That's a good way of putting it."

"That first meeting was seven years ago, and I've been attending ever since. I started making the meals, wanting to give the attendees some kind of comfort." Betty sighed a laugh. "You know us Southerners love to feed folks. It's my love language."

"Well, I really appreciate all you do. More than the food. You always welcome me with such warmth, like you're really happy to see me."

Betty's hand came to a rest on my forearm. "Because I am, sweetie. I can't bring my Ernest back, but it blesses me to be able to make a difference—no matter how small—to others struggling with addiction."

I dried my hands and wrapped my arms around Betty. She looked nothing like Olla, but she reminded me of my grandmother, nonetheless. The world needed more Bettys and Ollas.

With the dishes done, I made the tea about the time everyone started arriving. As I carried over a pitcher to the counter, I saw another person the world needed more of walk through the door.

"Gilbert! What are you doing here?"

"I wanted to check on you, especially after yesterday. You hangin' in there, kid?"

"By a thread, but yes." I filled a cup with ice and tea and handed it to him. Then I made myself one. "Wanna sit with Maren?"

Gilbert nodded. "Sure."

We joined Maren and a few others at one of the two tables and indulged in small talk until Reggie stood at the small podium.

"I know it's only Tuesday, but I hope you are all having a good week so far." Reggie smiled, making eye contact with each of us as he tended to do. He went over a few announcements and then we got in line to make our plates.

"Why don't you sit with us and eat, Betty?" I asked as she served me a spoonful of fruit.

"Oh, that's okay, dear."

"No, really. I'd love for you to sit and enjoy this food with us. Please." I glanced over at her two friends behind the counter, Nancy and Diane. "Y'all too."

They gave each other questioning looks, then Betty shrugged. "Why not?"

We recited the Serenity Prayer and once we were seated, Maren joined Reggie up front.

"Hello. My name is Maren and I've been sober for six months and one week." She stood a little taller tonight and made eye contact instead of staring at the floor. "I've been going to therapy with my ex-husband and my children. It was weird at first, but the last two weeks have been better. We're finally talking about things we should have talked about a long time ago. I'd like to encourage you to think about counseling too if you haven't." Maren looked around the room. "There's a reason we turned to substance abuse. And we need to figure that out. I understand that now. Or I'm starting to."

We clapped as she took her seat. I wondered if that's what Cy and I needed. Counseling, so we could figure things out together.

The meeting wrapped up early, seemed no one was much in the sharing mood. Gilbert walked me out.

"You coming to the house to test me?" I handed him my to-go plate and riffled for my keys.

"Nah. I'll sneak one on you soon, though." Gilbert gave me a smug grin. "Say, that was nice what you did with Betty and her friends."

"It just seemed like the right thing. I didn't like the division, plus they should be able to enjoy their meals too."

"So many times there's a line drawn between the 'us' and 'them' where it shouldn't be. I'm glad you're seeing that." Gilbert gave me my container, opened his and swiped a strawberry.

I placed my bag and container onto the passenger seat. "Why exactly are you my probation officer?"

"We already talked about this."

"Yeah, but you doing this as a favor for your judge friend seems kinda flimsy."

He leaned against the Caddy. "Even though I retired, I still felt like I could be of some use, so I told Archie to keep me in mind if he put someone on probation in my area. No more than thirty minutes. You fit the bill."

"What about being my sponsor too, though? Isn't that a conflict of interest?"

"Both roles are to help keep you in line, so no."

My eyes narrowed, still not buying it completely. "You ever sponsor anyone else while being their probation officer?"

He scrubbed a palm down his cheek. "You're just full of questions tonight. The answer is no."

"Why me then?"

"During that initial visit with you in prison, you reminded me of my younger self."

"What? We both had long blonde hair and boobs?" I joked but he glared.

"You want me to tell you or not?"

"Yes."

"Then shut that smart mouth of yours and listen."

Heat crept up my face. "Sorry."

"From the report, I learned you'd lost your husband and your grandmother in one fell swoop. I personally know that when grief piles up on someone like that, they can buckle under the weight. I didn't see an alcoholic criminal that day. I saw a young woman buckled underneath a pile of grief. It was much the same as me when I returned from Vietnam."

I swallowed the lump of grief that surfaced from his sentiment, then had to clear my throat. "I don't know much about that war."

"All you need to know is it was hell on earth and should have never happened. That's my opinion anyway. I lost a lot of people right in front of my eyes. Talking one minute, gone the next. It was brutal. I tried drinking those images away, but it only made it worse. I buckled. Had it not been for my Valerie, I would be dead long ago. I got another chance to live. *Really* live." Gilbert tapped my chin with his knuckle. "I want to make sure you get a chance to live too."

We stood in the dimming day, the sounds of traffic and a dog barking barely registered, because this old man just devastated me. Why would he care to help me?

Maybe it was best to stop questioning it. To just accept it and appreciate it. I could do that but in my own way, of course.

"Oh gosh, Gilly!" I dried my face with my sleeve. "You're making my eyes leak all over the place!"

"Help, someone! She's sprung a leak!" He waved his free hand, and Reggie started our way, but Gilbert flicked a wrist. "We just messin'."

Laughing, Reggie reversed and continued toward his truck.

I fiddled with my key chain, smoothing my thumb over Fern's tiny photo. "You mean more to me than I let on. Thank you, Gilbert. For everything."

"You're welcome, kid. Have a good night."

"You too."

"Oh, wait a minute. I forgot something." He fished in his pocket and pulled out a copper-colored coin. "Your seven-month chip. I'm a little late getting it to you."

I accepted the chip and rubbed my thumb over the raised words. *To thine own self be true.* "Thanks."

"You keeping them somewhere close? So you can have a visual of what you've achieved?"

I smiled. "Yes, sir. I'll add this one tonight."

"I'm proud of you, Junie." Gilbert got into his sports car and waited until I pulled out of the parking lot to leave.

Feeling better equipped to handle what was surely coming with Cy and the custody battle, I drove home with my shoulders no longer slumping. I thought about Maren and what she shared about attending therapy with her family. I decided to focus on finding a counselor first and worry about Cy later.

Once I arrived home, I took a moment to carry my chip and the painting upstairs to the workroom. I'd work on that later, but for now this sudden need to find a therapist was top priority. I opened my laptop and began researching counseling centers for family and substance abuse. There were plenty of places and I started feeling hopeful, but then I got a glimpse of the cost and my optimism plummeted. I couldn't ask my brother to attend counseling *and* ask him to pay for it. No way would he ever go for that.

Slapping the lid shut, I went to bed. A restless night followed, tossing and turning, trying to figure out a way to swing the cost of therapy.

Three in the morning, I finally gave up on sleep and decided to call my mother. If I had to grow up and parent then perhaps it was time to make my parents do the same.

Switching on the lamp, I sat up and settled my back against the headboard, then dialed Mom.

"Junie? Honey, everything okay?"

"I can't sleep."

"Obviously. It's, what, two . . . no, three there?"

"Yeah." I smoothed out the blanket. "I need to fix this mess with Cy."

She didn't speak right away and I feared she would figure out a way to dismiss my worries, or tell me about some rare plant they'd been able to propagate, but then she said, "What can I do to help?"

Perking up, I braved telling her about the therapy idea. "I've found a few places in Charleston that specialize in family therapy. I want to ask Cy to go with me, but I can't afford it. And I'm scared he'll say no anyway."

Mom grew quiet again. "Send me the link to whichever place you'd like to go to. I'll call Cy and see if I can talk him into it."

"You'll call him?"

"Yes. If he agrees, I'll pay for it." She sighed. "I feel like your father and I are partly to blame. I'm sorry we aren't there. It's just . . . we're right in the middle of a big project and—"

"Y'all are always in the middle of something. You have been all my life." I made myself shut up, worried she'd change her mind and not help.

A few beats passed in silence until Mom cleared her throat. "That sounded . . . resentful. I thought . . . I thought we were showing you and your brother it was okay to pursue your calling, to not let anything hold you back."

"Even your own children?"

"You're a fine one to talk." Her response hit harder than a slap across the face.

"I'm trying to fix my messes. You and Dad have never owned up to making any!"

"Well, I'm so sorry we were such horrible parents!"

My entire body started shaking and I felt like I was going to throw up. I jumped out of bed and paced around the room, trying to shake it off. This was the first time I'd ever come close to confronting my mother, and it was making me physically sick. I wondered if I could just backtrack and pretend we hadn't gone there.

I stopped in front of the mirror and stared at Fern's picture, remembering my purpose. The relationship with my parents may have been a lost cause, but I genuinely wanted and needed one with my brother and daughter.

"I'm sorry. I'm stressed and shouldn't be taking it out on you." I held my breath, silently begging her to take the bait.

"That's understandable. I'm sorry too."

I exhaled. "I really do appreciate you offering to help me with the therapy. Again, I'm really sorry for mouthing off."

"It's okay." She sighed, sounding relieved to put the pin back into the Wilder family grenade too. "I'll call Cy tomorrow. Why don't you try to get some rest?"

"Yes, ma'am. Love you."

"Love you too, Junie."

Too keyed up to sleep, I went to the workroom to add my new chip to the painting. I rummaged through my paint bin for white and yellows to help create a daisy, which was associated with motherhood. This chip would remind me I was a good mother, and even though I'd made a terrible mistake, I could overcome it. I'd prove it to my parents, to my brother, and especially to my daughter.

21

"I've cleaned you all up, old lady. Now be good and don't cause me any more trouble." I finished drying off the back window of the Caddy and admired her sparkly clean body.

Every time I turned around, some other issue came up with this vehicle. Thursday night, on my way home from the Magnolia Nephalist meeting, I was pulled over and came close to having a heart attack. Turned out the Caddy had a taillight out. The officer was kind, just giving me a warning. I went yesterday to Greg and gave him some more of my money, but it wasn't too costly of a fix this time.

I put away the car-cleaning supplies and went inside to get myself washed up. Despite the early hour, the humidity was already stifling.

My phone vibrated in my pocket. I pulled it out and stared at my brother's name for a split second before answering. "Hey."

"Junie!" His voice didn't hold the chipper excitement mine did. No, his held a frantic anger.

Instantly unsettled, I blurted, "What's wrong? Fern okay?"

"She is, but are you?"

"Why wouldn't I be?" Confused, I darted up the stairs to my room to gather a fresh set of clothes.

"What was it this time? Pills? Booze? Both?"

With my hand in the shirt drawer, I halted. "What the heck are you talking about?"

"I haven't heard from you all week. After my Nashville news, I assumed you went on a bender again." Sounded like that's exactly what he wanted me to do. Too bad.

Tossing the shirt back into the drawer and slamming it shut, I whirled around and slumped against the dresser. "Well, you assumed wrong, big brother. I've been giving you some space is all. Seemed you were sick of me calling." I needed the break more like it. I was so angry at him for even considering taking my daughter out of state. "We need to talk about Fern coming to live with me."

"We already did."

"Well, we need to talk about it again. I want to see her. And if you could see me, you'd *see* how good I'm doing." I stared at the ceiling. "I'm serious this time, Cy. I woke up. I'm changed."

"Something I've heard a million times with you! Such hyperbole." He groaned, closer to a growl. "I'm getting another call. We'll have to talk about this another time." And just like that, Cy hung up on me.

Fed up, I ran through the shower, got dressed, and set out toward Columbia. One way or the other, I would see my daughter this day. Enough was enough.

The thick weekend traffic didn't deter me from my mission. I'd considered stopping to get Fern a little gift, perhaps a doll or stuffed animal, but decided to just give her me this time.

A little over two hours later, I slowly drove through Cy's neighborhood and parked at the curb across the street from his house. I reached for the door handle but stopped when I spotted Cy, his eight-year-old son Alex, and Fern out on the front lawn playing a game of chase.

They hadn't noticed me, so I sat back and observed them, an outsider stealing a peek into this family. A family I was supposed to be a part of, but because of one epically failed day, I'd lost that privilege.

Sinking deeper into the driver's seat, I watched as Cy went down on his knees, allowing the two children to tackle him. Getting caught up in their silliness, I snickered, then full-on laughed. Fern's tiny self tackled Cy, hopping on his back like a bull rider about to take the grand championship. Even through the closed window, I heard Cy make what he must have thought sounded like a bull, but to me he sounded more like a dying animal. Fern squealed as he bucked, then Alex tried climbing on, only for all three to collapse in a heap.

I laughed but stopped abruptly as the bitter reality hit me: *they're better off without me.* Not just my brother and his family, but also my own child. I put the Caddy into drive and slinked away, undetected, which only drove home the point even further—I was insignificant, forgettable, a dud.

The first hour back to Sullivan's Island, I drove in silence. No radio. No phone call to my parents to beg them to come home for once and step up. Only my thoughts to keep me company, but they were doing a lousy job.

They are all better off without you.

Look! No frowns.

They are happy now.

You're the problem, it's you.

Just leave them alone.

I passed a few liquor stores. My mouth watered and this need to wheel in and quench my craving came over me, but I kept on driving. I managed for a little while until needing a restroom break. I pulled into a gas station. After filling up the Caddy, I walked inside with as much ambition as someone heading to the gas chambers.

I used the bathroom, washed my hands, and ordered myself to walk out the front doors of the store without any shopping. Snacks cost too much financially. And the beverage cooler could cost too much personally.

But then, the scene of Cy with his child and mine on his neatly mowed lawn came to mind. The lousy thoughts picked right up again.

They are all better off without you.

They don't need you.

You're the problem, it's you.

Just leave them alone.

Grinding my teeth, I took a step forward, then another until I stood in front of the beer and wine cooler. While scanning all the options that might help to numb the ache in my chest, I decided I'd get a liquid appetizer here and then move on to a liquor store for the main course.

I opened the glass door and grabbed the first thing my hand landed on. A tall can of light beer. The coolness of the can in my grip made my mouth water and I could almost hear the hissing sound it would make when I popped the tab, like a sigh of relief. Throat closing, body aching, I somehow managed to return the can to the shelf. To make sure I didn't pick it back up again, I slammed the door shut and wiped the condensation dampening my palm onto my jeans to get rid of the guilt. I reversed a step, only to lunge forward again. Reaching for the handle then dropping my trembling hand, I silently begged God, *Please, please take the taste of unhealthy out of my mouth. Please don't let me give in to this weak moment. Give me strength to walk away.*

A tinkling giggle interrupted my prayer, or maybe answered it. As I opened my eyes, a little girl around Fern's age plowed into me. Her tiny arms reached around my legs and gripped me with a fierceness I'd not expected from such a small human.

"Pop! I wanna pop!" The little girl let go of me, only to grab my hand and drag me over to the soda cooler and point to a bottle of Sprite.

"Good choice, but . . ." I scanned the store and spotted a haggard woman hurrying in our direction.

"Ellison! Honey, you cannot run off from Mommy like that!" She swooped the child up into her arms and started planting kisses all over her face, making Ellison squeal like a little piglet. "I would be so sad if I lost you."

The mother apologized to me, but I waved off her concern. "It's no problem. Glad she's okay."

"Little ones can be such a handful, ya know." The mom laughed. "Do you have any?"

"Yes. A little girl about Ellison's age." I stuttered through my response, tasting the bitterness of what could possibly be a lie. A lie because I no longer felt like my own daughter belonged to me.

"Oh, so you totally understand!" The young mother gave me a commiserating smile, then started down the chip aisle.

Once they were out of sight, my gaze bounced between the shelves of beer and bottles of wine just to the left. Swallowing with great effort, I refocused on the soda cooler. Sure, the chemicals it took to make the fizzy pop probably stole years off my life, but that would be better than the epic disaster the cooler to the left could inflict. I finally decided on a bottle of Sprite and got the heck out of there before changing my mind again.

Knowing I needed to talk to someone, to confess that I almost slipped, I walked over to Henry's once I made it home. I found him out back at the patio table, his attention fully on the laptop in front of him. "You busy?"

He looked up and met my gaze without answering, his fingers never slowing the rhythmic tap over the keyboard. I realized he was looking at me but only saw whatever world he was in the midst of creating. Moments passed until he looked down, I assumed to save his work. I imagined the click of that save icon was like him closing the door to his imagination and stepping back into reality.

Henry leaned back in the chair, his focus now clear and on me. Tilting his head, he gave me a thoughtful frown, reading the distress on my face. "Something wrong?"

"Yes."

"What do you need?"

"I need a drink."

He slowly shook his head. "No you don't. What do you really need?"

"My daughter. I need my daughter." The words barely made it past my lips, just in a puff of air as fragile as ash.

Henry stood and motioned for me to join him on the wicker sofa. "Tell me what happened?"

I collapsed beside him and started with the phone call from Cy that led to my spur-of-the-moment trip to Columbia to see my daughter, only to chicken out. As Henry listened quietly, I even confessed to standing in that convenience store, staring into a beer cooler.

"I'm sorry, Junie."

I shook my head and huffed. "You have nothing to be sorry for. This is all on me."

"Anything I can do?"

"No . . . I just have to see this through." I groaned again. "I want to scream or break something." I bowed my head and rested it in my palms. "Or both!"

"Do you have some closed-toe shoes?"

I dropped my hands. "For what?"

"You're stressed, right? Need to blow off some steam?"

"I'm not running in this heat."

"Me neither." He rose to his feet and beckoned me to do the same. "What we're doing is indoors."

I slowly stood. "What's indoors?"

"You'll see. Go change your shoes and meet at the Jeep." Barefooted, Henry turned to go inside, to put his own shoes on, I assumed.

I thought about the last time I went somewhere with him, the tattoo parlor, and how that had been a good distraction. Curious, I did as he said.

By the time we pulled up in front of a storefront inland, my curiosity had eased the craving for alcohol a good bit. *Bull in a China Shop*, I read on the topsy-turvy styled sign, letters going in wonky angles.

Henry led me inside where mosaics were on display.

"Oh wow . . ." I ran my fingers over a vase. The shiny shards of tile in various greens reminded me of mermaid scales. "Are we making mosaics?"

"Not this time." Henry walked over to a lady behind a counter. "Hi there. Two for demolition."

"Demolition?" I muttered behind him.

"You got it, hon." The lady handed him two pairs of goggles and two sets of gloves. "How many boxes a piece?"

Henry offered me one of the pairs of goggles and the smaller gloves. "One for me. Two for her."

"Boxes?" I asked.

Neither one of them answered me.

Henry paid, at my protest, then the lady led us to the back of the building. As we entered the room, things began clicking into place while I took in the space—a beat-up back wall full of scuffs and scars, a dusty cement floor, broken pieces of dishware and pottery scattered about. Letting off some steam never seemed so creative as this.

A guy wheeled in three boxes filled with all sorts of dishes and placed them at the yellow line painted on the floor. "Just load up the broken pieces into those crates and leave them on the table."

"Okay." Henry put the goggles over his glasses and then worked his hands into the gloves. "The object here, if it's not already clear, is to throw dishes at the wall. Easy enough, right?"

I eyed the box by my feet and decided on a pink floral-printed plate. "It doesn't feel right to break these pretty plates."

"But the broken pieces are used to create art. You're an artist, so you can appreciate that, yeah?"

"I guess . . ."

An explosion rang out. Startled, I looked up from my plate in time to watch a shower of pottery rain onto the floor. "Good grief. Warn a girl, will ya!"

Henry leaned down and plucked a chipped teacup from his box. Without saying a word, he reared his arm back and threw the cup like a baseball. This time I got to witness it exploding into a million pieces.

Wanting in on the action, I tossed the plate, but didn't get the same result. It practically bounced off the wall, only breaking when it hit the cement floor.

"You can do better than that." He slung a plate with great force as if it were a Frisbee and it smashed all to pieces.

I went for a cup and tried the baseball method. This time it exploded on impact. "Great day! That's satisfying." Exhilarated, I gave Henry a high-five.

"Good. You have two boxes to break." Henry nodded to the boxes on the floor, silently telling me to get to it, so I did.

For the next forty or so minutes, I took out my frustration on every poor unsuspecting piece of china. With each burst, bits of frustration erupted out of me, the release much the same as that day I whacked golf balls with Gilbert. The physical activity pulled the anxiety out of my body, piece by piece, until endorphins took over and banished it. For a short spell, at least.

On the way home, I talked nonstop about it, and Henry listened, only adding a head nod and smile. When he parked in his driveway, I figured that was that, but he walked me to my porch like the gentleman I knew him to be.

"Things are gonna work out, Junie. Not today, but they will. Just hang in there." Henry wrapped his arms around me and just held me for a long time. The man knew how to hug. Firm but gentle, in my space without dominating it. I looked up to thank him but he mistook my intentions and began leaning down with his eyes zeroed in on my lips.

"Whoa!" I planted a palm squarely in the middle of his face and pushed him away. "No!"

Brows furrowed and glasses sitting askew, he looked adorably confused. "I thought—"

"No thinking like that, mister!" I waggled a finger at him, as if it were all his fault. Had I felt that pull between us? Yes, but no way could I go anywhere near that. "No kissing!"

Squinting, he tipped his head to the side. "Are you sure?"

"Yes, I'm sure. We have to be sure!" I clutched my bag to my chest and backed away. "No kissing!"

He held his palms up. "Fine. No kissing."

"I better get inside." I pointed a thumb over my shoulder.

"Junie . . . If things were different and life more settled . . . would there be a possibility of kissing?" This sweet man looked so vulnerable that I wanted to wrap my arms around him and never let go.

Instead, I backed up several steps, hand reaching behind me for the door. "Yes, Henry. There would be so much kissing. But I can't. Fern has to be first from here on out. I'm sorry."

He took his glasses off and wiped a hand down his face. "Don't ever apologize for focusing on Fern. Please. Fern first. That's how it should be."

Him agreeing so easily made me want to rush back to him, so I turned and hurried inside before I did something stupid, like leap into his arms and kiss him anyway.

How could something feel so right, but show up at the wrong time?

22

Most every night this week I'd spent tossing and turning with a new loop of regrets—not getting out of the car to see my child last Saturday, coming dangerously close to giving in and buying something to numb my hurt, that almost kiss with Henry. Today, I needed to put all that out of my head and focus on this chance to face my brother for the first time in months.

I took my time getting ready, curling my hair, putting on a fresh pink dress. I wanted to look like someone who had her act together. I did have my act together, but I had a very stubborn man to convince.

"You can do this," I told my reflection before setting off to North Charleston.

During both stints in rehab, I'd become accustomed to therapy. They were fairly big on it, both in a group setting and one-on-one, so this should have been like second nature by this point. But sitting beside my brother, it was nothing but awkward. Rightfully so, since I was still a bit shocked that Cy actually agreed to this in the first place.

On the opposite end of the navy velvet couch from my stoic brother, my fingers glided over the soft fabric on the armrest. Almost absently, in a way of seeking comfort without realizing it, like smoothing a security blanket. As we waited for the therapist to join us, I made a swirling pattern. I wondered if they placed this couch here as some type of sensory therapy. Probably.

The door opened so I brought my hand to my lap, as if caught red-handed. A thirty-something woman walked in, wearing a flowy top and casual slacks. Even she knew summer in the Lowcountry was just too much to handle in fussy business attire.

"Hi. I'm Shari. You must be Juniper and Cypress."

My brother shook his head. "Just Cy, please."

"And you can call me Junie," I added.

"Lovely." Shari gave us a warm smile. "May I offer you a water or coffee?"

I shook my head, too nervous to drink anything. With how tight my throat was, I'd probably choke to death.

"Water is fine," Cy said, sounding a bit haughty. He had agreed to be here but he was making sure I knew he wasn't happy about it. "Chilled if you have it."

After Shari delivered Cy his *chilled* water, she moved to her desk and gathered a pen and leather notebook. Bringing both with her, she took the navy-and-cream-striped wingback chair across from us. "May I be honest with you for a moment before we get started?"

Shrugging, we both nodded.

"I normally have couples or family counseling sessions. This is my first sibling session. I'm quite excited to work with you."

I held back a snort. This woman had no idea what she was getting herself into. I sure didn't associate the word *excited* with me and my brother. *Uncomfortable* would be a better description.

Shari crossed one leg over the other, placed the notebook in her lap, and flipped it open. "So . . . I'm told you both have had a rocky few years . . ." She gave us an encouraging look, perhaps to provoke us to admit all the dark secrets.

We both remained mute. The poor woman would need a crowbar to pry information out of us that quick in the game.

Minutes ticked by on the wall clock. I glanced at it, taking in the details. Weathered white wood designed to look like a ship wheel.

The therapist cleared her throat with a soft cough, getting my attention. "Junie, would you like to start?"

Beads of perspiration broke out along my forehead and my leg began to bounce. In my peripheral vision, Cy shifted. A quick glance his way revealed him shooting death glares at my jumpy leg. I pressed my foot into the carpet to make it stop. "I, uh . . . as you know . . . I, uh . . ."

"Good grief. I don't have the time or the patience for this!" Cy's outburst made me jolt. "Just tell her how you drove drunk with your baby in the back seat, on the way to get *my child*, and got yourself arrested!"

Head whipping around, I gawked at my red-faced brother. I'd never seen him so livid, as if my stuttering had detonated a bomb of emotions in him. Not even when he bailed me out of jail that day had he reacted this way. Shame warming my cheeks, I returned my gaze to Shari. "I wasn't planning on driving that day but Lana called, frantic. Their son was sick and needed to be picked up from school. I should have told her I couldn't, but she and Cy had done so much for me, and I was ashamed to admit I had been drinking. It was my wedding anniversary and I was having a rough day and—"

"See!" Cy stabbed a finger my way. "Excuses. It's always the same with her."

I hiccupped, trying to hold back a sob. The hardest part of this new dynamic between my brother and me was that the two of us used to be a team, an "us versus them." But now it was him against us. I *hated so much* that I was now in a category with my parents.

"Let's take a breath." Shari's voice had taken on a soothing tone. I'm sure that came with training and years of experience. "Cy, you seem a little angry."

"A *little* angry?" He laughed, bitter and brittle.

Shari jotted something down in her notebook. "Would you like to talk about why you're so angry?"

"Where to start?" Cy laughed that non-laugh again. "This isn't Junie's first mess-up. It's been years of dealing with her. It's exhausting."

"What else has she done to cause you anger?"

"We're going to need a whole heckuva lot longer than an hour." I braced for the embarrassing answer I knew would follow. "How about my son's first birthday party. Junie showed up wasted and knocked the gift table over. In front of my friends and colleagues. Half of Alex's gifts fell into the pool."

My sarcasm showed up and spilled out of my mouth even as the sweat broke out along my hairline and my stomach twisted with nausea. "Good thing he was too young to remember, right?" Who was I kidding? I feared none of us would ever forget.

Cy continued talking as if I hadn't said a word, shifting on the couch so he could speak directly to me. "What about Lana's graduation from nursing school? You didn't show up but then blamed it on me because I forgot to remind you. Like I had nothing else in the world to worry about besides my spoiled brat of a sister. You caused a scene, going off on me in front of our family at Easter." He turned to Shari. "That's Junie for ya. When she's guilty of something, she somehow twists it in her delusional brain to make herself the victim."

My bottom lip quivered but I managed to keep the tears from spilling. He had all the right in the world to be angry with me, but still, I was his little sister, right? The one who depended on him. Maybe that was something else I'd gotten wrong, depending on him too much.

"Junie, is there anything you'd like to say?" Shari asked, continuing in that calm tone.

Swallowing past the rock lodged in my throat, I admitted, "I've messed up more times than I care to admit. I want to make things right between me and my family. That's why I'm here."

"Do you mind talking about what led to your mess-ups, as you put it?" Shari waited again, giving me time to think before responding.

"I'm an alcoholic in active recovery."

"When did your problem with alcohol begin?"

"I don't know, I had my first drink when I was thirteen. By sixteen, I was doing drugs and drinking most every day, even before school. I quit cold turkey when I found out I was pregnant, but I relapsed after my daughter was born." I stated that like a fact sheet, the same way I had done during sessions in rehab. "I've been to rehab twice because of it."

"And what did you learn?" Shari tipped her chin, encouraging me to continue down a path filled with painful truths.

"When things get too heavy, I used to turn to substances to lighten it up. To block some of it out." I shrugged. "But I've learned that was a delusion. It only caused more problems."

"What steps have you taken to not cause more problems?"

"I've been sober for seven months, two weeks, and six days. I go to weekly AA meetings and I keep in close contact with my sponsor."

"Junie, it's good that you have recognized what you need to work on." Shari turned her attention to my brother. "And, Cy, with time, I do believe you can forgive your sister. From my experience, this world is mostly us against them. Family doesn't have to be that way. It's your choice."

She echoed my earlier thoughts and I wanted so badly to be back on his side and be done with us being against each other. She was right though, this was up to Cy, not me.

Cy grumbled something unintelligible, shifting on the couch as if the velvet held an army of ants.

Shari wrote something else down just as a timer went off. Had we even managed to complete one thing in this rapid hour? I doubted it.

"I think this has been a good start." Shari looked at us expectantly, pausing to give us a chance to respond. We didn't. "Will this time next week work for you?"

Cy spoke first. "No. I live in Columbia. This is actually a big inconvenience, especially since my family and I are in the middle of packing up to move."

I think he added that last part as a dig, or I took it as one anyway.

"We provide counseling sessions via Zoom. Will that be more convenient?"

I liked that she didn't give him an out, but an option. I nodded. "Works for me. Whatever is best for Cy." And I meant that, not even a smidgen of sarcasm in there.

Cy heaved a heavy breath. "I guess. But can we make it a morning session? Eight would be best."

"Great. Junie? Does this suit your schedule?"

"I'll make it work, yes." My mornings were delegated to dog walking, but I kept my mouth shut. One time a week, I could rearrange my schedule.

We wrapped things up, stopping by Shari's assistant's desk in the small lobby to set up the Zoom meeting for next week. Then, in stiff silence we walked outside.

In the parking lot, neither of us seemed done speaking our piece.

Glaring at Cy over the hood of his car, I snapped, "Why does everything have to be so dang hard with you?"

He raked his fingers aggressively through his thinning hair. "You're the one who's always been hard to deal with. Years of it, Junie! It's formed calluses."

We had another glaring standoff while I gathered my feelings and filed them away so that I could speak evenly. "I may not ever be able to make things right by your high standards, but I have by the law's standards. So whether you like it or not, you *will* give me my child back before you move to Tennessee." Needing to get away from him before I said something I'd regret, I beelined to the Caddy.

I had known our problems wouldn't be fixed in one hour, that things would get worse before they got better, but it still felt like this had been a fool's errand.

23

Days had passed since my therapy session with Cy and I still hadn't shaken the funk it had put me in. I guess that was another part of recovery, facing the hard parts no matter how painful.

As I finished tying my shoe, my phone chirped with a new text.

I pulled it from the side pocket of my leggings and read Henry's prayer for the day.

God, please keep the taste of unhealthy out of Junie's mouth today. Please show her she is strong enough.

"How'd you know I needed this today?" I muttered, staring at the screen. I almost texted that to him, but we didn't do text conversations.

With the upcoming long holiday weekend, everyone wanted their dog walked this morning before heading out of town. That meant three big dogs, three small dogs, and only one human to manage them all. I began the morning by walking Poe separately, then went around the neighborhood and rounded up all the other dogs. I was completely outnumbered and a fool for thinking I could walk them all at the same time. But I somehow managed it fairly well until we reached the park and Winston decided he'd had enough exercise. He plopped down and pretty much played dead.

I wiped my sweaty forehead on my shoulder, wishing I had a free hand. "Come on, Winston. Let's go." I used my upbeat fun voice but got no response, then I made a terrible mistake. "I'll give you a treat!" Well, that got the stinker to his feet at the same time the other five dogs started jumping with excitement for a treat as well. Suddenly, I found myself stuck in a game of maypole where I was the pole and the dog leashes were the ribbons. We got all tangled up, but I refused to let one leash go. "Sit! Down! Sit!"

"Looks like you've got yourself in a fine mess."

I looked up and there Deaton James stood, a lopsided smirk on his face. "Yep." I rotated my wrist to unloop a tight leash.

"Here. Let me help." Deaton stepped forward, picking up Oliver, the butterball Maltipoo. He unclipped the leash long enough to unravel it from the tangle, then clipped it back on. Then he plucked another dog from the fray and did the same thing until all the small dogs were untangled. It freed me up enough to get Jazzy, Winston, and Beau apart.

"Thank you, Deaton." I gave out treats as promised while I had some help. "You saved the day."

"That's me. Your superhero." He looked up from rubbing Yari's belly and winked. The miniature German Shepherd seemed smitten with him.

"Yeah, yeah." I rolled my eyes. "Seriously though. Thanks."

"No problem." He straightened. "Are you about finished walking them?"

I checked the time on my phone. "We have another twenty minutes." I reached for the small dogs' leashes, but he shook his head.

"I'll help you finish, then get them home."

"No. I can't ask you to do that." I held my hand out but dropped it when he strode away with the darn dogs.

"It's really no problem. The only thing I have to do all day is water plants and check the mail. Enjoy the pool."

"Tough life."

"I know, right. I'm bored by it all, but Daddy Dearest says I can't bail." Deaton seemed aware enough of the dogs to keep them in the shade as much as possible. At only eleven in the morning, the heat was already pushing close to unbearable.

Once we had all my furry wards back to their rightful owners, a nice long sit with the air conditioner on full blast called my name. "I gotta get out of this heat. Thanks again, Deaton."

"I'm starving. Let's head back up the street and grab some lunch. My treat." Deaton looked unruffled by the humidity and exercise. Opposite of my sweaty mess.

"I don't feel like walking all that way again." I fished a hand wipe from the pouch and used it to mop my face.

"It's not even a quarter mile. You walk it all the time." Deaton scoffed, placing his hands inside the front pockets of his greenish gray shorts. I'm fairly certain the shorts and his T-shirt were designer athletic wear. The material looked buttery soft and airy, no sweat stains in sight.

I lowered the wipe and narrowed my eyes. "How do you know that?"

"It's a small island, Junie. I see you around."

I hesitated. "But I'm a sweaty mess and covered in dog hair."

"We'll walk right by your place. Just run in and grab a clean shirt." The man made an art of nagging until he got his way. I'm sure his boyish good looks and that darn crooked smile allotted him quite a bit. I knew it did back in rehab. The overseers seemed to never *see* any of his wrongdoing: stealing snacks out of the admin lounge, having a cell phone, sneaking out at night, coming back with little bags of uh-ohs and oh-nos. "You know you miss me. Please?"

I inclined my head and grumbled, "Fine. But I'm buying my own food. And I only have about an hour to spare."

Smiling, Deaton motioned for me to lead the way. "Okay, Sassy."

I jabbed a finger against the ticklish spot on his side, making him flinch. "And *don't* call me that."

"Yes, ma'am." He chuckled, batting my hand away.

With Deaton shadowing me, I darted up the steps and paused before entering the code. "Have a seat on the porch. I won't be but a minute." I glanced at him over my shoulder.

Lips pouted out, he flopped into a chair. "Southern hospitality at its finest."

Ignoring his sarcasm, I punched in the door code and went inside. I changed into a fresh shirt, retied my lopsided ponytail, and returned to the porch with the faint hope that Deaton had decided to bail. No such luck.

Deaton rose to his feet. "Where do you want to eat?"

I thought about each restaurant, weighing the prices. It was Sullivan's Island, after all, so not many low-cost options existed. Then I remembered where to get complimentary chips and salsa. "Let's go to Mex 1."

"Good choice."

We arrived at a nice quiet restaurant, a rare occurrence on the island.

"Table by the window," Deaton told the hostess, pointing to the exact one he wanted, which was near a ceiling fan.

Before we took a seat, a young lady dropped off iced waters, chips, and salsa, promising our server would be by shortly for our orders.

I sat across from Deaton and turned my face toward the ceiling. The cool breeze from the rotating fan worked wonders for my wilted mood. "What a day." I sighed.

"It's not even noon." Deaton sprawled in his chair—looking laid-back and relaxed—and swiped a chip from the basket.

"Tell me about it." I reached for my glass and took a long gulp. The ice shifted and splashed water onto the front of my shirt. I squealed.

"Dang, girl. It's too early in the day for wet T-shirt contests." Deaton tossed me his napkin.

I tucked my chin and tried to inspect my shirt while dabbing it with the napkin. "You can see through my shirt?"

He roared with laughter. "Ha! Made you look!"

I threw the wet napkin and nailed him on the cheek with it. "That's not funny!"

"Is too!" Deaton grinned, shaking his head. "Maybe I should hang out with you more often. My problem with boredom would be solved."

I laughed it off, instead of answering. That would not be happening. I picked up the menu and scanned the options.

"Hi there. I'm Derrick. Can I get y'all something besides water to start you off?"

"Just water for me."

"No mocktail this time?"

I looked up and found a familiar face. "Oh my gosh. I can't believe you remembered that."

The server offered a sheepish smile. "You made quite an impression that day."

My face went up in flames, recalling how I blurted that bit about being an alcoholic. That was almost two months ago and the poor guy still remembered.

"I'll take whatever local craft you have on draft," Deaton spoke up, irritation sharpening his tone.

"Sure, man. Just need to see your ID."

Deaton rolled his eyes and pulled out his thin leather wallet, then handed Derrick his driver's license.

"I've never seen a driver's license from Hawaii," Derrick commented as he inspected it.

"Hawaii?" I asked.

Deaton handed me the card once Derrick gave it back. "It's where my mother lives. I live there most of the time too."

I glanced over the license with a pretty rainbow on it, noticing he was only twenty-two. Right at four years younger than me. Guess that explained the low maturity level.

"Be right back." Derrick turned to leave.

"Actually, could I go ahead and order. I can't stay long . . ."

Derrick nodded. "What can I get you?"

I picked the cheapest item. "I'll take the cantina chicken taco."

"That's all?"

"Yes. I'm not very hungry." I smiled.

Deaton snapped his fingers to get Derrick's attention and ordered with an air of superiority, "A Baja bowl with grilled mahi and steak. And a side of street corn."

"Anything else?" Derrick asked politely but I could tell he had to put effort into it.

"I think we're good. Thanks." I collected the menus and handed them over. Once Derrick was out of earshot, I leaned across the table and lowered my voice. "We're in recovery. You shouldn't be drinking."

"Alcohol has never been my vice. I can take it or leave it." Deaton pulled the saltshaker to his side of the table and twisted it circle after circle. "Now . . . if you offered me a line of coke, well, that's another story."

"Don't even joke about this." I shook my head. "You know alcohol is one of mine. I don't feel comfortable with you drinking."

"Chill, Junie. It's just a beer." He flicked a lazy hand around the restaurant. "And people are drinking all around us. The bar isn't even three steps away from our table."

I scanned the room and more tables than not had adult beverages. At the bar, one of the bartenders filled a glass from the frozen margarita machine while another handed a colorful cocktail to a patron.

When Deaton put it that way, I guess I was overreacting. "You're right. Sorry."

This was something new to deal with, alcohol within reach all the time. It made me think of how after buying a new car, you start seeing that model everywhere. Used to, I didn't pay it any attention, but now, sober and trying to keep it that way, I saw the opportunity to consume everywhere. Grocery store, gas station, restaurant, on the beach.

Deaton nudged my leg with his. "Let's just relax and enjoy lunch, okay?"

"Okay."

Another server dropped off Deaton's beer, but I kept my eyes glued on the chips and salsa as I shoveled them in.

"I didn't think you were all that hungry," Deaton commented with his signature teasing tone.

"I'm trying to enjoy my lunch over here, sir. Now leave me to it." I chomped down loudly on a chip and began smacking.

He responded by making a goofy face, the one with lips twisted and eyes crossed. The same face he used to make every time I beat him in a game of King's Corners or reprimanded him about one of his crude jokes.

Derrick delivered our food. "Y'all need anything else?"

"Maybe more chips."

"Sure thing."

"Another beer for me." Deaton shoved his empty glass dangerously close to the edge of the table, but Derrick had quick reflexes and caught it in the nick of time. The guys' eyes met in some challenge and Derrick broke first and walked away. Deaton smirked as if he'd won some great battle.

Another beer arrived and Deaton wasted no time tucking into it. Feeling increasingly uncomfortable with that beer close enough I could smell it, I averted my eyes from the frosty mug and tried my darnedest to focus on my taco. *Eat your food, then leave. You can do this.*

"This fish is overcooked and dry," Deaton grumbled. He set his fork down and picked up his beer.

I surveyed his artfully arranged bowl. "It looks fine to me."

Deaton waved Derrick over and complained, asking for another bowl. "And another beer while I'm having to wait."

"Sorry about that." He picked up the bowl and asked me, "Is your food okay?"

"Yes. It's delicious. Thank you."

"I'll put a rush on this." Derrick held the bowl a little higher and rushed off.

I turned to meet Deaton's eyes, which were starting to take on a glassy appearance. "*Another* beer?"

"It's hot and I'm thirsty."

I gave his untouched water glass a measured look while taking a bite of my chicken taco.

Rolling his eyes, Deaton picked up the glass and chugged the entire thing in one shot. He did it to make a point, but it made me feel better, nonetheless. Or it did, until he approached his third beer in the same manner as the water. By then, his voice grew louder and his guffaws turned ridiculous, drawing the attention of other diners.

When Deaton went to the restroom, I waved Derrick over. "May I pay my bill?"

Derrick handed me the receipt. "That guy bothering you?"

I waved off his concerns. "No. He's just having one of those days . . ." I scrunched my nose.

"Okay."

I paid for my lunch plus a twenty-dollar tip. I hated to part with it, but felt like it was the least I could do. The poor guy had earned it for having to put up with Deaton.

I stood just as Deaton returned to the table. "I'll see you around."

"What?" He sat up straighter. "Where you going?"

"I have work to do. I already told you that."

"You're kidding, right? It's a holiday weekend. Let's have some fun today." He started waving for Derrick again. "Let's get you one of those cocktails he was flirting with you about."

Just one to calm your nerves wouldn't hurt.

"No!" I said to both Deaton and the maddening voice in my head. "No. I . . . I gotta go." I hurried around the table, knocking into it. Something clattered to the floor, but I didn't slow my escape to see what it was. The whole darn table could have crashed to the floor and it still wouldn't have slowed me down.

24

Independence Day represented more than just an occasion for hot dogs and fireworks. On this day back in 1776, the colonists held up their stubborn chin to Great Britain and said, "We good. We got this without you." I couldn't help but think of all the naive teenagers who had thought this very thing. That they were good and could handle things all on their own. I included myself. Not saying this great nation wasn't ready to handle things all on their own, but I know for a fact I sure wasn't ready at age eighteen when I agreed to become a wife. My record stood as testament.

I decided to get out of the house and commemorate the gift of freedom with the rest of the residents, as well as the hordes of tourists, on Sullivan's Island. Dressed in a red tank top and cutoff jean shorts, I went to the garage with a damp cloth and used it to wipe the dust off Olla's golf cart. I knew exactly where her Fourth of July décor was and thought maybe it would be fun to participate in this morning's parade. I remembered zipping around the island with her on this cart.

Olla always let me ride shotgun and had Cy sit on the back. That one little perk really made me feel like someone important.

I had come out here last night and plugged the cart in to charge, but when I turned the key now, it did nothing. I hopped off and lifted the seat and jiggled the battery cables. Cy used to do this to get it going, but it didn't work for me. I tightened some bolts, wiggled a few other cables, but nothing worked. It made me think about neglected relationships, if left alone to only collect dust, how difficult they could be to resurrect, much like the relationship with my brother.

Dusting my hands off, I made a promise to myself and to my daughter that by next year, the cart would have new batteries and she and I could decorate it together and be in that parade.

Leaving the dead cart in the back of the garage, I walked up the street and found a good spot to people watch and take in the festivities. Locals liked to dress up, which only added to the fun of the day. An array of Uncle Sam and Lady Liberty characters, lots of American-flag shirts, star-shaped sunglasses, and various red, white, and blue light-up accessories.

Golf cart after golf cart paraded by, all decked out in gaudy patriotic décor. One was fashioned into looking like a ship named the *Great Red, White, and Blue* with a shark bite on the hull. Another cart looked like a tiki hut with hula dancers. But my favorite had to be the one with an inflatable Uncle Sam riding a surfboard on top of the cart.

Following the golf cart parade, most folks were on a mission to find some lunch. The heavily scented smoke from grills clung in the air. I weaved in and out of the congested festivities to get to the park, mindfully keeping an eye out for Deaton. Alcohol was prohibited from the park so maybe that would keep him away.

"Junie!"

I turned to find Bekah walking over, holding hands with a red-headed guy with a constellation of freckles across his cheeks. "Hey."

"Junie, I'd like you to meet my fiancé, Leon. Leon, this is my old friend Junie."

"Nice to meet you." Leon offered his hand and I shook it.

"You too." I smiled.

"Momma and Daddy are setting up a picnic over there." Bekah pointed to a big oak tree with long limbs providing lots of shade. "You should join us."

"Oh, I uh . . . I'm just . . . That's okay." I tucked my hands in my back pockets and reversed a few steps. "I have other plans." *Plans to keep to myself.*

Bekah twisted her lips. "Bummer. At least come over and say hi. Momma would love to see you."

I followed Bekah and Leon over to her family's setup. It looked much like everyone else's in the park. Red-white-and-blue-themed tablecloths with matching plates and napkins. And an array of food.

Bekah's mother wrapped her arms around me. "Junie Wilder! It's so good to see you!"

Laughing, I returned her hug. "You too, Mrs. Gwen."

"You're just in time." She dropped one arm and used the other to steer me to the table. "Let's make a plate."

"Oh, no thanks. I just came by to say hello." I held my hands up when she tried to hand me a star-shaped plate. "I can't stay but a minute. Sorry."

Gwen gave up after a few rounds of me protesting and asked the typical questions. *How's your parents? Brother? Anyone special in your life?*

I plastered on a smile and responded with canned responses. *They're fine. Not at the moment.*

"Leon, honey," Gwen said, draping a hand on his shoulder, "you should be warned. These two used to be nothing but trouble." She nodded toward me and Bekah.

Bekah scoffed. "I don't know what you're talking about."

I laughed and it had a nervous hitch to it. Most people still considered me trouble.

Gwen clucked her tongue. "Oh yes you do." She turned toward Leon. "These two girls, along with a handful of their friends, became felons one summer."

"Momma! That is not true!" Bekah gasped and giggled, knowing her mom was teasing.

I forced a chuckle. More than likely, I was the only felon in this group.

"Well, then why did the sheriff bring y'all to the station and the entire group was put on probation and assigned community service for the rest of the summer?"

Bekah huffed. "That sheriff only brought us in to scare us."

Leon frowned, but the glint in his eyes gave away his amusement. "Bek, what crime did you commit?"

"They got caught stealing," Gwen interjected. Clearly she was getting a kick out of razzing Bekah in front of her fiancé.

I finally spoke up, "It wasn't a crime, just a prank. And we returned all the property. No harm. No foul."

Leon crossed his arms. "What property?"

"Most all the houses on the island have name plaques. You've seen the one on ours, right?" Bekah asked Leon.

He nodded. "High Tide Hideaway."

Mrs. Gwen huffed. "These two decided it would be fun to swap house names throughout the entire neighborhood. They went around late one night unscrewing the plaques and switching them."

"Yeah, and we wouldn't have gotten caught if it weren't for that kid Jonah. He tripped up the steps at one house and woke the residents. It was the last switcheroo too!" Bekah guffawed, and we all joined in.

"We spent the rest of the summer doing yard work for all those people whose plaques we switched." I shook my head. Finding the humor in it now felt strange, yet satisfying.

Before I could excuse myself, Gwen started chatting away about Bekah's upcoming wedding. Nodding my head in the right spots and sprinkling in a well-placed *aww* here and there, I took in the crowd around me. Families in lively conversations, eating and laughing. This should have been a great change from my day-to-day routine of work and solitude. Instead, it just emphasized what I didn't have. I felt out of place and not much in a celebratory mood, but I kept a smile carefully in place.

At the first chance, I slipped away but didn't make it far. A little boy, maybe around eight or nine, came stomping in my direction and stopped right in front of me.

"It broke!" He wailed, holding up what looked like a noisemaker made from a paper towel tube painted blue and red. I didn't know much about kids, but I thought he was a little too old for such a tantrum—or hissy fit, as Olla used to call them.

I took the noisemaker from his chubby hand and inspected it. "Looks like your top fell off."

He produced the broken, crumpled part from his pocket. "I lost all the bells."

"It's okay." I scanned the park. "Did you make this here today?"

"Over there." He pointed toward a tent-covered table with children gathered around it. "At the kids' tent."

"Let's go see about making another one."

"No! I want mine."

"Okay." I rolled my eyes. "Maybe we can fix yours." We walked over to the table and collected the necessary supplies to fix his noisemaker. Within minutes, it was back to making noise and the young boy skipped away without so much as a *thank you*.

Shrugging it off, I started to leave.

"Here!" A little girl with brown curly hair held out a coloring sheet. "You color with me." She waved the paper in the air until I accepted it.

"I, uh . . ." I looked across the table at another lady.

Smiling, she handed me a box of crayons. "You're trapped now." She *tsk*ed. "They lure you in and won't let you leave."

Laughing, I took a seat beside the bossy little girl. I figured she'd be content now that I'd sat down to color, but she undoubtedly wanted to be a teacher or dictator when she grew up. She gave me instructions the entire time. "Use the blue on that part of the flag. Red for the stripes. Blue and red for the fireworks. Not like that. Like this!"

The next thing I knew, I had been roped into making crafts with other children. I wasn't sure if I'd somehow gotten mistaken for a volunteer, but well, I guess that's what I ended up being. Some of the kids caught on that I actually knew how to draw, so for a while I had a little line waiting for me to draw designs on their noisemakers.

Another volunteer at the table, who looked to be in her sixties, laughed warmly. "You seem like a natural with children. I bet you'll be a good momma one day."

I figured a smile wasn't a lie, so I offered that instead of any comment. Starting to feel like a phony, I made excuses and left the craft booth.

The day was a sensory overload experience, with people pulling me in so many directions. Between spending time with Bekah's family and then all those children, it made me miss Fern even more.

Reaching my limit, I made my way home around dusk. I went into the kitchen and as I plugged my phone into the charger, my eye caught the dish towel on the floor. It must have slipped off the cabinet knob where I'd hung it that morning. I bent to pick it up and noticed I must have tracked in some sand in without realizing it. I tossed the towel into the laundry room and grabbed a broom to sweep up the sand. Keeping Olla's house spotless was my way of paying respect for her leaving it in my care. Once I finished the floor, I grabbed a duster and made a pass around the living room.

By the time I finished tidying up, the sky had darkened enough for fireworks. I made myself a glass of iced water and brought it with me out to the deck. I glanced next door, finding it completely dark. Henry had gone to his mom's for the holiday weekend and I tried not to envy him for that, considering family time was typically a given thing for people who knew how to behave. I hadn't behaved, so now I had to face the consequence of spending holidays alone. In the last year, that had included Thanksgiving, Christmas, New Year's, Valentine's Day, Easter, all of them. Only Gilbert had visited me on Christmas Eve, making me feel even more pathetic, having my probation officer as my only guest.

Scooting my chair closer to the railing and propping up my feet, I decided to focus on what I had instead of what I didn't. The warm breeze was pleasant, the view spectacular. I had a nice home, much nicer than most, even though it didn't feel like mine. I had my health. And I was blessed to be born in a country with so much freedom.

A loud boom followed by crackles filled the air as colorful bursts lit up the Charleston Harbor sky. Memories of Cy and me sitting out here with Olla had me softening toward my brother. I could almost taste the lemon and cherry flavors of the Rocket Popsicles she always bought us. No matter what we'd been through, I loved my brother. Missed him, even.

We hadn't talked much lately, aside from the tense therapy sessions, but tonight had me feeling nostalgic enough to reach out to him.

I went inside and walked over to the counter to unplug my phone, but it was no longer plugged in. Glancing around, I tried to remember if I'd actually plugged it in, or had the towel on the floor distracted me?

"I'm losing my ever-loving mind." Shaking my head, I checked to make sure the front door was locked—it was—then moved out to the deck.

After making a brief video of the fireworks, I texted it to Cy. **Doesn't this bring back memories?**

I waited for a reply, but put the phone down when one never came. Maybe those were my memories to cherish alone, like most everything else in my life.

25

"The bottom line is, in life, sometimes good things happen, sometimes bad things happen. But honey, if you don't take a chance nothing happens."

I clicked off the TV. "Those Golden Girls are some wise ladies."

Winston lifted his head from my lap and barked.

I smoothed my hand along his fluffy back and stood from the couch to stretch. "Enough TV for us, buddy. Three episodes is the limit. And I need to take Dorothy's advice and go take a chance."

Winston followed me to the door. I slid on my shoes, then snapped on his leash. "Your people said to have you back by two, so we better hustle."

We took off down the road and made it to his house within ten minutes. Alden had started allowing me to bring Winston over for some company, even giving me a key to the door, but it was getting harder and harder to return him.

Winston stopped on the stoop and gave me those big puppy eyes.

"They'll be home soon." I bent and gave the fluffball a big hug. "Go on now."

With a soft whine, he obeyed.

"I'd stay, but I have a list to start working on. First stop: Poe Library and you're not allowed inside. Sorry, buddy." It pained me knowing I couldn't take Winston on at the moment. But at least I could keep showing up for him. I knew how it felt not to have anyone show up. Alone at the hospital after having Fern, alone in that prison cell, alone on family day in rehab.

"I'll see you tomorrow. Promise." I waited until he stretched out in his dog bed, full-on pouting, then locked up.

I went back to the house to grab my bike. I rolled to a stop and eyed the odd building before me. Between you and me, Sullivan's Island had quite a collection of unsightly structures and this library was one of them. It didn't start its life as a house of books, so there was that. It used to be a former Spanish-American war gun battery. I surveyed the funky building with its white paint and black trim. Two sets of metal and concrete stairs leading to the roof formed an *A* right up front and in between the stairs, two air conditioning window units stuck out like buck teeth.

I listened to the units whine, trying to keep up with the demand of the hot day, as I found a shaded spot to leave the bike. I went around to the side entrance door and stepped inside. The musty scent of old books and damp air greeted me. Perhaps I was a weirdo, but I liked the smell of this library, it stirred memories of my youth. And every time I visited, it felt like I was being allowed into a secret club of sorts. If this secret club had a password to enter, it would surely be *Poe*. Tucked on the shelves were lots of nods to the famous poet. Paintings of his morose image, well-worn copies of his books on display, even a creepy Poe bobblehead. I reached out and tapped his comically big head, making it jiggle.

"Good afternoon."

I searched for the voice of greeting and noticed a petite woman behind the media desk. "Hello."

"Please let me know if you need any help."

I moved to stand before her and read her name tag. *Delores, Branch Manager.* "Actually, I wanted to check out your children's section and see about children's programs."

She handed me a pamphlet. "This is July and August's schedule. We keep this posted on our website as well."

I scanned the itinerary. *Storytime. Nature Crafting. Saturday at the Movies.* "Oh wow. This is great. Thank you." I motioned behind me. "I'm going to look around, if you don't mind."

"Not at all. Take your time." Delores went back to sorting a stack of books.

I started toward the children's section, but a book on the staff pick table caught my attention. I whipped out my phone and took a picture of *Too Far Gone* and sent it to Henry. **Look what I found in the famous Poe Library!** I immediately regretted it. We didn't exchange texts. Henry only sent the morning prayer. But before I could regret it too much, he replied.

I heard that book stinks. Wouldn't read it if I were you.

Snickering, I thumbed another text. **Ha! The staff beg to differ. We're talking people who read books for a living. Think they have great taste.**

Henry didn't reply and I was glad he wasn't one of those texters that had to get the last text.

I spent a while roaming around the small building, scanning the shelves. Then I renewed my way-out-of-date library card and set out for my next destination, just up the road from the library.

The triangular monster came into view well before I reached it. Top portion painted black and the bottom white, the lighthouse always reminded me of a robot with no arms or legs. I daydreamed of me and Fern exploring it, much like I did as a child. How she would be fascinated by the vastness and history.

I came to a halt at the base of it and the daydream came crashing down with the addition of a chain-link fence. "What the heck?"

"They closed it to public tours due to structural issues."

Still straddling the bike, I looked over my shoulder and found Henry sitting on the hill beside the lighthouse. His laptop rested on his lap. "Really? I wonder when this happened."

"I looked it up. It's been closed for the past seven years."

I turned the bike around and walked it over to the foot of the hill. Some sort of military building sat on top, probably within the hill too, but it had always been closed for exploration for as far back as I could remember. "I guess I'll have to take this off my list."

Henry closed his laptop but stayed sitting in the grass. "What list?"

I took a seat beside him. "I'm making a fun list for Fern. That's why I was just at the library, scoping out the children's programs."

"What else is on the list?"

"Not much so far. Just the park, the beach, the library. When she's older, we'll explore Fort Moultrie." I drew up my knees and draped my arms over them.

"I think most children would probably be happy with the park and beach."

"Yes. But I really hoped the lighthouse would be a part of it." I reclined my head and looked up at the tall building. "Us island kids used to hang out here letting our imaginations guide all sorts of adventures all summer long."

"Yeah. Like what?"

I huffed a laugh. "Mainly pirates hunting treasure."

Henry smiled. "Sounds like a great childhood."

My head bobbed side to side. "Mostly. Because of my Grandma Olla. Cy and I stayed with her most every summer of my childhood."

"All summer?"

"Yep."

"Wouldn't you miss your parents?"

"You have to have something first in order to miss it when it's gone." I closed my mouth firmly, for fear something else cynical would fall out.

Henry didn't say anything for a while. We just pretended to admire the ugly lighthouse.

A family of four rolled up on a golf cart and seemed just as bummed by the fence. They took a few pictures, then drove away.

Henry shooed a fly buzzing around my head. "Your list for Fern reminds me of something my mom used to do every summer. She bought a mini spiral-bound notebook each spring and we would add a list of things we wanted to do during summer break. We had to pick a theme for our list so everyone had something different."

"What would your list be?"

"During the school year, our TV time was extremely limited, so I mostly made a list of movies I wanted to watch. Some in the theater, some we could rent."

"How limited are we talking?"

"We could watch the evening news with my parents and on the weekend we were allowed three hours."

"Yikes."

"With my dad being a college professor, academia came before anything else, especially screen time." Henry placed the laptop beside him and reclined onto his elbows.

"What about your sister? What list did she like to make?"

"Ricki changed her list every year, but I remember one year she made a traveling list." He chuckled. "I'm talking Paris, Hawaii, places like that. Mom made it happen though."

"No way. Really?"

"Yes, but in our backyard. We had a luau one week, then the next we had lunch at a little bistro. Summers with Mom were the best."

"It sure sounds like it." I plucked a piece of grass. "Maybe I need to rethink my Fern Fun List."

"You could take it one step further and make a journal of all sorts of lists. Things you want the two of you to do together, now and in the future, like traveling. You could make lists of memories you want to share with her."

"I like the way you think, Mr. Mystery." I pushed my shoulder against his and he did the same in return. "By the way, what are you doing here?"

"I'm writing an action sequence where they're scaling the side of a tall building." He motioned toward the lighthouse. "I thought this would give me some perspective."

I stood and brushed the back of my shorts. "Well, I'm going to head to the house."

"Me too." Henry shoved his computer and notepad into his backpack. "My mom's birthday is coming up. I'd love to get her a pair of your earrings, maybe a bracelet to match."

I perked up at the idea. "I have time now if you'd like to shop through what I already have made or I can even custom-make them. It only takes like a day or two."

"Okay." Henry started walking down the street. "I'll meet you there."

I hated to take off on my bike, leaving him to walk. "I'll get everything pulled out for you to look at." I sped toward the house and hurried upstairs. Henry had seen me make earrings and such, but this was different so I took my time displaying the pieces like I would at Bek's.

Soon, Henry arrived and I showed him into the workroom.

"Let me know if you have any questions."

He straightened his glasses and leaned forward, inspecting my offerings. "She likes turquoise jewelry."

"She has good taste. Turquoise is my favorite too." I selected a pair made out of cream suede with small turquoise stones. "I can make a bracelet to match this or the other pair."

"I can't decide which pair she'd like best . . ."

As Henry carefully considered each pair, mumbling about his mother's preferences, I wondered why this man wasn't married. Any woman would be fortunate to be his wife.

"Both pairs please."

I stopped studying his profile and focused on the earrings in his hands. "Really?"

"Yes. She'll love both. You said you can make bracelets to go with them?"

"Absolutely." I motioned to the bracelets already made. "Any of those styles catch your fancy? Or do you have something else in mind?"

"I think she'll like the braided style, but whatever your creativity leads you to make is fine by me."

He started patting his pockets.

"We'll settle up once I have the bracelets finished."

"You sure?"

"Yes." I put his mother's earrings to the side and started putting away the other pairs. "Henry, can I ask you something personal?"

"Hmm. I don't know. You can give it a go and we'll see."

I glanced up and met his blue eyes. "Where's your wife?"

"Huh?"

"Surely there's a Mrs. Morrison. Where is she?"

"She's not showed up yet." He handed me a bracelet to put away. "I had a fiancée one time though."

"Did you misplace her?" I probably shouldn't have joked, but he was known for misplacing things. Just last week, I caught him searching the bushes out front of his house. Sure enough, he came out with a box of cereal. *I thought I left it on the porch somewhere.*

"Misplace her?" He huffed a low chuckle. "That's basically what she said." He picked up a spool of twine and fiddled with it. "I'd just started writing my first novel right after we were engaged. You may have noticed how I get lost in it and well, she wasn't a fan of that. She said she wasn't going to live her life competing for my attention with some dumb story."

"Ouch." I leaned against the edge of the table, thinking it was her loss. Sure, Henry was intensely focused on his manuscript, but nothing I did seemed to slip his notice. He was still present, aware of what was going on around him. I wished my parents understood they could have been the same way. "Does she know you're the famous H. M. Rossi?"

"No. She gave me the ring back and ditched me before I found an agent and publisher." Henry returned the twine to the table and picked up a long pheasant feather, running it through his fingers. "She lives upstate with a husband who knows how to pay her attention and two children that take all hers. She's happy and I'm happy for her."

"As long as everyone is happy, I guess . . ." I shrugged.

"What about your marriage? Were you happy?"

My chest tightened. "I got married when I was eighteen. Does any teenager know what makes them happy?" I crossed my ankles and spotted a pink paint splatter on the floor. "We were young and reckless, partying too much. The good times were good, but they never lasted for very long. We'd argue, Arlo would lay out all night, then I would leave him. Then he'd beg me to come back. I loved him and I know he loved me too. When I got pregnant I thought things would change, we'd grow up and settle down. But then he died and now I'll never know." Hot tears trekked down my trembling cheeks.

Henry came to stand in front of me and pulled me into his arms. "I shouldn't have asked. I'm sorry."

I buried my face into his soft shirt. "I asked first. It's okay. No one ever asks me about him and it makes me even sadder. Arlo had his faults, but don't we all?"

Henry's arms tightened around me. "Tell me something good about Arlo."

I angled my face so that my ear rested over Henry's heart. "He was a really talented artist. I'm talking realistic portraits." I sniffled a laugh. "One time he drew my brother and it was spot on, but Cy hated it."

"Why?"

I raised my head and looked at Henry to get his reaction. "Arlo drew Cy picking his nose."

Henry guffawed and I laughed with him until I began to cry again.

"I'm such a mess." I groaned, hiding my face against Henry's chest.

"We all are." He rested his cheek on top of my head, and I felt completely cared for in a way I wasn't sure I had ever felt.

No longer holding back, my body fell into the embrace. I'd fought against this pull for the last month, but for a moment I let that go and clung to him as the tension crackled around us. I knew Henry felt it too. His heart began beating faster as his fingers combed through my hair, the gesture a little beyond comforting.

The private moment we shared in the book nook weeks ago, the long-suffering hug after my failed trip to Columbia, the conversations . . . it was all leading to somewhere but right now I was south of somewhere and needed to keep that fact firmly in place, which meant I had to stop what was happening.

I stepped back and patted Henry on the shoulder. "Thanks. Sometimes a girl just needs a hug, ya know?"

Henry didn't return my smile, as if not completely accepting this brush-off.

"I'll let you know when I get the bracelets finished."

"Sounds good. Thanks." His voice was a bit raspy, close to a whisper.

Keeping plenty of space between us and my hands to myself, I walked Henry out, then moved my attention to making that list journal.

I hunted around until finding an unused journal. It was quite thick with plenty of space to add all sorts of lists as Henry had talked about.

My phone chimed with a message from an unknown number.

Are you done being mad at me, Sassy? I'm bored. Wanna hang out?

"No." I deleted it without replying, as I'd done with three other messages Deaton had sent in the last few days. In none of the previous messages had he offered to apologize for the scene he caused at the restaurant or the ugly word he called me.

Stop ignoring me!

Having my fill of it, I blocked his number. If he didn't get it from that gesture, then I didn't know what it would take.

26

Thursday passed in the same manner most days passed that summer. Dogs, hats, house prep. Once I finished the daily tasks, I took some time to work on Fern's journal before I had to leave for my meeting. So far, the journal included lists of things I wanted to teach or do with Fern. I also added a section for lists about our family, including a page for Arlo, Olla, Mom, Dad, and even Cy.

Closing the pen, I reread the list I just added.

Fun Facts about your daddy, Arlo:

1. He always wore mismatched socks.
2. He would only eat green candies.
3. He didn't eat any type of cheese.
4. He sometimes took on the voice of whoever he was talking to.
5. Instead of writing me letters, he would draw a rebus puzzle, a type of riddle. (I was terrible at solving them.)

I left extra space, as I'd done with each list so far, figuring I could add to them as memories or ideas came to me. I wanted to add more but needed to leave soon for my meeting.

I slid the journal into my bag, thinking I should keep it handy in case something inspired me. I fished for my keys as I stepped onto the porch. Movement caught me by surprise. "Ah!" I screamed and whacked the trespasser with my bag.

"Whoa!" Henry cowered in the chair and held a notepad up to protect his head.

I dropped the bag and clutched my chest. "You scared the tar out of me!"

Henry peeped at me from behind his notepad. "I didn't mean to."

"You can't just hang out on a neighbor's porch without letting them know." I bent down and picked up my bag, checking to make sure I hadn't cracked my phone screen. Luckily, it was fine.

"That wasn't my initial plan." He gestured to the backpack at his feet. "I wanted to go sit on the beach and write for a while."

I scanned the porch. "Did you get lost on the way?"

"No, smarty. I came over here to invite you, but then an idea for a scene came to me and I wanted to write it down before I forgot it."

"Oh. Makes sense." I plucked the keys from an empty planter where they'd landed when I accidently launched them in the air. "You're welcome to stay, but I'm heading out."

"Is the Magnolia meeting early today?" Henry asked, surprising me that he actually remembered it was Thursday and that I had a meeting. Maybe he paid more attention than he let on.

"No. It's the regular time."

"Really?" He pulled out his phone and checked the time. "How'd that happen?"

"How'd what happen?"

"It's after seven."

I adjusted the bag on my shoulder. "What time did you walk over here?"

Henry scratched his cheek. "I think around two."

"Oh wow. That's . . . a while."

He slowly stood and stretched and I heard his back pop. "No wonder I'm starving." He shoved his notepad and pen inside the backpack and zipped it up. "Do you wanna grab a burger with me from Poe's?"

"I can't, but maybe another time."

"Okay." Henry bent down and picked up my journal. "This yours?"

"Shoot. I didn't realize it fell out. Thanks." I studied the plain cover, thinking it needed some sprucing up. "This is my list journal. The one you encouraged me to make."

"Oh yeah. How's it going so far?"

"Great. I've added at least twenty list topics. Must read or listen or watch lists. I've added fun fact lists about my family members too."

"Fun facts?"

"Yes. Like for Olla, I listed that she used to sew dress-up costumes for me and Cy. I'm going to add some of her best recipes too."

"You have to add the tomato salad recipe."

"Oh, I'm definitely adding that one. I have room to add more lists. Since you gave me the idea, would you mind skimming through it and maybe giving me some more ideas for topics?" I held it out toward him.

"Sure." Henry started flipping pages, as if we had all the time in the world. Had he already forgotten I needed to leave? "Where's the list about yourself?"

"Huh?"

Henry lifted the journal. "Your fun fact list. Fern needs to know unique things about you too."

"It would be one short list." I checked the time. "I really need to go, but I'd appreciate some input anyway. Just leave it on the porch when you're done reading. Bye, Henry." I skipped down the steps.

"Later, Junie."

I headed to Downtown Charleston with very little time to spare, which is always a bad idea for the congested area of town. Not surprisingly, I arrived at Patsy's a little late. It didn't seem too big of a deal, but as I entered the garden and noticed everyone standing before small holes around the pineapple fountain's flower bed, I reconsidered. All eyes collided with me. "Uh, hi. Sorry I'm late. Traffic." I shrugged.

"It's okay, darlin'." Patsy waved me over to where she stood with a tall brunette. "Junie, this is Kierra. She's an addictions counselor and she usually joins us once a month. Except last month she took off to go get married."

"Congratulations."

Kierra smiled as her thumb touched the diamond ring on her finger. "Thank you. And you must be the newest member of the Magnolia Nephalist Society."

"Yes. For some reason they let me in."

"Of course we did. You're fabulous." Patsy waved her hand toward a vacant spot, her long orange nails arrowing in the direction. "Now, Junie, just find an empty hole."

I sidled up next to Chris Evans and inhaled the earthy smell of fresh-turned soil.

"Go ahead, Kierra. Tell us what we're doin' today." Patsy gestured to the counselor.

Kierra pointed a small shovel toward the hole in front of her. "We are each standing before a grave. Please focus on yours."

I looked down at the small hole—no bigger than maybe a foot deep and just as wide—and figured we were burying fairies. Or small animals, which I was not down for.

As if Jackée read my thoughts, she clucked her tongue. "I ain't buryin' no animal."

Kierra smiled. "No animals, I promise. These are graves for broken dreams."

A choking sound tore through the garden. All heads turned toward the usually reserved Axil as he crumbled to the ground.

"Is he having a heart attack?" Mei yelled as we all rushed over to him.

"Axil, honey, you okay?" Patsy placed her hand on his back but he shook her off.

"I killed my best friend!"

My eyes snapped up and met equally wide-eyed stares. Looking back to Axil, I'd never witnessed a more broken man than him in all my life. Broad shoulders slumped and shaking, flushed face streaked in tears.

"I killed Mitch!" Axil sobbed louder. He lowered his head and gripped it between his giant hands. "I didn't mean to!"

Patsy knelt beside him and we all followed suit, forming a circle around him. I wasn't sure if we were dealing with a murderer or what, but I went along with everyone else.

Kierra appeared with a wet washcloth and placed it on the back of Axil's neck. "Axil, I'm so sorry. I didn't realize this would be a trigger for you."

Axil cried for a long time and when he calmed enough to talk, he began telling a story so tragic I'd never be able to forget it.

"Me and Mitch . . . we went on a hunting trip with a group of buddies." His chest heaved in that stuttering way when someone has cried so much their body can't take any more. "I hate guns and only agreed to go when they said we'd crossbow. No guns. We'd be safe." Sniffing, he wiped his nose. "I guess after a few too many beers nothing's safe."

We waited for him to continue, knowing something awful was about to come next. When he cleared his throat for the second time, Jackée hopped up and grabbed him a water.

After a few swallows, Axil stared at the water bottle as he spoke. "None of us had shot a thing all day and it started getting dark but no one wanted to give up just yet. We had a bet that whoever made the first kill, the others had to buy him dinner. It was trivial, but we were a competitive bunch and I wanted to win so bad . . . When something came from behind a tree I fired the bow without thinking." He began crying again. "I killed my best friend instantly."

"Oh, Axil," Patsy whispered, but he seemed too lost in his pain to hear her.

He laughed bitterly. "I've never been drunk once in my entire life, including that night. The legal blood alcohol limit is .08 percent. Mine was only .04 percent."

"That means he's not even an alcoholic," Pearl whispered, making a face, but everyone dismissed her and kept our focus on Axil.

"It was an accident, Axil," Kierra said calmly. "Tragic, yes, but still an accident."

I'd read somewhere once that nearly one thousand people are shot yearly during hunting accidents in the United States. I recalled it, but didn't tell the others. I seriously doubted it would make Axil feel any less guilty.

"There weren't any charges but I wish there had been. I needed to pay something for what I did." Axil shook his head, still staring at the water bottle in his hand. "Mitch's wife and parents asked me to be a pallbearer. Can you imagine? Tonight reminded me of the funeral. Me helping our other friends carry his casket. It was this mahogany wood and the flowers on top were so strong the smell made me sick to my stomach. I watched them lower him in the ground and stayed until they'd smoothed the dirt over him. I wanted to trade places with him so bad. That night I snuck over to my old man's house and stole one of his handguns, but the stupid thing jammed."

Mei gasped, then reached for his hand, hers so tiny compared to his. "That was stupid of you!"

"I know. My wife found me on my knees in my shed, trying to get the gun to work. We've not been right since . . . That's why we moved here. For a fresh start, but I've learned ghosts can follow you anywhere."

Bruno scooted closer and gave Axil's back a manly clap. "I'm really glad that gun didn't work, my friend." He scanned the small group. "Most of you don't know, but it was Axil who made me get clean. We worked together on a few Habitat for Humanity projects and he caught me drunk on the worksite. Said he'd kick my butt if I didn't get help."

Kierra rose to her feet. "I'm so glad you're still here too, Axil." She eyed the hole, then the group. "Maybe we should call it a night."

"No." Axil stood next, looking more steady. "I need to bury some things. Go ahead."

"Are you sure?" Kierra asked.

"Yes."

Once we returned to our small graves, Kierra began passing out pieces of paper, along with pencils. "I'd like for you to take a few moments to write down some broken dreams. Dreams that you need to let go."

I focused on the blank paper and frowned, thinking about how I was always told not to give up on your dreams. What an odd thing for a counselor to instruct us to do. *Let go of your dreams.* It went against what I had heard on steady repeat while growing up. *Never give up on your dreams, Junie Bug.*

Out the corner of my eye, I noticed others were writing things down, so I quit overthinking it and started writing too.

My broken dreams: famous artist in NYC. Healthy marriage with Arlo. Healthy relationship with my bro—

My pencil stopped, then I flipped it and erased the last one. I couldn't give up on fixing my relationship with Cy just yet.

"Now," Kierra spoke above the gurgling of the fountain, "I want you to read those dreams one last time, then tear the paper into as many pieces as possible and scatter it into the grave. Because today we bury those dreams."

The first tear broke through NYC, then through Arlo's name. Arlo could have made it in the art world, though. He had true talent. I was always more of a crafter. The only reason I could draw flowers so well was I painstakingly practiced drawing plants and flowers so I could impress my parents.

I took my pencil out and wrote on the bottom of the paper, *making myself into what I thought my parents wanted.* I ripped through it and tossed the fruitless idea into the hole. I finished tearing the rest of the paper and opened my fist, allowing each jagged piece of my dreams to rain down into the small grave.

"Now I realize that was difficult, to give up on a dream. But what I want you to really focus on is the fact that those were not the right dreams for you. Think about that and then go select a flower from the cart." Kierra motioned toward a rolling cart off to the side with a colorful variety of flowers. "Pink petunias, purple gladiolus, white daisies, and blue cornflowers. Each flower's meaning is associated with hope."

I shuffled over, waiting my turn, then picked the first flower my hand landed on. Cornflowers. Leaning in, I smelled the flower and it reminded me of a grassy yard.

With Kierra's instruction, we planted our flowers. My cornflowers looked beautiful next to Chris Evans's white daisies and Jackée's pink petunias. "This new plant you've covered your grave with represents your new dreams. Although you didn't write them down, I want you to do that on your own tonight. Each time you come to this garden, I want you to water your flower and reflect a few moments on your new dreams. Make a plan for them and just as you water and tend to this flower, do the same for your new dreams."

"This reminds me of our state motto." Patsy spoke up, brushing her gloved hands together. When did the woman put those on? *"While I breathe, I hope."*

"Yes." Kierra beamed. "We are all still breathing, right?"

Murmurs of agreement trickled from the small group.

Kierra nodded. "Then we can still hope."

I fluffed and smoothed the soil around my flower, thinking about how not too long ago I sat in traffic and read our state's motto on a random license plate. That day I sure didn't feel like I had any hope, but surrounded by this group of people seeking their own hope, I had a renewed desire to keep trying anyway.

I drove home with all these thoughts drifting about in my mind. I decided I would add my list of dreams to Fern's journal. I found it on the table by the door. I scooped it up and went inside.

Kicking off my sandals, I flipped through the pages while trying to decide what I would put on the dreams list. A neat handwriting caught my attention on the movie list below my loopy scribbles. *All Marvel movies.*

Grinning, I wandered to the living room and sat on the couch. I searched for more additions, finding "Human" by Cody Johnson on the list of great songs. I placed the journal on my lap and pulled up the song on my phone and listened. *I'm still learnin' to be human.* "Same, sir, same."

I flipped until stopping on the future adult reading list, expecting to find the addition of an H. M. Rossi book. Instead, I found *The Storied Life of A. J. Fikry* by Gabrielle Zevin.

I reached the last list in the journal so far, the fun facts about Cy. Nothing was added to his, not surprising. Henry didn't know any of the people listed. I flipped the page, intending to add the dreams list, only to find an entire new list had been added.

Fun Facts about your mommy, Junie:

1. She baby talks to dogs. It's the funniest voice ever.
2. She gets paint in her hair all the time, but it doesn't seem to bother her.
3. She cares about others more than she cares about herself.
4. She has a dry sense of humor.
5. She has a beautiful smile, even though she's stingy with sharing it.

I had no idea he'd paid that close attention to me and it seemed he genuinely liked me. His words were almost too kind. I knew why I liked him. An endless list scrolled through my head. Funny, talented, thoughtful, kind, downright handsome . . . maybe Henry would someday have a page in this book too.

27

The Magnolia Nephalist Society meetings always provided me with helpful tools to face challenges in my sobriety. For the last few days, I kept going back to the new dream list. I even incorporated it into today's hat design by adding a garden of moonflowers and lavender, both symbolizing dreams. Once I finished drawing the flowers with the pyro pen, I prepped a strip of lavender fabric and layered it on top of cream-colored lace, wrapping both around the bottom of the crown. I was in the process of adding an antique gold brooch for a hat buckle when the FaceTime alert popped up on my phone.

Placing the hat on the table, I accepted the FaceTime and Dad's face filled the screen.

"Hi, sweetheart."

"Hey, Dad. What's up?"

He looked to his left and then to his right. "I wanted to talk to you while your mom is at a thing." He looked behind him, as if he expected her to accost him at any moment.

"Okay . . ."

"As you know, she turns sixty in November."

I exaggerated a gawking face. "Sixty? How'd that happen so fast? Feels like she just turned forty."

"I know." He chuckled. "Anyway, I thought it would be fun to throw her a surprise party. I'll pay for your and Cy's plane tickets."

I slumped in the chair, wanting to throw the danged phone across the room. "Dad, I'm on probation, remember? I can't leave the state, much less the country."

His smile vanished and he took on that cloudy expression. "Oh, I thought maybe you'd be done with that by then."

"Nope. Not until next May." The fact that he didn't know this was enough to tick me off, but him expecting me and my brother to just drop whatever we were doing to go along with his whim had me irate. They were the ones who left us. "You'll just have to celebrate without me. Sorry."

I wasn't sorry. At all. They'd missed my eighteenth and twenty-first birthdays. Clearly, my birthday milestones didn't matter to them, so why should theirs matter to me?

"I do hate that . . . You think Cy and his family will be able to come?"

My eyes slid over to the small area by the bookcases. Since the botched trip to Columbia, I'd spent hours painting a garden of poisonous plants. Oleander, foxglove, angel's trumpet, hemlock . . . All just as beautiful as they were deadly. I felt murderous at the moment, myself.

"I doubt it. Cy and *his* family will be busy getting settled in Nashville, but you'll have to talk to him to be sure."

"Nashville?"

"Yes, Dad. He's been offered a job at Vanderbilt." I huffed heavily enough to make a strip of lace ribbon sail off the table. "Do you and Mom seriously not keep up with us at all?"

"We've been busy, but that's no reason for you to be disrespectful, young lady."

Oh, the dad voice comes out now? Too late for that.

"Sorry. But like I said, you'll have to ask Cy." I glanced at the clock. Two hours before the Tuesday meeting. "I have to head out for my AA meeting, so I guess I'll talk to you later."

I punched the end button and tossed the phone to the side. Elbows on the table, I leaned my forehead into the palms of my hands, taking several cleansing breaths to calm down. When that didn't work, I dropped to the floor and went through some yoga poses, but I was too keyed up for that to be effective.

Standing, I picked up the phone and called Betty.

She answered right away. "Hello, sweetie. How are you?"

"Good. And you?" I paced over to the window and gazed out at the ocean. It seemed agitated today too, choppy waves rolling in with aggression.

"Oh, I'm just dandy."

"Great. I was wondering if I could come early to the meeting and help you."

"I'm making spaghetti, so some extra hands would be perfect."

"I just need to change and I'll be on my way."

"Okay. See you soon."

I left the unfinished hat and the unfinished argument with my father in the workroom and hurried to change out of my sweatpants and into a pair of jeans. I uncoiled my hair, gave it a few blasts of dry shampoo, brushed it out and retied it in a messy bun. Good enough. I locked up the house and jogged down the steps to the Caddy parked in the driveway.

As I opened the driver's door, a fancy silver SUV with the Porsche logo on the hood came to a stop beside me.

The window rolled down and Deaton popped his head out. "Hey you."

"You have some nerve, showing up here after how you acted the last time I saw you." I crossed my arms and glared.

He got out of his SUV and held up his palms, a look of pure innocence on his devilish face. "That's why I'm here. To apologize."

"Apologize for what?" I asked him this much in the same way Olla used to ask, to make sure we knew what we were at fault for. *No sense in sayin' you're sorry if you don't even accept your sorry actions,* she would say. What I would give to have her still here with me.

Deaton sighed dramatically. "I was having a bad day, drank too much, and acted like a jerk. I'm really sorry, okay? Can you forgive me?"

I could forgive him, but I wouldn't be forgetting. "Apology accepted. Now if you don't mind, I have somewhere I need to be." I motioned for him to move.

"Where you heading?"

"I have an appointment."

His eyes narrowed. "Kinda late for an appointment."

I laughed but it sounded nervous and unsure, exactly how this guy always made me feel. I hated that feeling. "I meant a meeting."

"Oh, you mean AA?"

"Yep." I placed a foot inside the vehicle, hoping he'd take the hint.

"Can I go with you?"

That totally threw me off. Deaton James wanting to go to a meeting? I remembered he hated group therapy in rehab, to the point of defiantly lying on the floor and taking a nap during sessions. "Why?"

He frowned. "You were right the other day at lunch. I shouldn't have been drinking. It's a slippery slope and now I'm craving things I shouldn't."

"You should probably find an NA meeting." I smoothed my thumb over my nails. "Didn't you say your problem is with drugs?"

"I haven't had time to find one."

"You know there's an NA and AA app that'll show you all the meetings in your area. You can download it for free."

"I'll look into it, but I'd like to go with you tonight."

Realistically, I couldn't prevent Deaton from going and I should be encouraging him in his sobriety, but darned if I didn't want to. "It's at the Methodist church right off the island. I'm going early to help set up. I can give you the address, that way you can go later."

"Nah. I don't have anything going on. I can go now too."

My shoulders slumped. "Fine. You want to follow me then?"

His frown eased into a small smile, one that seemed on the sly side. Something about it didn't sit right with me. "Follow you? Yeah, sure. I can do that." He returned to his SUV and backed out of the driveway, giving me enough space to back out too.

The fellowship hall smelled like an Italian restaurant, but the succulent aroma of garlic and herbs did nothing for me tonight. Dealing with Dad earlier and now Deaton, left me feeling queasy.

"Hey, sweetie." Betty waved me over. "You want to mix the tea?"

"Sure." I looked over my shoulder. "Deaton, just have a seat at one of those two tables."

Staring at the screen on his phone, he strode to the table like an obedient child.

Relieved he didn't want to stick to me like usual, I washed my hands and got to work, remaining busy until the meeting began. It didn't seem to bother him, though. I glanced one time and found that he'd had the attention of the entire table while he told some lively story. Enthusiastic facial expressions, talking with his hands. By the laughter, he was keeping himself in check as well as keeping the story clean.

After we recited the Serenity Prayer, an older gentleman with stark white hair and a long beard volunteered to speak. I'd noticed him at all the meetings, but he'd never spoken before now. With the aid of a cane, he shuffled up to the small podium. "My name is Lorenzo. I'm thirty-six days sober."

We clapped, but I was a bit confused.

"Yes, that means what you think it means." His voice sounded paper-thin and raspy. "I slipped after nineteen years without a drop of whiskey." Clutching the podium with his gnarled hands, he cleared his throat. "I lost my son forty-nine days ago. He was seventy years old. Not a spring chicken, but he was still my son. And my best friend. We went fishing every Saturday. Rain or shine. We had breakfast together most every day of the week. Heck, we did most everything together since we were both widowers. Losing him . . . I didn't handle it well. Figured I'd drink myself to death so I could join him." Fat tears trekked down his weathered face and disappeared into the cloud of his beard. "I'm not sure why God didn't take me, but after a week of it, I gave up and tossed the bottles. My boy would have been so disappointed in me." Lorenzo placed a shaky palm over his mouth and heaved a suppressed sob. "I hurt every day, but when I come to this meeting it's more bearable. I'll turn ninety in two weeks. My time on this earth is limited, but I want to finish it out in a way that'll make my boy proud." Lorenzo started to walk back to his seat. Reggie jumped up to help him as we clapped once again.

Sniffling, I batted a tear off my cheek. Fern had only been in my life for close to three years, but I already considered her my best friend. I wanted to look back in my old age and be able to say I made her proud.

At the end of the meeting, we all took turns giving Lorenzo a hug and offering condolences for his son and words of encouragement.

During the short drive home, my eyes wandered to the rearview mirror, watching Deaton follow closely behind me. That saying you draw more bees with honey than vinegar came to mind. Perhaps the time had come to bring out some vinegar. I didn't even want to admit how close I'd gotten to giving in and indulging with him at the restaurant. My counselor stressed the importance of surrounding myself with people who advocated for my sobriety. And that meant having to let some people go. Deaton had to go.

I parked in my driveway, and before I even turned the engine off, Deaton pulled in behind me. "Go away," I muttered, staring at his headlights in my rearview mirror. This was getting ridiculous. I got out and he joined me in the driveway. "Deaton, it's late and I'm tired."

"Could you just give me like ten minutes? Would that be too much to ask?" Deaton held his palms up.

I crossed my arms and made no move toward the porch. "Why do you need ten minutes? We just spent over a few hours together."

"That was a few hours of you playing keep-away." He huffed a laugh. "I think we need to clear the air between us."

Rolling my neck, I stared at the star-studded sky for a moment. Deaton, and the mistake I made with him, had haunted me all summer and I was ready to be exorcised of it once and for all. If we cleared the air, then maybe he'd realize the best thing for him to do was move on.

"Okay." I moved up the porch stairs and sat in the chair by the door, offering him the other on the opposite side. I expected him to give me a hard time and want to go inside, but he didn't, thank goodness.

"I thought we connected that first night—" Deaton started, but I interrupted.

"We were both high." I refrained from rolling my eyes. It seemed in my best interest not to bruise his ego. "You reminded me of my late husband. I was lonely. That's why I let you kiss me."

"We did more than kiss." He smirked, totally overlooking my mention of a dead husband.

Cringing, I shook my head. "Not much more." The choppy images of that night flickered through my mind, the two of us hiding in a cleaning supply closet, making out like the world was about to end. I guess at the time it felt that way, believing nothing would change so why keep trying. I had absolutely zero faith in getting my life sorted when I arrived that night from prison.

"Well, I don't see why we can't pick up where we left off." Deaton gave me a salacious grin, one that made me feel sick.

"We can't." I sliced a hand through the air, reinforcing my statement. "I don't know if you remember from our group therapy sessions, but I have a daughter and I'm working on regaining custody of her. I don't have any space in my life for a relationship."

Deaton frowned, his eyes moving to look next door. "What about your neighbor?"

I gripped the armrests with sweaty hands, wondering if his ten minutes were up yet. "What about him?"

"I see you over there a lot."

"How do you see that?"

"When I go for walks on the beach. What's up with the two of you?"

"Nothing more than neighbors, I promise you that." I stood, ready to end this. "I really don't have time in my life for unnecessary drama, Deaton. So . . . I'd like for you to leave and not come back. Please." I motioned toward the yard, but he didn't budge.

His defiant expression morphed to one of hurt. "But . . . I thought we were friends."

"Deaton . . . we were there for each other during a difficult time in rehab. I'm grateful for that, but we both know anything now would just end up toxic. You almost peer pressured me into drinking the other day. I almost gave in." I shook my head. "I can't chance ruining all the progress I've made. That means we can't be friends. I'm sorry."

"What's so wrong with me?" His frown deepened to something dark. "Not good enough for ya?"

Did the guy not hear a word I just said?!

"No. Not at all." I flicked my wrist to shoo that notion away. "You're out of my league, by miles. And I'm complicated. I have a dead husband

I'm still mourning. A daughter I've lost custody of. And I'm an alcoholic. You're better off finding someone with less baggage, trust me."

Deaton stood and peered down at me with his lips firmly pressed together. Did he finally get it? That what we did had been a mistake and it was time to move on?

I waited, wondering how he would respond, but he only gave me a slow resigned nod. Without another word, he simply left. Could it be that easy to be rid of him? *I sure hope so.*

28

Mowing the lawn has several health benefits. Great cardiovascular exercise, reduces stress, improves mental clarity. I had looked it up as motivation for getting the chore done, but I'd realized quickly back in May that I actually enjoyed mowing. The mindless task and exertion was quite soothing.

Pushing the mower across the last strip, I surveyed my manicured yard, proud of the straight lines. I wished I had more lawn. I checked Henry's yard. It was just as shaggy as it had been most of the summer. Needing more mowing therapy, I started in on his lawn too. I liked the burn along my shoulders, the grittiness on my skin, the instant gratification of completing the task.

As with my yard, Henry's was small and I finished in no time. Removing the key, I began rolling the mower toward the garage. A silver Porsche drove by slowly. Deaton waved but kept going.

Since my conversation with Deaton, we'd run into each other more often than I cared for. On the beach, at the park, walking down the sidewalk . . . He never approached me, nor did he try to engage in conversation, only offering a lift of his chin or a small wave.

I put away the mower and trucked it inside. My phone chimed. Distracted, I checked the notification, finding Bekah's name.

I sold the last pair of your earrings today. Can you bring more tomorrow?

"Now this is a problem I could get used to." **That's great. I'll drop some off in the morning.**

See you then.

Once I got myself cleaned up, I inventoried what I already had complete, figuring I could knock out a few more pairs this afternoon. I gathered the supplies and moved out to the back deck. Gilbert kept on me about isolation and getting out of the house, so this was me taking his advice. Normally, Henry would be next door typing away and I counted that as interaction with others, but as I spread the supplies on the patio table there was no sign of Henry.

I got busy anyway and worked on a pair of faux cowhide earrings, accented with round wooden discs.

The gritty slide of patio doors cut through the relatively quiet evening and I willed myself not to look over, to just keep threading the beads together and act like I wasn't aware of my neighbor moving around his patio. I heard a chair scrape against the concrete, then another. Did he have company?

Shaking my head, I mumbled to myself, "None of your business."

More scraping sounds and annoyed huffs, then bare feet slapping against the concrete finally won over my curiosity. I looked over and found Henry's firm backside in the air as he yanked beach towels out of the wicker trunk and tossed them aside like a clown pulling out an endless rainbow of handkerchiefs. With towels littering the ground around him, Henry straightened, placed his hands on his hips, and growled. Seriously, he growled. Then he slammed the lid and stepped over his mess, apparently with no thought of cleaning it up.

My eyes followed him as he stormed over to the pool and crouched down beside it, peering into the water as if it held the answer to something. I got up and carried my nosy self over there to see what was going on.

I stood behind him for a few beats watching him scan the pool. "What the heck are you doing?"

Yelping, Henry jumped, righting himself just in time before tumbling into the water. He turned around and I noticed he had a different pair of glasses on. His others reminded me of Clark Kent's black frames, but these were more like Harry Potter's round frames. Darned if he didn't pull these off too. "I lost my glasses."

I smiled, unable to help myself, considering my thoughts were about said glasses. "And you think they're in the pool?"

He gave the water a sideways glance and scratched the back of his head. "I may or may not have found them there a time or two."

"Okay, I need details on that."

He shrugged sheepishly. "I'll forget they're on my face and dive in and they fall off and I forget to retrieve them."

Absentminded Professor. That's what I should start calling him.

"Good thing you have this pair." I pointed toward his face.

He grimaced. "They're my old pair so the prescription is weaker. I'll get a headache if I have to wear them for too long."

Biting my lip, I stepped to the edge of the pool to help with the search. "Have you looked in your bathroom, maybe the nightstand?"

"Yeah. There and the front porch, in my Jeep, the fridge, the dish rack . . ." He motioned around the patio. "Out here."

I wondered how many times he'd found his glasses or whatever else he'd misplaced in the fridge or dish rack. The guy was unaware of just how charming he was, absentmindedness and all. I stopped staring at him and returned my attention to the bottom of the pool. Sure enough, I caught sight of a dark object in the deep end. "How deep is this pool?"

"Eight feet."

No wonder it was difficult to see the glasses in the rippling water. I pointed near the white drain. "Found them."

"Yeah?" Henry reached a hand behind his back and ripped off his shirt. Tossing it to the side, he dove in. In a blink, he reemerged holding up his black glasses like a prize, a giant relieved smile on his face. He swam effortlessly to the side and lifted himself out in one smooth motion. "Thanks!"

I snickered, unable to hold it in. "You're welcome. But now you may want to go ahead and get the other pair before you forget them too."

Henry looked confused but then it dawned on him. "Shoot. I forgot to take the others off too." He turned to dive in but this time I grabbed his arm and held out my hand for his other glasses. Laughing, he handed them over and dove in and I tried really hard not to admire his form. Straight-up, this man should have been an Olympian.

This time, when he emerged, the Harry Potter glasses were on his smiling face. He did that impressive lift out of the pool again.

I handed him the black frames and he switched them. "Maybe you should get one of those grandma chains to put on the legs of your glasses, that way you won't lose them so easily." I teased him, and the next thing I knew, I had been tossed into the pool! I breached the water and found Henry roaring in laughter. Not cool with that, I began choking on the water. "Help! Help!" Flailing, my body sunk under.

In a blink, strong, sure arms wrapped around my thrashing body and rocketed me to the surface. "Junie! You okay?"

The panic in his voice was the exact reaction I had wanted. "Sucker!" Now, I roared in laughter.

"That wasn't funny!" Glowering, Henry used his hold on me to dunk me back under.

Grinning like a doofus, I came up sputtering and splashed him. A water fight ensued, one trying to up the other in dunks and splashes.

That all came to a halt when his long arms wrapped around me, probably in an attempt to toss me, but my raucous laughter shut off quicker than a kinked water hose as reality came back into focus.

"Let go." I shoved out of his hold and started swimming toward the steps. Not an easy task while wearing a sopping wet shirt and jeans.

"Junie," Henry called out, close behind me.

I swiped one of the discarded towels near the wicker trunk and dried my face.

"What did I do wrong?"

"You didn't do anything wrong. It's just . . ." I lowered the towel and gave him a passing glance. "I can't do this."

"What do you mean?"

"That!" I jabbed a finger at the rippling pool, still showing the aftermath of our frolicking. "I don't deserve that."

Brow furrowed, his head tilted to the side. "What don't you deserve?"

"The fun. The laughter." I sniffed.

Hands on his hips, dripping water, Henry regarded me with a deep frown. "Why not?"

"This isn't a vacation stay. I'm here to get my act together so I can get my daughter back." Turning on my wet heels, I hightailed it, away from Henry and my embarrassment, and back to my solitary confinement next door. It had been stupid of me to even come over here in the first place.

29

Time-out on an island. Sounded like a pretty nice form of punishment, I'm sure, but with each day that passed without my daughter, it felt more like being back in that small prison cell. If it were left up to my brother, I'd probably still be there. But I was here instead.

Hearing someone pull up outside, I peered out the window and saw Cy's vehicle. "Speaking of the devil." I darted downstairs and met him in the yard. "Hey. Something wrong?"

"Yes. Your lawyer contacted me."

I glanced past him, disappointed when finding no mini-me in his back seat. "You left me no choice."

"How are you even affording such?"

"It's really none of your business, but there are legal services for those who need assistance at a discount rate. But if you'd just be decent about this and give me my daughter, then I wouldn't have to."

He moved around me. "Let's go inside and discuss this."

Huffing, I trailed behind him up the porch.

Cy looked to the right and lifted his hand without stopping his mission to get inside. "Hey, Henry."

Truly confused, my head snapped in the direction of Henry's porch just in time to see him lift his hand and mumble a hey. I stood frozen as our eyes connected. "What the . . . ?"

Henry appeared to be on his own mission, hurrying inside his house like his tail was on fire.

I stepped past the threshold and slammed the door. "You know Henry?"

Cy looked up from his phone as he took a seat on the couch, lines creasing between his eyebrows. "We used to work together. I asked him to keep an eye on you."

Frowning, I rested my hands on my hips. "You asked him to keep an eye on me? For what?"

My brother rolled his eyes. "Don't ask stupid questions. You know why. Forget that though." He turned his phone screen toward me, showing off an email from my lawyer. "We have more important things to talk about. Why are you trying to prohibit me from taking Fern out of the state?"

"I want to see my daughter. And I certainly don't want you taking her even farther away from me. Since you keep blowing me off, I had to take matters into my own hands."

Cy barked out a humorless laugh. "Into your own hands? We already know that always ends in disaster, little girl."

My face burned and my vision blurred, but I refused to let go of the tears. "Look, I'm sick of you belittling me, Cy! Yes, I screwed up in the worst way possible. You all have a right to be upset with me. I've never said you didn't, but this . . ." I motioned toward him, shaking my head. "This is just cruel. And I've had my fill of it!"

Cy scowled at me as we had a heated stare-off.

After several intense minutes, I ran out of steam and collapsed in the chair across from him. "I miss her, Cy. If you'd just grant me visitation."

He broke eye contact and fixed his gaze past my shoulder. "You remember your senior year, when Mom and Dad accepted that two-year position in Montreal?"

"Yeah?"

"Olla wouldn't let them take you with them. Said you deserved a stable senior year, so she stayed in Columbia during your school year. You remember?"

I knew his point before he finished, so I nodded without speaking.

"Lana and I want a safe, stable life for Fern. A structured childhood. Just like what Olla wanted for you." He leaned forward, elbows on his knees. "We can give her that, Junie. I'm just not sure you can yet."

"I'll never be able to thank you enough—"

"I didn't do it for you!" Cy's face turned red in a flash as he sat back.

"I know! And that's what makes me love you even more . . . That you love my daughter more than me. That you'd do everything to protect her, even if that includes keeping her away from me, but you have to know I've woken up! I have changed. I can give her what she needs now."

His eyes narrowed into a disapproving scowl. "You sure about that?"

"I—"

"Just think about what you've already put her through and what dragging us to court would further do." He stood and started toward the door.

"You just got here and you're already leaving?"

"I have other business to attend to in Charleston besides your mess."

I pressed my lips together to prevent myself from smarting off. Instead, I let him go without protest. What was the point in even trying with him anyway?

Everything Cy wanted for Fern, I did too. A stable, structured childhood, something that had never been in the cards for me. Each time a new once-in-a-lifetime opportunity came about for my parents, I'd end up in a new school or back at Grandma Olla's. I didn't mind the part of living with my grandmother, but I minded the uncertainty of it.

Cy slammed the door on his way out, causing me to jump. "Jerk." Slumping forward, I cupped my face in my hands and groaned. "What a mess . . ."

The doorbell rang, but I didn't move. A few seconds passed, then someone knocked. A tepid knock of a coward. One who had hid something from the get-go and now that he'd been exposed wanted to come clean.

Well. Forget him.

I rose from the chair, walked right up to the door, and threw the dead bolt with enough force to drive home the emphasis that I wouldn't be accepting any feeble attempt of an apology.

"Junie!" Another knock. "Let me explain!"

Leaving Henry outside, I stomped upstairs to my room, too ticked to even avoid the creaky step. Even though it was still daylight out, I didn't care. I'm not sure how I managed it, maybe my body just crashed out of mercy, but sleep found me quickly. As soon as my head hit the pillow, I was out.

*

"Mommy! Mommy!"

Among the cacophony of Fern's screams and the officer's harsh tone and the strobe-light flashes of blue light, I felt the cold, heavy metal clamp around my wrists. Pulled tight behind my back, sending a tight pain along my shoulders, but I barely registered it as I craned my neck to see my child. Only the bottom of her sparkly pink Crocs kicking out were within my view.

"Fern!"

"You have the right to remain silent . . ."

I messed up. I messed up. No, no, no, no . . . "Fern! Baby!"

"Anything you say can and will be used against you . . ."

"Mommy!" Her guttural sobs penetrated, as if a knife had been shoved deep in my chest.

"Fern! I'm so sorry, baby!" A hand gripped the top of my head, shoving me in the back of the car. The smell of urine, not my own but the leftovers from someone else ruining their lives, overwhelmed me.

"Mommy!"

*

I woke with a start.

Heart galloping, it took a minute for my eyes to adjust to the dark. I held my breath and listened, trying to figure out what pulled me from sleep so abruptly. The nightmare. My baby screaming for me.

I tapped the screen on my phone and checked the time. Two in the morning. I crashed around seven, so maybe I'd gotten all the sleep out of my system. No way would I be able to go back to sleep after reliving the worst day of my life.

I flipped the lamp on. After my eyes adjusted, I found the list written on the mirror. The most important thing to me right now. I scanned it until landing on number five. *Set up Fern's room.* I'd painted it and arranged the furniture, but the quilt still wasn't complete.

Deciding that was something I could do, considering everything else seemed impossible at the moment, I shoved the blanket off and went down to Olla's sewing room to get to work.

30

Olla didn't believe in cussing. *There's enough words in the English language to express yourself without using ugly words.* But there was one word my grandmother let slip every now and then, like a wayward burp, sneaking up on you out of the blue.

She claimed it wasn't a *real* bad word but something about the pronunciation of it told me otherwise. Ain't no way of making that word sound acceptable.

Apparently, I took after my grandmother in the sense I wasn't much on inappropriate language either, but I couldn't deny how effective the word *pissed* was when capturing the exact reaction I felt when realizing my next-door neighbor who was starting to look a whole heckuva lot like my superhero—albeit dorky in fashion—was in cahoots with my arch nemesis—aka my brother.

Seriously! They. Knew. Each. Other.

Wanting to stay away from Henry's lying, stupid, handsome face, I set up shop in the crow's nest. Even though it was tighter quarters than the patio below, I felt safer. Safer from my hurt feelings and the man who helped cause them. Even from this elevated vantage point, I could still hear the rapid rhythm of Henry's keyboard but far enough away to not actually have to see him.

I began drawing a fern pattern on the sage-green Western hat. I wanted to eventually purchase a branding iron with a fern frond on the end to personalize each of my pieces. Thinking bigger, I decided one day I would have my own boutique and make it my mission to showcase work from others who had fallen on hard times. I'd give them a chance like Bekah had given me.

A noise below drew me out of my thoughts. Holding the pen midair, I turned in my seat and listened. Footsteps were moving across my sandy deck. Then, someone knocked. The typing from next door also stopped, but no one spoke.

Easing to the edge of the rail, I glanced over and saw a fedora hat that I wished to never see again. I heard the squeak of the back door opening, then he disappeared from my sight.

"Hey!" Henry shouted. "You can't just go into someone's house like that!"

Deaton emerged from my house at the same time Henry stormed up the steps.

"It's okay, man. I'm Junie's friend. We go *way* back." Deaton shrugged with a devil-may-care attitude. He motioned behind him. "Besides, it was unlocked."

Henry crossed his arms. "Doesn't matter. It's still trespassing."

"Whatever." Deaton started toward the deck stairs. "You happen to know where Junie is?"

Henry's eyes lifted just long enough to meet mine, then returned his glare to Deaton. "She's at my house."

Deaton stopped descending the stairs and glanced over his shoulder at Henry. "You mind telling her she has company?"

"Can't. She's taking a nap. Sorry." Henry certainly didn't sound sorry. At least the liar had put his fibbing skills to good use.

"The two of you hooking up or something?"

"Or something. You need to leave."

Deaton chuckled, low and gravelly. "No worries. I'll give her a call."

I scooted completely out of sight and held my breath, scared to death my phone was about to start ringing and give me away. It shouldn't, since I'd blocked his number, but I wasn't exactly sure how that worked. Several long moments passed, then the typing started up again next door. I blew out a long sigh of relief.

Collecting my belongings, I rushed inside. After putting the hat and supplies in the workroom, I went downstairs to see if Deaton had bothered anything. He was only in the house for less than a minute but I still needed to check. Nothing seemed amiss. With a shaky hand, I locked the back door, then went into the kitchen to get a glass of water. I opened the cabinet and a plastic Cool Whip bowl toppled out.

Inspecting the cluttered shelves, evidence that my grandmother didn't like to throw things away, I decided it was time to do something about it. Cy and I hadn't changed much in the last three years since she passed away. On Olla's nightstand in her bedroom, her colorful reading glasses remained sitting on top of *The Lady's Mine* by Francine Rivers. Only three chapters remained. That didn't seem fair, her being so close to finishing it but never would.

I hadn't been able to bring myself to put the book or her glasses away. But this, the Cool Whip containers and butter bowls, I could start here. It gave me a way of working off some frustration anyway. Grabbing a garbage bag, I got to work, pulling everything out of the cabinets, sorting, tossing the unnecessary items, then putting away the keepers.

Once I finished that cabinet, I moved to the next, then the next, pausing only long enough to make a trip to the garbage bin outside.

I saved the cabinet above the refrigerator for last. Grabbing a chair, I climbed up but before I could open the door a tickling attacked my nose.

"Achoo!" I sneezed several times and nearly toppled off the chair. Climbing down, I blew my nose, then grabbed a damp cloth.

After dusting the top of the fridge, I opened the cabinet and was startled to find a treasure that I had no business discovering. An unopened bottle of Fireball.

Pulling the heavy bottle from the cabinet, I hopped down and sat in the chair and stared at the amber liquid. Smoothing a fingertip over the edges of the scorched label, an indicator of what it was capable of, I swallowed with difficulty. I could just about taste the hot sweetness, feel the burn of the whiskey down my throat and the coating warmth in my belly. Grandma Olla always kept a bottle stashed away, claiming a small shot of it would chase away a cold or cough. That was the difference between me and her. She could take a tiny swig and walk away from the bottle, but not me. It would worry me slap to death until every last drop was gone.

Just drink it. No one will know.

Mad at myself for even considering it, I left the kitchen. Bottle clutched in my fist, I marched it over to Henry's.

I slammed the bottle onto the patio table. "I was cleaning and found this. Since you're my babysitter, I thought I should turn it in to you. It's still sealed, so be sure to report that to my brother." I spun on my heels and started retracing my steps.

"Junie!" Henry called, but it did nothing to slow my retreat.

Back inside, I finished cleaning the kitchen with the burdening weight of that darn bottle of booze on my mind. I couldn't quit thinking about it. Even with the bottle out of the house, I itched for it.

Hands shaking, throat burning, I felt my control slipping. Needing to get a grip, I called Gilbert.

"I'm having a bad day." I rubbed my forehead. "I really want a drink."

"I'll make us a tee time. I'm on my way. Be ready."

We both knew whacking golf balls at Topgolf wouldn't fix anything, but at least it would be a good distraction. I was starting to realize that staying sober required lots and lots of distractions.

31

Back in the quaint office with coastal-blue walls and nautical décor, I felt no more comfortable than the first visit.

"This is a nice surprise, having you both back in my office."

I'd been just as surprised as Shari when we both received the email from Cy three days ago, asking for this in-person session. Frankly, it scared me.

Cy sat up a little straighter. "I'm about to move to Tennessee, so I thought we should do one more in person before then."

His statement punched me hard in the gut and took the breath right out of me for a painful moment.

Finding my voice, I spoke up. "He's trying to take my daughter to Tennessee with him even though I've asked him not to."

Shari jotted something down in her notebook, probably something on the lines of *Junie wants what she can't have*. Three weeks of Zoom sessions, she knew about the custody battle and what I did to lose custody in the first place. "Cy, why do you feel it's necessary to continue to keep custody of Fern?"

"I don't think Junie is ready to take a child on full-time by herself."

Now I sat up straighter. Turning on the couch, I faced my brother head-on. "But I am, Cy. If you'd just come by the house and stay longer than a hot minute, you'd see. I have her room ready. I even finished the quilt Olla was making her."

Cy scoffed. "It takes more than a bedroom remodel to be a parent."

"I know that!"

"You haven't had to be a parent. It's taking care of your child on your good days *and* the hard ones. Making sure they're fed, bathed, educated, loved. It's not putting them in danger." He combed his fingers through his hair. "Parenting is twenty-four seven. You don't get weekends off. You have no idea."

"What makes you the authority on parenting?"

"I've had to be one ever since I was eleven years old. That's roughly twenty-six years of experience."

I flinched at his sharp tone and the brutal truth. Sitting back, I started drawing circles in the velvet material on the armrest. A drink would calm me better, but the textured sofa would have to do.

He turned to Shari. "Junie has no experience in parenting."

"What about before her incarceration? Didn't Junie have custody of Fern then?"

"She came straight to my house from the hospital. She and the baby both had babysitters practically around the clock. Me and my wife. A few ladies from our community came over to help her while we were at work."

"Junie, why did you need so much help?"

Biting the inside of my lip, I tried to come up with a response that didn't make me sound like the victim. My brother and I had that in common. We hated me being viewed in that role. "I was diagnosed with postpartum depression at my six-week check-up. The doctor didn't know about my struggle with substance abuse and gave me meds I had no business taking. I should have spoken up, but I didn't. I just wanted to feel normal again. That's on me. Most days I couldn't get out of bed."

"That's understandable. You'd just lost your husband and your grandmother," Shari offered, but I was tired of accepting this reasoning.

"It's not understandable at all. I started taking double doses of my meds until the doctor caught on and wouldn't refill my prescription. So I started drinking again. I realize now how selfish I was."

"Why do you say that?"

"My brother had just lost Olla too. He had to take care of her estate, take care of me, take care of Fern, take care of his family, and work full-time." I looked at my brother. "I've never fully apologized for all that. I'm sorry, Cy. I really am."

He met my eyes briefly, then returned to studying his hands.

Shari shifted in her chair. "Cy, you said you've been parenting for over twenty years. Would you elaborate on that?"

He looked up at her. "My parents . . ." He sighed. "They've always been career-driven and that's taken them all over the place. We didn't have much of a stable homelife with them gone so much. My grandmother stayed with us when she could and we spent summers with her, but it has always been left up to me to take care of Junie."

Shari began writing again, but I wanted her to realize the extent of Cy raising me more than his blanketed answer.

"Cy isn't just saying that. It's the truth." I thought back over the years for examples. "I remember him cooking our meals in the kitchen, not one of my parents. I had a bad habit of scraping my knees. Cy was the one to always patch me back up. And when I started my period, I went to him, not my mom. That's how natural it felt, him being in the parenting role for me. He didn't tease me. Instead, he did a few Internet searches, then he went to the store and brought home the supplies I needed." I quickly swiped away a wayward tear and glanced at my brother, his shoulders hunched and his chest rising a little faster now. "He's always been my person. I can't even imagine how much of a burden it's been on you, Cy."

"Junie, what led up to you living with Cy?" Shari didn't even look up from her notepad, writing a novel it seemed.

Cy spoke before I could. "Junie and our grandmother were thick as thieves. Olla had been taking care of Junie after her husband died and the plan was for Junie and the baby to live with her. Then Olla died suddenly and Junie's blood pressure went through the roof. It sent Junie into labor two and a half weeks early." Cy did something that shocked me so severely that tears splashed down my cheeks. He reached for my hand. "It scared me. I thought we were going to lose you and the baby too."

We shared a rare sibling moment that only needed significant eye contact and a slight head nod. It made me want to wrap my arms around him, to cling to the one steady rock I'd ever known, but his body language told me to tread lightly, so I stayed on my side of the couch.

He refocused on Shari as I sat there and quietly wept. "Olla would have wanted me to take care of Junie and Fern . . . I wanted that too, so we brought them home."

"And where were your parents when all this happened?"

"Overseas. It took them a few days to get here, in time for the funeral. They stayed long enough to help me get Junie and the baby moved in, then they took off again, only coming back for Junie's court hearing."

"So . . . you haven't seen them in almost a year?"

"Yes, but that's what we're used to." Cy let go of my hand and grabbed me a tissue, ever the caretaker.

"Have either of you expressed to your parents how you feel about them being away so much of your lives?"

I cleared the lump from my throat. "It's hard to when they're so happy with what they do. How do you talk against their dreams?"

"You're the children, not the parents. Shouldn't they be the ones encouraging you to chase your dreams?"

Now I felt defensive on my parents' behalf. "How could they encourage us to chase our dreams if they didn't do the same?" I lifted my shoulders, releasing them on a stuttered breath. "Yes, I've resented them at times, a lot of times, but I can't hold it against them."

"Cy?" Shari motioned toward him. "Is this how you feel too?"

"More or less. Like, what's the point in bringing it up to them now? What's done is done. And honestly, I'm used to them not being around. When they are, it's like trying to get to know strangers."

"Maybe if you write them a letter? They need to know how their choices have affected you. It may go a long way in patching up your relationship with each other."

"Why worry with our relationship? He's leaving me too." My throat closed and another stupid sob tried squeaking through.

"You've had a lot of that in your life. People leaving."

I dried my face with another tissue. "Doesn't everybody?"

Cy didn't say anything and I was tired of talking too. I checked the time on the ship wheel clock. Only ten minutes to go.

Shari seemed to catch on that we were done, so she closed her notepad and tapped her pen on the cover. "It's your choice, but I want to encourage you to give some thought to writing those letters to your parents. You don't have to ever mail them, just do it as a venting exercise." She stood. "If either of you want to talk one-on-one, I'd be happy to make that happen."

We both stood too, and after saying our goodbyes, we left in a more somber state than we had arrived. This therapy was like going to the doctor to get stitches for a cut, but instead, the doctor takes out a knife and deepens the wound.

32

Dear Mom and Dad,

I hated my childhood. I hated having to attend five different schools, because your careers had us moving so much. I hated that you memorized the scientific names for plants, but you couldn't remember to make it to my school play.

And that one time, the gala at Brookgreen Gardens, I hated the most. I was maybe eight years old and got tired of standing around while you two were busy mingling well into the night. I hunkered down by one of those statues in the garden and fell asleep. Y'all FORGOT me! Just went home and didn't realize until a maintenance worker found me and called you. I remember sitting in that gatehouse by the entrance and being relieved to see Cy's car pull up and not yours. I think I began hating you a little after that night.

I tossed the pen on the desk and crumpled the paper. How could this be helpful? Stirring up all those memories just made me more upset. Made me want to scream. Made me want to take a drink.

My parents were not present in my life, even while standing right in front of me. I tried filling those voids with things that I shouldn't. Alcohol, pills, partying. Looking back on it now, I probably did it for attention too.

After throwing away the letter, I moved to Fern's room and started making her bed with the new sheet set. The color reminded me of pale orange sherbet and would complement the colors of the quilt.

After placing the finished quilt on Fern's bed, I took a step back and surveyed the room. It was ready for her, but was I ready for the responsibility? The first two years of her life, I had lived in a constant state of foggy grief, worsened by alcohol. And as Cy stated, I had a lot of help with taking care of her.

Friday's therapy session had me facing some hard truths with my parents but also facing the hard truth Cy pointed out. I didn't know how to be a parent. The fact of the matter was that no judge was going to keep Fern away from me. I'd looked it up, and the goal is always to rehabilitate the parent and return the child to them. In the eyes of the judicial system I was, in fact, rehabilitated. That meant I needed to learn how to parent. ASAP! But first I needed to get to Seacoast.

On the way to church, I contemplated how to go about learning to be a parent. YouTube, obviously, but maybe an in-person class would be better. A good fifteen minutes early for the service, I parked in the shade, rolled down the window, and took a moment to do a search for parenting classes on my phone.

"Whatcha doin' out here by ya'self?"

I jumped, nearly flinging the phone but managed to hold on to it. "Good grief, Pearl! You just took a decade off my life!"

She hobbled off and I thought the odd lady was gone but then the passenger side door flung open. "Come help me up."

I doubted questioning her would do any good, so I hopped out and did as she instructed. Once I was settled back into my seat, she started jabbering.

"The youth these days." She *tsk*ed. "Always got ya faces buried in ya phones. So much so you didn't even hear me call ya name."

I cut her a sideways glare and picked up my phone from the cup holder. "I was looking up something very important, I'll have you know."

She squinted at my phone. "What's so important? A new Facebook friend request?"

"No. It's . . ." I had not shared about the custody battle with the Magnolia group, but maybe that was part of my issue. Not sharing. Not leaning on the support network around me. I looked over at the little lady waiting for an answer and decided to take a chance and give her one. "I'm working on getting custody of my daughter back and . . . honestly I'm scared I'm not going to know how to take care of her, so I was looking up parenting classes."

She clucked her tongue. "In my day, we didn't have books or classes. We just had our instincts."

I lowered the phone to my lap. "You think that's all I need? My instincts?"

Pearl gave my question some thought, tapping her chin. "Probably not. You already screwed it up once."

My shoulders hunched. "I can't afford to screw it up again. I can't do that to Fern."

"Fern." Pearl nodded. "That's a good name." She patted my shoulder. "Sit up straight and let's find a class we can go to."

I eyed her. "You're going to go with me?"

"Sure," Pearl said.

"Why?"

She gave me a haughty frown. "You rather go by ya'self?"

"No ma'am. Not really."

"Then find one and we'll go."

And that's what I did, and Pearl held true to her word and went with me. The class ended up being helpful—I learned about child safety and appropriate car seats. We also ended up attending a CPR class together the following week. Pearl was a hoot, cracking jokes in class, and I felt normal again, just a mother wanting to learn how to take proper care of my child.

In the midst of everything this summer, I'd come to understand just how extraordinary *normal* could be. I also realized that living like a hellion wasn't really living. That lifestyle was oppressing, but living a quiet, steady life was freeing.

33

God, please keep the taste of unhealthy out of Junie's mouth today. Please show her she is strong enough.

The text showed up every morning with the sun, but Henry no longer added any silly comment at the end. We both knew we were beyond that. I wanted to respond and tell him to just stop, but I honestly needed his prayers.

Like every Tuesday this summer, I read Henry's text, prayed my own prayer, got dressed and walked the dogs, came home and showered, worked on custom hats and pieces for my Etsy shop and Bekah's store until four. Then I would head over to the Methodist church to help Betty.

"What's on the menu for tonight?" I asked Betty while washing my hands in the kitchen sink.

"It's been so blamed hot, I figured we'd do something a little lighter. We're having a salad night." Betty smiled, happy with the idea.

"Sounds good to me," I said, picturing us setting up a salad bar of sorts.

Turns out, salad night in a Southern church meant potato salad, pasta salad, egg salad, chicken salad, tuna salad, tomato cracker salad (of course), fruit salad, and Watergate salad. Served with various crackers and bread.

"You gonna share tonight?" Betty gave me a meaningful look as she placed a serving spoon beside the pasta salad.

"I'm not sure." I grabbed a cloth and wiped away a splash of tea on the counter.

Betty and I had grown closer in the last few weeks and I'd confided in her that I'd been thinking about sharing with the group.

"You've said so yourself, how listening to others share their story has encouraged you. Just think how wonderful it would be for you to return some of that."

"Yes, ma'am." I left it at that and got back to work.

Once most were finished eating, Reggie took his place behind the small podium and asked everyone to stand. "Please join me in reciting the Serenity Prayer." He waited until we were all to our feet, then began leading us. *"God grant me the serenity to accept the things I cannot change, the courage to change the things I can, and the wisdom to know the difference."*

While everyone else took their seats, I walked up to the podium before I chickened out. I smoothed my sweaty palms down the side of my jeans and offered a wobbly smile. "Hi . . . I umm . . . I'm Junie."

"Hi Junie," the group said in unison.

I took a deep breath and blinked to clear my blurry vision. How embarrassing would it be to pass out! Before I did that or just lost my nerve, I began speaking. "I died once. You'd think that would be hard to do." I shook my head. "Turns out, it's pretty easy to die. The coming back though. Well, that's another story. You'd also think surviving an overdose would be enough to straighten me out, but surviving meant I had to face the fallout from it." I scanned the group and landed on Betty.

"Go ahead," Betty mouthed, tipping her head.

"I mostly gave up pills after that but leaned heavily on alcohol. I kept thinking I just needed to numb things, ya know?" I searched for Maren. "The only thing that accomplished was me losing everything important to me. I lost respect for myself. I lost the trust of my family. I lost track of my life. And, most importantly, I lost custody of my daughter after I drove drunk with her in the car." I fidgeted, shifting my weight from one foot to the other. "What I've come to learn is my alcoholism has taken so much away from me . . . I'm tired of losing."

"Me too," Kason spoke up, crossing his arms.

I nodded. "In the eight months since sobering up, I've realized the only way to stop losing is to stop using. I've had to admit my wrongs and right them. I'm slowly gaining respect for myself, working on regaining my family's trust and custody of my daughter. I pray every day that God would take the taste of unhealthy out of my mouth and I encourage you to do the same. Thank you." Cheeks hot, I darted back to my seat while everyone clapped.

I didn't know—and probably never would—if my words mattered to anyone. I guessed that wasn't the point. My story—as humiliating and tragic as it was—needed to be shared. I'd never told Maren how much her sharing her story helped me, so I just hoped someone here heard what needed to be heard and that it had the same effect on them.

Kason, lanky and sullen, made his way to the podium. *He thinks the sun comes up just to hear him crow.* I'd heard Olla use this expression once or twice and it definitely fit Kason. Mr. The World Owes Me.

"Dad found a bottle underneath the seat in my car, so he took my keys. I swear it's old, but he won't listen." Kason rubbed his red eyes and groaned. "I can't do nothing right." Clearly, he hadn't heard anything useful from me tonight.

My phone vibrated with a new text from Patsy in the MNS group chat. **SOS. Emergency meeting tonight. Please attend if available.** I looked around the fellowship hall as Kason continued to whine about the unfairness.

Making my apologies, I slipped out of the meeting as soon as Kason wrapped up his bemoaning. By the time I arrived, most everyone else was there gathered around Patsy's dining room table.

"What's the emergency?" Pearl asked, easing her arthritic body into a chair, grunting as she did.

All eyes were on Jackée as she silently cried.

Patsy exchanged a look with Jackée and patted her on the shoulder. "Jackée fell off the wagon."

We waited a long pause, then Jackée told us in a hoarse voice, "Both boys are at sports camp and . . . well, I missed them and I was alone and lonely and bored. I was grocery shopping and walked right down the beverage aisle and before I knew it, I was back home with a case of Seagram's. I chugged three of them before I got myself under control." Jackée wiped her cheeks with a trembling hand and said through gritted teeth, "I'm so mad at myself!"

I mainly kept quiet during meetings, but tonight it seemed I was in a talkative mood. "You stopped, didn't you?"

She nodded.

"And then you came straight to us." I eased around the table and knelt beside her chair. "Jackée, you're so brave. I have so much respect for you for doing that." I wrapped my arms around her and felt the trembling of her body. I wished I were one of those people who could come up with wise comforting words on the fly, but that person I was not, so I hugged her tightly.

Gilbert showed up and elbowed his way to get to Jackée. "You screwed up. That don't make you special." *Leave it to Gilbert.* "But you coming here to get back on track immediately, now that, young lady, makes you special." He winked at her and offered her a hug.

While we sat around the table in silence, Jackée started venting. It was the first time I heard her entire story.

"I had a volleyball scholarship. Nearly a full ride to the University of Southern California. But I screwed that up by sophomore year. Too much partying and very little studying. I failed a drug test and was kicked off the team. I moved back home with my parents and started stealing and pawning their belongings to pay for drugs and alcohol. They gave me an ultimatum: either go to rehab and get clean or they were kicking me out."

"Did rehab help?" Bruno asked.

Jackée shrugged. "At first yes. I managed to get clean but made other dumb choices. I ended up having back-to-back pregnancies with two different men. Neither wanted to be fathers. Go figure." She huffed a laugh. "I did what I had to do. I took night classes for web design while raising my boys alone. I was exhausted all the time and a friend of mine shared her kid's ADHD meds with me, saying it would give me the energy to be a mom and student. She was right, but not long, that turned into a mess and I had to do an outpatient treatment for a while. The constant up and down . . . It's never going to get easier, is it?" Her face crumbled as she sagged forward and began to sob.

We gathered close. I took one hand and Patsy the other while others placed a hand on her back. No one offered platitudes nor judgment, just showed her grace. That in itself gave me a lot to think about. How the church was formed to be a place of grace for those needing healing of all kinds. Physical. Spiritual. Emotional. This group didn't look like the conventional AA meeting or church, but it certainly embodied the heart of both.

34

"Aren't we a little too old for field trips?" Axil asked in his grumbly voice as I drove us down I-26 in Olla's Escalade—the perfect vehicle for field trips. He was my copilot with Pearl, Bruno, Mei, and Jackée in the back.

"It's a food festival and we get to support Chris. Not a bad way to spend a Saturday," Pearl said. "Besides, you're never too old for anything."

"Except maybe sucking your thumb," I offered, checking my rearview mirror and seeing Chris Evans right behind me driving his brand-new mobile bakery truck. Gilbert was bringing up the rear in his Corvette with Patsy as his copilot.

"Or coloring on your walls," Bruno piped in and made me laugh.

"I still do that one." I smiled, catching his eye in the mirror.

"Just don't tell my little boy. We caught him last week scribbling on the bathroom wall with a red Sharpie. Looked like a crime scene." Bruno *tsk*ed. "Toddlers are a handful."

My smile wobbled then slipped away. I wished I knew what he was talking about. Sure, I had a toddler, but I had no idea if she was a handful or not. With only three weeks until Cy had to be in Tennessee, I hoped I would be finding out real soon.

Axil pointed to the left. “There’s a car coming up hot behind you.”

I checked the fast lane and noticed a sporty car zooming up beside me. Not sure why I needed him pointing that out, considering we were in the right lane, but Mr. Copilot was taking his job seriously and who was I to question him.

“Did I hear someone say this place used to be a ghost town?” I asked.

“It made national news about six years ago when a construction company came in and brought the entire town back to life,” Jackée said.

“It’s the biggest revitalization project in the state’s history,” Bruno added. “I like that they named the town Somewhere. The woman overseeing the project said it’s so folks will always have somewhere to go.”

“I like that too.” I slowed down and took a right. “So, what’s the plan? Chris is going to set up his truck and we help him?”

“Jackée is going to help Chris, but we can be on hand if he needs anything,” Bruno said. “Mainly, we’re showing him our support, so plan on relaxing and enjoying the festival.”

“I told Chris I’d help too. I’m a great salesperson,” Pearl commented. She was a bossy little thing and there was no telling what would come out of her mouth.

“I think we can handle it, Pearl,” Jackée said. “He’s been giving me extra bread and treats for Omar and Najee. Those two are bottomless pits. Chris won’t take any money, so I’d really like to help to pay him back.”

“It won’t hurt to have extra help,” Pearl kept on. I had a feeling she’d end up in that food truck by the end of the day anyway. She tended to get her way with us, mainly just to hush her up about it.

Passing a water tower with a fancy logo and the town name, Somewhere, written on it, I joined the line of cars rolling into town. “Ain’t this place so quaint.”

"It looks like a new old town," Mei said, her face glued to the window as we passed by the Grocery Depot, then a community center that looked like it had once been an old-time saloon. "For some reason I thought it was going to look like one of those ghost towns in an old Western. You know, decrepit and spooky."

"I saw an interview with Avalee Murray," Pearl said. "She led the redevelopment project and their goal was to keep the integrity of the town while restoring it."

"Well, I think they nailed it," Jackée commented.

We all mumbled our agreement. It definitely had the charm of a small Southern town, much like Beaufort or Summerville.

I located a parking spot and we all exited the Caddy. "Where will Chris set up?"

"Main Street is closed for table vendors and the trucks will be parked over by the Farmer's Market area." Bruno pointed out toward the right. "Behind the deli and library. I heard they have an award-winning barbeque truck that's here permanently." The breeze picked up, as if on cue, carrying hints of woodsmoke and spices.

We made our way over there to make sure Chris didn't need a hand with anything. The black truck with cedar accents and gold scripted lettering that spelled out *Loafing Around* was easy to spot among the pastel and brightly colored trucks.

"His is the nicest," Pearl commented, sounding like a proud grandmother.

Pearl seemed a bit unsteady today, leaning heavily on her cane, so I grabbed her a foldout chair. After getting her set up in the shade with a bottle of water, I helped to load beautifully wrapped breads and pastries on a portable rack.

"Move the rack closer to the order window, will ya." Pearl pointed her cane toward the right of the window. "That'll make it easier for customers to buy more."

"Good thinking," Chris said cheerfully.

"Looks like you have it under control. Just shoot us a text if you need anything," Patsy said. She turned and began strolling away in her peachy-pink caftan, bracelets jingling, and we followed like obedient ducklings. "Let's start over by the old saloon and work our way up Main Street."

The first vendor, a woman with a kind smile, handed each of us a canvas bag. Her name tag said Nita. "Hey y'all. Welcome to Somewhere Food Festival. There's an itinerary in your bag for the day and some goodies."

We took our bags, thanking her, and started toward the next vendor. Not long into our exploration, everyone began going their own way until just Mei and I were walking together.

We'd only made it halfway up Main Street when I felt my bag being tugged out of my hand. "Hey!" I turned in time to see a dog make off with it. "That dog swiped my bag," I complained to Mei, who found it funny.

A minute later, a young boy with wild blond hair came over with that dog trailing behind him. "Here's your bag back." He thrust the bag toward me. "Preacher only stole the pecan brittle."

My eyes narrowed. "Preacher?"

"That's his name."

"Oh. Well, you got yourself a thieving dog."

The dog happily snacked on his stolen treat, no cares to give about getting caught for his crimes.

"He's the mayor."

"Preacher is the mayor?" Mei questioned, reaching down to pat the brown-and-black-spotted dog.

"Not officially, but yeah." He shrugged, like it made perfect sense. "I'm Koda. We're both the grand marshals of the festival." He tapped the large button fastened on his shirt.

"Well, I'm honored to meet you both." I surveyed the busy street. "Maybe you could direct us where to find ice cream."

Koda spun around and pointed at an old, galvanized grain bin that had been remodeled into a small shop. "Sweet Silo is where the ice cream's at. My favorite is the red velvet ice cream. You gotta try it."

I angled away from Preacher, catching him going for my bag again. "Oh yeah? I love red velvet. Thanks for the recommendation."

"No problem. Have a good one." Koda patted his leg and the thieving mayor named Preacher followed him until they disappeared into the crowd.

"That was . . . entertaining." Mei giggled.

I shook my head and laughed too.

We stepped up to the order window at the ice cream shop. "I'll take a scoop of red velvet, please."

"And I'll take a scoop of peach," Mei added.

Someone sighed heavily behind us. "Y'all done and messed up."

We whirled around and had to crane our necks back to see the guy's face. Tall, blond, and close to our age.

"We messed up?" Mei said, playing with the necklace around her neck. "Please do enlighten us." The flirt in her tone wasn't lost on me.

His blue eyes twinkled as his lips lifted in a friendly smile. "Somewhere is known for its pecans." He directed our attention toward the pecan grove on the other side of the road. "The butter pecan ice cream is the best. It has a ribbon of caramel too. Are either of you allergic to nuts?"

We shook our heads.

He sidestepped us. "Dana, can I get two samples of butter pecan for these two ladies?"

"Sure thing, Bash." The girl dug two generous spoonfuls out and handed them to us.

A bit salty and nutty and a whole lot delicious, he wasn't kidding about it being the best. "Wow, this *is* the best ice cream I've ever tasted. Is it too late to change my order?"

"No problem," the young girl said, happily accommodating. She handed us ice cream cones piled high with butter pecan.

"I'm Bash, by the way," the handsome host told us as he accepted his ice cream cone.

We introduced ourselves, then I shared the funny run-in with the grand marshals.

"Koda is my little brother." Now that Bash mentioned it, I could see the resemblance.

Bash also shared that he helped renovate this town. I found it quite interesting but even more interesting was that Mei and Bash seemed to have really hit it off. Not wanting to be the third wheel, I slipped away.

Enjoying another lick of ice cream, I turned to walk over to the picnic tables and nearly plowed into someone. Protecting my ice cream, I looked up into a familiar face and glared.

"Now you're spying on me all the way out here for my brother?"

Henry held his hands up, blocking that notion and my escape. "No. It's not like that. Your life coach told me about the festival. It sounded fun."

I didn't know whether to believe Henry or not. Searching the crowd for Gilbert, I mumbled, "He's so fired."

"I just wanted to say hey. And to see how you're doing."

"I'm fine." I thought about walking away full of attitude, but I couldn't muster any. Truthfully, I was still hurt by what he did but I also missed him. What a conundrum . . . "I'm surprised you were able to leave your computer long enough for a food festival."

Henry bumped his glasses up his nose and gazed around. "I really like to eat. Gilbert said your friend the baker has a truck here today. I've been dreaming about that bread you shared with me. I thought I'd buy some."

"You know he's got a shop Downtown where you can purchase bread anytime, right?"

"I do now, but I also needed a break."

"Well, have fun with that." I shouldered past him.

"Wait. Before you run away from me, I need to tell you something."

I turned to face him. "So tell me."

"I . . ." He checked over his shoulder, as if searching for someone.

"Spit it out already."

"I told Cy and Lana about the festival and . . ."

My heart dropped. "They're here?"

"Yes." He rubbed the back of his neck.

"Alex and Fern here too?"

"Yes."

I had a good mind to reach over and pinch him. "Is Gilbert in on this?"

Henry quickly shook his head. "No. Gilbert just wanted us to fix our friendship. I think."

I didn't have the patience to point out we had no friendship. "Does Cy know I'm here?" I tossed my ice cream into the trash and joined him in searching the crowd.

"Uh . . ."

"Henry," I snapped through gritted teeth.

"No."

I threw my hands up, then dropped them hard against my thighs. "Why would you do that?"

He stepped closer and lowered his voice. "I thought if you could see each other . . . I don't know . . . Maybe you could spend some time—"

"No. He's going to think I did this to ambush them and he's just going to resent me even more."

"Maybe not. Don't you want to see Fern?"

"More than anything, but not like this." I stepped into the alleyway between two buildings. "I'm trying to do things the right way."

"I'll explain and—"

"No." I leveled him with a glare. "You've done enough. Seriously, Henry, stay out of it." Tucking my chin and keeping my eyes to the ground, I did a mad dash to the Caddy. Thankfully, I didn't run into Cy and the rest of my family. I hunched down in the driver's seat and pushed a palm against my chest. My daughter was in reach and I knew if I tried to seek her out in this crowd, it would only work against me.

What had Henry been thinking? And why was he still involving himself in my business? I sat stewing over all of this for quite some time, wishing I could just leave instead of hiding out in my vehicle.

Eventually, I spotted Chris Evans and Jackée walking over. I rolled the window down and called out to them. "Hey. Who's managing the truck?"

"No one. I sold out." Chris looked baffled. That made two of us. His truck had been loaded with bread and other treats less than two hours ago.

"That was fast. Did you have a mob of people show up after we left?"

"We had a good line, but a friend of yours came by and bought me out of everything."

I squinted up at him. "A friend of mine?"

"Yes." Jackée smirked. "*Henry.* I think the man is in love."

I snorted. "Not hardly. He's not my friend either."

She shot me a look, lips twisting into a smirk. "Sure could've fooled me."

I changed the subject. "Does that mean we can go home now?"

"Pearl sent us to buy her an elephant ear." Jackée checked the time on her phone. "But we can leave after that. You want us to get you one too?"

"No thanks. I'll be here when everyone is ready to go."

Jackée eyed me. "Are you okay?"

"I have a bit of a stomachache, but I'll be okay."

She frowned. "You sure?"

"Yeah."

"Okay. We'll be back soon."

I nodded and mustered up a smile, waving them off when they hesitated to leave.

The drive home was full of chatter. The group raved about the town and the festival, but I only contributed head nods and smiles. Everyone else had enough to say that I got away with it.

After dropping everyone off, I made my way to Sullivan's Island. Walking up the porch steps, I found a box filled with bread and pastries sitting in the rocking chair.

"That man," I grumbled, swiping the box and carrying it inside. I knew I needed to forgive him, I just didn't know how to let the deceit of his actions go. Not yet anyway.

I put away the food in the kitchen and checked the time, thinking it should be close to bedtime, but it was just past six, way too early to call it a day.

The thing I couldn't get used to about being alone all the time was *all the time* I had on my hands. I settled onto my bed and picked up the *Life Recovery Workbook*. Each time, I started by rereading the twelve steps I'd paraphrased on the inside of the book cover.

1. I'm powerless over my problems. They're unmanageable.
2. Only God can restore me.
3. I've turned my life over to God.
4. Inventory myself.
5. Admit my wrongs to myself, to God, and to someone else.

6. I want God to remove my defects.
7. Ask God to remove my shortcomings.
8. List the people I've harmed.
9. Make amends with them.
10. Stay accountable to wrongs and quickly admit to them.
11. Pray to God and ask for his will.
12. Share what I've learned with others and continue to practice it.

I looked over the list and stopped on numbers eight and nine. I'd already apologized to my brother and parents, but one name stuck out today. Lana. I'd never given her an official apology.

Moving to the small writing desk, I selected a few sheets of plain stationary. I used colored pencils to decorate the top with Lana's favorite flowers—magnolias and sunflowers—while I considered what I wanted to write to her. By the time I'd created a lush bouquet, I'd worked up my nerve to apologize for dragging her into my mistakes.

Dear Lana,

I screwed up my life and in the process, I screwed up yours too. The day I made my awful, inexcusable, stupid mistake of driving drunk with my daughter in the back seat, I was on my way to putting your son in danger too. I'm not sure I'll ever forgive myself, so I don't blame you if you don't.

I'm sorry. So, so sorry.

And I'm sorry that even though it was my mistake, you're one of the people living with the consequences of it. You nor my brother deserve what I've put you through.

For a few years, after losing Arlo and Olla, I lost myself. That's not an excuse, just a fact. I fell into a dark place. Now

I'm digging my way out of it, even though it's taking a lot longer than I'd hoped.

Thank you for stepping up and becoming a mother to my daughter when I failed at it. I know you love her and she's in good care. I will never be able to repay you for that. It is the most precious gift someone has ever given me, loving my child as your own.

I'm sorry. I thank you. I love you.

Junie

I carefully folded the note and tucked it inside an envelope. I may have gone through all twelve steps, but I'd come to realize I would never be done learning from them. I also started to understand that life is hard, but we must live the hard parts to become a better person. A healthier person. Writing Lana's name and address on the front of the envelope, I wasn't sure about being a better person but I did feel healthier.

35

You are cordially invited to Mei Lee's violin recital

Sunday, July 30 at 7:00 p.m.

Charleston Music Hall

I stared at the invitation on my refrigerator door. It would be Mei's first concert in over a year. Tonight was about Mei, and as a member of the Magnolia Nephalist Society, I would be there to cheer her on.

I ventured into Olla's walk-in closet in search of a dress I remembered her wearing to a wedding one time. She didn't like to part with anything, so I knew it had to still be in there. I stood in the middle and took a minute, my hands trailing over the clothes. Eyes closed, I could almost imagine her standing right here with me. I leaned my face into one of her button-down shirts and breathed in the faint scent of her perfume that still clung to the fabric. I knew the time was fast approaching that I'd have to go through all this, considering my father chose not to and this was three years past due, but today wasn't that day.

Straightening, I moved to the back where a section of outfits hung in garment bags, unzipping and rezipping until my eyes landed on lilac and cornflower blue. The material crinkled as I pulled the gown out of the bag and inspected it. It still looked as good as new. I removed the dry-cleaning receipt and tried it on, already knowing it would fit since my grandmother and I were the same size.

Shuffling out of the closet, I stood in front of her antique mirror and smoothed a hand down the front. Even though the gown was long with Juliet sleeves, the chiffon material was light and airy. My favorite part of the dress was the dark-purple velvet ribbon around the waist, which fancied it up. Perfect for a violin performance, I'd hoped.

With that sorted, I carefully undressed and laid the gown on Olla's bed, then moved to my room. I managed to work my long hair into a soft updo and kept the makeup minimal but for the winged eyeliner, making my green eyes more vibrant than usual. After I slipped the dress back on and wiggled my feet into a pair of strappy silver-heeled sandals, I felt much more in a festive mood.

I switched my wallet and keys, along with mints and light-pink lip gloss, from my slouchy bag to Olla's sleek silver clutch. Channeling my grandmother's genteel Southern manner, I headed out, making a quick stop at Trader Joe's to pick up a beautiful bouquet of flowers for Mei.

Getting into the downtown area wasn't so bad, surprising for a Saturday evening, so I arrived an entire thirty minutes early. The theater was mostly empty, which I chalked up to my punctuality. I sat in the fourth row near the middle to make sure I had a good view. The only thing on the big stage was a violin case on a stand and some type of speaker with a foot pedal. I should have studied up on this type of performance before today, but other things had consumed me lately.

"You're early."

I glanced over my shoulder and saw Gilbert making his way down the center aisle, a bouquet of flowers in his hands. Patsy and Jackée were right behind him. "I wanted a good seat."

"Ain't you all gussied up." Gilbert nodded in approval.

"You are too." I motioned toward his tan summer suit. "Everyone, for that matter. Jackée, you look like a million bucks."

"Thanks, hon." Jackée shimmied a bit, causing the light overhead to catch on the sparkly gold-and-black swirls of her strapless dress. "But not as fabulous as our Patsy." She nodded at Patsy, who wore what had to be the fanciest caftan I'd ever seen. Royal blue silk with beading around the flowy sleeves. Gold and diamond jewelry dressed it up even more.

Patsy winked at Jackée and they tapped hips before she took a seat beside me. "I'm so nervous for her." Patsy looked through the program we were handed at the door. "This is a big step."

Gilbert nodded. "Yeah, especially since she's swore for months now that she'd never play again."

Jackée leaned over Patsy and whispered to us as a few other people trickled in. "Nothing against our Mei, but I'm not into classical music." She scrunched her nose, making the diamond stud in her nose catch the overhead lights.

Patsy rested her hand on Jackée's arm and whispered, "It's okay, suga'. I'm not crazy about sourdough, but we don't have to tell Chris that. Same with Mei. She doesn't have to know this isn't our thing, we just need to be supportive."

I looked at Patsy in a whole new light. Who didn't like sourdough?

Axil walked up with Pearl clinging to his arm for support. The elderly lady was a little unsteady on her feet lately and it seemed to worsen when Axil was near enough she could hold on to him. He settled her in the seat at the end of our aisle, then he took the empty seat beside me. Chris Evans and Bruno arrived shortly after.

"There was an accident just past the bridge. We both got stuck in it," Bruno explained.

I glanced around and noticed more empty rows than not. I believed the place had close to a thousand seats but not even a hundred were occupied. "You think the accident is holding up this many guests?" I motioned behind us.

"No. Mei only wanted family and close friends here tonight," Patsy said as the lights began to lower. "This is a test run to see if performing is something she wants to pursue again."

"Oh. That makes sense."

A tall guy walked past us carrying a gigantic arrangement of white roses and joined Mei's parents up front. Gasping, I nudged Patsy's arm. "I know that guy!"

"You do? Who is he?"

"His name is Bash and I'm pretty sure he's Mei's future husband. They met at the food festival in Somewhere."

Jackée leaned around Patsy and said, "Aww . . . That is so sweet."

Patsy studied Bash and hummed. "He's mighty good-looking. Our girl has excellent taste. And how brave of her to invite him tonight. I'm so proud of her."

"Me too," I said with Jackée echoing my sentiments. Mei was twenty years old and had made more progress with getting her life together than most her age, even with the excessive drinking handicap she had overcome. Proud we were.

A tiny Mei Lee wearing a choir robe walked onto the stage, carrying a beautiful wooden violin. I expected someone to introduce her or maybe Mei say a few words before she began, but neither happened. She simply placed the bow against the strings and started playing.

I heard Axil sigh loudly, clearly not a fan of classical music either. I hadn't listened to much in my life, but I didn't mind the soothing music. Whatever song she played was bittersweet, the notes drawing out a longing inside me that made me weepy.

It was quite a long song and Axil fidgeted in the seat beside me, sighing frequently.

The song finally came to a slow end. Mei placed the violin on the vacant stand and flicked open the second case to reveal a metallic hot-pink violin with black accents. I didn't know much about instruments but it looked like the Cadillac of violins.

Mei tapped the foot pedal, making a thumping beat swell throughout the theater. Whipping off the robe, the demure young woman transformed into a showstopper. She was wearing a fitted tuxedo jacket with tails over a striped T-shirt, black tulle ballerina-style skirt, fishnet stockings, and black combat boots. She yanked the clip out of her hair, letting the tousled locks fall as they may, and the once-quiet audience roared to life at the same time the stage lights came to life in bursts of colors.

Not wasting any time, Mei settled the hot-pink violin under her chin and started plucking the strings to the beat of "Runaway" by OneRepublic, then she switched to using the bow. The song transitioned to "9 to 5" by the legendary Dolly Parton.

Axil did one of those earsplitting whistles, causing me to jump. Laughing, I joined in with everyone else, clapping to the beat as our heads bobbed.

Mei played other contemporary songs, some I didn't know, but most I did. "Used To Be Young" by Miley Cyrus. "Shotgun" by George Ezra. "Dog Days Are Over" by Florence & The Machine. That girl played her heart out! Dancing around, she seemed to be genuinely enjoying herself, thank goodness, because I couldn't imagine a world without her sharing this extraordinary gift.

Too soon, Mei pressed the foot pedal to stop the accompaniment, transitioning into a soft rendition of "Fall into Me" by Forest Blakk.

"This is one of my favorite songs!" I whisper-yelled to Patsy.

Nodding, she just grinned, looking toward the stage proudly.

The song drew to a close, a perfect conclusion to the performance. After a moment of silence, we erupted into applause, everyone shooting to their feet.

Rosy-cheeked, Mei smiled and curtsied.

"Mei is a rock star!" Jackée shouted, doing a little shimmy with her hands in the air.

Bruno started chanting, "Encore! Encore!" And we all joined in, but Mei darted off the stage.

Stunned, the theater grew quiet.

As quickly as Mei disappeared, she reappeared, skipping to the middle of the stage. "Oh, all right." She rolled her eyes, making us laugh. She fiddled with a small device, then tapped the foot pedal and the melody was easily recognizable. "Happy" by Pharrell Williams.

We all clapped along and danced in place—that song just beckoned you to—until the song transitioned into another. "Cheap Thrills" by Sia. She alternated from tapping the back of the violin like a drum, running the bow over the strings, to plucking the strings like a guitar.

Sadly, the song ended way too soon and Mei curtsied for one last time.

"My mind is blown. No wonder they call Mei a prodigy," I said in awe.

"That girl ort to be in the New York Philharmonic," Pearl added, straightening her giant purple glasses.

Pasty nodded her head. "She was the first-chair violinist with the Chicago Symphony Orchestra from age twelve to seventeen, but I think she's right where she should be."

Eventually, we took our turns congratulating Mei and giving her our bouquets.

"You did good, young lady," Gilbert said with his arm wrapped around her shoulders. "I'm proud of you."

"Thanks." Mei grinned. "I had fun."

"As you should." He squeezed her close before stepping away so Chris Evans could give her a hug.

When I got my turn, I chose to tease her a bit while pulling her in for a hug. "I'm surprised he didn't bring you butter pecan ice cream."

"He brought me a gallon last week." Mei giggled and I knew right then and there she was a goner.

After celebrating with everyone, I floated home on the high of Mei's success. I had almost reached the porch when I heard Henry call my name. Grin vanishing, I glanced over my shoulder and saw him returning from his mailbox. He still looked like absent-minded Henry with rumpled clothes and glasses sitting askew, but he seemed a little stunned.

"Wow. You look so lovely."

I glanced down at the dress. "Uh, thanks."

Henry moved closer and I scolded myself for pausing. Clearly, he took that as an invite. "Please let me apologize."

"Henry, not today." I backed away.

"I've given you time to cool off. Please."

I closed my eyes and sighed. "Fine."

"You want to go inside or next door? I actually made sweet tea earlier."

My eyes popped open as I regarded him. I was impressed, and a glass of iced tea sounded refreshing after all that cheering at Mei's concert, but . . .

"Just one glass, then I'll leave you alone, okay?" Henry ticked his head toward his house.

Saying nothing, I walked beside him, noticing he kept stealing glances at my outfit and hair. "I went to a violin recital to support a friend."

"That's nice. How'd it go?" Henry opened the door and held it for me and I did my best to not let any part of us touch as I passed him.

"Fine." I continued to the kitchen and was surprised no dishes or empty cereal boxes were littering the counters. "Your house is clean."

"Yeah. I finished my book so now I can focus on domestic things, like cleaning and making tea." He busied himself with pulling out two glasses from the cabinet and filling them with ice, then tea. "Lemon?"

I settled on a stool at the kitchen island, marveling over the sparkling clean granite. "You actually have lemons?"

He made a show of opening his fridge, waving a hand in game show fashion at the fully stocked shelves.

"Lemon would be great."

Henry retrieved one from the produce drawer and brought it to a small cutting board.

"What'd you do with all that bread you bought from Chris Evans?"

"Most of it is in the freezer. He gave me instructions on how to thaw it and all that."

"I can't believe you bought him out that day."

"It's good bread." Henry placed a wedge of lemon in my glass and handed it over. We both took a long drink. He set his glass down and took in a deep inhale. "I didn't mean to lie to you."

I studied him for a moment. "How so?"

"Cy asked me to keep an eye out for you in case you needed anything. The day I introduced myself I planned on telling you that, but then I met you and I just wanted to get to know you as my neighbor, not my colleague's sister."

"Why?"

He ran his hand through his messy dark hair. "Honestly, I was drawn to you immediately." He dropped his hand. "You realize you lied to me first, right?"

I scoffed, setting the glass down in preparation for a fight. "How do you figure?"

"You told me Gilbert was your personal trainer instead of your probation officer."

"How did you know that?"

"Cy gave me his number too, just in case."

"I don't think you can compare my lie to yours." I smoothed my thumb over my fingernails. "I confided in you about things and you just sat there like you didn't know any of it. That's just wrong, Henry."

"It wasn't like that. Cy only told me you'd gotten into some trouble and were on probation."

"Seriously?"

"Seriously. Your brother didn't tell me the important parts. I didn't know about Fern or that you'd lost your husband." Henry came around the island, hunching down until we were eye level. "Cy didn't tell me how incredibly talented you are or how caring you are or how beautiful . . ." He paused, shaking his head. "I started to tell you so many times, but I knew once that was between us, you'd stop opening up to me."

I scoffed. "Scared you wouldn't have anything to report back to my brother?" I slid off the stool, hearing all I needed to.

"The only thing I reported back to him was that you were working your butt off, attending support groups regularly, and that he had no right keeping your daughter from you." Henry stopped me at his door. "I'm on your side, Junie. Please believe that, if nothing else." Henry placed his hand on my shoulder. "I miss you."

I met his gaze and held it for a long moment. I was sad that his lies were now wedged between us, because I missed him too. "Thank you for your daily prayers and whatever you've said to Cy on my behalf, but I think it's best we keep to ourselves from here on out." I scooted around him and out the door, leaving a lot unsaid for the sake of moving forward.

36

Rainbow Row in Charleston's historic district was made up of thirteen brightly colored homes that were constructed around 1740. The Caribbean color scheme didn't come about until a preservation project in the late 1920s set out to restore the historical homes. All in all, they'd survived a civil war, flooding, earthquakes, and monstrous hurricanes such as Hurricane Hugo in 1989. I'd learned a lot about Rainbow Row in school, so I couldn't help but be a bit awestruck every time I visited Patsy. As we gathered in her sky-blue part of the rainbow, I sure hoped this old house was ready to face another storm. By the door a line of raincoats, umbrellas, and rain boots sat dripping onto the floor. Much like we were doing, locals loved sitting around debating whether a tropical cyclone would visit us, unwelcomed, or skirt up the coast to where North Carolina's hand liked to reach out and greet it more properly.

"It can't be that bad," Jackée commented nonchalantly.

"How do you know?" Pearl asked. Her purple glasses were barely hanging on to the tip of her tiny nose. How could she even breathe? I wanted to reach over and push them up.

"If it was real bad, the Waffle House would close down. They're better at forecasting the weather than those weathermen." Jackée pointed to the TV where a red banner rolled along the bottom of the screen while a woman in ridiculously tall heels motioned toward the circular nuisance on the radar.

"They like to be called meteorologists," Bruno piped in.

Jackée clucked her tongue. "Them fools don't know nothin' about meteors either! But Waffle House does. They still open, so we're good."

All that Waffle House talk had me hankering for an order of hash browns smothered in sautéed onions and covered in American cheese.

"What do you think, Junie?" Pearl asked.

I snapped to and wiped the drool from the corner of my mouth. "I think we need to go to Waffle House."

The group chuckled.

"I know y'all need to get home soon, but I'm glad everyone was able to make it. I'll keep our meeting brief." Patsy gave us a kind smile. "Storms can leave us isolated and that can be difficult. Please reach out if you find yourself struggling."

I'd flipped my calendar to August earlier this week, making me aware of another looming storm—my brother leaving town with my child.

"Patsy's right," Gilbert said. "You can call me too if you need to. I've got a canoe. I'll come to you if need be." You'd think he was joking but the man said it in all seriousness. "Just because this storm might cause a calamity, doesn't give you a pass to cause one too."

"I have bread, Danishes, and croissants for everyone, so at least we won't starve." Chris Evans placed a large box on the table and started passing around steaming bags filled with freshly baked goods. "I've been nervous-baking all day."

"Well good, because I've been nervous-munching all day and already polished off most of our storm snacks." Jackée lifted the loaf of sourdough and inhaled the aroma with great appreciation. Chris

Evans slid her two extra loaves and she gave him a giant smile. "My boys are gonna be fightin' over this. Thank you."

It was almost undetectable with his dark skin, but I caught a hint of Chris Evans blushing. I met Patsy's eyes and we shared a knowing smile.

Patsy went over a few pointers to help us stay distracted during the storm. "Play card games. Read a book. Or just take naps. It's the perfect time to catch up on your rest. Self-care and all that, ya know."

We said our goodbyes but Gilbert stopped me at the door. "Will Henry be around just in case the storm gets rough?"

I held back the retort that a man could protect me from a hurricane no better than anyone else. "No. He's out of town, but I'll be fine." I'd received my daily prayer text three days ago with the addition of him letting me know he was visiting family for the next week. Still not quite over him lying to me, I simply sent a thumbs-up emoji.

"Well, you know I'm just up the road if you need me." Gilbert gave me a sturdy side hug and it was all I could do not to lean in. I hoped Gilbert's son knew how lucky he was to call this man *Dad*.

"Yes, sir. And if you need me, I'm just down the road." I gave him one last squeeze and let go. I flipped the hood of my raincoat up and did a mad dash to the Caddy.

A thick sheet of rain made the task of getting home safely a little more tricky, but I made it in one piece. I parked as close to the house as possible, did my best at tucking the food underneath the raincoat, and darted up the porch steps. Placing the bread and pastries onto the chair by the door, I shucked the coat and draped it over the back of the chair. As I kicked off the rainboots, a shiver raced up my neck. I turned and peered out at the dark front yard, only finding the palmetto trees swaying in the brisk wind.

Shaking my head, I keyed in the code for the door and eased it open, silently reprimanding myself for forgetting to turn some lights on before I left. The clouds had shown up and ran off the sun early, leaving me with a dark house full of thick shadows. Gathering my belongings from the chair, I walked inside and stood there for a moment, listening to the house groan its grievances with the weather.

I think it's gonna be a long, long time . . .

The line from "Rocket Man" popped in my head and started on repeat.

I think it's gonna be a long, long time . . .

I wondered if it was too late to beg Cy to let me go stay with them during the storm. I'd had my opportunity this morning when he called to check on me but I'd chickened out. Heaving an antsy sigh, I moved away from the door and headed for the kitchen.

A shadow shifted just as I turned into the kitchen. Blinking to refocus my eyes, I peered at it again, only to find it charging my way. I choked on a scream as arms wrapped around me, knocking the bread and pastries to the floor.

"Boo!" Deaton's mocking voice struck me like a hot iron. He laughed.

Furious, I shoved him off and flipped on the light switch. "What are you doing in my house?"

"To surprise you!" He laughed. "We need a hurricane party."

"Are you high?" I asked, knowing the answer. His twitching and blown pupils gave it away. I reversed a step. "You're trespassing. Either get out or I'm calling the police."

"But I'm bored. I wanna play a game." The crooked smirk disappeared and a dark expression came over him. I turned to run as he lunged for me, knocking into my back and nearly sending us both to the floor.

"Let go!" I wrestled with him, trying to wiggle free. The treats ended up mushed in the tussle and that made me even madder. I shoved my hand into my bag to search for my phone, but Deaton snatched it and threw it across the room.

"Let's have some fun, Sassy." Using his entire body, Deaton propelled me forward. His arm wrapped around me until his hand rested on my shoulder and then I felt the cold press of metal to the side of my neck.

I began to tremble. "Is that a g-gun? Are you *crazy*?"

"Just a little." He chuckled, raspy like brittle fall leaves. His hold on my shoulder became more of a pinch.

"You're hurting me."

Deaton leaned closer, filling the space with the sharp scent of sweat and something else that reminded me of rehab. A sourness that didn't wash off so easily. "You brought this on yourself."

"How?" I blinked rapidly but my eyes refused to focus.

"I only wanted you to give me a freaking chance." He skimmed his nose along my hair, the action too intimate. "I've tried all summer to get you to just talk to me. We could be fun together if you'd just loosen up."

I highly doubted talking was the only thing he wanted but went along with it. "Fine. We can talk. J-just put the gun away and . . ."

"Be a good girl and go sit on the couch." He shoved me in that direction and I shuffled to the couch on weak legs. With the gun still aimed at my head, he pulled out a pair of handcuffs.

I choked on air. "You don't need to cuff me."

He laughed, cackling. "Yeah, right. You're too sassy for submission." Licking his lips, his eyes skimmed my body. "That's too bad . . . Now hold out your hands."

With no other choice, I did as Deaton said and he secured the handcuffs around my wrists. At least he placed them in front of me and not behind my back. I regarded him as he sat on the coffee table in front of me. Wild red eyes, bottom lip chewed raw, a sore beneath his right nostril, dark circles under his eyes. He'd lost weight since I saw him last.

"Deaton . . . are you okay?"

He sniffed and hitched a shoulder, not quite a shrug, more like a twitch. "Yeah, babe. I thought we could have us a hurricane party." Gun in one hand, he fiddled with his phone until music started playing ridiculously loud.

"When's the last time you've slept?" I asked, raising my voice over the song.

Tilting his head, Deaton stared at the ceiling and chewed on his bottom lip. "Not sure."

"Why don't we have some hurricane snacks, then rest a while before the storm arrives."

"Nah . . . I'm not hungry." He jumped to his feet and began an anxious pace around the room.

"These cuffs . . ." I wiggled my wrists, the metal clanking together, biting into my skin. "They're too tight. Can you loosen them some?"

Deaton shook his head in an exaggerated motion. "It's the only way I can make you get still. You've been like a scared little mouse, sneaking around and scurrying away every time you've seen me lately." Squinting his glassy eyes, he chuckled. "Gotta keep you still somehow."

Anger scorched through me, but I forced a wobbly smile, figuring my best bet was to play along. "You could've sprung for the fur-lined cuffs at least."

"I thought about it." He chuckled again, nearly tipping sideways, and went back to pacing.

"Come on, Deaton. Take these off, please."

"You've ignored me all summer. I don't like to be ignored." Mouth twisted, he waved the gun toward me from across the room. "Do you think you're too good for me?"

Was this really about a case of a bruised ego more than anything else?

"No! I'm the one not good enough for *you*. Seriously, we've talked about this. You need someone who doesn't have the baggage like—"

"That's enough!" Deaton stormed over and glared down at me, the gun pointing to my chest. A reminder for me to tread carefully. "I'm so sick of your brush-offs."

I buttoned my lips and nodded.

"Good. Just shut up. Shut up, shut up, shut up."

With the music still blaring, he returned to circling around the living room. Like a caged animal, agitated and unable to get still. The sensation of things moving too fleetingly to process had me off-kilter. At some point, I lost the feeling in my hands.

"Deaton, I can't feel my hands. Please loosen them a little."

It took me asking a few more times, but he finally did. He studied the red marks blooming around the metal, as if he couldn't fathom what caused it.

"Poor baby," he murmured, kissing each wrist.

I withdrew from his touch and let out a heavy yawn, feeling my body sway. "I'm really tired."

Tucking the gun in the waist of his pants, Deaton pulled out a small vial and tapped a small mound of white powder on top of his hand. He leaned forward and sniffed and the mound disappeared in a flash. He sighed, then licked the residue away. "You want a bump, babe? It'll wake you up."

I shook my head, a bitterness rising into my throat.

"Come on . . . Don't be a party pooper."

"I need to pass my drug test or I'll go back to prison, but you enjoy."

"More for me then!" Deaton cranked the music up. My sore wrists forgotten, he grabbed them and yanked me off the couch. Wincing, I held back a yelp and danced as he instructed, just thankful he didn't force the drugs on me. "Come on, Sassy. Gotta wake you up for our hurricane party!"

If this guy says hurricane party one more time . . . !

With no other choice, I danced with him, listening to his cackling laughter and repeated words over the loud music. It was maddening and my head spun.

Sometime around three in the morning, the storm showed up in a rage, knocking the power out. Finally, Deaton turned the music off, leaving my ears ringing. We listened to the wind howl and rain squalls slap against the windows. I was beyond the point of sleepy, that otherworldly place where you're too exhausted to feel the fatigue.

"There are some flameless candles on the shelf in the laundry room," I told him, not wanting to sit in the dark with a tweaking drug addict. I contemplated making a run for it while he left the room, but the threat of a bullet stopping me kept me pinned to the couch.

Deaton fetched the candles and set them around the living room. "This is romantic." He looked over his shoulder and winked at me.

Kidnapping me is romantic? I think not.

He returned to the couch and placed his hand on my knee.

My body stiffened. "Please don't do that, Deaton."

He shoved off my knee and glared at me. "We could have a good time, enjoy each other like we did that one night, if you'd just loosen up!" He started up pacing the room again, hurling explicit names at me. *Stuck-up this, snobby that . . .* Fine by me, as long as he kept his hands to himself he could call me all the names.

Eventually he shut up and just marched around in a zig-zag pattern. Mid-pace he stopped and cocked his head to the side. "What is that noise?"

I listened for a few beats. "Rain and wind."

He shook his head and stumbled a bit sideways. "No. The other noise."

I angled my head and listened again. "I don't hear anything else."

"Yes, you do!"

Oh shoot. Was he starting to hallucinate?

His eyes darted wildly around the room. "That ticking! Something's ticking! Tick, tick, tick!"

I finally picked up on the sound. "It's just the clock."

"Well, it's driving me crazy! Where is it?"

"The back hall."

Grabbing a candle, Deaton stormed out of the room. I jumped up and followed him and watched in horror as he reared back and punched the clockface.

"Deaton! No!"

In a blind rage, he punched it again and this time the glass shattered.

"Stop! I'll turn it off. Please stop!" I took a chance and pulled him by the back of his shirt.

His hand flew to his waistband and yanked out the gun.

"J-just step back and I'll make it stop. P-please!"

He stumbled out of the way. "Shut it off! I can't take much more!"

With trembling hands, I opened the bottom case and pulled the weights until they rested on the bottom of the clock floor, then I stopped the pendulum. I wanted to scream at him and punch him as hard as he punched my clock, but I took a breath and calmed myself as best as I could.

"See. It stopped." I looked behind me when he didn't respond. "Deaton?"

"I'm bleeding," he said in a bewildered tone, his attention on his hand.

I took a cautious step closer and saw a stream of blood dripping down his arm. I had a good mind not to bandage him up but I didn't want blood all over the place, ruining even more of my grandmother's precious home. "Let's move to the kitchen. There's a first aid kit in there."

"'Kay."

"Does it feel like there's glass in the cuts?" I plundered under the sink and pulled out the red box.

"Dunno."

"Okay. Well, let's rinse it and then I can wrap it with gauze." I cleaned the wounds the best I could. The dim light made it hard to assess the cuts but I thought they weren't too deep. The idiot would survive. I wrapped his hand, then secured it with tape.

"You're too good to me, Junie," Deaton slurred. "You fixed my hand."

Wanting to keep him calm, I said, "Of course. You're my friend."

"That's all I've wanted." He looked so sad that I wanted to reach out and comfort him, but decided against it. Deaton moved me to the couch and sat next to me, his knee bobbing up and down, jostling the entire couch. "I'm heading out of town soon. Got some friends up in Colorado."

"What do you plan on doing in Colorado?" I figured I just needed to keep him talking until the high wore off enough for him to pass out.

"My buddy is starting up a river excursion business. I'm thinking about going in on it with him." Deaton scooted closer, sadness gone with excitement in its place. "You should come with me."

"I can't. My daughter is here."

He snorted. "No she isn't. You lost custody of her."

That stung so deep, it made my eyes water. I bowed my head to avoid his scrutiny. "I'm working on getting her back."

"Don't you think she's better off where she's at?" Deaton brushed my hair out of my face, gripped my chin, and forced me to meet his eyes. "We can just disappear. Start over, yeah?"

Hating that he stirred my doubts and insecurities, I bit down on the inside of my lip to the point it should have hurt but I felt nothing. Too numb to do anything but bite down hard.

"Now you're bleeding!" His bloodshot eyes widened.

I licked my lips. "I'm okay."

"Stop that." Deaton rose to his feet. "I'll grab a washcloth."

Watching him go straight to the bathroom, something niggled in the back of my lethargic mind. He was way too familiar with my house. When he returned with a washcloth, I said, "You've been in my house before."

He hitched a shoulder. "A few times."

"How?"

"I saw you put in the code that day we went to Mex 1."

"But that didn't give you the right to break into my home."

He didn't seem to hear me or just didn't care. Instead, he crouched in front of me and started cleaning my chin and lips. There was goodness in him, in a twisted way.

Deaton leaned closer. "What are you thinking, Sassy?"

"You're not a bad person, Deaton. The gun and handcuffs . . . this isn't you."

He frowned. "How do you know?"

"Most people aren't bad, I don't think. Just good people who have done bad things. Me included. I'm a good person who's done bad. Arlo, my late husband, was a good person too. Just made a lot of bad choices. You remind me of him."

Deaton's expression morphed into a more somber one. "You really think I'm good?"

"Yes. But you're making some bad choices." I raised my cuffed wrists.

He stared at the handcuffs for several long beats and I thought maybe I'd reached him, but then he handed me the washcloth and went to stand by the window. His silence didn't last long, nor did him standing still. Moving around the room for hours, he retold me about going to Colorado to start up a business venture with his friend.

A dim morning showed up, barely making itself known as the storm churned over the top of us. Seemed it had no plans on leaving us alone. As Deaton twirled the gun in his grasp, over and over, I concluded he had no plans of leaving me alone either.

Sometime midmorning, I heard my phone go off in my bag somewhere on the floor and wondered who was calling. Gilbert? Cy? Would they think it odd that I didn't answer? Would they come out in the storm to check on me?

"When is that power coming back on? It's so hot in here." Deaton wiped his sweaty face with the back of his hand, the gun still in his grip. He'd yet to put it down. "I can't breathe!" Tremors overtook his body.

"Why don't you sit down and rest a bit?"

He slammed his fist down hard against an end table, making me jump. "Why don't you shut up!"

The mood swings grew worse by midday and Deaton took up rambling about how terrible his father was.

"That man has never loved me. He's always treated me like I was an embarrassment! He's a bigwig, thinks I'm not good enough!" Deaton yelled and ranted until his voice grew hoarse. The day had started slipping away by the time that happened and he finally shut up, just sitting beside me, swaying.

My eyes burned but I didn't take them off of him or the gun as he rocked, even when his motion threatened to lull me. I'd worked out a pattern of blinking, widening my eyes, blinking again, watching, waiting, blinking, praying for this to be over.

Deaton finally picked up a pattern of his own. His head bobbed forward a few times before he'd jolt awake. His pattern didn't last too long. One last bob, then his body slumped like a felled tree against the armrest.

I contemplated just lying back and giving in to sleep too. My body felt like lead weights were holding me to the couch, but eventually I managed to scoot off. I checked to make sure he didn't wake and sighed when he hadn't budged. The gun had slipped out of his hand and was now wedged between the cushions. I was terrified of the gun but more terrified to leave it with him, so I went at it like a game of Jenga, ever so slowly sliding the gun free. Deaton shifted and his leg brushed against my arm. I froze, studying his face. Thankfully, his eyes remained shut.

Without bothering to look for a key for the handcuffs, I tiptoed over to my bag. Another glance over my shoulder showed he remained asleep. Holding my breath, I tucked the gun into my bag. On shaky legs that felt close to buckling, I moved to the front door and almost knocked over the lamp on the entry table. It wobbled but I placed my palms on either side to steady it. With sweat trickling between my shoulder blades, my instinct urged me to run screaming, but I tamped it down and, quiet as the mouse Deaton claimed me to be, I scurried right outside.

Dodging broken tree limbs and other debris I didn't take the time to catalog, I stumbled over to Henry's porch and dialed 911.

The next hour turned into a blur of blue lights and commotion. As a uniformed man put Deaton into the back of a cop car, I thought about Gilbert telling us not to cause a calamity during the storm, yet that was exactly what happened. He was going to be so disappointed in me.

"Ma'am," a police officer spoke, drawing me out of my haze. He held the gun I'd handed over to them earlier. "Just wanted to let you know this is a pellet gun and it didn't even have any pellets in it."

I rubbed my sore wrist. "Is that supposed to make me feel better? That I was held against my will with a fake gun?"

He had enough grace to blush. "No, ma'am. What he did is against the law, the federal law at that. I just wanted you to know."

"Thank you for telling me."

"Sure thing." He tipped his head and walked away. "Oh, and the power's back on."

After the police left with Deaton, I locked the house up as securely as I could, going as far as shoving chairs underneath the doorknobs. I moved upstairs at a snail's pace. The adrenaline from earlier had seared through my system and now I was close to crashing. I turned the shower on and then stood staring into the bathroom mirror while waiting for the water to heat.

It made no sense to have someone like Deaton James infatuated with me. My green eyes weren't dull but far from sparkling. Lips formed well enough to do their job assisting me with eating, drinking, and talking, but neither plump nor pillow soft. Chapped most of the time. At the moment my plain blonde hair was much more ratty than normal due to the night's horrific events.

Shaking my head, I moved away from the unassuming reflection and stepped into the shower. Clearly, Deaton's infatuation spawned from wanting something he couldn't have. Like me wanting a muscle relaxer or pain pill or shot of tequila at the moment to alleviate all the hurts currently housed inside and outside me.

37

It's darkest before the dawn. I'm not sure it's scientifically correct, considering I'd sat outside in the dark and watched the sky gradually lighten before dawn, but I understood the expression, nonetheless. I'd just lived out the darkest part and could only hope things were about to get better somehow.

The light of a new day revealed the aftermath of the storm. Palm fronds littered the muddy yard and puddled street. A broken tree limb, a beach ball that didn't belong to me. The aftermath of my own storm still lingered. Bruised with a weariness that I wished didn't belong to me too.

I blinked against the grittiness of my eyes. I needed to go inside and get some rest, but my brain was like a live wire as it tried processing everything I'd just gone through. I could hardly believe it actually happened. Easing my sleeve up, I studied the red and purple rings around my wrist, proof that it had.

A black Suburban with blacked-out windows pulled into my driveway, barely missing the downed tree limb. Too late to dart inside, I stayed put and slid my sleeve back down.

Three men exited the vehicle and started toward the porch.

"May I help you?" I asked as they reached the stairs.

"I'm Congressman George Michaels."

A snicker slipped out and I blamed it on sleep deprivation. "George Michael?"

"Michael*s*." He stressed the *s*, making a hissing sound. He yanked off his aviator sunglasses and leveled me with a look. "I'd like to talk with you about last night's incident."

My guard instantly went up. Why would a politician be about police business? "The authorities have taken care of it." I tried to inflect some steel in my declaration but I was too drained to properly pull it off. More like a flimsy piece of floral wire that had been twisted and unwound one too many times.

Before I could ask them to leave, I heard the rumble of a fast-approaching sports car, loud enough it drew all of our attention. The Corvette wheeled into Henry's empty driveway and came to an abrupt stop, then Gilbert sprung from the driver's side. He broke out in an angry-man fast walk as if on a mission to kick butts and take names. My waning confidence rallied.

"Who are you?" Gilbert demanded as he came to a stop in the muddy yard.

"I'm Congressman Michaels and I'm here to speak with Miss Wilder on what transpired here last night."

I noticed he forwent sharing his first name this time.

Gilbert didn't seem impressed. "Last night? I just read the police report. Try two and a half days, not counting the other incidents where your son broke into Miss Wilder's house."

"Son?" My eyes volleyed between Gilbert and the congressman.

"And you are?" Michaels asked Gilbert.

"You know who she is and how to find her, so I'm pretty sure you know who I am as well." Gilbert moved up the steps and stood beside me.

Michaels huffed, unimpressed. "You're the probation officer?"

Gilbert didn't confirm. "The police are handling what your son did. You have no right being here."

"Deaton is your son?" I asked Michaels, since no one answered me the last time.

"Yes. My son goes by his mother's last name. We thought that was for the best, considering the stupid stuff he likes to pull." He rolled his eyes.

"Stupid stuff . . . like kidnapping?" I asked, furious that he would downplay such crimes.

"Amongst other things, yes."

"Oh, you mean the gun?" I tried again and got another eye roll.

"It was a pellet gun," one of the other suits muttered.

"She didn't know that!" Gilbert balled his fists.

Michaels glanced around the yard. "May we go inside and discuss this?"

"No," Gilbert and I said at the same time.

I eased slightly behind Gilbert. "I'm not comfortable with strangers in my home, not after what Deaton just did."

Michaels sighed. "I just want to make things right. What will it take for you to not press charges?"

I thought about it for a second and the answer came fairly quickly. "Just make sure he never steps foot in Charleston County again, or South Carolina for that matter."

"He's on his way to a facility in Hawaii. Shouldn't be a problem."

My eyes narrowed, not quite believing him. "Hawaii? The police left with him in handcuffs just hours ago."

One of the suits spoke. "Didn't take long to put him on a private flight. You should be happy about that."

"*Happy?* Oh, thank you so much." I crossed my arms but flinched in pain and dropped them back to my sides. "How can you guarantee he won't jump on another plane and be back here tonight?"

"I've taken his credit cards, his license, and passport. He's basically stuck there." Michaels ran a hand through his thinning hair. He appeared as exhausted as I felt. "I'm really hoping this new treatment facility will help him."

"For what it's worth, I do too." I remembered the rehab counselor saying that around forty to sixty percent of people in treatment for substance abuse will relapse. Not a very encouraging estimate at all.

I turned to go inside but paused as Gilbert spoke up. "Your son stole Junie's sense of security. I think the least you can do is pay to restore it."

Michaels hesitated, eyes flicking to me then to Gilbert. "How?"

"New locks and a security system for her house. And you can pay for the security services for as long as you remain in office."

"That might be years," one of the goons grouched.

"I'm sure it will still be the cheapest cover-up Congressman Michaels will ever have to pay for." Gilbert gave him a stern glare.

"Fine." Michaels looked at me. "Is that it?"

"He broke the glass in my grandmother clock. I need that fixed."

Michaels sighed and scrubbed a hand down his face, the diamond in his signet ring flashing in the sunlight. "Did he break anything else?"

Deaton broke something in me, but I didn't think any amount of money could patch that up. "No. Just the clock."

Michaels turned to the guy on the left. "Do a quick estimate on the cost and write her a check."

The guy walked over to the SUV, splashing mud on the back of his suit pants. Minutes later, he returned with a check from some private corporation I'd never heard of, I'm assuming so it couldn't be traced back to the congressman. I gladly took it, needing to reestablish safety in a house that would soon be home to my daughter if all went well.

"I really am sorry for what Deaton put you through." Michaels handed me a business card. "My personal number is on the back. If you hear anything from him at all, you let me know and I'll take care of it."

I glanced at the card, then stacked it on top of the check. "Thank you."

Gilbert and I remained on the porch until the SUV disappeared out of sight.

Walking into the living room, I placed the check and business card on the coffee table and sat on the couch. I rubbed my eyes and yawned. "Thank you for being here."

He waved my appreciation off, as if it were no big deal. "You have the mobile deposit app?"

"Yes, sir."

"Good. Get that check deposited while I go grab new locks." He started toward the door. "And try to get a little rest while I'm gone."

"You don't have to. I'll go do that." I rose too fast and swayed a bit on my feet.

Gilbert shook his head and left without responding, so I sat back down before I keeled over. There I remained until gathering enough gumption to grab my phone and deposit the check.

I hated to face the destruction in the back hallway, but that glass needed to be cleaned up, so I grabbed the broom and dustpan. I kept my focus on the floor, sweeping up the shards, but once that was done I lifted my gaze and took in the broken top glass.

"It's fixable," I assured myself. I opened the bottom case and wrapped my fist around the first chain, pulling until the weight reached the top, then doing the same with the other two chains. With a shaky hand, I nudged the pendulum. Seconds later, the ticktock began as tears streamed down my cheeks. I wished Cy were here, instructing me on how to fix what just occurred here, but I couldn't involve him. This was my mess to clean up. Even though my life seemed just as shattered as this glass, I felt it was all fixable. I'd come too far for it not to be.

After throwing the broken glass away, I took some ibuprofen and hurried through another shower in hopes it would wake me up enough to help Gilbert change the locks. By the time I made it down the stairs, Gilbert had returned.

He handed me the heavy hardware-store bag. "There's more. Be right back."

I placed the bag on the kitchen island and looked for the receipt but didn't find it. "I need the receipt so I can pay you back," I said as I heard the door reopen. I turned when he didn't answer, finding him carrying two Taco Bell Party Packs. "I'm hungry but not that hungry."

Gilbert handed the boxes off and left out again. This time he came back with two more Party Packs and a group of my favorite people. The entire Magnolia Nephalist Society crew shuffled in, carrying stuff I couldn't make out due to the tears flooding my eyes.

"What are y'all doing here?"

"We're in the mood for Taco Bell," Bruno said, giving me a side hug.

"And cookies," I heard Chris Evans say as Jackée wrapped me in a fierce hug. "I've already made the salted caramel dough. We just need to bake them."

"Great," Gilbert commented. "Let's eat the tacos, then the ladies can help Chris with the cookies while Bruno and Axil help me change the locks."

I eased away from Jackée, only to be accosted by Patsy.

"Are you okay, darlin'?"

"I think so . . ." I rested my head on Patsy's shoulder, taking in the comforting scent of her fancy perfume. "I'm more mad than anything." I straightened. "And having to use the bathroom in handcuffs? Zero out of ten, would not recommend."

Pearl hobbled over, relying heavily on her cane, and wrapped an arm around my waist. "If you can make jokes, then you'll be okay."

"Maybe you're the one we need to worry about being okay or not. How'd you manage getting up the tall steps outside?"

"I'm fine. Gilbert said I just have a hitch in my giddy-up." Pearl straightened her purple glasses. "I'll be even better after a few tacos."

"I brought Things!" Mei held up the game box, one I'd never played before. "We can play it after we eat and while the cookies bake. It's so fun!"

By the time we all had plates heaping with tacos, my world began to feel a little more level.

With the room filled with the delicious aroma of freshly baked cookies and lots of lighthearted chatter, I realized by early evening what this group had done. They'd chased away the bad memories from the last few days and replaced them with the warmth of friendship, support, and comfort.

While cleaning up, Patsy and Mei went outside, then returned with small suitcases.

"What are you two doing?" I asked, tossing a wayward taco wrapper and napkin into the trash.

"We're having a sleepover," Patsy answered, looking around. "Where can we put our stuff, suga'?"

"Y'all have already done so much. You don't have to stay with me too."

Patsy started toward the stairs. "All the rooms upstairs?"

I followed, knowing her mind was made up. "Yes, ma'am."

I offered Patsy Olla's room and put Mei in Cy's. By the time I went downstairs to lock up, the guys were gone and Gilbert was settling on the couch. He'd changed into a pair of lounge pants and a T-shirt.

"You staying too?"

"Just for tonight. You need some sleep and we thought you'd be more likely to do that if you had some company."

Close to tears again, I went to the laundry room and pulled a pillow and quilt from the linen cabinet and brought them to Gilbert. "Gilbert, you know you're my best friend, right?"

"Sure am, kid." Gilbert wrapped his arms around me and I felt protected in a way a daughter would in the arms of her father. "You're gonna be okay." He held me at arm's length, meeting my eyes, and said, "The Bible says, *We can rejoice, too, when we run into problems and trials, for we know that they help us develop endurance.*"

I huffed a laugh. "I have to be in the best shape of my life then."

"Of course you are. I'm your personal trainer, after all."

I grimaced. "How'd you know I called you that?"

"Henry told me."

"Figures, the snitch." I dried my face on my shirtsleeve, yawning loudly.

"Go get some rest. When you're all caught up, us two are going to have a heart-to-heart on forgiving that boy."

I didn't consider a thirty-four-year-old man a *boy* but didn't feel up to arguing with Gilbert. "I'll think about it."

I went to bed and slept for a solid year straight. Well, not really, but it felt that way.

38

Some people say they were born knowing what they wanted to do with their lives, having a direction from the get-go. Not me. I was born without a compass and it had taken me quite some time to develop one, but I truly felt I was on my way to figuring out my direction. Even while walking Jazzy and Beau, I could sense it happening. No more drifting.

After returning the dogs, I went out to the deck for a little break. Moving to the edge, I reached out to grip the railing and flinched away from a sharp sting, realizing too late that the rosebush had claimed that section.

"Ouch." I flipped my hand over and noticed a thorn stuck in the center of my palm. Mom would have corrected me, saying this was a prickle, not a thorn. Either way, I held my breath, pinched the sharp nuisance between my finger and thumb and plucked it out. As a small bead of blood formed, I recalled that verse about a thorn in the flesh. Somewhere in Second Corinthians, I think. I'd heard varying thoughts on what troubled Paul. Some said the thorn was a sickness, some said it was a sin. Others pointed out that Paul actually told us what the thorn was to some degree, that it was a messenger from Satan to torment him. I didn't claim to be a theologian, but I could relate to the messenger tormenting me. Not a day went by that the devil wasn't in my ear, tearing me down.

You're a nobody.

A screwup.

You'll never stay clean.

You're the worst mother ever.

Some days I believed my tormentor's lies. That I would fail again and again. That Fern deserved better than me. That I had no right to want her. But I was finally starting to realize those days I had to lean into the truths even more. No matter how many mistakes, fails, stumbles, thorns, I was still a child of the heavenly Father and nothing could pluck me out of his hands.

I placed my thumb over the wound, applying pressure, and moved inside.

On the coffee table, my phone screen lit up with an incoming text message from Henry. He'd been out of town but never missed his morning prayer text. He'd already sent the daily text, so I wasn't certain about this one. Curious, I thumbed it open.

I'm on your porch. I have a surprise but you have to PROMISE not to freak out. Brace yourself and answer the door.

I reread it twice and wasn't all that certain how one braces themselves. Winging it, I took a few deep breaths and rotated my shoulders. Opening the door, I said, "Please don't have me a dog . . ." I froze at the sight before me.

"I thought this was the only way to properly apologize to you." Henry placed his hand on Fern's tiny shoulder. I began to get choked up but he shook his head. "Not in front of your little company. You can do that afterwards."

Gasping for air, I knelt in front of her and grinned, taking in her neat pigtails and pink floral sundress. "Fernie!"

She clung to Henry's leg, looking uncertain in a way that tore my heart out. *My child doesn't even know me.*

"So we stopped by Walmart and got lots of sand toys and Aunt Lana packed us a picnic. Would you like to spend the day on the beach with us?"

Sniffing, I nodded, then cleared the knot from my throat. "I'd love to."

"Great." Henry patted Fern's shoulder. "Fernie, how about you stay here with your mom and I'll go get your toys."

Fern looked at me curiously, her green eyes so assessing, reminding me so much of myself and Arlo. Then she reached for me and my world tilted so severely that I think it righted for the first time. I picked up my daughter, pressed a kiss to her smooth cheek, and carried her inside, marveling at how I could so easily carry my whole world right here in my arms.

"I love you, Fernie." I kissed the side of her forehead and breathed in the sweet almond scent, pleasantly surprised that Lana still used my favorite baby shampoo.

Henry came through the door with a small toilet seat. "Lana said to have Fernie try to use the bathroom as soon as we got here. She said this fits right on top of the regular toilet."

"Oh, Fernie, you're potty training. That's so great!" I'd missed so much.

"While you do that, I'm going to run next door to change. Be right back."

I helped Fern in the bathroom, praising her for doing a good job. She smiled, showing off her daddy's dimples. "I a big girl."

"Yes, you are!"

Soon Henry returned and I went upstairs to change too, choosing an old long-sleeved rash guard shirt to wear over my bikini top. Most of the bruises around my wrists had healed and only a few spots remained yellow, but I didn't want to explain them. It still seemed surreal what transpired here just a week ago.

After we gathered everything, we made our way to the beach. From the outside, I'm sure we looked like a perfect family and I would have loved it to be true.

"Okay, who wants to help me build a sea turtle?"

Henry straightened his glasses. "A sea turtle?"

"Yep." I grabbed a bucket and started filling it with wet sand. "Come on. We'll need lots of sand."

We filled and dumped the wet sand into a pile and as we worked, my little girl hummed and it was the most precious thing.

"She does that a lot," Henry commented, noticing me watching her.

I sat back on my haunches and wiped the sweat off my brow. "You've spent a lot of time with her?"

Henry continued digging. "I have recently, yes."

"Why?"

He stopped and used the back of his hand to push his glasses up his nose. "I wanted to get to know her and also . . ." He glanced at Fern. She seemed lost in her own world, humming and digging. "I wanted to try talking some sense into your stubborn brother."

At a loss for words, I went back to forming a wide dome of sand. Fern eventually scooted into my lap and placed her hands near mine and we both worked together, smoothing the sand. I tried staying in the moment, cherishing each minute gifted to me, but my heart ached, knowing I'd have to let her go at the end of the day.

"I hungwy."

I glanced down at her and smiled. "You are?"

She nodded, making her pigtails bounce around.

"Let's see what Aunt Lana made us." I helped Fern to her feet and stood, taking the time to brush off as much sand as possible, then moved to the blanket where the cooler bag sat. I began pulling everything out—neatly packed ham sandwiches, sliced cucumbers, bags of chips, sliced peaches, and a little container filled with ketchup. "What's the ketchup for?"

"Cukes!" Fern said, scooping up the bag of cucumbers.

I laughed. "Oh my gosh. Cucumbers dipped in ketchup is what I craved while I was pregnant with you, Fernie girl."

"Seriously?" Henry joined us on the blanket, looking right doubtful.

"Don't knock it until you try it." I opened the container and dunked a piece of cucumber into the ketchup, then handed it to Fern. She didn't even hesitate before popping it into her mouth.

Henry curled his lip.

Unperturbed, I dunked a slice and chomped down. The flavor brought back so many memories: my first bout of morning sickness, the first time I felt the butterfly dance that was my baby inside me, the first strong kick—thankfully, Arlo got to experience her kicks before he died—the first contraction, the first time I held my baby in my arms.

"Are you okay? Is that weird mess making you sick?"

Blinking back tears, I looked up at Henry and shook my head. "Just memories visiting me. Lots and lots of memories." Needing to ground myself, I leaned over and kissed the side of Fern's head and handed her another cucumber. Getting my act together, I divvied out our lunches.

Once we were done eating, Fern began to yawn.

Henry placed the empty containers into the cooler bag. "We probably need to let the little lady rest some."

"There's an umbrella in the garage. You want to go get it, and we could take a break out here?"

"Sounds like a plan." Henry dusted his hands and hurried up the beach to the garage. He rejoined us with the blue-striped beach umbrella. He placed it over the blanket and the three of us stretched out. Surprisingly, Fern gave us no trouble, just curled next to me and started playing in my hair as if each strand made up her favorite security blanket—something else she used to do before I lost her.

Henry rolled to his side and smoothed her pigtail away from her face. "She's special."

Smiling, I tucked Fern closer to me. "Yeah?"

"Of course. She's a lot like her mother." Henry reached to smooth my hair, much like he just did Fern's. "She loves to draw. Cy's fridge is covered in squiggly pictures. And she does that thing like you do where you run your thumb over the top of your fingernails." He touched the tips of my nails.

"I can't believe you even noticed that."

"There's not much about you I haven't noticed." Entwining our hands, Henry whispered, "There's something else you two have in common."

Grinning like a fool, I whispered, "What's that?"

He scooted a little closer, as if he were about to share the grandest secret ever. "She really hates coffee."

I snorted out a laugh, jostling Fern a bit, but she kept on snoozing.

With a slow wink, Henry yawned, and soon his eyes closed for a while. The lull of the ocean waves and the caress of the sunshine tempted me to sleep too, but I didn't dare give in to it. I remained attentive, taking in my two favorite people sleeping so contentedly, and prayed a miracle would show up where I could keep them both. Sure, Henry had hurt me, but now I'd begun to see what he did from his perspective. If he'd not concealed his connection with Cy, I may never had gotten to know him on the level I did this summer.

Soon, too soon, it was time to return Fern to Columbia.

We put away the beach day and after changing Fern into some dry clothes for the trip home, I started crying. The tears wouldn't stop falling out of my eyes, but I kept on smiling, probably looking a bit deranged.

"Why don't you ride with us?" Henry suggested.

I looked up from folding Fern's beach towel. "You sure?"

"Absolutely." He picked up Fern and bopped her on the tip of her nose, making her giggle. "Fernie, would you like Mommy to ride with us?"

"Yep, yep!"

"Okay." I finished packing her bag and gladly jumped in Henry's Jeep.

We sang nursery rhymes most of the way, and completely off-key.

All too soon, we pulled into Cy's driveway and he met us outside.

"Hi," Cy said awkwardly.

"Hey," I said much in the same weird tone.

"Unka Cy!" Fern nearly squealed. "We got a sea turtle!"

He scooped her up and gave us a quizzical look. "You did?"

"We made a *sand* sea turtle," I corrected.

Henry whipped out his phone to show off pictures he took of our creation. "Pretty neat, right?"

Cy glanced in my direction, then back to the phone. "Yeah."

Lana appeared at the door and ushered us inside. "Fern, let's go potty." She held Fern's hand and started down the hallway with me following.

I should have thought of that, taking my daughter first thing, and felt chastised even though I hadn't been. "Fern did a great job today. No accidents."

Lana grinned at my daughter. "She's been so much easier to potty train than Alex was. I didn't think he'd ever get the hang of it. But not this little lady. She's caught on really quick."

"Thank you, Lana, for . . . everything. Fern's blessed to have you."

Lana's grin settled into more of a thoughtful smile. "Fern is a blessing to us. We love her."

I nodded, wanting to say I loved her too, but this wasn't a competition and I feared I'd get upset. I was already walking a fine line with my emotions.

Once we were finished in the bathroom, we joined the guys and Alex in the living room where a wall of moving boxes reminded me of their impending departure. Instead of sitting on the couch or in a chair, everyone stood, making it clear we were not invited to stay awhile.

"I guess we better head back. Cy, thanks for today." Henry placed a hand on my shoulder and gave me a soft nudge, the gesture making it clear it was time to go, but that was the last thing I wanted to do.

I squatted in front of Fern. "I love you, Fernie," I said, giving her what I'd hoped was an easy smile. She wrapped her little arms around my neck and squeezed. I hugged her until Cy cleared his throat. "I'll see you soon," I whispered, then let go, even though my heart begged me not to. I unglued my feet and allowed Henry to steer me out the door.

We had just made it down the steps when the door opened and shut behind us. I turned and saw Cy standing there.

Cy cleared his throat. "I was thinking . . . If it's okay with you, we want to spend the weekend at the beach house."

I perked up. "Of course. It's your house too."

Cy nodded. "Okay. Well, we'll see you Friday."

"Okay." I heard the Jeep crank behind me. "I guess I better go."

"Junie . . ."

I paused and looked over my shoulder. "Yeah?"

"You know I love you, right?"

I mustered a smile. "I love you too." Close to coming undone, I gave him a quick wave and climbed into the Jeep.

We remained quiet until Henry drove out of the neighborhood. "I think that went well—"

A bloodcurdling wail tore through my chest and all the pent-up emotions brought on by the day erupted out of me. Instead of trying to soothe me, Henry drove home and just let me sob.

We made it back to Sullivan's Island. By then the sobs had trickled down to a mere whimper, but Henry wouldn't let me go home.

"Just . . . Let's sit outside and get some fresh air, okay?"

Not knowing what to do with myself, I agreed, and Henry led me over to his patio where we sat staring off at the shore. He placed an arm around my shoulders and held me for a good long while until I managed to pull myself together.

"Thank you," I whispered.

"Does this mean you accept my apology?"

"Yeah. What you did today . . . that was a pretty solid apology." I unraveled myself from his arms and stood. "I better head home."

He grasped my hand before I got very far. "Once the dust settles, what do you think about me asking you out?"

"There's a lot of dust that needs settling."

"I'm a patient man."

I met his eyes and smiled. "Then I'd like that." I gave his hand a gentle squeeze and walked away.

39

Dark clouds had showed up this afternoon and brought along a rainy mess. I tried not to flash back to the night of the hurricane as I arrived at Patsy's, but it was almost impossible. Flashes of driving here in the rain, then back to Sullivan's Island where a nightmare had awaited. Taking a few breaths, I reassured myself that Gilbert was keeping tabs on Deaton and he was, in fact, in a rehab facility on the Big Island.

I flipped up the hood of my raincoat, jumped out of the Caddy, and made a run for it.

"Over here!" Gilbert waved me toward the gate and we both darted past it and met the rest of the group standing underneath the side portico. "Eww-wee, it's a real frog strangler out here."

"A what?" Pearl asked.

"He means that's a serious downpour." I pointed toward the heavy sheet of rain.

Pearl sucked her teeth, shaking her head. "Yous have the weirdest sayings in the South. Just say what ya mean."

"Now, Pearl, you're welcome here, and all, but don't go tryin' to change us." Gilbert dipped his chin. "Besides, the way we say things is much more interesting."

The door swung open. "Y'all come on in!" Patsy, barefoot in a pink hibiscus-printed caftan, waved us inside. "I have a special room to show you!" Where we all looked like drowned rats, she resembled a freshly blossomed flower with fresh highlights in her curly hair.

Our wet shoe soles squeaked against the floor as we followed her to a set of interior French doors.

Patsy turned to face us, the skirt of her dress swishing from her abrupt movement. "Wait till you see this fabulous room. It has the potential to change your lives." She reached behind her and opened the double doors, revealing a completely empty space. Nothing but plain white walls and richly stained wood floors.

Pearl let out a cranky huff. "It's just an empty room, for crying out loud!"

"But, honey, it's filled with all the people who have walked in your shoes." Stepping backwards, Patsy ushered us inside the vacant room. "It's filled with all the people who control your future. Y'all see 'em?"

With puzzled looks, we scanned the room, shaking our heads.

"No," Axil answered for all of us.

"Neither do I!" Patsy beamed. "In that same regard, these are the people who you should allow to determine your identity, to influence your life."

Standing beside Gilbert, I let that resonate, how I'd spent most of my life letting someone else decide my identity. Scanning the empty room, I saw flashes of my neglectful parents too busy to see the real me, too distracted to notice my cries for help. Blinking Mom and Dad away, I saw flashes of Cy and his criticism, his disappointment, his stern judgment. Then I caught a glimpse of Arlo in the corner, a mischievous smile on his face. He'd painted me in a warped image of my true self, enticing me to rebel against anyone and anything. With each slow blink, I banished them all until no ghostly images remained.

"The next time you go wasting your time on worrying about the opinion of other people, I want you to picture this room right here." Patsy stabbed a pink-tipped index finger in every direction. "This *empty* room. You are loved, you are cherished, and you are chosen by our Savior, and your identity is far greater than any label someone tries to place on you. Don't ever forget that."

Patsy allowed us time to absorb the lesson she'd laid plainly before us. Then she clapped her hands, in true Patsy fashion. "Alright! Now who's ready for some cake?"

Content with a full belly and my spirits lifted, I went home, but as soon as I pulled into the driveway my heart plummeted when I found Lana on the front porch. I shoved out of the Caddy and hurried to meet her. "What's wrong?"

"Nothing. I wanted to come up a day early so you and I could spend some time together." Lana stood. "I'm locked out."

"Oh. Sorry about that. I changed the locks. The . . . uh, door codes weren't working very well." I hurried up the steps. "I had a spare key made for you and Cy." I unlocked the door and disarmed the new alarm system, then led her into the kitchen. I fished out the extra keys from the drawer and handed them to her. "Are you sure there's nothing wrong?"

Lana perched on a stool and surveyed the kitchen. "I've done my best to stay out of this . . ." She returned her blue eyes to me. "But before Cy and the children get here, I wanted you and me to have a talk."

I settled on the stool beside her. "Whatever is bothering you, please just tell it to me straight."

A few tense moments passed before Lana spoke in a quiet voice. "Fern . . . She cried for you that first month. No child should have to go through what you've put her through. It's almost unforgivable."

That hit as hard as a runaway train. I rubbed my chest and tried to catch a breath. "I—"

"No. Let me finish." Lana sniffed. "After Arlo died, Olla had a heart-to-heart with me and Cy. She told us, *Junie's young, pregnant, and now a widow. We are going to have to help her pull up her bootstraps. Don't ever leave her to do it on her own.*" Lana ran her finger along a vein of gray in the marble. She looked over at me with watery eyes. "Cy thought that maybe some tough love was what you needed this year after what you did, but that's not what Olla would have wanted. We failed her too."

"No. The blame is all on me. It's taken a while, but I understand that now. Yeah, I had some awful things happen but it's on me for how I handled it all so poorly." I reached over and placed my hand on top of hers. "Lana, I'm so sorry for everything I've put you and our family through. Genuinely, I'm sorry."

"You already apologized in your letter, so don't apologize again." She placed her other hand on top of mine. "No matter how furious we've been with you, it's time to let that go. Our family needs to start moving forward, and we can't do that if we keep dragging up the past and dwelling on our mistakes."

"Mistakes are like ghosts, though. They haunt me."

"Speaking of haunting, I thought you should know Henry has spent most of the summer trying to convince Cy to let you see Fern. He's been quite persistent."

"I can't believe y'all had someone spying on me." Huffing a laugh, I let go of her arm.

"I didn't know Cy hadn't told Henry about Fern or much about your situation until he showed up back in June and gave Cy an earful. For what it's worth, he's really advocating for you. Telling us how dedicated you've been to your meetings, working, staying sober."

"Thank you for telling me."

"I'm going to make sure Fern is back with you before we move to Tennessee."

I shook my head, trying not to get my hopes up. "I doubt Cy will go for that."

"Your brother is stubborn, but he's coming around. You should know, this weekend is a test to see if you're ready. That's really why I'm here early, to help you, but . . ." She peered around the room. "It looks like you have things under control."

Had she expected to find the place trashed?

"Fern's room is ready and I bought a car seat. I've taken a CPR class too. What else should I do?"

Lana smiled. "Fern's a little thing, so you'll need a gate for the top and bottom of the stairs, child safety locks for the cleaning supply cabinets, and I'd put any of Olla's things you don't want broken out of Fern's reach."

Excitement welled inside me, making it hard to sit still. This was happening. Really happening! I was getting another shot. "I'll go to the store first thing in the morning."

"Oh, and regular laundry detergent irritates Fern's skin. You'll need to use one that's dye- and perfume-free."

I grabbed my notepad and jotted down Lana's preferred detergent brand. I fired off question after question, wanting to know Fern's routine, her favorite books, foods, shows, activities. "What about hobbies? What does she like to do?"

"She loves to color, just like her mommy and daddy." Smiling, Lana swiveled her stool to face me. "I know Fern is still young, but I think she may be musically talented. She doesn't just hum along to songs, she harmonizes with them. Just something to keep in mind, and if she shows interest, you might want to explore it."

I nodded, impressed by my child, and thought about Mei. "I know just the right person to help me if she does." Hearing myself say that with such confidence caught me off guard for a moment. I had a lot of right people in my life now. People I could trust, lean on, depend on, people who could turn to me for the same kind of support. Such a satisfying truth. "What else?"

We sat at the kitchen island making a list of all the things I needed to get done. I was so ready to get on with it, loved that my life was about to become the opposite of boring and lonely. I glanced around the kitchen, picturing the fridge covered in drawings and smudges from little hands, sippy cups in the sink, tiny shoes piled by the door. I pictured a house lived in, noisy, and chaotic, knowing all that chaos would transform it into a home.

Lana made it clear, we were turning the page on the past and starting fresh. It felt good to not dwell on the mistakes, but focus on plans for a healthier future.

Moving forward, I decided to stop living in the past of *shoulda, woulda, coulda,* and start living in the now with *I shall, I will, I can.*

40

NINE MONTHS LATER

The warm morning breeze rustled through my low ponytail as Winston and I made our way along the sidewalk just past Stith Park. The playground was deserted but with summer break right around the corner, it wouldn't be for long.

"All right, slowpoke. I've got a list a mile long to do today. Come on. Let's speed it up." My upbeat tone and playful jog was all it took for the goofy dog to play along. "I have orders for four new hats! Can you believe it? And I have to drop off stock for the boutique too. Fernie's Fancifuls is keeping me busy."

Winston let out a spirited bark, sounding right happy for me.

"And I'm leading the meeting tomorrow night for Patsy. She's gone on a cruise," I tell my companion, glad that I still had time to walk him, Jazzy, and Beau. My days were too hectic to keep a full dog walking schedule, but I considered that a really good thing. "I gotta figure out the object lesson I want to share with them. You got any ideas?"

Winston looked up, his tongue hanging out of the side of his mouth in that smiling way. I patted his head and we kept trotting along. He was still my favorite dog, but we'd made a pact not to ever tell the others.

I unlocked my front door and let myself and Winston in. Some silly song on TV and giggling welcomed us. Winston went straight to his water bowl in the laundry room and began lapping it up. Sounded like more was hitting the floor than making it into his mouth.

I'd adopted Winston last fall, but it felt like he'd always been here. Much like those two in the living room.

On the couch with cereal bowls in hand sat two bedheads. Leaving them to their cartoons, I went to the kitchen, washed my hands, then grabbed a handful of oat cereal. I stood behind the couch for a moment and watched as Fern pointed to the screen with her spoon and giggled. Snickering, Henry crammed another bite into his mouth. He'd been such a loyal friend, happily spending an hour or so in the mornings with Fern while I walked the dogs. He'd subscribed to some healthy cereal subscription box so that he could share his love of cereal with my daughter without filling her full of sugar and preservatives, saying he had to be a good cereal role model.

"Hey, you two." I popped the last bits of cereal into my mouth and dusted my hands together. "Whatcha watching?"

"Curious George," Henry answered. Still holding the spoon, he pushed his glasses up with the back of his hand. "It's a classic and Fernie here has excellent taste in cartoons." He nodded at her and she beamed ear to ear at his praise. "How was dog walking today?"

Fern perked up and barked proudly.

Henry held his palm out and she gave him five. Those two . . . This was one of the little games they played. If either mentioned an animal, the other had to make that animal's sound. They even had a sound for fish. *Bubble, bubble.* And in true Henry fashion, he did all his silly notions with her in utmost seriousness, making it all the more funny.

At the sound of her barking, Winston came barreling around the couch and plopped at Fern's feet.

"It was fine until Winston chased a squirrel for a hot minute before the little thing turned to confront him. The big goof ran away from it in pure terror."

Henry and Fernie squeaked like a squirrel.

Shaking my head, I joined them on the couch and accepted a bite of Fern's cereal. She thought it was the most fun to feed me, so of course, I indulged her. "Thanks for hanging out with my girl."

"No problem." Henry made no move to leave, continued watching the cartoon while slurping up the last of the cereal and milk from the bowl.

Fern followed suit and spilled some on the front of her pajama top.

Already prepared, Henry picked up the dish towel from his lap and dabbed it dry. "Today is the last day of the semester, so I'll be a little late getting back, but . . ." He placed the towel into his Papa Bear-sized bowl, eyes on it instead of me. "I was wondering—and Fernie already said it's a good idea—and if you think it's a good idea too, I'd like to take you on a date tonight."

Eyes wide, I sat up a little straighter. "Oh?"

"Yeah." He shrugged. "You told me later when the dust settled you'd give us a shot." He gazed around the room before giving Fern a meaningful look. "Seems pretty settled to me."

I nodded, thinking about how far we'd come since last August. Cy finally relinquished custody of Fern without much of a fight before they moved to Tennessee. I think our therapy sessions helped us both to get past our past enough so that we could move on from it. Fern actually settled in rather quickly, as if picking up right where we left off. At first, I caught myself thinking how children were just so resilient, but then I remembered no one noticed how un-resilient I was with my parents' absence, so I set up counseling sessions with Shari for just me and Fern to make sure she was okay. I was in a much better place in my recovery, but I still attended both group meetings every week and had no plans on stopping. Between the meetings and church, I felt surrounded by an ironclad support system. The dust had settled. So maybe it was finally time to agree to a date with Henry.

"Okay, but Fernie will have to join us."

Henry blinked, looking taken aback. "That felt too easy."

I shrugged, fighting a smile. "A year felt too easy?"

"You're right. It's been quite difficult putting up with you." His lip twitched with tease, but he didn't allow the smile freedom. "Bekah will be here at five to pick up Fernie. They're having a girls' night, but maybe Fernie can come with us next time."

I loved that he was already talking about a next time. "A girls' night?"

"Cookie class," Fern answered, her attention on the silly monkey on the TV.

"Cooking?"

She shook her head. *"Cookie."*

"They're going to a cookie decorating class." Clearing his throat, Henry stood. From his shift in posture, slightly hunched, I already knew what was coming before he started speaking in his Count von Count accent. "It's time for the number of the day. *Ah, ah, ah.*" He held up his bowl. "That's one, one bowl." Fern happily handed hers to him. "Two! Two bowls, *ah, ah, ah* . . . The number of the day is . . ."

"Two!" Fern jumped up and did a little dance while Henry continued the *ah, ah, ah* laughing, mimicking the Sesame Street character.

Snickering, I sat there and took in the sight of them. This counting was another one of their games. Yesterday, the number of the day had been eight, because that was the number of washable markers in the new pack Henry gave her. Those were as much a gift to me as to my daughter since it made for easy cleanup.

Admittedly, I had no idea what children her age should know but I considered my three-and-a-half-year-old daughter a level of genius all on her own. She knew colors, could count to twenty, could sing the ABC song, knew how to brighten any dark day just by smiling.

Henry placed the bowls in the sink, then headed inside the laundry room off the kitchen. "Junie, you mind coming here for a minute?"

I placed a kiss on the top of Fern's head and then went into the laundry room, finding Henry leaning against the dryer. "You mean it? You'll go on a date with me?"

"Yes. But what if I had said no?"

"I would have had to crash Fernie and Bekah's girls' night and drown my sorrows in pink frosting and sprinkles. I'm really glad I don't have to do that." He reached for me, pulling me in for a hug. "You think this date tonight could end with a kiss, perhaps?" Henry said, his lips against my neck. We both knew that counted as a kiss, just not the kind he wanted.

"No."

He leaned back to meet my eyes. "No kissing, still?"

"No, I don't want to wait until the date. I'd like for you to kiss me now." I pouted my lips, making myself clear.

Growing serious, he took his glasses off and laid them on top of the dryer. Even with his dark hair sticking up every which way and him wearing a rumpled T-shirt and joggers, Henry Morrison was the most handsome man I'd ever met. His was the best kind of handsome too, the kind that came from within first.

As his lips met mine I knew something that I'd known for quite some time and would wait a little while longer before admitting out loud. I loved him, first as a great friend, but then much more than that.

"Mommy, we gotta check on Grandma!" Fern burst through the door and we managed to jump apart at the same time.

"Okay. Let's go check on her." I winked at Henry, who was blushing, and let Fern lead me to the grandmother clock. I opened the glass case and stepped out of the way so she could pull the chains down. As I listened to her cute little grunts and the zipping sound of the chains, I thought about Olla and wondered just how proud she would be of me and how far I'd come in the last year. Between doing right by my daughter and wanting to honor my grandmother, I would give it my all to continue down this road of sobriety, to be someone my grandmother would be proud of.

"Look, Henry! I did it all by myself!" Fern pointed to the clock.

"Well done, Fernie." Henry held his hand up and she slapped it with enthusiasm. "Okay, ladies, I must be on my way." He placed a kiss on Fern's cheek and then mine.

Once Henry headed out the door to get ready for work, Fern and I got ready for our day. First, taming her hair and brushing her teeth. Then moving upstairs to our workroom. I'd set up her own little table with interactive puzzles and educational coloring sheets appropriate for her age and she absolutely loved working alongside Mommy. We would work until lunch and then she would nap while I worked a little more. Our afternoons were spent at the park or beach until Henry returned home from the college and we'd either swim in his pool or play some game of their choosing. Life was simple but so good.

I settled down at my table to begin another hat, but I took a moment to gaze at my child. I'd learned the hard way not to take even a second with her for granted.

"What you want me to color, Mommy?" Fern uncapped one of her new markers.

"Whatever you want to." I smiled wistfully.

"Hmm . . . Winston!" She replaced the blue marker and selected the brown one.

At the mention of his name, our dog trotted over to her table and stretched out beside her chair.

Fern started dragging the marker down a fresh piece of paper. The concentrated expression on her sweet face—lips twisted, eyes slightly narrowed—reminded me of her father. My chest tightened every time I caught a glimpse of Arlo in our daughter, knowing he'd missed out on meeting the most perfect gift we were ever given. Sober and determined, I would love her enough for the both of us.

My phone buzzed with an incoming message from the MNS group text.

Mark your calendars for Somewhere's Food Festival June 29 with Chris Evans!

I gave it a thumbs-up and put a reminder in my calendar app before I forgot. I loved that quaint town. Loved that people could go there and it could be their *somewhere*.

"I'm gonna give this one to Gilly and that one to Henry."

I glanced up from the phone screen and saw Fern holding up two colorful drawings. "They'll love that. So pretty, Fernie."

She went back to marking up the page, as if trying to cover every speck of white. As I watched her color, I reflected on my *somewhere* and decided it wasn't an actual place, but the people surrounding me. Fern, Henry, Gilbert, the Magnolia Nephalist Society, Betty and the group at the Methodist church. Even Cy and his family. They were my somewhere.

Despite the rocky journey, I was no longer south of somewhere but exactly where I was meant to be.

Acknowledgments

As I wrap up my twenty-first book, I want to take a moment to reflect on all those who support my passion for storytelling. I'm blessed to be surrounded by the right people. People I can trust, lean on, and depend on.

My heavenly Father, why you allow such a mess as myself to share such stories, I may never know on this side of glory, but I am so thankful you allow it. Please don't let me get in the way of it.

The Lowe Bunch: Bernie, Nate, and Lu. Life is sweeter with each of you in it. I asked God a long time ago to give me my very own family to love, and he gave me so much more. You make each breath, each second, worth it. I love you. I love you. Simple as that. I love you.

There is a very select group of friends who enter your life and refuse to leave you, no matter how bad you screw up. Trina Cooke, Jennifer Strickland, Teresa Moise, and Stephanie Wilhelm, you are that group. You love me, as is, and I love you, as is, and that is a true gift from God. In a world full of inconsistencies, you are consistent. Thank you.

My creative friends Vicki Baty and Marybeth Whalen, I love spitballing story ideas with you both. You challenge my imagination and help me see the possibilities tucked along the edges of a scene. You're pretty fun travel companions too!

I have the best literary agent and I'm seriously not sure I deserve her, but please don't tell her that! Danielle Egan-Miller, you are my rock star. I don't ever have to worry beyond creating the story I want to tell, because you take care of the rest. I am one lucky girl to have you in my corner.

Tyndale House Publishers, you are so much more than a publishing house. You are a supportive team, a caring family, a generous ministry, and I'm honored to be a part of it. I have so much gratitude for my gifted editor, Kathy Olson. You helped me lean in to the difficult parts of Junie's story, trekking through the rocky terrain of addiction, loss, and recovery. I'm proud of the story we will share with the world. Stephanie Broene and Karen Watson, you both are a joy to work with. Thank you for advocating for me and my stories.

To all of the bookstore, book club, and library friends I've made throughout the years: you are amazing. Thank you for your encouragement and support. You are a blessing I do not take for granted.

When I was looking for research material for this book, I happened upon *The Life Recovery Workbook* and *The Life Recovery Bible* without even realizing they were produced by my very own publisher. How wild is that? No, not wild, just another God wink. This workbook helped me understand the complexities of addiction so much better. If you are dealing with addiction of any sort or have a loved one in that battle, I encourage you to check out this Bible and workbook.

And I encourage you to love and to forgive those in your life who are struggling. Just love them where they are at, even if they do things you don't agree with. No one is promised tomorrow.

South of Somewhere Recipes

Henry's Loaded Cereal Treats

6 tbsp. (¾ stick) unsalted butter, plus additional butter for pan
6 cups mini marshmallows, divided
3 cups Rice Krispies cereal
1 cup Fruity Pebbles cereal
1 cup Lucky Charms cereal
1 cup Froot Loops cereal

Butter a 9x13 cake pan. Melt the 6 tbsp. of butter in a large pot over low heat. Add 5 cups of mini marshmallows and stir until completely melted. Remove from heat and add Rice Krispies, Fruity Pebbles, and Lucky Charms. Fold in the remaining mini marshmallows. Once combined, press mixture into prepared pan. Let cool, then cut into squares.

Recipe Variations:

S'mores Cereal Treats: Use 3 cups Rice Krispies, 2 cups Golden Grahams, 1 cup Cocoa Pebbles.

Peanut Butter Treat: Add ½ cup smooth peanut butter to the melted butter and marshmallow mixture. Use 3 cups Rice Krispies, 2 cups Reese's Puffs, 1 cup Cocoa Pebbles. Add ½ cup semisweet chocolate chips with the cereal.

Olla's Tomato Cracker Salad

2 large tomatoes, diced
1 green onion, chopped
2 tbsp. Duke's Mayonnaise
1 tsp. ranch seasoning
1 sleeve of saltine crackers, coarsely crushed
Pepper to taste

In a bowl, mix mayonnaise and ranch seasoning. Then add tomatoes, onions, and saltines. Give it a good mix and eat immediately.

Add-in options:

Chopped hard-boiled egg
Chopped bacon
Cubed ham

South of Somewhere Playlist

"Human" by Cody Johnson

"Seasons" by Bebe Rexha & Dolly Parton

"Runaway" by OneRepublic

"Breakdown" by Andrew Ripp

"Used To Be Young" Miley Cyrus

"Sun to Me" by Zach Bryan

"Fall Into Me" by Forest Blakk

"The Other Side" by Cindy Morgan

"People" by Jervis Campbell

"Worn" by Tenth Avenue North

"Narrow Road" by Chris Renzema

"Somebody Prayed" by Crowder

"Revival" by Judah & the Lion

"Brighter Days" by Blessing Offor

"Perfectly Loved" by Rachael Lampa and TobyMac

"Fear Is Not My Future" by Maverick City Music

"Shotgun" by George Ezra

"Dog Days Are Over" by Florence & The Machine

Discussion Questions

1. The author typically focuses on a redemption theme in her stories. How was the redemption in this story different from or similar to her other books?

2. An important lesson the characters learn is that you have to love people where they are, even if they do things you don't agree with. How have you encountered this challenge in your own life?

3. Did this story provide any insights into the substance abuse recovery process that you didn't expect?

4. The author introduces us to two different types of support groups—one more traditional and the other nontraditional. What did you think about both of them? Did you like one better than the other?

5. Another theme of this story is exploring sibling relationships, both estrangement and reconciliation. Why are sibling relationships sometimes complicated?

6. Junie's brother Cy gives her a hard row to hoe. Was he right to do that? Could he have responded differently?

7. Junie's therapist suggests writing a letter to her parents about how their choices have impacted her—not to mail, but just as a venting exercise. Is there someone you'd like to write such a letter to, even if you will never mail it?

8. Henry is dishonest with Junie about knowing her brother, but he defends his actions, thinking it's in her best interest. Do you agree or disagree with his choice? When, if ever, is it okay to lie?

9. Junie begins a journal including lists of things she hopes to share with Fern one day. What list would you add to the journal?

10. This is a heavy story, but were there any lighthearted moments you liked in particular?

About the Author

T. I. Lowe is an ordinary country girl who loves to tell extraordinary stories. She is the author of 21 novels, including the #1 international bestseller and critically acclaimed *Under the Magnolias* and her debut breakout *Lulu's Café*. Her novel *Indigo Isle* won the prestigious Christy Award in the contemporary romance category and was subsequently named Christy Award Book of the Year. She lives in coastal South Carolina with her husband and family. Find her at tilowe.com or on Facebook (T.I.Lowe), Instagram (tilowe), and X (@TiLowe).

CONNECT WITH T. I. LOWE ONLINE AND SIGN UP FOR HER NEWSLETTER AT

tilowe.com

OR FOLLOW HER ON

f T.I.Lowe

tilowe

TiLowe

g T_I_Lowe

CP1684